EX LIBRIS

VINTAGE CLASSICS

Stories To Get You Through The Night

Stories to get you through the Night

Katherine Mansfield, Anton Chekhov, Oscar Wilde,
Wilkie Collins, Arthur Conan Doyle, Virginia Woolf,
Rudyard Kipling, Helen Simpson, Richard Yates, James Lasdun,
Alice Munro, Martin Amis, Haruki Murakami, Angela Carter,
Kate Chopin, Elizabeth Gaskell, W. Somerset Maugham,
The Brothers Grimm, Julian Barnes and John Cheever

AND WITH AN INTRODUCTION BY
Helen Dunmore

VINTAGE BOOKS
London

Published by Vintage Classics 2010

6 8 10 9 7

'Her First Ball' by.Katherine Mansfield, first published in *The Sphere*, 1921; 'The Student'
by Anton Chekhov (trans. Constance Garnett), first published in *The Cook's Wedding
and Other Stories*, 1922; 'The Selfish Giant' by Oscar Wilde, first published in *The Happy
Prince and Other Tales*, 1888; 'A Terribly Strange Bed' by Wilkie Collins, first published
in *Household Words*, V, no. 109, April 1852; 'The Story of an Hour' by Kate Chopin,
first published in *Vogue*, 1894; 'The Half-Brothers' by Elizabeth Gaskell, first published
in *The Dublin University* Magazine, 1859; 'King Thrushbeard' by The Brothers Grimm
(trans. Jack Zipes), first published in *The Collected Fairy Tales*, 1987; 'The Adventure
of the Blue Carbuncle' by Arthur Conan-Doyle, first published in *Strand Magazine*, 1892;
'Kew Gardens' by Virginia Woolf, first published in 1919; 'The Cat That Walked by
Himself' by Rudyard Kipling, first published in *Just So Stories for Little Children*, 1902;
'Charm for a Friend with a Lump' by Helen Simpson, first published in *Geography
Boy*, 2010; 'A Convalescent Ego' by Richard Yates, published in *The Collected Stories
of Richard Yates*, 2004; 'An Anxious Man' by James Lasdun, first published in *The Paris
Review*, Spring 2005 and in *It's Beginning to Hurt*, Jonathan Cape, 2009; 'The Moons
of Jupiter' by Alice Munro, first published in *The Moons of Jupiter*, 1983; 'The Coincidence
of the Arts' by Martin Amis, first published in *Heavy Water*, 1998; 'On Seeing the
100% Perfect Girl One Beautiful April Morning' by Haruki Murakami (trans. Alfred
Birnbaum & Jay Rubin), first published in *The Elephant Vanishes*, 2001; 'The Tiger's
Bride' by Angela Carter, first published in *The Bloody Chamber and Other Stories*,
1979; 'Mabel' by W. Somerset Maugham, published in *The Gentleman in the Parlour*,
1930; 'Hermitage' by Julian Barnes, first published in *Cross Channel*, 1996;
'Clementina' by John Cheever, first published in *The New Yorker*, 1960.

This collection first published in 2010 by
Vintage Classics Random House
20 Vauxhall Bridge Road, London SW1V 2SA

www.vintage-classics.info

Addresses for companies within The Random House Group Limited
can be found at: www.randomhouse.co.uk/offices.htm

The Random House Group Limited Reg. No. 954009

A CIP catalogue record for this book is available from the British Library

ISBN 9780099541073

The Random House Group Limited supports The Forest Stewardship
Council (FSC®), the leading international forest certification organisation.
Our books carrying the FSC label are printed on FSC® certified paper.
FSC is the only forest certification scheme endorsed by the leading environmental
organisations, including Greenpeace. Our paper procurement policy can be found at
www.randomhouse.co.uk/environment

MIX
Paper from
responsible sources
FSC
www.fsc.org   FSC® C016897

Typeset by Palimpsest Book Production Limited, Grangemouth, Stirlingshire
Printed and bound in Great Britain by
Clays Ltd, St Ives plc

Contents

Introduction *by* Helen Dunmore   ix

Stories to make you glad to be alive

Her First Ball *by* Katherine Mansfield   3
The Student *by* Anton Chekhov   13
The Selfish Giant *by* Oscar Wilde   21

Stories to send a shiver down your spine

A Terribly Strange Bed *by* Wilkie Collins   31
The Adventure of the Blue Carbuncle
    by Arthur Conan Doyle   51

Stories to help you rejoice in the beauty of nature

Kew Gardens *by* Virginia Woolf   77
The Cat That Walked By Himself *by* Rudyard Kipling   87

Stories to read when it's all going wrong

Charm for a Friend with a Lump *by* Helen Simpson   103
A Convalescent Ego *by* Richard Yates   109
An Anxious Man *by* James Lasdun   125
The Moons of Jupiter *by* Alice Munro   147

Stories to intrigue and excite

The Coincidence of the Arts *by* Martin Amis 169
On Seeing the 100% Perfect Girl One Beautiful April
    Morning *by* Haruki Murakami 209
The Tiger's Bride *by* Angela Carter 217

Stories to remind you that love conquers all

The Story of an Hour *by* Kate Chopin 241
The Half-Brothers *by* Elizabeth Gaskell 247
Mabel *by* W. Somerset Maugham 263
King Thrushbeard *by* The Brothers Grimm 271

And stories to celebrate the joys of growing old

Hermitage *by* Julian Barnes 281
Clementina *by* John Cheever 301

Introduction

STORY WAS BORN in dark caves, lit by a splash of firelight. Every winter, once the brief hours of day were over, the long hours came when no one could work. In those hours storytelling grew strong, filling the dark with drama, passion, conflict, adventure, comedy and intimacy. Huddled listeners held their breath as the tension of the plot tightened and the storyteller's craft played on their imaginations. Leaping shadows became ships' prows beating through wine-dark waters, knights wrestling with dragons, lovers escaping together in the dead of night, or a poor boy in search of a magic lamp. Subtle, vigorous, funny, heartbreaking, the stories flowed until they faded into sleep.

The human longing for story is so powerful, so primitive, that it seems like something not learned, but locked into our genes. Our world is flooded with electric light to the point that true darkness is as rare as silence, but even as we punch the remote for a midnight film, or forlornly wander the neon aisles of 24-hour supermarkets, we crave a richer stimulus, and a deeper comfort. We are creatures of story, and passive consumption suits us only up to a certain point. We can gulp down any amount of what the computer industry calls 'content' and yet remain unsatisfied, even jaded, because not enough has been asked of us and we have a great deal to give.

The best stories work because they kindle the reader's imagination into its fullest life. In our mind's eye we summon up the horror of a bed's canopy descending in absolute silence, swathed in stifling drapery. We share the frozen terror of the intended victim, as Wilkie Collins intended us to share it in his chilling story 'A Terribly Strange Bed'. In 'The Tiger's Bride', Angela Carter's narrative whirls us round and round until we are lost in a disorientating forest of sensuous experience. We imagine the heavy, monstrous, beguiling head of the Tiger who has won his bride on a bet. All our own histories of vulnerability, nakedness and desire fuse into the story's words. The images are not there to be received passively; we have to re-make them as the words spring into life in our heads. It is through taking part in the creation of the story that we make it our own for ever.

This anthology is entitled *Stories to Get You Through the Night*, and the title suggests the many meanings of night in a human life. Everyone knows the meaning of 'a bad night', with its dragging hours of darkness, restlessness and an increasing exhaustion which seems to push sleep away from itself. Night is the cousin of death; perhaps it prepares us for it. But night is also the place where the richness of our inner lives is exposed to our astounded consciousness. Our minds relax their grip on common sense and accelerate into the deeper logic of dreams. Sometimes it seems that the truth of our imaginations belongs to the night.

At other times night becomes a metaphor for the loneliness of the human being. Such a night might bring solitary depths of reflection, a hospital vigil, the memory of the dead or anguish over the living. So often it's the book at the bedside that makes such a night bearable, because among the many gifts of fiction is its power to reassure us that we are not alone in what we think and feel. The best stories crystallise experience with such clarity that we seem to recognise it as it truly is, perhaps for the first time. The short story form is intensely personal. It speaks into our inner ear, to and through our solitude. The precision and compression of the short story give it power to cut through to the heart. It is this quality that gives certain favourite short stories such a lasting place in the reader's affection.

Many of the short stories in this anthology have already won generations of readers. Arthur Conan Doyle's 'The Adventure of the

Blue Carbuncle' was first published in *Strand Magazine* in January 1892. Rudyard Kipling's 'The Cat That Walked By Himself' was published in 1905, as one of the *Just-So Stories* which have enchanted children ever since, and inspired illustrators, film-makers and cartoonists around the world. The worlds from which these two stories sprang may have vanished – Conan Doyle's fog-bound London, where a man's character may be deduced from his hat and geese are bred in Brixton, now possesses the charm of fable. But his steely understanding of human motivation and behaviour is timeless, as are Kipling's warm, playful humour and perfect pitch for how children want to hear a story told. The listener, yielding to Kipling's rhythms, becomes the storyteller's Best Beloved, for whom the story is shaped and made.

In Katherine Mansfield's story she contrasts the old world of European manners with the new world of the Antipodes. In 'Her First Ball', Leila's excitement, anticipation and dread are made brilliant by her heightened perceptions. For Leila, a provincial New Zealand drill hall is as fabulous as the ballroom entered by Natasha Rostova in *War and Peace*. In the dazzle, her mind registers key details: the leaping of the gas jet in the ladies' cloakroom, the quivering of the coloured flags across the ceiling, or the endearing way her cousin Laurie leans forward and says to his sister, 'Look here, darling, the third and ninth as usual. Twig?' To Leila, these words sum up the brother-and-sister intimacy which she has never known, and contrast with her own 'forsaken up-country home, listening to the baby owls crying "more pork" in the moonlight'.

The most exciting thing about this story is that its brightly-lit interior – glittering, as it seems to Leila, with glamour and possibility – is also haunted by the vast darkness of the surrounding bush, to which this European-style revelry is an irrelevance.

I have read this story perhaps ten times in my life, and each time it seems to change a little, as if Katherine Mansfield knew how to cut her lines so sharply that they always catch a different light. She learned much of this art from Chekhov, who taught her that a short story does not have to strive for a sleek plot in order to be full of character, change and event. Like Mansfield, Chekhov is one of the most intense creators of mood, and of key moments which burn themselves into the reader's memory. 'The Student' is a very short story – it comes and goes within four pages – and a good third of it is taken up by the student seminarian's retelling of a Gospel story, Peter's denial of Christ on the night of his arrest in the Garden of Gethsemane.

On a bitterly cold spring night, the student is drawn to the campfire of Vasilisa and her daughter. These three human beings come together in random but terribly powerful intimacy, stretching out their hands to the flames and thinking of the 'still, still, dark, dark garden, and in the stillness, faintly audible, smothered sobbing . . .' They meet, they share this moment of naked communication, they shed tears and then they part. The student looks back and sees the women's light still burning in the desolate village, and 'the inexpressible sweet expectation of happiness, of unknown mysterious happiness, took possession of him little by little, and life seemed to him enchanting, marvellous, and full of lofty meaning.'

The economy of 'The Student' is startling. With a few strokes, Chekhov summons up the vast, desolate Russian landscape as winter returns to swallow up spring; he captures character and place in a couple of sentences, and above all he expresses the interior landscape of the student in all its complexity, as his emotions swerve from gloom to exaltation.

The revelation of character through fleeting moments and actions is typical of the short story. James Lasdun's 'An Anxious Man' drives its chief character, Joseph Nagel, through a thicket of self-doubt and fear because he has completely lost confidence in his own perceptions. The financial markets are down, and his wife's inheritance is melting away. Like many of his time and place, Joseph has shared the dream that modest capital could be key to 'real riches', if he and his wife play the markets right. But the markets fail him. The dream was false, and suspicion clouds into a 'thick grief' which comes close to destroying him.

Lasdun picks out detail to show how much Joseph has lost faith in himself. He sees a woman jump the queue in an upmarket Cape Cod fishmonger, to make sure that she gets the last two lobsters. Her serene ruthlessness repels Joseph. He makes a judgment which is later suspended when he meets the woman socially and finds that she is not only a neighbour, but that she flatters, flirts and disconcerts until he doesn't know if he's on his head or his heels. Throughout the story, Joseph fails to trust what he sees, hears and knows. Riddled with anxiety, he is hyper-sensitive and hyper-aware. He notices too much but cannot interpret anything to his own satisfaction. Instead, he goes over and over each incident, trying to extract from it every possible shade of meaning. It is a story in the tradition of F. Scott Fitzgerald, dealing with money and status, and what happens when these are taken away. Like Fitzgerald, Lasdun anatomises an era when material success became confused with moral virtue.

There are stories here by writers who are renowned for their work in the genre, such as Helen Simpson or Alice Munro, and others by writers who are more familiar as novelists, such as Elizabeth Gaskell or Kate Chopin. Some are innovative, stretching language, using it impressionistically, testing its boundaries. Virginia Woolf's 'Kew Gardens' uses a painterly, layered technique to create a dazzle that mimics the heat-hazed brilliance of the summer day:

> . . . the glass roofs of the palm house shone as if a whole market full of shiny green umbrellas had opened in the sun; and in the drone of the aeroplane the voice of the summer sky murmured its fierce soul. Yellow and black, pink and snow white, shapes of all these colours, men, women and children were spotted for a second upon the horizon, and then, seeing the breadth of yellow that lay upon the grass, they wavered and sought shade beneath the trees, dissolving like drops of water in the yellow and green atmosphere, staining it faintly with red and blue.

'Kew Gardens' is a story to be savoured slowly. It lays the summer day down on the page, stroke by stroke, so that it becomes a sensation to be relished by all the senses. The story is packed with heat, noise, texture, scent, light. It is probably hard for us to appreciate quite how daring Woolf was, now that we have become used to her influence working on later generations of writers, but it's easy to give way to the seduction of her style. The stroke of genius here is the introduction of the aeroplane, high up in the summer sky. A lesser writer might have complained about its mechanical noise interrupting the pastoral delights of summer. Woolf's ear is more acute. This is a human-made landscape, a thing of metal and glass as well as trees and flowers. Its soul is lyrical, yet also fiercely mechanical. It needs an aeroplane.

Interestingly, Helen Simpson also plays with ideas of the natural and the unnatural in her deceptively simple story 'Charm For A Friend With A Lump'. The narrator addresses a friend who has been diagnosed with cancer – a recurring theme in Simpson's short stories. We don't know whether or not the friend will ever hear these words; perhaps they are part of what will one day become a conversation, perhaps they are a soliloquy in which the narrator tries to make sense of her own fear and anguish at the prospect of loss.

Both characters, it seems, are gardeners. (Perhaps it's bold to assume that Simpon's characters are women, but the word 'lump' has such a particular resonance for women of a certain age that this seems credible.) The narrator lingers over the names of plants: striped Rond de Nice courgettes, Invincible pears, Marmande tomatoes and Titania blackcurrants. It's understood that these two friends share the language of gardening, as they share so much else. Lightly, Simpson glances on the fact that cancer treatments also come from plants. Mistletoe extract may be fringe medicine, but Tamoxifen, which derives from the yew, is a standard drug for breast cancer.

Behind all the language of germination, growth and fruition there is the shadowy presence of another, unwanted cell proliferation, ripening towards the destruction of its host. The writing is clear but subtle, held together by the depth of feeling which one friend shows for the other. 'First let me take a piece of chalk and draw a circle around you, so you're safe.' This is a realistic, even earthy story, but it is also a piece of magic which calls on the strongest runes of fiction to protect its own.

Another story uses the guise of realism to develop a fantastic idea to its logical conclusion, and to raise a subject which could not be discussed frankly at the date of its publication. In 'Mabel' W. Somerset Maugham takes the well-known theme of the romantic quest, in which a knight undertakes a long, dangerous journey to win his elusive lady. He inverts it by making the love-object a reluctant young colonial in Burma, who has arranged to marry a girl from 'Home'. The marriage is delayed, and 'suddenly, without warning, his nerve failed him. He had not seen Mabel for seven years. He had forgotten what she was like. She was a total stranger . . . He couldn't go through with it.' Seized with 'the courage of despair' George sets out on a journey which takes him all over Asia, with the questing Mabel just a step behind. The comedy of Mabel's improbably accurate hunting-down of her man is beautifully judged, in a fictional crescendo of letters, telegrams and timetables. Maugham just glances at the psychological torment of George, who is in a cold sweat lest she catch him. Within the story's texture lies Maugham's own profound unease about his homosexuality and his marriage. George cannot shake Mabel off; she is his personal and social nemesis. Maugham's crisp, satiric sentences mask anguish while they build suspense:

> Mabel stepped out. She was neat and cool and fresh. There was nothing in her appearance to suggest that she had just come in after a fortnight on the road. George was petrified. He was as pale as death.

Maugham could not write openly about his homosexuality, because the laws and conventions of his time forbade it. His hidden emotion gives a charge to the story which belies its tidy conclusion.

In this story, as in many others, what is not quite said becomes even more powerful than what is made explicit. The economy of the short story drives both writer and reader to weigh every word, and make it count. This is probably the reason why short stories are memorable in the same way as poems are memorable. They are also endlessly re-readable.

Short stories become old friends whose familiarity breeds content; but at the same time they retain their power to startle and to disclose new facets of themselves. I am happy to spend years catching up with the intentions of the writers whose work I love and admire, because reading to the end of a short story is not the same as finishing it. There is always something more to discover: a shade of meaning, a hidden joke, a vibration of feeling or a play on words, a revealing line of dialogue or a breathtaking turn of phrase. The best short stories will take a reader through the night, and through a life-time.

Helen Dunmore, 2010

Stories
to make you
glad to be
alive

Her First Ball
by
Katherine Mansfield

Katherine Mansfield was born Kathleen Mansfield Beauchamp in 1888 in New Zealand. In 1903 she moved to London, where she attended Queen's College alongside her two sisters. When she finished her education she returned to New Zealand where she began to write short stories and had several works published in the *Native Companion,* which was the first time she used the pseudonym K. Mansfield. After the success of Mansfield's first collection of stories, *In the German Pension* (1911), she returned to London and wrote regularly for the periodical, *The New Age*. Diagnosed as suffering from tuberculosis, Mansfield moved to the south of France where she continued to write and publish until her death in 1923. After her death two further collections of short stories were published: *The Dove's Nest* (1923) and *Something Childish* (1924).

Her First Ball

EXACTLY WHEN THE ball began Leila would have found it hard to say. Perhaps her first real partner was the cab. It did not matter that she shared the cab with the Sheridan girls and their brother. She sat back in her own little corner of it, and the bolster on which her hand rested felt like the sleeve of an unknown young man's dress suit; and away they bowled, past waltzing lamp-posts and houses and fences and trees.

'Have you really never been to a ball before, Leila? But, my child, how too weird—' cried the Sheridan girls.

'Our nearest neighbour was fifteen miles,' said Leila softly, gently opening and shutting her fan.

Oh dear, how hard it was to be indifferent like the others! She tried not to smile too much; she tried not to care. But every single thing was so new and exciting . . . Meg's tuberoses, Jose's long loop of amber, Laura's little dark head, pushing above her white fur like a flower through snow. She would remember for ever. It even gave her a pang to see her cousin Laurie throw away the wisps of tissue paper he pulled from the fastenings of his new gloves. She would like to have kept those wisps as a keepsake, as a remembrance. Laurie leaned forward and put his hand on Laura's knee.

'Look here, darling,' he said. 'The third and the ninth as usual. Twig?'

Oh, how marvellous to have a brother! In her excitement Leila felt that if there had been time, if it hadn't been impossible, she couldn't have helped crying because she was an only child, and no brother had ever said 'Twig?' to her; no sister would ever say, as Meg said to Jose that moment, 'I've never known your hair go up more successfully than it has to-night!'

But, of course, there was no time. They were at the drill hall already; there were cabs in front of them and cabs behind. The road was bright on either side with moving fan-like lights, and on the pavement gay couples seemed to float through the air; little satin shoes chased each other like birds.

'Hold on to me, Leila; you'll get lost,' said Laura.

'Come on, girls, let's make a dash for it,' said Laurie.

Leila put two fingers on Laura's pink velvet cloak, and they were somehow lifted past the big golden lantern, carried along the passage, and pushed into the little room marked 'Ladies.' Here the crowd was so great there was hardly space to take off their things; the noise was deafening. Two benches on either side were stacked high with wraps. Two old women in white aprons ran up and down tossing fresh armfuls. And everybody was pressing forward trying to get at the little dressing-table and mirror at the far end.

A great quivering jet of gas lighted the ladies' room. It couldn't wait; it was dancing already. When the door opened again and there came a burst of tuning from the drill hall, it leaped almost to the ceiling.

Dark girls, fair girls were patting their hair, tying ribbons again, tucking handkerchiefs down the fronts of their bodices, smoothing marble-white gloves. And because they were all laughing it seemed to Leila that they were all lovely.

'Aren't there any invisible hair-pins?' cried a voice. 'How most extraordinary! I can't see a single invisible hair-pin.'

'Powder my back, there's a darling,' cried some one else.

'But I must have a needle and cotton. I've torn simply miles and miles of the frill,' wailed a third.

Then, 'Pass them along, pass them along!' The straw basket of programmes was tossed from arm to arm. Darling little pink-and-silver programmes, with pink pencils and fluffy tassels. Leila's fingers shook as she took one out of the basket. She wanted to ask some one, 'Am I meant to have one too?' but she had just time to read: 'Waltz 3. "Two, Two in a Canoe." Polka 4. "Making the Feathers Fly,"' when Meg cried, 'Ready, Leila?' and they pressed their way through the crush in the passage towards the big double doors of the drill hall.

Dancing had not begun yet, but the band had stopped tuning, and the noise was so great it seemed that when it did begin to play it would never be heard. Leila, pressing close to Meg, looking over Meg's shoulder, felt that even the little quivering coloured flags strung across the ceiling were talking. She quite forgot to be shy; she forgot how in the middle of dressing she had sat down on the bed with one shoe off and one shoe on and begged her mother to ring up her cousins and say she couldn't go after all. And the rush of longing she had had to be sitting on the veranda of their forsaken up-country home, listening to the baby owls crying 'More pork' in the moonlight, was changed to a rush of joy so sweet that it was hard to bear alone. She clutched her fan, and, gazing at the gleaming, golden floor, the azaleas, the lanterns, the stage at one end with its red carpet and gilt chairs and the band in a corner, she thought breathlessly, 'How heavenly; how simply heavenly!'

All the girls stood grouped together at one side of the doors, the men at the other, and the chaperones in dark dresses, smiling rather foolishly, walked with little careful steps over the polished floor towards the stage.

'This is my little country cousin Leila. Be nice to her. Find her partners; she's under my wing,' said Meg, going up to one girl after another.

Strange faces smiled at Leila – sweetly, vaguely. Strange voices answered, 'Of course, my dear.' But Leila felt the girls didn't really see her. They were looking towards the men. Why didn't the men begin? What were they waiting for? There they stood, smoothing their gloves, patting their glossy hair and smiling among themselves. Then, quite suddenly, as if they had only just made up their minds that that was what they had to do, the men came gliding over the parquet. There was a joyful flutter among the girls. A tall, fair man flew up to Meg, seized her programme, scribbled something; Meg passed him on to Leila. 'May I have the pleasure?' He ducked and smiled. There came a dark man wearing an eyeglass, then cousin Laurie with a friend, and Laura with a little freckled fellow whose tie was crooked. Then quite an old man – fat, with a big bald patch on his head – took her programme and murmured, 'Let me see, let me see!' And he was a long time comparing his programme, which looked black with names, with hers. It seemed to give him so much trouble that Leila was ashamed. 'Oh, please don't bother,' she said eagerly. But instead of replying the fat man wrote something, glanced at her again. 'Do I remember this bright little face?' he said softly. 'Is it known to me of yore?' At that moment the band began playing; the fat man disappeared. He was tossed away on a great wave of music that came flying over the gleaming floor, breaking the groups up into couples, scattering them, sending them spinning . . .

Leila had learned to dance at boarding school. Every Saturday afternoon the boarders were hurried off to a little corrugated iron mission hall where Miss Eccles (of London) held her 'select' classes. But the difference between that dusty-smelling hall – with calico texts on the walls, the poor terrified little woman in a brown velvet toque with rabbit's ears thumping the cold piano, Miss Eccles poking the girls' feet with her long white wand – and this was so tremendous that Leila was sure if her partner didn't come and she had to listen to that marvellous music and to watch the others sliding, gliding over the golden floor, she would die at least, or faint, or lift her arms and fly out of one of those dark windows that showed the stars.

'Ours, I think—' Some one bowed, smiled, and offered her his arm; she hadn't to die after all. Some one's hand pressed her waist, and she floated away like a flower that is tossed into a pool.

'Quite a good floor, isn't it?' drawled a faint voice close to her ear.

'I think it's most beautifully slippery,' said Leila.

'Pardon!' The faint voice sounded surprised. Leila said it again. And there was a tiny pause before the voice echoed, 'Oh, quite!' and she was swung round again.

He steered so beautifully. That was the great difference between dancing with girls and men, Leila decided. Girls banged into each other, and stamped on each other's feet; the girl who was gentleman always clutched you so.

The azaleas were separate flowers no longer; they were pink and white flags streaming by.

'Were you at the Bells' last week?' the voice came again. It sounded tired. Leila wondered whether she ought to ask him if he would like to stop.

'No, this is my first dance,' said she.

Her partner gave a little gasping laugh. 'Oh, I say,' he protested.

'Yes, it is really the first dance I've ever been to.' Leila was most fervent. It was such a relief to be able to tell somebody. 'You see, I've lived in the country all my life up till now . . .'

At that moment the music stopped, and they went to sit on two chairs against the wall. Leila tucked her pink satin feet under and fanned herself, while she blissfully watched the other couples passing and disappearing through the swing doors.

'Enjoying yourself, Leila?' asked Jose, nodding her golden head.

Laura passed and gave her the faintest little wink; it made Leila wonder for a moment whether she was quite grown up after all. Certainly her partner did not say very much. He coughed, tucked his handkerchief away, pulled down his waistcoat, took a minute thread off his sleeve. But it didn't matter. Almost immediately the band started and her second partner seemed to spring from the ceiling.

'Floor's not bad,' said the new voice. Did one always begin with the floor? And then, 'Were you at the Neaves' on Tuesday?' And again Leila explained. Perhaps it was a little strange that her partners were not more interested. For it was thrilling. Her first ball! She was only at the beginning of everything. It seemed to her that she had never known what the night was like before. Up till now it had been dark, silent, beautiful very often – oh yes – but mournful somehow. Solemn. And now it would never be like that again – it had opened dazzling bright.

'Care for an ice?' said her partner. And they went through the swing doors, down the passage, to the supper room. Her cheeks burned, she was fearfully thirsty. How sweet the ices looked on little glass plates and how cold the frosted spoon was, iced too! And when they came back to the hall there was the fat man waiting for her by the door. It gave her quite a shock again to see how old he was; he ought to have been on the stage with the fathers and mothers. And when Leila compared him with her other partners he looked shabby. His waistcoat was creased, there was a button off his glove, his coat looked as if it was dusty with French chalk.

'Come along, little lady,' said the fat man. He scarcely troubled to clasp her, and they moved away so gently, it was more like walking than dancing. But he said not a word about the floor. 'Your first dance, isn't it?' he murmured.

'How did you know?'

'Ah,' said the fat man, 'that's what it is to be old!' He wheezed faintly as he steered her past an awkward couple. 'You see, I've been doing this kind of thing for the last thirty years.'

'Thirty years?' cried Leila. Twelve years before she was born!

'It hardly bears thinking about, does it?' said the fat man gloomily. Leila looked at his bald head, and she felt quite sorry for him.

'I think it's marvellous to be still going on,' she said kindly.

'Kind little lady,' said the fat man, and he pressed her a little closer, and hummed a bar of the waltz. 'Of course,' he said, 'you can't hope to last anything like as long as that. No-o,' said the fat man, 'long before that you'll be sitting up there on the stage, looking on, in your nice black velvet. And these pretty arms will have turned into little short fat ones, and you'll beat time with such a different kind of fan – a black bony one.' The fat man seemed to shudder. 'And you'll smile away like the poor old dears up there, and point to your daughter, and tell the elderly lady next to you how some dreadful man tried to kiss her at the club ball. And your heart will ache, ache' – the fat man squeezed her closer still, as if he really was sorry for that poor heart – 'because no one wants to kiss you now. And you'll say how unpleasant these polished floors are to walk

10

on, how dangerous they are. Eh, Mademoiselle Twinkletoes?' said the fat man softly.

Leila gave a light little laugh, but she did not feel like laughing. Was it – could it all be true? It sounded terribly true. Was this first ball only the beginning of her last ball, after all? At that the music seemed to change; it sounded sad, sad; it rose upon a great sigh. Oh, how quickly things changed! Why didn't happiness last for ever? For ever wasn't a bit too long.

'I want to stop,' she said in a breathless voice. The fat man led her to the door.

'No,' she said, 'I won't go outside. I won't sit down. I'll just stand here, thank you.' She leaned against the wall, tapping with her foot, pulling up her gloves and trying to smile. But deep inside her a little girl threw her pinafore over her head and sobbed. Why had he spoiled it all?

'I say, you know,' said the fat man, 'you mustn't take me seriously, little lady.'

'As if I should!' said Leila, tossing her small dark head and sucking her underlip . . .

Again the couples paraded. The swing doors opened and shut. Now new music was given out by the bandmaster. But Leila didn't want to dance any more. She wanted to be home, or sitting on the veranda listening to those baby owls. When she looked through the dark windows at the stars, they had long beams like wings . . .

But presently a soft, melting, ravishing tune began, and a young man with curly hair bowed before her. She would have to dance, out of politeness, until she could find Meg. Very stiffly she walked into the middle; very haughtily she put her hand on his sleeve. But in one minute, in one turn, her feet glided, glided. The lights, the azaleas, the dresses, the pink faces, the velvet chairs, all became one beautiful flying wheel. And when her next partner bumped her into the fat man and he said, 'Pardon,' she smiled at him more radiantly than ever. She didn't even recognise him again.

The Student
by
Anton Chekhov

Anton Chekhov was born in Russia, on 29 January 1860, the third of six surviving children. He began writing short stories during his time at the University of Moscow and after graduating in 1884 with a degree in medicine worked as a journalist and writer of comic sketches. In 1887 his short story collection *At Dusk (V Sumerkakh)* won Chekhov the coveted Pushkin Prize and he produced his first full-length play, *Ivanov*. The first performance of *The Seagull* (1896) was a disaster but a new adaptation by the Moscow Art Theatre was a critical and commercial success. Soon after they staged triumphant adaptations of *Uncle Vanya* (1899), *The Three Sisters* (1900) and *The Cherry Orchard* (1904). By May, 1904 Chekhov was terminally ill with tuberculosis and died on 15 July, 1904.

The Student

A<small>T FIRST THE</small> weather was fine and still. The thrushes were
calling, and in the swamps close by something alive droned
pitifully with a sound like blowing into an empty bottle. A snipe
flew by, and the shot aimed at it rang out with a gay, resounding
note in the spring air. But when it began to get dark in the forest
a cold, penetrating wind blew inappropriately from the east, and
everything sank into silence. Needles of ice stretched across the
pools, and it felt cheerless, remote, and lonely in the forest. There
was a whiff of winter.

Ivan Velikopolsky, the son of a sacristan, and a student of the
clerical academy, returning home from shooting, walked all the time
by the path in the water-side meadow. His fingers were numb and
his face was burning with the wind. It seemed to him that the cold
that had suddenly come on had destroyed the order and harmony
of things, that nature itself felt ill at ease, and that was why the
evening darkness was falling more rapidly than usual. All around it
was deserted and peculiarly gloomy. The only light was one gleaming
in the widows' gardens near the river; the village, over three miles
away, and everything in the distance all round was plunged in the
cold evening mist. The student remembered that, as he went out
from the house, his mother was sitting barefoot on the floor in the
entry, cleaning the samovar, while his father lay on the stove coughing;
as it was Good Friday nothing had been cooked, and the student
was terribly hungry. And now, shrinking from the cold, he thought

that just such a wind had blown in the days of Rurik and in the time of Ivan the Terrible and Peter, and in their time there had been just the same desperate poverty and hunger, the same thatched roofs with holes in them, ignorance, misery, the same desolation around, the same darkness, the same feeling of oppression – all these had existed, did exist, and would exist, and the lapse of a thousand years would make life no better. And he did not want to go home.

The gardens were called the widows' because they were kept by two widows, mother and daughter. A camp fire was burning brightly with a crackling sound, throwing out light far around on the ploughed earth. The widow Vasilisa, a tall, fat old woman in a man's coat, was standing by and looking thoughtfully into the fire; her daughter Lukerya, a little pock-marked woman with a stupid-looking face, was sitting on the ground, washing a cauldron and spoons. Apparently they had just had supper. There was a sound of men's voices; it was the labourers watering their horses at the river.

'Here you have winter back again,' said the student, going up to the camp fire. 'Good evening.'

Vasilisa started, but at once recognised him and smiled cordially.

'I did not know you; God bless you,' she said.

'You'll be rich.'

They talked. Vasilisa, a woman of experience, who had been in service with the gentry, first as a wet-nurse, afterwards as a children's nurse, expressed herself with refinement, and a soft, sedate smile never left her face; her daughter Lukerya, a village peasant woman, who had been beaten by her husband, simply screwed up her eyes at the student and said nothing, and she had a strange expression like that of a deaf mute.

'At just such a fire the Apostle Peter warmed himself,' said the student, stretching out his hands to the fire, 'so it must have been cold then, too. Ah, what a terrible night it must have been, Granny! An utterly dismal long night!'

He looked round at the darkness, shook his head abruptly and asked:

'No doubt you have been at the reading of the Twelve Gospels?'

16

'Yes, I have,' answered Vasilisa.

'If you remember at the Last Supper Peter said to Jesus, "I am ready to go with Thee into darkness and unto death." And our Lord answered him thus: "I say unto thee, Peter, before the cock croweth thou wilt have denied Me thrice." After the supper Jesus went through the agony of death in the garden and prayed, and poor Peter was weary in spirit and faint, his eyelids were heavy and he could not struggle against sleep. He fell asleep. Then you heard how Judas the same night kissed Jesus and betrayed Him to His tormentors. They took Him bound to the high priest and beat Him, while Peter, exhausted, worn out with misery and alarm, hardly awake, you know, feeling that something awful was just going to happen on earth, followed behind . . . He loved Jesus passionately, intensely, and now he saw from far off how He was beaten . . .'

Lukerya left the spoons and fixed an immovable stare upon the student.

'They came to the high priest's,' he went on; 'they began to question Jesus, and meantime the labourers made a fire in the yard as it was cold, and warmed themselves. Peter, too, stood with them near the fire and warmed himself as I am doing. A woman, seeing him, said: "He was with Jesus, too" – that is as much as to say that he, too, should be taken to be questioned. And all the labourers that were standing near the fire must have looked sourly and suspiciously at him, because he was confused and said: "I don't know Him." A little while after again someone recognised him as one of Jesus's disciples and said: "Thou, too, art one of them," but again he denied it. And for the third time someone turned to him: "Why, did I not see thee with Him in the garden to-day?" For the third time he denied it. And immediately after that time the cock crowed, and Peter, looking from afar off at Jesus, remembered the words He had said to him in the evening . . . He remembered, he came to himself, went out of the yard and wept bitterly – bitterly. In the Gospel it is written: "He went out and wept bitterly." I imagine it: the still, still, dark, dark garden, and in the stillness, faintly audible, smothered sobbing . . .'

The student sighed and sank into thought. Still smiling, Vasilisa suddenly gave a gulp, big tears flowed freely down her cheeks, and she screened her face from the fire with her sleeve as though ashamed of her tears, and Lukerya, staring immovably at the student, flushed crimson, and her expression became strained and heavy like that of someone enduring intense pain.

The labourers came back from the river, and one of them riding a horse was quite near, and the light from the fire quivered upon him. The student said good-night to the widows and went on. And again the darkness was about him and his fingers began to be numb. A cruel wind was blowing, winter really had come back and it did not feel as though Easter would be the day after to-morrow.

Now the student was thinking about Vasilisa: since she had shed tears all that had happened to Peter the night before the Crucifixion must have some relation to her . . .

He looked round. The solitary light was still gleaming in the darkness and no figures could be seen near it now. The student thought again that if Vasilisa had shed tears, and her daughter had been troubled, it was evident that what he had just been telling them about, which had happened nineteen centuries ago, had a relation to the present – to both women, to the desolate village, to himself, to all people. The old woman had wept, not because he could tell the story touchingly, but because Peter was near to her, because her whole being was interested in what was passing in Peter's soul.

And joy suddenly stirred in his soul, and he even stopped for a minute to take breath. 'The past,' he thought, 'is linked with the present by an unbroken chain of events flowing one out of another.' And it seemed to him that he had just seen both ends of that chain; that when he touched one end the other quivered.

When he crossed the river by the ferry boat and afterwards, mounting the hill, looked at his village and towards the west where the cold crimson sunset lay a narrow streak of light, he thought that truth and beauty which had guided human life there in the garden and in the yard of the high priest had continued without interruption to this day, and had evidently always been the chief thing in human life and in all earthly life, indeed; and the feeling of youth, health, vigour – he was only twenty-two – and the inexpressible sweet expectation of happiness, of unknown mysterious happiness, took possession of him little by little, and life seemed to him enchanting, marvellous, and full of lofty meaning.

The Selfish Giant
by
Oscar Wilde

Oscar Fingal O'Flahertie Wills Wilde was born in Dublin on 16 October, 1854. He studied classics at Trinity College, Dublin, where he was an outstanding student and was awarded a scholarship to Magdalen College, Oxford, where he studied from 1874 to 1878. After he graduated, he moved to London to pursue a literary career. A first volume of his poetry was published in 1881 and as well as composing verse, he contributed to publications such as the *Pall Mall Gazette*, wrote fairy stories, published a novel, *The Picture of Dorian Gray* (1891), and several plays, *Lady Windermere's Fan* (1892), *An Ideal Husband* (1895) and *The Importance of Being Earnest* (1895). In April 1895, Wilde sued the Marquis of Queensberry for libel, after the Marquis accused him of being homosexual. Wilde lost and, after details of his private life were revealed during the trial, was tried for gross indecency and sentenced to two years of hard labour. While in prison he composed a long letter to his close friend Lord Alfred Douglas, posthumously published under the title *De Profundis*. Wilde was released with his health irrevocably damaged and his reputation ruined. He spent the rest of his life in Europe, publishing *The Ballad of Reading Gaol* in 1898. He died in Paris on 30 November 1900.

The Selfish Giant

EVERY AFTERNOON, AS they were coming from school, the children used to go and play in the Giant's garden.

It was a large lovely garden, with soft green grass. Here and there over the grass stood beautiful flowers like stars, and there were twelve peach-trees that in the spring-time broke out into delicate blossoms of pink and pearl, and in the autumn bore rich fruit. The birds sat on the trees and sang so sweetly that the children used to stop their games in order to listen to them. 'How happy we are here!' they cried to each other.

One day the Giant came back. He had been to visit his friend the Cornish ogre, and had stayed with him for seven years. After the seven years were over he had said all that he had to say, for his conversation was limited, and he determined to return to his own castle. When he arrived he saw the children playing in the garden.

'What are you doing here?' he cried in a very gruff voice, and the children ran away.

'My own garden is my own garden,' said the Giant; 'any one can understand that, and I will allow nobody to play in it but myself.' So he built a high wall all round it, and put up a notice-board.

TRESPASSERS
WILL BE
PROSECUTED

He was a very selfish Giant.

The poor children had now nowhere to play. They tried to play on the road, but the road was very dusty and full of hard stones, and they did not like it. They used to wander round the high wall when their lessons were over, and talk about the beautiful garden inside. 'How happy we were there,' they said to each other.

Then the Spring came, and all over the country there were little blossoms and little birds. Only in the garden of the Selfish Giant it was still winter. The birds did not care to sing in it as there were no children, and the trees forgot to blossom. Once a beautiful flower put its head out from the grass, but when it saw the notice-board it was so sorry for the children that it slipped back into the ground again, and went off to sleep. The only people who were pleased were the Snow and the Frost. 'Spring has forgotten this garden,' they cried, 'so we will live here all the year round.' The Snow covered up the grass with her great white cloak, and the Frost painted all the trees silver. Then they invited the North Wind to stay with them, and he came. He was wrapped in furs, and he roared all day about the garden, and blew the chimney-pots down. 'This is a delightful spot,' he said, 'we must ask the Hail on a visit.' So the Hail came. Every day for three hours he rattled on the roof of the castle till he broke most of the slates, and then he ran round and round the garden as fast as he could go. He was dressed in grey, and his breath was like ice.

'I cannot understand why the Spring is so late in coming,' said the Selfish Giant, as he sat at the window and looked out at his cold white garden; 'I hope there will be a change in the weather.'

But the Spring never came, nor the Summer. The Autumn gave golden fruit to every garden, but to the Giant's garden she gave none. 'He is too selfish,' she said. So it was always Winter there, and the North Wind, and the Hail, and the Frost, and the Snow danced about through the trees.

One morning the Giant was lying awake in bed when he heard some lovely music. It sounded so sweet to his ears that he thought it must be the King's musicians passing by. It was really only a little linnet singing outside his window, but it was so long since he had heard a bird sing in his garden that it seemed to him to be the most beautiful music in the world. Then the Hail stopped dancing over his head, and the North Wind ceased roaring, and a delicious perfume came to him through the open casement. 'I believe the Spring has come at last,' said the Giant; and he jumped out of bed and looked out.

What did he see?

He saw a most wonderful sight. Through a little hole in the wall the children had crept in, and they were sitting in the branches of the trees. In every tree that he could see there was a little child. And the trees were so glad to have the children back again that they had covered themselves with blossoms, and were waving their arms gently above the children's heads. The birds were flying about and twittering with delight, and the flowers were looking up through the green grass and laughing. It was a lovely scene, only in one corner it was still winter. It was the farthest corner of the garden, and in it was standing a little boy. He was so small that he could not reach up to the branches of the tree, and he was wandering all round it, crying bitterly. The poor tree was still quite covered with frost and snow, and the North Wind was blowing and roaring above it. 'Climb up! little boy,' said the Tree, and it bent its branches down as low as it could; but the boy was too tiny.

And the Giant's heart melted as he looked out. 'How selfish I have been!' he said; 'now I know why the Spring would not come here. I will put that poor little boy on the top of the tree, and then I will knock down the wall, and my garden shall be the children's playground for ever and ever.' He was really very sorry for what he had done.

So he crept downstairs and opened the front door quite softly, and went out into the garden. But when the children saw him they were so frightened that they all ran away, and the garden became winter again. Only the little boy did not run, for his eyes were so full of tears that he did not see the Giant coming. And the Giant stole up behind him and took him gently in his hand, and put him up into the tree. And the tree broke at once into blossom, and the birds came and sang on it, and the little boy stretched out his two arms and flung them round the Giant's neck, and kissed him. And the other children, when they saw that the Giant was not wicked any longer, came running back, and with them came the Spring. 'It is your garden now, little children,' said the Giant, and he took a great axe and knocked down the wall. And when the people were going to market at twelve o'clock they found the Giant playing with the children in the most beautiful garden they had ever seen.

All day long they played, and in the evening they came to the Giant to bid him good-bye.

'But where is your little companion?' he said: 'the boy I put into the tree.' The Giant loved him the best because he had kissed him.

'We don't know,' answered the children; 'he has gone away.'

'You must tell him to be sure and come here to-morrow,' said the Giant. But the children said that they did not know where he lived, and had never seen him before; and the Giant felt very sad.

Every afternoon, when school was over, the children came and played with the Giant. But the little boy whom the Giant loved was never seen again. The Giant was very kind to all the children, yet he longed for his first little friend, and often spoke of him. 'How I would like to see him!' he used to say.

Years went over, and the Giant grew very old and feeble. He could not play about any more, so he sat in a huge armchair, and watched the children at their games, and admired his garden. 'I have many beautiful flowers,' he said; 'but the children are the most beautiful flowers of all.'

One winter morning he looked out of his window as he was dressing. He did not hate the Winter now, for he knew that it was merely the Spring asleep, and that the flowers were resting.

Suddenly he rubbed his eyes in wonder, and looked and looked. It certainly was a marvellous sight. In the farthest corner of the garden was a tree quite covered with lovely white blossoms. Its branches were all golden, and silver fruit hung down from them, and underneath it stood the little boy he had loved.

Downstairs ran the Giant in great joy, and out into the garden. He hastened across the grass, and came near to the child. And when he came quite close his face grew red with anger, and he said, 'Who hath dared to wound thee?' For on the palms of the child's hands were the prints of two nails, and the prints of two nails were on the little feet.

'Who hath dared to wound thee?' cried the Giant; 'tell me, that I may take my big sword and slay him.'

'Nay!' answered the child; 'but these are the wounds of Love.'

'Who art thou?' said the Giant, and a strange awe fell on him, and he knelt before the little child.

And the child smiled on the Giant, and said to him, 'You let me play once in your garden, to-day you shall come with me to my garden, which is Paradise.'

And when the children ran in that afternoon, they found the Giant lying dead under the tree, all covered with white blossoms.

Stories
to send a
shiver down
your spine

A Terribly Strange Bed
by
Wilkie Collins

William Wilkie Collins was born in London in 1824. After the death of his father, a landscape artist, in 1847 Collins published his first book, *Memoirs of the Life of William Collins, Esq., R.A.* He considered a career in painting, exhibiting a picture at the Royal Academy summer exhibition in 1849, but it was with the publication of his first novel, *Antonina*, in 1850 that his career as a writer began in earnest. Collins was a lifelong friend of Charles Dickens and several of his novels were serialised in Dickens's weekly publication, *All the Year Round* including *The Woman in White* (1860) and *The Moonstone* (1866), which was described by T. S. Eliot as the 'first and greatest of English detective novels'. Always in delicate health, on 30 June 1889 Collins suffered a stroke and died on 23 September.

A Terribly Strange Bed

SHORTLY AFTER MY education at college was finished, I happened to be staying at Paris with an English friend. We were both young men then, and lived, I am afraid, rather a wild life, in the delightful city of our sojourn. One night we were idling about the neighbourhood of the Palais Royal, doubtful to what amusement we should next betake ourselves. My friend proposed a visit to Frascati's; but his suggestion was not to my taste. I knew Frascati's, as the French saying is, by heart; had lost and won plenty of five-franc pieces there, merely for amusement's sake, until it was amusement no longer, and was thoroughly tired, in fact, of all the ghastly respectabilities of such a social anomaly as a respectable gambling-house. 'For Heaven's sake,' said I to my friend, 'let us go somewhere where we can see a little genuine, blackguard, poverty-stricken gaming with no false gingerbread glitter thrown over it all. Let us get away from fashionable Frascati's, to a house where they don't mind letting in a man with a ragged coat, or a man with no coat, ragged or otherwise.' 'Very well,' said my friend, 'we needn't go out of the Palais Royal to find the sort of company you want. Here's the place just before us; as blackguard a place, by all report, as you could possibly wish to see.' In another minute we arrived at the door and entered the house.

When we got upstairs, and had left our hats and sticks with the doorkeeper, we were admitted into the chief gambling-room. We did not find many people assembled there. But, few as the men

were who looked up at us on our entrance, they were all types –
lamentably true types – of their respective classes.

We had come to see blackguards; but these men were something
worse. There is a comic side, more or less appreciable, in all
blackguardism – here there was nothing but tragedy – mute, weird
tragedy. The quiet in the room was horrible. The thin, haggard,
long-haired young man, whose sunken eyes fiercely watched the
turning up of the cards, never spoke; the flabby, fat-faced, pimply
player, who pricked his piece of pasteboard perseveringly, to register
how often black won, and how often red – never spoke; the dirty,
wrinkled old man, with the vulture eyes and the darned greatcoat,
who had lost his last *sou*, and still looked on desperately, after he
could play no longer – never spoke. Even the voice of the croupier
sounded as if it were strangely dulled and thickened in the atmosphere
of the room. I had entered the place to laugh, but the spectacle before
me was something to weep over. I soon found it necessary to take
refuge in excitement from the depression of spirits which was fast
stealing on me. Unfortunately I sought the nearest excitement, by
going to the table and beginning to play. Still more unfortunately, as
the event will show, I won – won prodigiously; won incredibly; won
at such a rate that the regular players at the table crowded round me;
and staring at my stakes with hungry, superstitious eyes, whispered
to one another that the English stranger was going to break the bank.

The game was *Rouge et Noir*. I had played at it in every city in
Europe, without, however, the care or the wish to study the Theory
of Chances – that philosopher's stone of all gamblers! And a gambler,
in the strict sense of the word, I had never been. I was heart-whole
from the corroding passion for play. My gaming was a mere idle
amusement. I never resorted to it by necessity, because I never knew
what it was to want money. I never practised it so incessantly as to
lose more than I could afford, or to gain more than I could coolly
pocket without being thrown off my balance by my good luck. In
short, I had hitherto frequented gambling-tables – just as I frequented
ballrooms and opera-houses – because they amused me, and because
I had nothing better to do with my leisure hours.

But on this occasion it was very different – now, for the first time in my life, I felt what the passion for play really was. My success first bewildered, and then, in the most literal meaning of the word, intoxicated me. Incredible as it may appear, it is nevertheless true, that I only lost when I attempted to estimate chances, and played according to previous calculation. If I left everything to luck, and staked without any care or consideration, I was sure to win – to win in the face of every recognised probability in favour of the bank. At first some of the men present ventured their money safely enough on my colour; but I speedily increased my stakes to sums which they dared not risk. One after another they left off playing, and breathlessly looked on at my game.

Still, time after time, I staked higher and higher, and still won. The excitement in the room rose to fever pitch. The silence was interrupted by a deep-muttered chorus of oaths and exclamations in different languages, every time the gold was shovelled across to my side of the table – even the imperturbable croupier dashed his rake on the floor in a (French) fury of astonishment at my success. But one man present preserved his self-possession, and that man was my friend. He came to my side, and whispering in English, begged me to leave the place, satisfied with what I had already gained. I must do him the justice to say that he repeated his warnings and entreaties several times, and only left me and went away after I had rejected his advice (I was to all intents and purposes gambling drunk) in terms which rendered it impossible for him to address me again that night.

Shortly after he had gone, a hoarse voice behind me cried: 'Permit me, my dear sir – permit me to restore to their proper place two napoleons which you have dropped. Wonderful luck, sir! I pledge you my word of honour, as an old soldier, in the course of my long experience in this sort of thing, I never saw such luck as yours – never! Go on, sir – *Sacre mille bombes!* Go on boldly, and break the bank!'

I turned round and saw, nodding and smiling at me with inveterate civility, a tall man, dressed in a frogged and braided surtout.

If I had been in my senses, I should have considered him, personally, as being rather a suspicious specimen of an old soldier. He had goggling bloodshot eyes, mangy moustaches, and a broken nose. His voice betrayed a barrack-room intonation of the worst order, and he had the dirtiest pair of hands I ever saw – even in France. These little personal peculiarities exercised, however, no repelling influence on me. In the mad excitement, the reckless triumph of that moment, I was ready to 'fraternise' with anybody who encouraged me in my game. I accepted the old soldier's offered pinch of snuff; clapped him on the back, and swore he was the honestest fellow in the world – the most glorious relic of the Grand Army that I had ever met with. 'Go on!' cried my military friend, snapping his fingers in ecstasy – 'Go on, and win! Break the bank – *Mille tonnerres!* My gallant English comrade, break the bank!'

And I *did* go on – went on at such a rate, that in another quarter of an hour the croupier called out, 'Gentlemen, the bank has discontinued for tonight.' All the notes, and all the gold in that 'bank', now lay in a heap under my hands; the whole floating capital of the gambling-house was waiting to pour into my pockets!

'Tie up the money in your pocket-handkerchief, my worthy sir,' said the old soldier, as I wildly plunged my hands into my heap of gold. 'Tie it up, as we used to tie up a bit of dinner in the Grand Army; your winnings are too heavy for any breeches-pockets that ever were sewed. There! That's it – shovel them in, notes and all! *Credie!* What luck! Stop! Another napoleon on the floor! *Ah! Sacre petit polisson de Napoleon!* Have I found thee at last? Now then, sir – two tight double knots each way with your honourable permission, and the money's safe. Feel it! Feel it, fortunate sir! Hard and round as a cannon-ball – *Ah, bah!* If they had only fired such cannon-balls at us at Austerlitz – *nom d'une pipe!* If they only had! And now, as an ancient grenadier, as an ex-brave of the French army, what remains for me to do? I ask what? Simply this: to entreat my valued English friend to drink a bottle of champagne with me, and toast the goddess Fortune in foaming goblets before we part!'

'Excellent ex-brave! Convivial ancient grenadier! Champagne by all means! An English cheer for an old soldier! Hurrah! Hurrah! Another English cheer for the goddess Fortune! Hurrah! Hurrah! Hurrah!'

'Bravo! The Englishman; the amiable, gracious Englishman, in whose veins circulates the vivacious blood of France! Another glass? *Ah, bah!* – the bottle is empty! Never mind! *Vive le vin!* I, the old soldier, order another bottle, and half a pound of *bonbons* with it!'

'No, no, ex-brave; never – ancient grenadier! *Your* bottle last time; *my* bottle this. Behold it! Toast away! The French Army! The great Napoleon! The present company! The croupier! The honest croupier's wife and daughters – if he has any! The Ladies generally! Everybody in the world!'

By the time the second bottle of champagne was emptied, I felt as if I had been drinking liquid fire – my brain seemed all aflame. No excess in wine had ever had this effect on me before in my life. Was it the result of a stimulant acting upon my system when I was in a highly excited state? Was my stomach in a particularly disordered condition? Or was the champagne amazingly strong?

'Ex-brave of the French Army!' cried I, in a mad state of exhilaration, '*I* am on fire! How are *you*? You have set me on fire. Do you hear, my hero of Austerlitz? Let us have a third bottle of champagne to put the flame out!'

The old soldier wagged his head, rolled his goggle-eyes, until I expected to see them slip out of their sockets; placed his dirty forefinger by the side of his broken nose; solemnly ejaculated 'Coffee!' and immediately ran off into an inner room.

The word pronounced by the eccentric veteran seemed to have a magical effect on the rest of the company present. With one accord they all rose to depart. Probably they had expected to profit by my intoxication; but finding that my new friend was benevolently bent on preventing me from getting dead drunk, had now abandoned all hope of thriving pleasantly on my winnings. Whatever their motive might be, at any rate they went away in a body. When the old soldier returned, and sat down again opposite to me at the table, we had the room to ourselves. I could see the croupier, in a sort of vestibule which opened out of it, eating his supper in solitude. The silence was now deeper than ever.

A sudden change, too, had come over the 'ex-brave'. He assumed a portentously solemn look; and when he spoke to me again, his speech was ornamented by no oaths, enforced by no finger-snapping, enlivened by no apostrophes or exclamations.

'Listen, my dear sir,' said he, in mysteriously confidential tones – 'listen to an old soldier's advice. I have been to the mistress of the house (a very charming woman, with a genius for cookery!) to impress on her the necessity of making us some particularly strong and good coffee. You must drink this coffee in order to get rid of your little amiable exaltation of spirits before you think of going home – you *must* my good and gracious friend! With all that money to take home tonight, it is a sacred duty to yourself to have your wits about you. You are known to be a winner to an enormous extent by several gentlemen present tonight, who, in a certain point of view, are very worthy and excellent fellows; but they are mortal men, my dear sir, and they have their amiable weaknesses. Need I say more? Ah, no, no! You understand me! Now, this is what you must do – send for a cabriolet when you feel quite well again – draw up all the windows when you get into it – and tell the driver to take you home only through the large and well-lighted thoroughfares. Do this; and you and your money will be safe. Do this; and tomorrow you will thank an old soldier for giving you a word of honest advice.'

Just as the ex-brave ended his oration in very lachrymose tones, the coffee came in, ready poured out in two cups. My attentive friend handed me one of the cups with a bow. I was parched with thirst, and drank it off at a draught. Almost instantly afterwards, I was seized with a fit of giddiness, and felt more completely intoxicated than ever. The room whirled round and round furiously; the old soldier seemed to be regularly bobbing up and down before me like the piston of a steam-engine. I was half deafened by a violent singing in my ears; a feeling of utter bewilderment, helplessness, idiocy, overcame me. I rose from my chair, holding on by the table to keep my balance; and stammered out that I felt dreadfully unwell – so unwell that I did not know how I was to get home.

'My dear friend,' answered the old soldier – and even his voice seemed to be bobbing up and down as he spoke – 'my dear friend, it would be madness to go home in *your* state; you would be sure to lose your money; you might be robbed and murdered with the greatest ease. *I* am going to sleep here; do *you* sleep here, too – they make up capital beds in this house – take one; sleep off the effects of the wine, and go home safely with your winnings tomorrow – tomorrow, in broad daylight.'

I had but two ideas left: one, that I must never let go hold of my handkerchief full of money; the other, that I must lie down somewhere immediately, and fall off into a comfortable sleep. So I agreed to the proposal about the bed, and took the offered arm of the old soldier, carrying my money with my disengaged hand. Preceded by the croupier, we passed along some passages and up a flight of stairs into the bedroom which I was to occupy. The ex-brave shook me warmly by the hand, proposed that we should breakfast together, and then, followed by the croupier, left me for the night.

I ran to the wash-hand stand; drank some of the water in my jug; poured the rest out, and plunged my face into it; then sat down in a chair and tried to compose myself. I soon felt better. The change for my lungs, from the fetid atmosphere of the gambling-room to the cool air of the apartment I now occupied, the almost equally refreshing change for my eyes, from the glaring gaslights of the 'salon' to the dim, quiet flicker of one bedroom-candle, aided wonderfully the restorative effects of cold water. The giddiness left me, and I began to feel a little like a reasonable being again. My first thought was of the risk of sleeping all night in a gambling-house; my second, of the still greater risk of trying to get out after the house was closed, and of going home alone at night through the streets of Paris with a large sum of money about me. I had slept in worse places than this on my travels; so I determined to lock, bolt, and barricade my door, and take my chance till the next morning.

Accordingly, I secured myself against all intrusion; looked under the bed, and into the cupboard; tried the fastening of the window; and then, satisfied that I had taken every proper precaution, pulled off my upper clothing, put my light, which was a dim one, on the hearth among a feathery litter of wood-ashes, and got into bed, with the handkerchief full of money under my pillow.

I soon felt not only that I could not go to sleep, but that I could not even close my eyes. I was wide awake, and in a high fever. Every nerve in my body trembled – every one of my senses seemed to be preternaturally sharpened. I tossed and rolled, and tried every kind of position, and perseveringly sought out the cold corners of the bed, and all to no purpose. Now I thrust my arms over the clothes, now I poked them under the clothes; now I violently shot my legs straight out down to the bottom of the bed; now I convulsively coiled them up as near my chin as they would go; now I shook out my crumpled pillow, changed it to the cool side, patted it flat, and lay down quietly on my back; now I fiercely doubled it in two, set it up on end, thrust it against the board of the bed, and tried a sitting posture. Every effort was in vain; I groaned with vexation as I felt that I was in for a sleepless night.

What could I do? I had no book to read. And yet, unless I found out some method of diverting my mind, I felt certain that I was in the condition to imagine all sorts of horrors; to rack my brain with forebodings of every possible and impossible danger; in short, to pass the night in suffering all conceivable varieties of nervous terror.

I raised myself on my elbow, and looked about the room – which was brightened by a lovely moonlight pouring straight through the window – to see if it contained any pictures or ornaments that I could at all clearly distinguish. While my eyes wandered from wall to wall, a remembrance of Le Maistre's delightful little book, *Voyage autour de ma Chambre*, occurred to me. I resolved to imitate the French author, and find occupation and amusement enough to relieve the tedium of my wakefulness, by making a mental inventory of every article of furniture I could see, and by following up to their sources the multitude of associations which even a chair, a table, or a wash-hand stand may be made to call forth.

In the nervous unsettled state of my mind at that moment, I found it much easier to make my inventory than to make my reflections, and thereupon soon gave up all hope of thinking in Le Maistre's fanciful track – or, indeed, of thinking at all. I looked about the room at the different articles of furniture, and did nothing more.

There was, first, the bed I was lying in; a four-post bed, of all things in the world to meet with in Paris – yes, a thorough clumsy British four-poster, with the regular top lined with chintz – the regular fringed valance all round – the regular stifling, unwholesome curtains, which I remembered having mechanically drawn back against the posts without particularly noticing the bed when I first got into the room. Then there was the marble-topped wash-hand stand, from which the water I had spilled, in my hurry to pour it out, was still dripping, slowly and more slowly, on to the brick floor. Then two small chairs, with my coat, waistcoat, and trousers flung on them. Then a large elbow-chair covered with dirty-white dimity, with my cravat and shirt collar thrown over the back. Then a chest of drawers with two of the brass handles off, and a tawdry, broken china inkstand placed on it by way of ornament for the top. Then the dressing-table, adorned by a very small looking-glass, and a very large pincushion. Then the window – an unusually large window. Then a dark old picture, which the feeble candle dimly showed me. It was a picture of a fellow in a high Spanish hat, crowned with a plume of towering feathers. A swarthy, sinister ruffian, looking upward, shading his eyes with his hand, and looking intently upward – it might be at some tall gallows at which he was going to be hanged. At any rate, he had the appearance of thoroughly deserving it.

This picture put a kind of constraint upon me to look upward too – at the top of the bed. It was a gloomy and not an interesting object, and I looked back at the picture. I counted the feathers in the man's hat – they stood out in relief – three white, two green. I observed the crown of his hat, which was of conical shape, according to the fashion supposed to have been favoured by Guido Fawkes. I wondered what he was looking up at. It couldn't be at the stars; such a desperado was neither astrologer nor astronomer. It must be at the high gallows, and he was going to be hanged presently. Would the executioner come into possession of his conical crowned hat and plume of feathers? I counted the feathers again – three white, two green.

While I still lingered over this very improving and intellectual employment, my thoughts insensibly began to wander. The moonlight shining into the room reminded me of a certain moonlight night in England – the night after a picnic party in a Welsh valley. Every incident of the drive homeward, through lovely scenery, which the moonlight made lovelier than ever, came back to my remembrance, though I had never given the picnic a thought for years; though, if I had *tried* to recollect it, I could certainly have recalled little or nothing of that scene long past. Of all the wonderful faculties that help to tell us we are immortal, which speaks the sublime truth more eloquently than memory? Here was I, in a strange house of the most suspicious character, in a situation of uncertainty, and even of peril, which might seem to make the cool exercise of my recollection almost out of the question; nevertheless remembering, quite involuntarily, places, people, conversations, minute circumstances of every kind, which I had thought forgotten for ever; which I could not possibly have recalled at will, even under the most favourable auspices. And what cause had produced in a moment the whole of this strange, complicated. mysterious effect? Nothing but some rays of moonlight shining in at my bedroom window.

I was still thinking of the picnic – of our merriment on the drive home – of the sentimental young lady who *would* quote 'Childe Harold' because it was moonlight. I was absorbed by these past scenes and past amusements, when, in an instant, the thread on which my memories hung snapped asunder; my attention immediately came back to present things more vividly than ever, and I found myself, I neither knew why nor wherefore, looking hard at the picture again.

Looking for what?

Good God! The man had pulled his hat down on his brows! No! The hat itself was gone! Where was the conical crown? Where the feathers – three white, two green? Not there! In place of the hat and feathers – what dusky object was it that now hid his forehead, his eyes, his shading hand?

Was the bed moving?

I turned on my back and looked up. Was I mad? Drunk? Dreaming? Giddy again? Or was the top of the bed really moving down – sinking slowly, regularly, silently, horribly, right down throughout the whole of its length and breadth – right down upon me, as I lay underneath?

My blood seemed to stand still. A deadly paralysing coldness stole all over me as I turned my head round on the pillow and determined to test whether the bed-top was really moving or not, by keeping my eye on the man in the picture.

The next look in that direction was enough. The dull, black, frowzy outline of the valance above me was within an inch of being parallel with his waist. I still looked breathlessly. And steadily and slowly – very slowly – I saw the figure, and the line of frame below the figure, vanish, as the valance moved down before it.

I am, constitutionally, anything but timid. I have been on more than one occasion in peril of my life, and have not lost my self-possession for an instant; but when the conviction first settled on my mind that the bed-top was really moving, was steadily and continuously sinking down upon me, I looked up shuddering, helpless, panic-stricken, beneath the hideous machinery for murder, which was advancing closer and closer to suffocate me where I lay.

I looked up, motionless, speechless, breathless. The candle, fully spent, went out; but the moonlight still brightened the room. Down and down, without pausing and without sounding, came the bed-top, and still my panic-terror seemed to bind me faster and faster to the mattress on which I lay – down and down it sank, till the dusty odour from the lining of the canopy came stealing into my nostrils.

At that final moment the instinct of self-preservation startled me out of my trance, and I moved at last. There was just room for me to roll myself sidewise off the bed. As I dropped noiselessly to the floor, the edge of the murderous canopy touched me on the shoulder.

Without stopping to draw my breath, without wiping the cold sweat from my face, I rose instantly on my knees to watch the bed-top. I was literally spellbound by it. If I had heard footsteps behind me, I could not have turned round; if a means of escape had been miraculously provided for me, I could not have moved to take advantage of it. The whole life in me was, at that moment, concentrated in my eyes.

It descended – the whole canopy, with the fringe round it, came down – down – close down; so close that there was not room now to squeeze my finger between the bed-top and the bed. I felt at the sides, and discovered that what had appeared to me from beneath to be the ordinary light canopy of a four-post bed was in reality a thick, broad mattress, the substance of which was concealed by the valance and its fringe. I looked up and saw the four posts rising hideously bare. In the middle of the bed-top was a huge wooden screw that had evidently worked it down through a hole in the ceiling, just as ordinary presses are worked down on the substance selected for compression. The frightful apparatus moved without making the faintest noise. There had been no creaking as it came down; there was now not the faintest sound from the room above. Amid a dead and awful silence I beheld before me – in the nineteenth century, and in the civilised capital of France – such a machine for secret murder by suffocation as might have existed in the worst days of the Inquisition, in the lonely inns among the Hartz Mountains, in the mysterious tribunals of Westphalia! Still, as I looked on it, I could not move, I could hardly breathe, but I began to recover the power of thinking, and in a moment I discovered the murderous conspiracy framed against me in all its horror.

My cup of coffee had been drugged, and drugged too strongly. I had been saved from being smothered by having taken an overdose of some narcotic. How I had chafed and fretted at the fever-fit which had preserved my life by keeping me awake! How recklessly I had confided myself to the two wretches who had led me into this room, determined, for the sake of my winnings, to kill me in my sleep by the surest and most horrible contrivance for secretly accomplishing my destruction! How many men, winners like me, had slept, as I had proposed to sleep, in that bed, and had never been seen or heard of more! I shuddered at the bare idea of it.

But, ere long, all thought was again suspended by the sight of the murderous canopy moving once more. After it had remained on the bed – as nearly as I could guess – about ten minutes, it began to move up again. The villains who worked it from above evidently believed that their purpose was now accomplished. Slowly and silently, as it had descended, that horrible bed-top rose towards its former place. When it reached the upper extremities of the four posts, it reached the ceiling, too. Neither hole nor screw could be seen; the bed became in appearance an ordinary bed again – the canopy an ordinary canopy – even to the most suspicious eyes.

Now, for the first time, I was able to move – to rise from my knees – to dress myself in my upper clothing – and to consider how I should escape. If I betrayed by the smallest noise that the attempt to suffocate me had failed, I was certain to be murdered. Had I made any noise already? I listened intently, looking towards the door.

No! No footsteps in the passage outside – no sound of a tread, light or heavy, in the room above – absolute silence everywhere. Besides locking and bolting my door, I had moved an old wooden chest against it, which I had found under the bed. To remove this chest (my blood ran cold as I thought of what its contents *might* be!) without making some disturbance was impossible; and, moreover, to think of escaping through the house, now barred up for the night, was sheer insanity. Only one chance was left me – the window. I stole to it on tiptoe.

My bedroom was on the first floor, above an *entresol*, and looked into a back street. I raised my hand to open the window, knowing that on that action hung, by the merest hair-breadth, my chance of safety. They keep vigilant watch in a House of Murder. If any part of the frame cracked, if the hinge creaked, I was a lost man! It must have occupied me at least five minutes, reckoning by time – five *hours*, reckoning by suspense – to open that window. I succeeded in doing it silently – in doing it with all the dexterity of a house-breaker – and then looked down into the street. To leap the distance beneath me would be almost certain destruction! Next, I looked round at the sides of the house. Down the left side ran a thick water-pipe – it passed close by the outer edge of the window. The moment I saw the pipe I knew I was saved. My breath came and went freely for the first time since I had seen the canopy of the bed moving down upon me!

To some men the means of escape which I had discovered might have seemed difficult and dangerous enough – to *me* the prospect of slipping down the pipe into the street did not suggest even a thought of peril. I had always been accustomed, by the practice of gymnastics, to keep up my schoolboy powers as a daring and expert climber; and knew that my head, hands, and feet would serve me faithfully in any hazards of ascent or descent. I had already got one leg over the window-sill, when I remembered the handkerchief filled with money under my pillow. I could well have afforded to leave it behind me, but I was revengefully determined that the miscreants of the gambling-house should miss their plunder as well as their victim. So I went back to the bed and tied the heavy handkerchief at my back by my cravat.

Just as I had made it tight and fixed it in a comfortable place, I thought I heard a sound of breathing outside the door. The chill feeling of horror ran through me again as I listened. No! Dead silence still in the passage – I had only heard the night air blowing softly into the room. The next moment I was on the window-sill – and the next I had a firm grip on the water-pipe with my hands and knees.

I slid down into the street easily and quietly, as I thought I should, and immediately set off at the top of my speed to a branch 'Prefecture' of Police, which I knew was situated in the immediate neighbourhood. A 'Sub-prefect', and several picked men among his subordinates, happened to be up, maturing, I believe, some scheme for discovering the perpetrator of a mysterious murder which all Paris was talking of just then. When I began my story, in a breathless hurry and in very bad French, I could see that the Sub-prefect suspected me of being a drunken Englishman who had robbed somebody; but he soon altered his opinion as I went on, and before I had anything like concluded, he shoved all the papers before him into a drawer, put on his hat, supplied me with another (for I was bareheaded), ordered a file of soldiers, desired his expert followers to get ready all sorts of tools for breaking open doors and ripping up brick flooring, and took my arm, in the most friendly and familiar manner possible, to lead me with him out of the house. I will venture to say that when the Sub-perfect was a little boy, and was taken for the first time to the play, he was not half as much pleased as he was now at the job in prospect for him at the gambling-house!

Away we went through the streets, the Sub-prefect cross-examining and congratulating me in the same breath as we marched at the head of our formidable *posse comitatus*. Sentinels were placed at the back and front of the house the moment we got to it; a tremendous battery of knocks was directed against the door; a light appeared at a window; I was told to conceal myself behind the police – then came more knocks and a cry of 'Open in the name of the law!' At that terrible summons bolts and locks gave way before an invisible hand, and the moment after the Sub-prefect was in the passage, confronting a waiter half-dressed and ghastly pale. This was the short dialogue which immediately took place:

'We want to see the Englishman who is sleeping in this house.'

'He went away hours ago.'

'He did no such thing. His friend went away; *he* remained. Show us to his bedroom!'

'I swear to you, Monsieur le Sous-Préfect, he is not here! He –'

'I swear to you, Monsieur le Garcon, he is. He slept here – he didn't find your bed comfortable – he came to us to complain of it – here he is among my men – and here am I ready to look for a flea or two in his bedstead. Renaudin!' calling to one of the subordinates, and pointing to the waiter – 'collar that man and tie his hands behind him. Now, then, gentlemen, let us walk upstairs!'

Every man and woman in the house was secured – the 'Old Soldier' the first. Then I identified the bed in which I had slept, and then we went into the room above.

No object that was at all extraordinary appeared in any part of it. The Sub-prefect looked round the place, commanded everybody to be silent, stamped twice on the floor, called for a candle, looked attentively at the spot he had stamped on, and ordered the flooring there to be carefully taken up. This was done in no time. Lights were produced, and we saw a deep raftered cavity between the floor of this room and the ceiling of the room beneath. Through this cavity there ran perpendicularly a sort of case of iron thickly greased; and inside the case appeared the screw, which communicated with the bed-top below. Extra lengths of screw, freshly oiled; levers covered with felt; all the complete upper works of a heavy press – constructed with infernal ingenuity so as to join the fixtures below, and when taken to pieces again, to go into the smallest possible compass – were next discovered and pulled out on the floor. After some little difficulty the Sub-prefect succeeded in putting the machinery together, and, leaving his men to work it, descended with me to the bedroom. The smothering canopy was then lowered, but not so noiselessly as I had seen it lowered. When I mentioned this to the Sub-prefect, his answer, simple as it was, had a terrible significance. 'My men,' said he, 'are working down the bed-top for the first time – the men whose money you won were in better practice.'

We left the house in the sole possession of two police agents – every one of the inmates being removed to prison on the spot. The Sub-prefect, after taking down my *procès-verbal* in his office, returned with me to my hotel to get my passport. 'Do you think,' I asked, as I gave it to him, 'that any men have really been smothered in that bed, as they tried to smother *me*?'

'I have seen dozens of drowned men laid out at the Morgue,' answered the Sub-prefect, 'in whose pocketbooks were found letters stating that they had committed suicide in the Seine, because they had lost everything at the gaming table. Do I know how many of those men entered the same gambling-house that *you* entered? Won as *you* won? Took that bed as *you* took it? Slept in it? Were smothered in it? And were privately thrown into the river, with a letter of explanation written by the murderers and placed in their pocketbooks?

No man can say how many or how few have suffered the fate from which you have escaped. The people of the gambling-house kept their bedstead machinery a secret from *us* – even from the police! The dead kept the rest of the secret for them. Good night, or rather good-morning, Monsieur Faulkner! Be at my office again at nine o'clock – in the meantime, *au revoir!*'

The rest of my story is soon told. I was examined and re-examined; the gambling-house was strictly searched all through from top to bottom; the prisoners were separately interrogated; and two of the less guilty among them made a confession. I discovered that the Old Soldier was the master of the gambling-house – *justice* discovered that he had been drummed out of the army as a vagabond years ago; that he had been guilty of all sorts of villainies since; that he was in possession of stolen property, which the owners identified; and that he, the croupier, another accomplice, and the woman who had made my cup of coffee, were all in the secret of the bedstead. There appeared some reason to doubt whether the inferior persons attached to the house knew anything of the suffocating machinery; and they received the benefit of that doubt, by being treated simply as thieves and vagabonds. As for the Old Soldier and his two head myrmidons, they went to the galleys; the woman who had drugged my coffee was imprisoned for I forget how many years; the regular attendants at the gambling-house were considered 'suspicious' and placed under 'surveillance'; and I became, for one whole week (which is a long time) the head 'lion' in Parisian society. My adventure was dramatised by three illustrious playmakers, but never saw theatrical day-light; for the censorship forbade the introduction on the stage of a correct copy of the gambling-house bedstead.

One good result was produced by my adventure, which any censorship must have approved: it cured me of ever again trying *Rouge et Noir* as an amusement. The sight of a green cloth, with packs of cards and heaps of money on it, will henceforth be for ever associated in my mind with the sight of a bed canopy descending to suffocate me in the silence and darkness of the night.

The Adventure of the Blue Carbuncle
by
Arthur Conan Doyle

Sir Arthur Conan Doyle was born on 22 May 1859 in Edinburgh. He studied medicine at the University of Edinburgh and began to write stories while he was a student. Over his life he produced more than thirty books, 150 short stories, poems, plays and essays across a wide range of genres. His most famous creation is the detective Sherlock Holmes, who he introduced in his first novel *A Study in Scarlet* (1887). This was followed in 1889 by an historical novel, *Micah Clarke*. In 1893 Conan Doyle published 'The Final Problem' in which he killed off his famous detective so that he could turn his attention more towards historical fiction. However Holmes was so popular that Conan Doyle eventually relented and published *The Hound of the Baskervilles* in 1901. The events of *The Hound of the Baskervilles* are set before those of 'The Final Problem' but in 1903 new Sherlock Holmes stories began to appear that revealed that the detective had not died after all. He was finally retired in 1927. Sir Arthur Conan Doyle died on 7 July 1930.

The Adventure of the Blue Carbuncle

I HAD CALLED UPON my friend Sherlock Holmes upon the second morning after Christmas, with the intention of wishing him the compliments of the season. He was lounging upon the sofa in a purple dressing-gown, a pipe-rack within his reach upon the right, and a pile of crumpled morning papers, evidently newly studied, near at hand. Beside the couch was a wooden chair, and on the angle of the back hung a very seedy and disreputable hard felt hat, much the worse for wear, and cracked in several places. A lens and a forceps lying upon the seat of the chair suggested that the hat had been suspended in this manner for the purpose of examination.

'You are engaged,' said I; 'perhaps I interrupt you.'

'Not at all. I am glad to have a friend with whom I can discuss my results. The matter is a perfectly trivial one' (he jerked his thumb in the direction of the old hat), 'but there are points in connection with it which are not entirely devoid of interest, and even of instruction.'

I seated myself in his armchair, and warmed my hands before his crackling fire, for a sharp frost had set in, and the windows were thick with the ice crystals. 'I suppose,' I remarked, 'that, homely as it looks, this thing has some deadly story linked on to it – that it is the clue which will guide you in the solution of some mystery, and the punishment of some crime.'

'No, no. No crime,' said Sherlock Holmes, laughing. 'Only one of those whimsical little incidents which will happen when you have four million human beings all jostling each other within the space of a few square miles. Amid the action and reaction of so dense a swarm of humanity, every possible combination of events may be expected to take place, and many a little problem will be presented which may be striking and bizarre without being criminal. We have already had experience of such.'

'So much so.' I remarked, 'that, of the last six cases which I have added to my notes, three have been entirely free of any legal crime.'

'Precisely. You allude to my attempt to recover the Irene Adler papers, to the singular case of Miss Mary Sutherland, and to the adventure of the man with the twisted lip. Well, I have no doubt that this small matter will fall into the same innocent category. You know Peterson, the commissionaire?'

'Yes.'

'It is to him that this trophy belongs.'

'It is his hat.'

'No, no; he found it. Its owner is unknown. I beg that you will look upon it, not as a battered billycock, but as an intellectual problem. And, first, as to how it came here. It arrived upon Christmas morning, in company with a good fat goose, which is, I have no doubt, roasting at this moment in front of Peterson's fire. The facts are these. About four o'clock on Christmas morning, Peterson, who, as you know, is a very honest fellow, was returning from some small jollification, and was making his way homewards down Tottenham Court-road. In front of him he saw, in the gaslight, a tallish man, walking with a slight stagger, and carrying a white goose slung over his shoulder. As he reached the corner of Goodge-street, a row broke out between this stranger and a little knot of roughs. One of the latter knocked off the man's hat, on which he raised his stick to defend himself, and, swinging it over his head, smashed the shop window behind him. Peterson had rushed forward to protect the stranger from his assailants, but the man, shocked at having broken the window, and seeing an official-looking person in uniform rushing towards him, dropped his goose, took to his heels, and vanished amid the labyrinth of small streets which lie at the back of Tottenham

Court-road. The roughs had also fled at the appearance of Peterson, so that he was left in possession of the field of battle, and also of the spoils of victory in the shape of this battered hat and a most unimpeachable Christmas goose.'

'Which surely he restored to their owner?'

'My dear fellow, there lies the problem. It is true that "For Mrs. Henry Baker" was printed upon a small card which was tied to the bird's left leg, and it is also true that the initials "H. B." are legible upon the lining of this hat; but, as there are some thousands of Bakers, and some hundreds of Henry Bakers in this city of ours, it is not easy to restore lost property to any one of them.'

'What, then, did Peterson do?'

'He brought round both hat and goose to me on Christmas morning, knowing that even the smallest problems are of interest to me. The goose we retained until this morning, when there were signs that, in spite of the slight frost, it would be well that it should be eaten without unnecessary delay. Its finder has carried it off, therefore, to fulfil the ultimate destiny of a goose, while I continue to retain the hat of the unknown gentleman who lost his Christmas dinner.'

'Did he not advertise?'

'No.'

'Then, what clue could you have as to his identity?'

'Only as much as we can deduce.'

'From his hat?'

'Precisely.'

'But you are joking. What can you gather from this old battered felt?'

'Here is my lens. You know my methods. What can you gather yourself as to the individuality of the man who has worn this article?'

I took the tattered object in my hands, and turned it over rather ruefully. It was a very ordinary black hat of the usual round shape, hard, and much the worse for wear. The lining had been of red silk, but was a good deal discoloured. There was no maker's name; but, as Holmes had remarked, the initials 'H.B.' were scrawled upon one side. It was pierced in the brim for a hat-securer, but the elastic was missing. For the rest, it was cracked, exceedingly dusty, and spotted in several places, although there seemed to have been some attempt to hide the discoloured patches by smearing them with ink.

'I can see nothing,' said I, handing it back to my friend.

'On the contrary, Watson, you can see everything. You fail, however, to reason from what you see. You are too timid in drawing your inferences.'

'Then, pray tell me what it is that you can infer from this hat?'

He picked it up, and gazed at it in the peculiar introspective fashion which was characteristic of him. 'It is perhaps less suggestive than it might have been,' he remarked, 'and yet there are a few inferences which are very distinct, and a few others which represent at least a strong balance of probability. That the man was highly intellectual is of course obvious upon the face of it, and also that he was fairly well-to-do within the last three years, although he has now fallen upon evil days. He had foresight, but has less now than formerly, pointing to a moral retrogression, which, when taken with the decline of his fortunes, seems to indicate some evil influence, probably drink, at work upon him. This may account also for the obvious fact that his wife has ceased to love him.'

'My dear Holmes!'

'He has, however, retained some degree of self-respect,' he continued, disregarding my remonstrance. 'He is a man who leads a sedentary life, goes out little, is out of training entirely, is middle-aged, has grizzled hair which he has had cut within the last few days, and which he anoints with lime-cream. These are the more patent facts which are to be deduced from his hat. Also, by the way, that it is extremely improbable that he has gas laid on in his house.'

'You are certainly joking, Holmes.'

'Not in the least. Is it possible that even now when I give you these results you are unable to see how they are attained?'

'I have no doubt that I am very stupid; but I must confess that I am unable to follow you. For example, how did you deduce that this man was intellectual?'

For answer Holmes clapped the hat upon his head. It came right over the forehead and settled upon the bridge of his nose. 'It is a question of cubic capacity,' said he; 'a man with so large a brain must have something in it.'

'The decline of his fortunes, then?'

'This hat is three years old. These flat brims curled at the edge came in then. It is a hat of the very best quality. Look at the band of ribbed silk, and the excellent lining. If this man could afford to buy so expensive a hat three years ago, and has had no hat since, then he has assuredly gone down in the world.'

'Well, that is clear enough, certainly. But how about the foresight, and the moral retrogression?'

Sherlock Holmes laughed. 'Here is the foresight,' said he, putting his finger upon the little disc and loop of the hat-securer. 'They are never sold upon hats. If this man ordered one, it is a sign of a certain amount of foresight, since he went out of his way to take this precaution against the wind. But since we see that he has broken the elastic, and has not troubled to replace it, it is obvious that he has less foresight now than formerly, which is a distinct proof of a weakening nature. On the other hand, he has endeavoured to conceal some of these stains upon the felt by daubing them with ink, which is a sign that he has not entirely lost his self-respect.'

'Your reasoning is certainly plausible.'

'The further points, that he is middle-aged, that his hair is grizzled, that it has been recently cut, and that he uses lime-cream, are all to be gathered from a close examination of the lower part of the lining. The lens discloses a large number of hair ends, clean cut by the scissors of the barber. They all appear to be adhesive, and there is a distinct odour of lime-cream. This dust, you will observe, is not the gritty, grey dust of the street, but the fluffy brown dust of the house, showing that it has been hung up indoors most of the time; while the marks of moisture upon the inside are proof positive that the wearer perspired very freely, and could, therefore, hardly be in the best of training.'

'But his wife – you said that she had ceased to love him.'

'This hat has not been brushed for weeks. When I see you, my dear Watson, with a week's accumulation of dust upon your hat, and when your wife allows you to go out in such a state, I shall fear that you also have been unfortunate enough to lose your wife's affection.'

'But he might be a bachelor.'

'Nay, he was bringing home the goose as a peace-offering to his wife. Remember the card upon the bird's leg.'

'You have an answer to everything. But how on earth do you deduce that the gas is not laid on in the house?'

'One tallow stain, or even two, might come by chance; but, when I see no less than five, I think that there can be little doubt that the individual must be brought into frequent contact with burning tallow – walks upstairs at night probably with his hat in one hand and a guttering candle in the other. Anyhow, he never got tallow stains from a gas jet. Are you satisfied?'

'Well, it is very ingenious,' said I, laughing; 'but since, as you said just now, there has been no crime committed, and no harm done save the loss of a goose, all this seems to be rather a waste of energy.'

Sherlock Holmes had opened his mouth to reply, when the door flew open, and Peterson the commissionaire rushed into the apartment with flushed cheeks and the face of a man who is dazed with astonishment.

'The goose, Mr. Holmes! The goose, sir!' he gasped.

Eh? What of it, then? Has it returned to life, and flapped off through the kitchen window?' Holmes twisted himself round upon the sofa to get a fairer view of the man's excited face.

'See here, sir! See what my wife found in its crop!' He held out his hand, and displayed upon the centre of the palm a brilliantly scintillating blue stone, rather smaller than a bean in size, but of such purity and radiance that it twinkled like an electric point in the dark hollow of his hand.

Sherlock Holmes sat up with a whistle. 'By Jove, Peterson!' said he, 'this is treasure trove indeed. I suppose you know what you have got?'

'A diamond, sir! A precious stone! It cuts into glass as though it were putty.'

'It's more than a precious stone. It's *the* precious stone.'

'Not the Countess of Morcar's blue carbuncle!' I ejaculated.

'Precisely so. I ought to know its size and shape, seeing that I have read the advertisement about it in *The Times* every day lately. It is absolutely unique, and its value can only be conjectured, but the reward offered of a thousand pounds is certainly not within a twentieth part of the market price.'

'A thousand pounds! Great Lord of mercy!' The commissionaire plumped down into a chair, and stared from one to the other of us.

'That is the reward, and I have reason to know that there are sentimental considerations in the background which would induce the Countess to part with half of her fortune, if she could but recover the gem.'

'It was lost, if I remember aright, at the Hotel Cosmopolitan,' I remarked.

'Precisely so, on the twenty-second of December, just five days ago. John Horner, a plumber, was accused of having abstracted it from the lady's jewel case. The evidence against him was so strong that the case has been referred to the Assizes. I have some account of the matter here, I believe.' He rummaged amid his newspapers, glancing over the dates, until at last he smoothed one out, doubled it over, and read the following paragraph:—

'Hotel Cosmopolitan Jewel Robbery. John Horner, 26, plumber, was brought up upon the charge of having upon the 22nd inst. abstracted from the jewel case of the Countess of Morcar the valuable gem known as the blue carbuncle. James Ryder, upper-attendant at the hotel, gave his evidence to the effect that he had shown Horner up to the dressing-room of the Countess of Morcar upon the day of the robbery, in order that he might solder the second bar of the grate, which was loose. He had remained with Horner some little time, but had finally been called away. On returning, he found that Horner had disappeared, that the bureau had been forced open, and that the small morocco casket in which, as it afterwards transpired, the

Countess was accustomed to keep her jewel was lying empty upon the dressing-table. Ryder instantly gave the alarm, and Horner was arrested the same evening; but the stone could not be found either upon his person or in his rooms. Catherine Cusack, maid to the Countess, deposed to having heard Ryder's cry of dismay on discovering the robbery, and to having rushed into the room, where she found matters as described by the last witness. Inspector Bradstreet, B division, gave evidence as to the arrest of Horner, who struggled frantically, and protested his innocence in the strongest terms. Evidence of a previous conviction for robbery having been given against the prisoner, the magistrate refused to deal summarily with the offence, but referred it to the Assizes. Horner, who had shown signs of intense emotion during the proceedings, fainted away at the conclusion, and was carried out of court.'

'Hum! So much for the police-court,' said Holmes, thoughtfully, tossing aside the paper. 'The question for us now to solve is the sequence of events leading from a rifled jewel case at one end to the crop of a goose in Tottenham Court-road at the other. You see, Watson, our little deductions have suddenly assumed a much more important and less innocent aspect. Here is the stone; the stone came from the goose, and the goose came from Mr Henry Baker, the gentleman with the bad hat and all the other characteristics with which I have bored you. So now we must set ourselves very seriously to finding this gentleman, and ascertaining what part he has played in this little mystery. To do this, we must try the simplest means first, and these lie undoubtedly in an advertisement in all the evening papers. If this fail, I shall have recourse to other methods.'

'What will you say?'

'Give me a pencil, and that slip of paper. Now then: 'Found at the corner of Goodge-street, a goose and a black felt hat. Mr Henry Baker can have the same by applying at 6.30 this evening at 221B, Baker-street.' That is clear and concise.'

'Very. But will he see it?'

'Well, he is sure to keep an eye on the papers, since, to a poor man, the loss was a heavy one. He was clearly so scared by his mischance in breaking the window, and by the approach of Peterson, that he thought of nothing but flight; but since then he must have bitterly regretted the impulse which caused him to drop his bird. Then, again, the introduction of his name will cause him to see it, for every one who knows him will direct his attention to it. Here you are Peterson, run down to the advertising agency, and have this put in the evening papers.'

'In which, sir.'

'Oh, in the *Globe, Star, Pall Mall, St James's Gazette, Evening News, Standard, Echo*, and any others that occur to you.'

'Very well, sir. And this stone?'

'Ah, yes, I shall keep the stone. Thank you. And, I say, Peterson, just buy a goose on your way back, and leave it here with me, for we must have one to give to this gentleman in place of the one which your family is now devouring.'

When the commissionaire had gone, Holmes took up the stone and held it against the light. 'It's a bonny thing,' said he. 'Just see how it glints and sparkles. Of course it is a nucleus and focus of crime. Every good stone is. They are the devil's pet baits. In the larger and older jewels every facet may stand for a bloody deed. This stone is not yet twenty years old. It was found in the banks of the Amoy River in Southern China, and is remarkable in having every characteristic of the carbuncle, save that it is blue in shade, instead of ruby red. In spite of its youth, it has already a sinister history. There have been two murders, a vitriol-throwing, a suicide, and several robberies brought about for the sake of this forty-grain weight of crystallised charcoal. Who would think that so pretty a toy would be a purveyor to the gallows and the prison? I'll lock it up in my strong-box now, and drop a line to the Countess to say that we have it.'

'Do you think this man Horner is innocent?'

'I cannot tell.'

'Well, then, do you imagine that this other one, Henry Baker, had anything to do with the matter?'

'It is, I think, much more likely that Henry Baker is an absolutely innocent man, who had no idea that the bird which he was carrying was of considerably more value than if it were made of solid gold. That, however, I shall determine by a very simple test, if we have an answer to our advertisement.'

'And you can do nothing until then?'

'Nothing.'

'In that case I shall continue my professional round. But I shall come back in the evening at the hour you have mentioned, for I should like to see the solution of so tangled a business.'

'Very glad to see you. I dine at seven. There is a woodcock, I believe. By the way, in view of recent occurrences, perhaps I ought to ask Mrs Hudson to examine its crop.'

I had been delayed at a case, and it was a little after half-past six when I found myself in Baker-street once more. As I approached the house I saw a tall man in a Scotch bonnet, with a coat which was buttoned up to his chin, waiting outside in the bright semicircle which was thrown from the fanlight. Just as I arrived, the door was opened, and we were shown up together to Holmes' room.

'Mr Henry Baker, I believe,' said he, rising from his armchair, and greeting his visitor with the easy air of geniality which he could so readily assume. 'Pray take this chair by the fire, Mr Baker. It is a cold night, and I observe that your circulation is more adapted for summer than for winter. Ah, Watson, you have just come at the right time. Is that your hat, Mr Baker?'

'Yes, sir, that is undoubtedly my hat.'

He was a large man, with rounded shoulders, a massive head, and a broad, intelligent face, sloping down to a pointed beard of grizzled brown. A touch of red in nose and cheeks, with a slight tremor of his extended hand, recalled Holmes' surmise as to his habits. His rusty black frock-coat was buttoned right up in front, with the collar turned up, and his lank wrists protruded from his sleeves without a sign of cuff or shirt. He spoke in a low staccato fashion, choosing his words with care, and gave the impression generally of a man of learning and letters who had had ill-usage at the hands of fortune.

'We have retained these things for some days,' said Holmes, 'because we expected to see an advertisement from you giving your address. I am at a loss to know now why you did not advertise.'

Our visitor gave a rather shame-faced laugh. 'Shillings have not been so plentiful with me as they once were,' he remarked. 'I had no doubt that the gang of roughs who assaulted me had carried off both my hat and the bird. I did not care to spend more money in a hopeless attempt at recovering them.'

'Very naturally. By the way, about the bird, we were compelled to eat it.'

'To eat it!' Our visitor half rose from his chair in his excitement.

'Yes, it would have been no use to any one had we not done so. But I presume that this other goose upon the sideboard, which is about the same weight and perfectly fresh, will answer your purpose equally well?'

'Oh, certainly, certainly!' answered Mr Baker, with a sigh of relief.

'Of course, we still have the feathers, legs, crop, and so on of your own bird, so if you wish—'

The man burst into a hearty laugh. 'They might be useful to me as relics of my adventure,' said he, 'but beyond that I can hardly see what use the *disjecta membra* of my late acquaintance are going to be to me. No, sir, I think that, with your permission, I will confine my attentions to the excellent bird which I perceive upon the sideboard.'

Sherlock Holmes glanced sharply across at me with a slight shrug of his shoulders.

'There is your hat, then, and there your bird,' said he. 'By the way, would it bore you to tell me where you got the other one from? I am somewhat of a fowl fancier, and I have seldom seen a better-grown goose.'

'Certainly, sir,' said Baker, who had risen and tucked his newly-gained property under his arm. 'There are a few of us who frequent the "Alpha" Inn, near the Museum – we are to be found in the Museum itself during the day, you understand. This year our good host, Windigate by name, instituted a goose club, by which, on consideration of some few pence every week, we were each to receive a bird at Christmas. My pence were duly paid, and the rest is familiar to you. I am much indebted to you, sir, for a Scotch bonnet is fitted neither to my years nor my gravity.' With a comical pomposity of manner he bowed solemnly to both of us, and strode off upon his way.

'So much for Mr Henry Baker,' said Holmes, when he had closed the door behind him. 'It is quite certain that he knows nothing whatever about the matter. Are you hungry, Watson?'

'Not particularly.'

'Then I suggest that we turn our dinner into a supper, and follow up this clue while it is still hot.'

'By all means.'

It was a bitter night, so we drew on our ulsters and wrapped cravats about our throats. Outside, the stars were shining coldly in a cloudless sky, and the breath of the passers-by blew out into smoke like so many pistol shots. Our footfalls rang out crisply and loudly as we swung through the Doctors' quarter, Wimpole-street, Harley-street, and so through Wigmore-street into Oxford-street. In a quarter of an hour we were in Bloomsbury at the 'Alpha' Inn, which is a small public-house at the corner of one of the streets which runs down into Holborn. Holmes pushed open the door of the private bar, and ordered two glasses of beer from the ruddy-faced, white-aproned landlord.

'Your beer should be excellent if it is as good as your geese,' said he.

'My geese!' The man seemed surprised.

'Yes. I was speaking only half an hour ago to Mr Henry Baker, who was a member of your goose-club.'

'Ah! yes, I see. But you see, sir, them's not *our* geese.'

'Indeed! Whose, then?'

'Well, I got the two dozen from a salesman in Covent Garden.'

'Indeed! I know some of them. Which was it?'

'Breckinridge is his name.'

'Ah! I don't know him. Well, here's your good health, landlord, and prosperity to your house. Good-night.'

'Now for Mr. Breckinridge,' he continued, buttoning up his coat, as we came out into the frosty air. 'Remember, Watson, that though we have so homely a thing as a goose at one end of this chain, we have at the other a man who will certainly get seven years' penal servitude, unless we can establish his innocence. It is possible that our inquiry may but confirm his guilt; but, in any case, we have a line of investigation which has been missed by the police, and which a singular chance has placed in our hands. Let us follow it out to the bitter end. Faces to the south, then, and quick march!'

We passed across Holborn, down Endell-street, and so through a zigzag of slums to Covent Garden Market. One of the largest stalls bore the name of Breckinridge upon it, and the proprietor, a horsey-looking man, with a sharp face and trim side-whiskers, was helping a boy to put up the shutters.

'Good evening. It's a cold night,' said Holmes.

The salesman nodded, and shot a questioning glance at my companion.

'Sold out of geese, I see,' continued Holmes, pointing at the bare slabs of marble.

'Let you have five hundred to-morrow morning.'

'That's no good.'

'Well, there are some on the stall with the gas flare.'

'Ah, but I was recommended to you.'

'Who by?'

'The landlord of the "Alpha."'

'Oh, yes; I sent him a couple of dozen.'

'Fine birds they were, too. Now where did you get them from?'

To my surprise the question provoked a burst of anger from the salesman.

'Now, then, mister,' said he, with his head cocked and his arms akimbo, 'what are you driving at? Let's have it straight, now.'

'It is straight enough. I should like to know who sold you the geese which you supplied to the "Alpha."'

'Well, then, I sh'an't tell you. So now!'

'Oh, it is a matter of no importance; but I don't know why you should be so warm over such a trifle.'

'Warm! You'd be as warm, maybe, if you were as pestered as I am. When I pay good money for a good article there should be an end of the business; but it's "Where are the geese?" and "Who did you sell the geese to?" and "What will you take for the geese?" One would think they were the only geese in the world, to hear the fuss that is made over them.'

'Well, I have no connection with any other people who have been making inquiries,' said Holmes carelessly. 'If you won't tell us the bet is off, that is all. But I'm always ready to back my opinion on a matter of fowls, and I have a fiver on it that the bird I ate is country bred.'

'Well, then, you've lost your fiver, for it's town bred,' snapped the salesman.

'It's nothing of the kind.'

'I say it is.'

'I don't believe it.'

'D'you think you know more about fowls than I, who have handled them ever since I was a nipper? I tell you, all those birds that went to the "Alpha" were town bred.'

'You'll never persuade me to believe that.'

'Will you bet, then?'

'It's merely taking your money, for I know that I am right. But I'll have a sovereign on with you, just to teach you not to be obstinate.'

The salesman chuckled grimly. 'Bring me the books, Bill,' said he.

The small boy brought round a small thin volume and a great greasy-backed one, laying them out together beneath the hanging lamp.

'Now then, Mr. Cocksure,' said the salesman, 'I thought that I was out of geese, but before I finish you'll find that there is still one left in my shop. You see this little book?'

'Well?'

'That's the list of the folk from whom I buy. D'you see? Well, then, here on this page are the country folk, and the numbers after their names are where their accounts are in the big ledger. Now, then! You see this other page in red ink? Well, that is a list of my town suppliers. Now, look at that third name. Just read it out to me.'

'Mrs. Oakshott, 117, Brixton-road – 249,' read Holmes.

'Quite so. Now turn that up in the ledger.'

Holmes turned to the page indicated. 'Here you are, "Mrs. Oakshott, 117, Brixton-road, egg and poultry supplier."'

'Now, then, what's the last entry?'

'"December 22. Twenty-four geese at 7s. 6d."'

'Quite so. There you are. And underneath?'

'"Sold to Mr Windigate of the 'Alpha' at 12s."'

'What have you to say now?'

Sherlock Holmes looked deeply chagrined. He drew a sovereign from his pocket and threw it down upon the slab, turning away with the air of a man whose disgust is too deep for words. A few yards off he stopped under a lamp-post, and laughed in the hearty, noiseless fashion which was peculiar to him.

'When you see a man with whiskers of that cut and the "pink 'un" protruding out of his pocket, you can always draw him by a bet,' said he. 'I daresay that if I had put a hundred pounds down in front of him that man would not have given me such complete information as was drawn from him by the idea that he was doing me on a wager. Well, Watson, we are I fancy, nearing the end of our quest, and the only point which remains to be determined is whether we should go on to this Mrs. Oakshott to night, or whether we should reserve it for to-morrow. It is clear from what that surly fellow said that there are others besides ourselves who are anxious about the matter, and I should—'

His remarks were suddenly cut short by a loud hubbub which broke out from the stall which we had just left. Turning round we saw a little rat-faced fellow standing in the centre of the circle of yellow light which was thrown by the swinging lamp, while Breckinridge the salesman, framed in the door of his stall, was shaking his fists fiercely at the cringing figure.

'I've had enough of you and your geese,' he shouted. 'I wish you were all at the devil together. If you come pestering me any more with your silly talk I'll set the dog at you. You bring Mrs. Oakshott here and I'll answer her, but what have you to do with it? Did I buy the geese off you?'

'No; but one of them was mine all the same,' whined the little man.

'Well, then, ask Mrs. Oakshott for it.'

'She told me to ask you.'

'Well, you can ask the King of Proosia for all I care. I've had enough of it. Get out of this!' He rushed fiercely forward, and the inquirer flitted away into the darkness.

'Ha, this may save us a visit to Brixton-road,' whispered Holmes. 'Come with me, and we will see what is to be made of this fellow.' Striding through the scattered knots of people who lounged round the flaring stalls, my companion speedily overtook the little man and touched him upon the shoulder. He sprang round, and I could see in the gaslight that every vestige of colour had been driven from his face.

'Who are you, then? What do you want?' he asked in a quavering voice.

'You will excuse me,' said Holmes, blandly, 'but I could not help overhearing the questions which you put to the salesman just now. I think that I could be of assistance to you.'

'You? Who are you? How could you know anything of the matter?'

'My name is Sherlock Holmes. It is my business to know what other people don't know.'

'But you can know nothing of this?'

'Excuse me, I know everything of it. You are endeavouring to trace some geese which were sold by Mrs. Oakshott, of Brixton-road, to a salesman named Breckinridge, by him in turn to Mr. Windigate, of the "Alpha," and by him to his club, of which Mr. Henry Baker is a member.'

'Oh, sir, you are the very man whom I have longed to meet,' cried the little fellow, with outstretched hands and quivering fingers. 'I can hardly explain to you how interested I am in this matter.'

Sherlock Holmes hailed a four-wheeler which was passing. 'In that case we had better discuss it in a cosy room rather than in this windswept market-place,' said he. 'But pray tell me, before we go further, who it is that I have the pleasure of assisting.'

The man hesitated for an instant. 'My name is John Robinson,' he answered, with a sidelong glance.

'No, no; the real name,' said Holmes, sweetly. 'It is always awkward doing business with an *alias*.'

A flush sprang to the white cheeks of the stranger. 'Well, then,' said he, 'my real name is James Ryder.'

'Precisely so. Head attendant at the Hotel Cosmopolitan. Pray step into the cab, and I shall soon be able to tell you everything which you would wish to know.'

The little man stood glancing from one to the other of us with half-frightened, half-hopeful eyes, as one who is not sure whether he is on the verge of a windfall or of a catastrophe. Then he stepped into the cab, and in half an hour we were back in the sitting-room at Baker-street. Nothing had been said during our drive, but the high, thin breathing of our new companion, and the claspings and unclaspings of his hands, spoke of the nervous tension within him.

'Here we are!' said Holmes, cheerily, as we filed into the room. 'The fire looks very seasonable in this weather. You look cold, Mr. Ryder. Pray take the basket chair. I will just put on my slippers before we settle this little matter of yours. Now, then! You want to know what became of those geese?'

'Yes, sir.'

'Or rather, I fancy, of that goose. It was one bird, I imagine, in which you were interested – white, with a black bar across the tail.'

Ryder quivered with emotion. 'Oh, sir,' he cried, 'can you tell me where it went to.'

'It came here.'

'Here?'

'Yes, and a most remarkable bird it proved. I don't wonder that you should take an interest in it. It laid an egg after it was dead – the bonniest, brightest little blue egg that ever was seen. I have it here in my museum.'

Our visitor staggered to his feet, and clutched the mantelpiece with his right hand. Holmes unlocked his strong box, and held up the blue carbuncle, which shone out like a star, with a cold, brilliant, many-pointed radiance. Ryder stood glaring with a drawn face, uncertain whether to claim or to disown it.

'The game's up, Ryder,' said Holmes, quietly. 'Hold up, man, or you'll be into the fire. Give him an arm back into his chair, Watson. He's not got blood enough to go in for felony with impunity. Give him a dash of brandy. So! Now he looks a little more human. What a shrimp it is, to be sure!'

For a moment he had staggered and nearly fallen, but the brandy brought a tinge of colour into his cheeks, and he sat staring with frightened eyes at his accuser.

'I have almost every link in my hands, and all the proofs which I could possibly need, so there is little which you need tell me. Still that little may as well be cleared up to make the case complete. You had heard, Ryder, of this blue stone of the Countess of Morcar's?'

'It was Catherine Cusack who told me of it,' said he, in a crackling voice.

'I see. Her ladyship's waiting-maid. Well, the temptation of sudden wealth so easily acquired was too much for you, as it has been for better men before you; but you were not very scrupulous in the means you used. It seems to me, Ryder, that there is the making of a very pretty villain in you. You knew that this man Horner, the plumber, had been concerned in some such matter before, and that suspicion would rest the more readily upon him. What did you do, then? You made some small job in my lady's room – you and your confederate Cusack – and you managed that he should be the man sent for. Then, when he had left, you rifled the jewel case, raised the alarm, and had this unfortunate man arrested. You then—'

Ryder threw himself down suddenly upon the rug, and clutched at my companion's knees. 'For God's sake, have mercy!' he shrieked. 'Think of my father! Of my mother! It would break their hearts. I never went wrong before! I never will again. I swear it. I'll swear it on a Bible. Oh, don't bring it into court! For Christ's sake, don't!'

'Get back into your chair!' said Holmes, sternly. 'It is very well to cringe and crawl now, but you thought little enough of this poor Horner in the dock for a crime of which he knew nothing.'

'I will fly, Mr Holmes. I will leave the country, sir. Then the charge against him will break down.'

'Hum! We will talk about that. And now let us hear a true account of the next act. How came the stone into the goose, and how came the goose into the open market? Tell us the truth, for there lies your only hope of safety.'

Ryder passed his tongue over his parched lips. 'I will tell you it just as it happened, sir,' said he. 'When Horner had been arrested, it seemed to me that it would be best for me to get away with the stone at once, for I did not know at what moment the police might not take it into their heads to search me and my room. There was no place about the hotel where it would be safe. I went out, as if on some commission, and I made for my sister's house. She had married a man named Oakshott, and lived in Brixton-road, where she fattened fowls for the market. All the way there every man I met seemed to me to be a policeman or a detective, and for all that it was a cold night, the sweat was pouring down my face before I came to the Brixton-road. My sister asked me what was the matter, and why I was so pale; but I told her that I had been upset by the jewel robbery at the hotel. Then I went into the back yard, and smoked a pipe, and wondered what it would be best to do.

'I had a friend once called Maudsley, who went to the bad, and has just been serving his time in Pentonville. One day he had met me, and fell into talk about the ways of thieves and how they could get rid of what they stole. I knew that he would be true to me, for I knew one or two things about him, so I made up my mind to go right on to Kilburn, where he lived, and take him into my confidence. He would show me how to turn the stone into money. But how to get to him in safety. I thought of the agonies I had gone through in coming from the hotel. I might at any moment be seized and searched, and there would be the stone in my waistcoat pocket. I was leaning against the wall at the time, and looking at the geese which were waddling about round my feet, and suddenly an idea came into my head which showed me how I could beat the best detective that ever lived.

'My sister had told me some weeks before that I might have the pick of her geese for a Christmas present, and I knew that she was always as good as her word. I would take my goose now, and in it I would carry my stone to Kilburn. There was a little shed in the yard, and behind this I drove one of the birds, a fine big one, white with a barred tail. I caught it, and, prising its bill open, I thrust the stone down its throat as far as my finger could reach. The bird gave a gulp, and I felt the stone pass along its gullet and down into its crop. But the creature flapped and struggled, and out came my sister to know what was the matter. As I turned to speak to her the brute broke loose, and fluttered off among the others.

'"Whatever were you doing with that bird, Jem?" says she.

'"Well," said I, "you said you'd give me one for Christmas, and I was feeling which was the fattest."

'"Oh," says she, "we've set yours aside for you. Jem's bird, we call it. It's the big, white one over yonder. There's twenty-six of them, which makes one for you, and one for us, and two dozen for the market."

'"Thank you, Maggie," says I; "but if it is all the same to you I'd rather have that one I was handling just now."

'"The other is a good three pound heavier," she said, "and we fattened it expressly for you."

'"Never mind. I'll have the other, and I'll take it now," said I.

'"Oh, just as you like," said she, a little huffed. "Which is it you want, then?"

'"That white one, with the barred tail, right in the middle of the flock."

'"Oh, very well. Kill it and take it with you."

'Well, I did what she said, Mr. Holmes, and I carried the bird all the way to Kilburn. I told my pal what I had done, for he was a man that it was easy to tell a thing like that to. He laughed until he choked, and we got a knife and opened the goose. My heart turned to water, for there was no sign of the stone, and I knew that some terrible mistake had occurred. I left the bird, rushed back to my sister's, and hurried into the back yard. There was not a bird to be seen there.

"'Where are they all, Maggie?' I cried.

"'Gone to the dealer's.'

"'Which dealer's?'

"'Breckinridge, of Covent Garden.'

"'But was there another with a barred tail?' I asked, "the same as the one I chose?'

"'Yes, Jem, there were two barred-tailed ones, and I could never tell them apart.'

'Well, then, of course, I saw it all, and I ran off as hard as my feet would carry me to this man Breckinridge; but he had sold the lot at once, and not one word would he tell me as to where they had gone. You heard him yourselves to-night. Well, he has always answered me like that. My sister thinks that I am going mad. Sometimes I think that I am myself. And now – and now I am myself a branded thief, without ever having touched the wealth for which I sold my character. God help me! God help me!' He burst into convulsive sobbing, with his face buried in his hands.

There was a long silence, broken only by his heavy breathing, and by the measured tapping of Sherlock Holmes' finger-tips upon the edge of the table. Then my friend rose, and threw open the door.

'Get out!' said he.

'What, sir! Oh, heaven bless you!'

'No more words. Get out!'

And no more words were needed. There was a rush, a clatter upon the stairs, the bang of a door, and the crisp rattle of running footfalls from the street.

'After all, Watson,' said Holmes, reaching up his hand for his clay pipe, 'I am not retained by the police to supply their deficiencies. If Horner were in danger it would be another thing, but this fellow will not appear against him, and the case must collapse. I suppose that I am commuting a felony, but it is just possible that I am saving a soul. This fellow will not go wrong again. He is too terribly frightened. Send him to gaol now, and you make him a gaol-bird for life. Besides, it is the season of forgiveness. Chance has put in our way a most singular and whimsical problem, and its solution is its own reward. If you will have the goodness to touch the bell, Doctor, we will begin another investigation, in which also a bird will be the chief feature.'

Stories
to help you rejoice
in the
beauty of nature

Kew Gardens
by
Virginia Woolf

Virginia Woolf was born Adeline Virginia Stephen in London in 1882, the daughter of Sir Leslie Stephen, first editor of *The Dictionary of National Biography*. The sudden death of her mother in 1895, when Virginia was 13, and that of her half-sister Stella two years later, led to the first of Virginia's several nervous breakdowns. From 1915, when she published her first novel, *The Voyage Out*, Virginia Woolf maintained an astonishing output of fiction, literary criticism, essays and biography including *Mrs Dalloway* (1925) and *To The Lighthouse* (1927). In 1912 she married Leonard Woolf, and in 1917 they founded The Hogarth Press. Virginia Woolf suffered a series of mental breakdowns throughout her life, and on 28 March 1941 she committed suicide.

Kew Gardens

FROM THE OVAL-SHAPED flower-bed there rose perhaps a hundred stalks spreading into heart-shaped or tongue-shaped leaves half way up and unfurling at the tip red or blue or yellow petals marked with spots of colour raised upon the surface; and from the red, blue or yellow gloom of the throat emerged a straight bar, rough with gold dust and slightly clubbed at the end. The petals were voluminous enough to be stirred by the summer breeze, and when they moved, the red, blue and yellow lights passed one over the other, staining an inch of the brown earth beneath with a spot of the most intricate colour. The light fell either upon the smooth, grey back of a pebble, or, the shell of a snail with its brown, circular veins, or falling into a raindrop, it expanded with such intensity of red, blue and yellow the thin walls of water that one expected them to burst and disappear. Instead, the drop was left in a second silver grey once more, and the light now settled upon the flesh of a leaf, revealing the branching thread of fibre beneath the surface, and again it moved on and spread its illumination in the vast green spaces beneath the dome of the heart-shaped and tongue-shaped leaves. Then the breeze stirred rather more briskly overhead and the colour was flashed into the air above, into the eyes of the men and women who walk in Kew Gardens in July.

The figures of these men and women straggled past the flower-bed with a curiously irregular movement not unlike that of the white and blue butterflies who crossed the turf in zig-zag flights from bed

79

to bed. The man was about six inches in front of the woman, strolling carelessly, while she bore on with greater purpose, only turning her head now and then to see that the children were not too far behind. The man kept this distance in front of the woman purposely, though perhaps unconsciously, for he wished to go on with his thoughts.

'Fifteen years ago I came here with Lily,' he thought. 'We sat somewhere over there by a lake and I begged her to marry me all through the hot afternoon. How the dragonfly kept circling round us: how clearly I see the dragonfly and her shoe with the square silver buckle at the toe. All the time I spoke I saw her shoe and when it moved impatiently I knew without looking up what she was going to say: the whole of her seemed to be in her shoe. And my love, my desire, were in the dragonfly; for some reason I thought that if it settled there, on that leaf, the broad one with the red flower in the middle of it, if the dragonfly settled on the leaf she would say "Yes" at once. But the dragonfly went round and round: it never settled anywhere – of course not, happily not, or I shouldn't be walking here with Eleanor and the children – Tell me, Eleanor. D'you ever think of the past?'

'Why do you ask, Simon?'

'Because I've been thinking of the past. I've been thinking of Lily, the woman I might have married . . . Well, why are you silent? Do you mind my thinking of the past?'

'Why should I mind, Simon? Doesn't one always think of the past, in a garden with men and women lying under the trees? Aren't they one's past, all that remains of it, those men and women, those ghosts lying under the trees, . . . one's happiness, one's reality?'

'For me, a square silver shoe buckle and a dragonfly—'

'For me, a kiss. Imagine six little girls sitting before their easels twenty years ago, down by the side of a lake, painting the water-lilies, the first red water-lilies I'd ever seen. And suddenly a kiss, there on the back of my neck. And my hand shook all the afternoon so that I couldn't paint. I took out my watch and marked the hour when I would allow myself to think of the kiss for five minutes only – it was so precious – the kiss of an old grey-haired woman with a wart on her nose, the mother of all my kisses all my life. Come, Caroline, come, Hubert.'

They walked on past the flower-bed, now walking four abreast, and soon diminished in size among the trees and looked half transparent as the sunlight and shade swam over their backs in large trembling irregular patches.

In the oval flower-bed the snail, whose shell had been stained red, blue, and yellow for the space of two minutes or so, now appeared to be moving very slightly in its shell, and next began to labour over the crumbs of loose earth which broke away and rolled down as it passed over them. It appeared to have a definite goal in front of it, differing in this respect from the singular high stepping angular green insect who attempted to cross in front of it, and waited for a second with its antennæ trembling as if in deliberation, and then stepped off as rapidly and strangely in the opposite direction. Brown cliffs with deep green lakes in the hollows, flat, blade-like trees that waved from root to tip, round boulders of grey stone, vast crumpled surfaces of a thin crackling texture – all these objects lay across the snail's progress between one stalk and another to his goal. Before he had decided whether to circumvent the arched tent of a dead leaf or to breast it there came past the bed the feet of other human beings.

This time they were both men. The younger of the two wore an expression of perhaps unnatural calm; he raised his eyes and fixed them very steadily in front of him while his companion spoke, and directly his companion had done speaking he looked on the ground again and sometimes opened his lips only after a long pause and sometimes did not open them at all. The elder man had a curiously uneven and shaky method of walking, jerking his hand forward and throwing up his head abruptly, rather in the manner of an impatient carriage horse tired of waiting outside a house; but in the man these gestures were irresolute and pointless. He talked almost incessantly; he smiled to himself and again began to talk, as if the smile had been an answer. He was talking about spirits – the spirits of the dead, who, according to him, were even now telling him all sorts of odd things about their experiences in Heaven.

'Heaven was known to the ancients as Thessaly, William, and now, with this war, the spirit matter is rolling between the hills like thunder.' He paused, seemed to listen, smiled, jerked his head and continued:—

'You have a small electric battery and a piece of rubber to insulate the wire – isolate? – insulate? – well, we'll skip the details, no good going into details that wouldn't be understood – and in short the little machine stands in any convenient position by the head of the bed, we will say, on a neat mahogany stand. All arrangements being properly fixed by workmen under my direction, the widow applies her ear and summons the spirit by sign as agreed. Women! Widows! Women in black—'

Here he seemed to have caught sight of a woman's dress in the distance, which in the shade looked a purple black. He took off his hat, placed his hand upon his heart, and hurried towards her muttering and gesticulating feverishly. But William caught him by the sleeve and touched a flower with the tip of his walking-stick in order to divert the old man's attention. After looking at it for a moment in some confusion the old man bent his ear to it and seemed to answer a voice speaking from it, for he began talking about the forests of Uruguay which he had visited hundreds of years ago in company with the most beautiful young woman in Europe. He could be heard murmuring about forests of Uruguay blanketed with the wax petals of tropical roses, nightingales, sea beaches, mermaids, and women drowned at sea, as he suffered himself to be moved on by William, upon whose face the look of stoical patience grew slowly deeper and deeper.

Following his steps so closely as to be slightly puzzled by his gestures came two elderly women of the lower middle class, one stout and ponderous, the other rosy cheeked and nimble. Like most people of their station they were frankly fascinated by any signs of eccentricity betokening a disordered brain, especially in the well-to-do; but they were too far off to be certain whether the gestures were merely eccentric or genuinely mad. After they had scrutinised the old man's back in silence for a moment and given each other a queer, sly look, they went on energetically piecing together their very complicated dialogue:

'Nell, Bert, Lot, Cess, Phil, Pa, he says, I says, she says, I says, I says, I says—'

'My Bert, Sis, Bill, Grandad, the old man, sugar,

Sugar, flour, kippers, greens,

Sugar, sugar, sugar.'

The ponderous woman looked through the pattern of falling words at the flowers standing cool, firm, and upright in the earth, with a curious expression. She saw them as a sleeper waking from a heavy sleep sees a brass candlestick reflecting the light in an unfamiliar way, and closes his eyes and opens them, and seeing the brass candlestick again, finally starts broad awake and stares at the candlestick with all his powers. So the heavy woman came to a standstill opposite the oval-shaped flower-bed, and ceased even to pretend to listen to what the other woman was saying. She stood there letting the words fall over her, swaying the top part of her body slowly backwards and forwards, looking at the flowers. Then she suggested that they should find a seat and have their tea.

The snail had now considered every possible method of reaching his goal without going round the dead leaf or climbing over it. Let alone the effort needed for climbing a leaf, he was doubtful whether the thin texture which vibrated with such an alarming crackle when touched even by the tip of his horns would bear his weight; and this determined him finally to creep beneath it, for there was a point where the leaf curved high enough from the ground to admit him. He had just inserted his head in the opening and was taking stock of the high brown roof and was getting used to the cool brown light when two other people came past outside on the turf. This time they were both young, a young man and a young woman. They were both in the prime of youth, or even in that season which precedes the prime of youth, the season before the smooth pink folds of the flower have burst their gummy case, when the wings of the butterfly, though fully grown, are motionless in the sun.

'Lucky it isn't Friday,' he observed.

'Why? D'you believe in luck?'

'They make you pay sixpence on Friday.'

'What's sixpence anyway? Isn't it worth sixpence?'

'What's "it" – what do you mean by "it"?'

'O, anything – I mean – you know what I mean.'

Long pauses came between each of these remarks; they were uttered in toneless and monotonous voices. The couple stood still on the edge of the flower-bed, and together pressed the end of her parasol deep down into the soft earth. The action and the fact that his hand rested on the top of hers expressed their feelings in a strange way, as these short insignificant words also expressed something, words with short wings for their heavy body of meaning, inadequate to carry them far and thus alighting awkwardly upon the very common objects that surrounded them, and were to their inexperienced touch so massive; but who knows (so they thought as they pressed the parasol into the earth) what precipices aren't concealed in them, or what slopes of ice don't shine in the sun on the other side? Who knows? Who has ever seen this before? Even when she wondered what sort of tea they gave you at Kew, he felt that something loomed up behind her words, and stood vast and solid behind them; and the mist very slowly rose and uncovered – O, Heavens, what were those shapes? – little white tables, and waitresses who looked first at her and then at him; and there was a bill that he would pay with a real two shilling piece, and it was real, all real, he assured himself, fingering the coin in his pocket, real to everyone except to him and to her; even to him it began to seem real; and then – but it was too exciting to stand and think any longer, and he pulled the parasol out of the earth with a jerk and was impatient to find the place where one had tea with other people, like other people.

'Come along, Trissie; it's time we had our tea.'

'Wherever *does* one have one's tea?' she asked with the oddest thrill of excitement in her voice, looking vaguely round and letting herself be drawn on down the grass path, trailing her parasol, turning her head this way and that way, forgetting her tea, wishing to go down there and then down there, remembering orchids and cranes among wild flowers, a Chinese pagoda and a crimson crested bird; but he bore her on.

Thus one couple after another with much the same irregular and aimless movement passed the flower-bed and were enveloped in layer after layer of green-blue vapour, in which at first their bodies had substance and a dash of colour, but later both substance and colour dissolved in the green-blue atmosphere. How hot it was! So hot that even the thrush chose to hop, like a mechanical bird, in the shadow of the flowers, with long pauses between one movement and the next; instead of rambling vaguely the white butterflies danced one above another, making with their white shifting flakes the outline of a shattered marble column above the tallest flowers; the glass roofs of the palm house shone as if a whole market full of shiny green umbrellas had opened in the sun; and in the drone of the aeroplane the voice of the summer sky murmured its fierce soul. Yellow and black, pink and snow white, shapes of all these colours, men, women, and children were spotted for a second upon the horizon, and then, seeing the breadth of yellow that lay upon the grass, they wavered and sought shade beneath the trees, dissolving like drops of water in the yellow and green atmosphere, staining it faintly with red and blue. It seemed as if all gross and heavy bodies had sunk down in the heat motionless and lay huddled upon the ground, but their voices went wavering from them as if they were flames lolling from the thick waxen bodies of candles. Voices. Yes, voices. Wordless voices, breaking the silence suddenly with such depth of contentment, such passion of desire, or, in the voices of children, such freshness of surprise; breaking the silence? But there was no silence; all the time the motor omnibuses were turning their wheels and changing their gear; like a vast nest of Chinese boxes all of wrought steel turning ceaselessly one within another the city murmured; on the top of which the voices cried aloud and the petals of myriads of flowers flashed their colours into the air.

The Cat That Walked By Himself
by
Rudyard Kipling

Joseph Rudyard Kipling was born in India in 1865 and sent to England, alongside his three-year-old sister, when he was six. He returned to India in 1882 and published his first prose collection, *Plain Tales from the Hills*, in 1888. His famous children's book, *The Jungle Book*, was published in 1894 and was followed by *The Second Jungle Book* (1895), *Just So Stories* (1902), and *Puck of Pook's Hill* (1906). He also published a novel, *Kim* (1901); poems, including *Mandalay* (1890), *Gunga Din* (1890), and 'If—' (1910); and many short stories, including 'The Man Who Would Be King' (1888) and the collections *Life's Handicap* (1891), *The Day's Work* (1898), and *Plain Tales from the Hills* (1888). He kept writing until the early 1930s and died in 1936.

The Cat That Walked By Himself

HEAR AND ATTEND and listen; for this befell and behappened and became and was, O my Best Beloved, when the Tame animals were wild. The Dog was wild, and the Horse was wild, and the Cow was wild, and the Sheep was wild, and the Pig was wild – as wild as wild could be – and they walked in the Wet Wild Woods by their wild lones. But the wildest of all the wild animals was the Cat. He walked by himself, and all places were alike to him.

Of course the Man was wild too. He was dreadfully wild. He didn't even begin to be tame till he met the Woman, and she told him that she did not like living in his wild ways. She picked out a nice dry Cave, instead of a heap of wet leaves, to lie down in; and she strewed clean sand on the floor; and she lit a nice fire of wood at the back of the Cave; and she hung a dried wild-horse skin, tail-down, across the opening of the Cave; and she said, 'Wipe your feet, dear, when you come in, and now we'll keep house.'

That night, Best Beloved, they ate wild sheep roasted on the hot stones, and flavoured with wild garlic and wild pepper; and wild duck stuffed with wild rice and wild fenugreek and wild coriander; and marrow-bones of wild oxen; and wild cherries, and wild grenadillas. Then the Man went to sleep in front of the fire ever so happy; but the Woman sat up, combing her hair. She took the bone of the shoulder of mutton – the big fat blade-bone – and she looked at the wonderful marks on it, and she threw more wood on the fire, and she made a Magic. She made the First Singing Magic in the world.

Out in the Wet Wild Woods all the wild animals gathered together where they could see the light of the fire a long way off, and they wondered what it meant.

Then Wild Horse stamped with his wild foot and said, 'O my Friends and O my Enemies, why have the Man and the Woman made that great light in that great Cave, and what harm will it do us?'

Wild Dog lifted up his wild nose and smelled the smell of roast mutton, and said, 'I will go up and see and look, and say; for I think it is good. Cat, come with me.'

'Nenni!' said the Cat. 'I am the Cat who walks by himself, and all places are alike to me. I will not come.'

'Then we can never be friends again,' said Wild Dog, and he trotted off to the Cave. But when he had gone a little way the Cat said to himself, 'All places are alike to me. Why should I not go too and see and look and come away at my own liking.' So he slipped after Wild Dog softly, very softly, and hid himself where he could hear everything.

When Wild Dog reached the mouth of the Cave he lifted up the dried horse-skin with his nose and sniffed the beautiful smell of the roast mutton, and the Woman, looking at the blade-bone, heard him, and laughed, and said, 'Here comes the first. Wild Thing out of the Wild Woods, what do you want?'

Wild Dog said, 'O my Enemy and Wife of my Enemy, what is this that smells so good in the Wild Woods?'

Then the Woman picked up a roasted mutton-bone and threw it to Wild Dog, and said, 'Wild Thing out of the Wild Woods, taste and try.' Wild Dog gnawed the bone, and it was more delicious than anything he had ever tasted, and he said, 'O my Enemy and Wife of my Enemy, give me another.'

The Woman said, 'Wild Thing out of the Wild Woods, help my Man to hunt through the day and guard this Cave at night, and I will give you as many roast bones as you need.'

'Ah!' said the Cat, listening. 'This is a very wise Woman, but she is not so wise as I am.'

Wild Dog crawled into the Cave and laid his head on the Woman's lap, and said, 'O my Friend and Wife of my Friend, I will help Your

Man to hunt through the day, and at night I will guard your Cave.'

'Ah!' said the Cat, listening. 'That is a very foolish Dog.' And he went back through the Wet Wild Woods waving his wild tail, and walking by his wild lone. But he never told anybody.

When the Man waked up he said, 'What is Wild Dog doing here?' And the Woman said, 'His name is not Wild Dog any more, but the First Friend, because he will be our friend for always and always and always. Take him with you when you go hunting.'

Next night the Woman cut great green armfuls of fresh grass from the water-meadows, and dried it before the fire, so that it smelt like new-mown hay, and she sat at the mouth of the Cave and plaited a halter out of horse-hide, and she looked at the shoulder of mutton-bone – at the big broad blade-bone – and she made a Magic. She made the Second Singing Magic in the world.

Out in the Wild Woods all the wild animals wondered what had happened to Wild Dog, and at last Wild Horse stamped with his foot and said, 'I will go and see and say why Wild Dog has not returned. Cat, come with me.'

'Nenni!' said the Cat. 'I am the Cat who walks by himself, and all places are alike to me. I will not come.' But all the same he followed Wild Horse softly, very softly, and hid himself where he could hear everything.

When the Woman heard Wild Horse tripping and stumbling on his long mane, she laughed and said, 'Here comes the second. Wild Thing out of the Wild Woods what do you want?'

Wild Horse said, 'O my Enemy and Wife of my Enemy, where is Wild Dog?'

The Woman laughed, and picked up the blade-bone and looked at it, and said, 'Wild Thing out of the Wild Woods, you did not come here for Wild Dog, but for the sake of this good grass.'

And Wild Horse, tripping and stumbling on his long mane, said, 'That is true; give it me to eat.'

The Woman said, 'Wild Thing out of the Wild Woods, bend your wild head and wear what I give you, and you shall eat the wonderful grass three times a day.'

'Ah,' said the Cat, listening, 'this is a clever Woman, but she is not so clever as I am.' Wild Horse bent his wild head, and the Woman slipped the plaited hide halter over it, and Wild Horse breathed on the Woman's feet and said, 'O my Mistress, and Wife of my Master, I will be your servant for the sake of the wonderful grass.'

'Ah,' said the Cat, listening, 'that is a very foolish Horse.' And he went back through the Wet Wild Woods, waving his wild tail and walking by his wild lone. But he never told anybody.

When the Man and the Dog came back from hunting, the Man said, 'What is Wild Horse doing here?' And the Woman said, 'His name is not Wild Horse any more, but the First Servant, because he will carry us from place to place for always and always and always. Ride on his back when you go hunting.'

Next day, holding her wild head high that her wild horns should not catch in the wild trees, Wild Cow came up to the Cave, and the Cat followed, and hid himself just the same as before; and everything happened just the same as before; and the Cat said the same things as before, and when Wild Cow had promised to give her milk to the Woman every day in exchange for the wonderful grass, the Cat went back through the Wet Wild Woods waving his wild tail and walking by his wild lone, just the same as before. But he never told anybody. And when the Man and the Horse and the Dog came home from hunting and asked the same questions same as before, the Woman said, 'Her name is not Wild Cow any more, but the Giver of Good Food. She will give us the warm white milk for always and always and always, and I will take care of her while you and the First Friend and the First Servant go hunting.'

Next day the Cat waited to see if any other Wild thing would go up to the Cave, but no one moved in the Wet Wild Woods, so the Cat walked there by himself; and he saw the Woman milking the Cow, and he saw the light of the fire in the Cave, and he smelt the smell of the warm white milk.

Cat said, 'O my Enemy and Wife of my Enemy, where did Wild Cow go?'

The Woman laughed and said, 'Wild Thing out of the Wild Woods, go back to the Woods again, for I have braided up my hair, and I have put away the magic blade-bone, and we have no more need of either friends or servants in our Cave.'

Cat said, 'I am not a friend, and I am not a servant. I am the Cat who walks by himself, and I wish to come into your cave.'

Woman said, 'Then why did you not come with First Friend on the first night?'

Cat grew very angry and said, 'Has Wild Dog told tales of me?'

Then the Woman laughed and said, 'You are the Cat who walks by himself, and all places are alike to you. You are neither a friend nor a servant. You have said it yourself. Go away and walk by yourself in all places alike.'

Then Cat pretended to be sorry and said, 'Must I never come into the Cave? Must I never sit by the warm fire? Must I never drink the warm white milk? You are very wise and very beautiful. You should not be cruel even to a Cat.'

Woman said, 'I knew I was wise, but I did not know I was beautiful. So I will make a bargain with you. If ever I say one word in your praise you may come into the Cave.'

'And if you say two words in my praise?' said the Cat.

'I never shall,' said the Woman, 'but if I say two words in your praise, you may sit by the fire in the Cave.'

'And if you say three words?' said the Cat.

'I never shall,' said the Woman, 'but if I say three words in your praise, you may drink the warm white milk three times a day for always and always and always.'

Then the Cat arched his back and said, 'Now let the Curtain at the mouth of the Cave, and the Fire at the back of the Cave, and the Milk-pots that stand beside the Fire, remember what my Enemy and the Wife of my Enemy has said.' And he went away through the Wet Wild Woods waving his wild tail and walking by his wild lone.

That night when the Man and the Horse and the Dog came home from hunting, the Woman did not tell them of the bargain that she had made with the Cat, because she was afraid that they might not like it.

Cat went far and far away and hid himself in the Wet Wild Woods by his wild lone for a long time till the Woman forgot all about him. Only the Bat – the little upside-down Bat – that hung inside the Cave, knew where Cat hid; and every evening Bat would fly to Cat with news of what was happening.

One evening Bat said, 'There is a Baby in the Cave. He is new and pink and fat and small, and the Woman is very fond of him.'

'Ah,' said the Cat, listening, 'but what is the Baby fond of?'

'He is fond of things that are soft and tickle,' said the Bat. 'He is fond of warm things to hold in his arms when he goes to sleep. He is fond of being played with. He is fond of all those things.'

'Ah,' said the Cat, listening, 'then my time has come.'

Next night Cat walked through the Wet Wild Woods and hid very near the Cave till morning-time, and Man and Dog and Horse went hunting. The Woman was busy cooking that morning, and the Baby cried and interrupted. So she carried him outside the Cave and gave him a handful of pebbles to play with. But still the Baby cried.

Then the Cat put out his paddy paw and patted the Baby on the cheek, and it cooed; and the Cat rubbed against its fat knees and tickled it under its fat chin with his tail. And the Baby laughed; and the Woman heard him and smiled.

Then the Bat – the little upside-down bat – that hung in the mouth of the Cave said, 'O my Hostess and Wife of my Host and Mother of my Host's Son, a Wild Thing from the Wild Woods is most beautifully playing with your Baby.'

'A blessing on that Wild Thing whoever he may be,' said the Woman, straightening her back, 'for I was a busy woman this morning and he has done me a service.'

That very minute and second, Best Beloved, the dried horse-skin Curtain that was stretched tail-down at the mouth of the Cave fell down – whoosh! – because it remembered the bargain she had made with the Cat, and when the Woman went to pick it up – lo and behold! – the Cat was sitting quite comfy inside the Cave.

'O my Enemy and Wife of my Enemy and Mother of my Enemy,'

said the Cat, 'it is I: for you have spoken a word in my praise, and now I can sit within the Cave for always and always and always. But still I am the Cat who walks by himself, and all places are alike to me.'

The Woman was very angry, and shut her lips tight and took up her spinning-wheel and began to spin. But the Baby cried because the Cat had gone away, and the Woman could not hush it, for it struggled and kicked and grew black in the face.

'O my Enemy and Wife of my Enemy and Mother of my Enemy,' said the Cat, 'take a strand of the wire that you are spinning and tie it to your spinning-whorl and drag it along the floor, and I will show you a magic that shall make your Baby laugh as loudly as he is now crying.'

'I will do so,' said the Woman, 'because I am at my wits' end; but I will not thank you for it.'

She tied the thread to the little clay spindle whorl and drew it across the floor, and the Cat ran after it and patted it with his paws and rolled head over heels, and tossed it backward over his shoulder and chased it between his hind-legs and pretended to lose it, and pounced down upon it again, till the Baby laughed as loudly as it had been crying, and scrambled after the Cat and frolicked all over the Cave till it grew tired and settled down to sleep with the Cat in its arms.

'Now,' said the Cat, 'I will sing the Baby a song that shall keep him asleep for an hour.' And he began to purr, loud and low, low and loud, till the Baby fell fast asleep. The Woman smiled as she looked down upon the two of them and said, 'That was wonderfully done. No question but you are very clever, O Cat.'

That very minute and second, Best Beloved, the smoke of the fire at the back of the Cave came down in clouds from the roof – puff! – because it remembered the bargain she had made with the Cat, and when it had cleared away – lo and behold! – the Cat was sitting quite comfy close to the fire.

'O my Enemy and Wife of my Enemy and Mother of My Enemy,' said the Cat, 'it is I, for you have spoken a second word in my praise, and now I can sit by the warm fire at the back of the Cave for always and always and always. But still I am the Cat who walks by himself, and all places are alike to me.'

Then the Woman was very very angry, and let down her hair and put more wood on the fire and brought out the broad blade-bone of the shoulder of mutton and began to make a Magic that should prevent her from saying a third word in praise of the Cat. It was not a Singing Magic, Best Beloved, it was a Still Magic; and by and by the Cave grew so still that a little wee-wee mouse crept out of a corner and ran across the floor.

'O my Enemy and Wife of my Enemy and Mother of my Enemy,' said the Cat, 'is that little mouse part of your magic?'

'Ouh! Chee! No indeed!' said the Woman, and she dropped the blade-bone and jumped upon the footstool in front of the fire and braided up her hair very quick for fear that the mouse should run up it.

'Ah,' said the Cat, watching, 'then the mouse will do me no harm if I eat it?'

'No,' said the Woman, braiding up her hair, 'eat it quickly and I will ever be grateful to you.'

Cat made one jump and caught the little mouse, and the Woman said, 'A hundred thanks. Even the First Friend is not quick enough to catch little mice as you have done. You must be very wise.'

That very moment and second, O Best Beloved, the Milk-pot that stood by the fire cracked in two pieces – ffft – because it remembered the bargain she had made with the Cat, and when the Woman jumped down from the footstool – lo and behold! – the Cat was lapping up the warm white milk that lay in one of the broken pieces.

'O my Enemy and Wife of my Enemy and Mother of my Enemy,' said the Cat, 'it is I; for you have spoken three words in my praise, and now I can drink the warm white milk three times a day for always and always and always. But still I am the Cat who walks by himself, and all places are alike to me.'

Then the Woman laughed and set the Cat a bowl of the warm white milk and said, 'O Cat, you are as clever as a man, but remember that your bargain was not made with the Man or the Dog, and I do not know what they will do when they come home.'

'What is that to me?' said the Cat. 'If I have my place in the Cave by the fire and my warm white milk three times a day I do not care what the Man or the Dog can do.'

That evening when the Man and the Dog came into the Cave, the Woman told them all the story of the bargain while the Cat sat by the fire and smiled. Then the Man said, 'Yes, but he has not made a bargain with me or with all proper Men after me.' Then he took off his two leather boots and he took up his little stone axe (that makes three) and he fetched a piece of wood and a hatchet (that is five altogether), and he set them out in a row and he said, 'Now we will make our bargain. If you do not catch mice when you are in the Cave for always and always and always, I will throw these five things at you whenever I see you, and so shall all proper Men do after me.'

'Ah,' said the Woman, listening, 'this is a very clever Cat, but he is not so clever as my Man.'

The Cat counted the five things (and they looked very knobby) and he said, 'I will catch mice when I am in the Cave for always and always and always; but still I am the Cat who walks by himself, and all places are alike to me.'

'Not when I am near,' said the Man. 'If you had not said that last I would have put all these things away for always and always and always; but I am now going to throw my two boots and my little stone axe (that makes three) at you whenever I meet you. And so shall all proper Men do after me!'

Then the Dog said, 'Wait a minute. He has not made a bargain with me or with all proper Dogs after me.' And he showed his teeth and said, 'If you are not kind to the Baby while I am in the Cave for always and always and always, I will hunt you till I catch you, and when I catch you I will bite you. And so shall all proper Dogs do after me.'

'Ah,' said the Woman, listening, 'this is a very clever Cat, but he is not so clever as the Dog.'

Cat counted the Dog's teeth (and they looked very pointed) and he said, 'I will be kind to the Baby while I am in the Cave, as long as he does not pull my tail too hard, for always and always and always. But still I am the Cat that walks by himself, and all places are alike to me.'

'Not when I am near,' said the Dog. 'If you had not said that last I would have shut my mouth for always and always and always; but now I am going to hunt you up a tree whenever I meet you. And so shall all proper Dogs do after me.'

Then the Man threw his two boots and his little stone axe (that makes three) at the Cat, and the Cat ran out of the Cave and the Dog chased him up a tree; and from that day to this, Best Beloved, three proper Men out of five will always throw things at a Cat whenever they meet him, and all proper Dogs will chase him up a tree. But the Cat keeps his side of the bargain too. He will kill mice and he will be kind to Babies when he is in the house, just as long as they do not pull his tail too hard. But when he has done that, and between times, and when the moon gets up and night comes, he is the Cat that walks by himself, and all places are alike to him. Then he goes out to the Wet Wild Woods or up the Wet Wild Trees or on the Wet Wild Roofs, waving his wild tail and walking by his wild lone.

> PUSSY can sit by the fire and sing,
>   Pussy can climb a tree,
> Or play with a silly old cork and string
>   To 'muse herself, not me.
> But I like Binkie my dog, because
>   He knows how to behave;
> So, Binkie's the same as the First Friend was,
>   And I am the Man in the Cave.
>
> Pussy will play man-Friday till
>   It's time to wet her paw
> And make her walk on the window-sill

(For the footprint Crusoe saw);
Then she fluffles her tail and mews,
      And scratches and won't attend.
But Binkie will play whatever I choose,
      And he is my true First Friend.

Pussy will rub my knees with her head
      Pretending she loves me hard;
But the very minute I go to my bed
      Pussy runs out in the yard,
And there she stays till the morning-light;
      So I know it is only pretend;
But Binkie, he snores at my feet all night,
      And he is my Firstest Friend!

*Stories
to read
when it's
all going wrong*

Charm for a friend with a lump
by
Helen Simpson

Helen Simpson was born in Bristol in 1959. She worked at *Vogue* for five years before her success in writing short stories meant she could afford to leave and concentrate full-time on her writing. She is the author of the short-story collections *Four Bare Legs in a Bed* (1990), *Dear George* (1995), *Hey Yeah Right Get a Life* (2000), *Constitutional* (2005) and *Geography Boy* (2010). In 1991 she was chosen as the *Sunday Times* Young Writer of the Year and won the Somerset Maugham Award. In 1993 she was chosen as one of *Granta*'s twenty Best of Young British Novelists. She lives in London.

Charm For A Friend With A Lump

FIRST LET ME take a piece of chalk and draw a circle round you, so you're safe. There. Now I'll stand guard, keeping a weather eye open for anything threatening, and we can catch up with each other while we wait.

Have a glance through this garden catalogue if you would. I need your help in choosing what to plant this spring. I thought the little yellow Peacevine tomatoes, so sweet and sharp, along with Gardener's Delight and Tiger Toms; but there's a lot to be said for Marmande too.

I'll have a word with the powers-that-be. The Health Czar. Ban parabens. I'll keep away the spotted snakes with double tongues, I'll be like Cobweb and Mustardseed in the play; I'll make sure the beetles black approach not near. By naming the bad things I'll haul them up into the light and shrivel their power over you. Hence, malignant tumour, hence; carcinoma, come not here.

Then I thought I'd try those stripy round courgettes this year, Ronds de Nice. You have to pick them as soon as they reach the size of tennis balls, you mustn't let them get any bigger than that or they won't be worth eating. They'll swell and grow as big as footballs if you let them. As for fruit, what do you think of Conference pears? Or, the catalogue recommends the Invincible, a very hardy variety which crops heavily and blooms twice a year.

Let's not even start on those predictable but useless paths which lead to nowhere. If only I hadn't smoked at fifteen, if only there hadn't been that betrayal, if only I hadn't spent so much time putting up with the insupportable – whyever did I think endurance was a virtue? Didn't I *want* to stay alive? If only I hadn't sipped wine, or drunk water from plastic bottles. If only I hadn't gone jogging the day Chernobyl exploded. Oh, give it a rest! We live in the world as it is, we all have to breathe its contagious fogs. It's wrong of them to claim it must somehow be our own fault when our health is under attack.

Let's get back to the catalogue. Help me choose some soft fruit. If I had more space I might try gooseberries again now there's this new cultivar that cheats American blight. But it's probably wiser to add to the existing blackcurrant patch; here's a new one, Titania, 'large fruit and good flavour. Crops very heavily over a long period. Good resistance to mildew and rust.'

We're advised to build up an arsenal of elixirs if we want to strengthen our own resistance. We're told we ought to call in light boxes, amulets, Echinacea drops and oily fish, we should fix on organic free-range grass-fed meat, Japanese green tea and a daily dose of turmeric. And if we're really serious about protecting ourselves we must avoid dry-cleaners, getting fat, aluminium, insecticides; shun transfats as the devil's food; forswear polystyrene cups. We've got to fight shy of white bread, a sedentary life-style, perfume and anger, if we truly want to save ourselves. And even if we tick off every item on the list, there's absolutely no guarantee that it'll lengthen our span by a single day.

On your last birthday, with your natural dislike of being reminded of the passing years, we skirted round the subject for a while. I asked what you'd be doing to celebrate. You scoffed. You said you'd rather forget about it. Do you remember? Then I reached down into myself and managed to say, 'You *should* celebrate, your birthday *should* be celebrated, because the world's a better place with you in it.' May you continue to pile on the years, but with more pleasure from now on. In time may you embrace fallen arches and age spots, and may you smilingly observe the arrival of batwing arms and a frankly vieux jeu décolletage. Decades from now may your joints creak and your ears hiss, may your crows' feet laugh back into the mirror at your quivering dewlaps.

Nobody in their right mind looks at an old oak tree growing in strength and richness and thinks, you'll be dead soon. They just admire and draw strength from its example. May you keep your hair on and your eyebrows in place. May you never have to wear a hat indoors. May you and your other half tuck two centuries under your belts between you, and then, like the old couple in the tale, when some kind god in disguise grants you a wish may you go together, hand in hand, in an instant.

I'm willing you to be well. Do you hear me? If there does happen to be some disorder in your blood I'm like Canute – I'll stay here by you and turn the tide. You're my persona grata.

And if they find that some weed or canker has gained hold after all – Japanese Knotweed, it might be, that ruthless invader and ignorer of boundaries – well, then, we'll deal with it. There are powerful new weed-killers these days, and they work. Doctors are like gardeners in the way they know how to distinguish between healthy growth and uncontrollable proliferation. There's a fine line, and what I am casting a spell for is that nothing inside you has stepped over it.

In my spell we are dreaming our way forward through the year into the green and white of May, and on into the deep green lily-ponds of June. The lushness of June, its new heat and subdued glitter of excitement at dusk, its scent and roses, that's what we'll aim for. I do love roses, their scent and beauty, particularly my Souvenir du Dr. Jamain and the thorny pink Eglantine beside the vegetable patch.

We'll have a party there this Midsummer's Eve, up by the tomato plants and ranks of cos lettuce, just the two of us. Let's write it in our diaries now. I can't spare you. You're indispensable! We'll have a party, and pledge your health by moonlight on the one night of the year when plants consumed or planted have magical powers.

There is a great deal of talk about the benefits of mistletoe extract and so on, but I'm not convinced. You can spend a lot of time and energy chasing magic potions, when you might be better occupied weaving your own spells over the future. En route, sleep will help. Everyone has their own private walled garden at night where they can prune their troubles and dream change into some sort of shape. That's what I'm trying to say, a dream can be a transformer, as well as providing a margin or grassy bank where you can rest while the outside world goes on. Active dreaming, which is what I would prescribe, can be a powerful form of enchantment.

You're not out of the woods yet, that's clear; but a little while from now I want you to walk out of the woods and into the June garden. Leave the black bats hanging upside down; they'll stay asleep. While we wait for summer, let's choose to be patient and hopeful. And soon, not really long from now at all, I aim to smile at you and say, Come into the garden, friend of my heart.

A Convalescent Ego
by
Richard Yates

Richard Yates was born in 1926 in New York and lived in California. His prize-winning stories began to appear in 1953 and his first novel, *Revolutionary Road*, was nominated for the National Book Award in 1961. He subsequently taught writing at Columbia University, the New School for Social Research, Boston University (where his papers are archived), at the University of Iowa Writers' Workshop, at Wichita State University, and at the University of Southern California Master of Professional Writing Program. He is the author of eight other works, including the novels *A Good School*, *The Easter Parade*, and *Disturbing the Peace*, and two collections of short stories, *Eleven Kinds of Loneliness* and *Liars in Love*. He died in 1992 from emphysema and complications from minor surgery.

A Convalescent Ego

'ONE THING YOU might do while I'm gone,' Jean said, 'is rinse out those new teacups. Did you hear me, Bill?'

Her husband looked up from a magazine. 'Sure I heard you. Wash the teacups.' And he could tell by the shape of her shoulders and back as she bent to zip up little Mike's jacket that this was one of her days for feeling overworked and unappreciated. 'Anything else you want me to do?' he asked.

She straightened up and turned around, sweeping back her hair with a tired hand. 'Oh, no, I don't think so, Bill. You just – rest, or whatever it is you're doing.'

'Park!' Mike demanded. 'Park, park!'

'Yes, darling, we're *going* to the park. Now, let's see,' she said vaguely, 'have I got everything? Keys, money, grocery list . . . yes. All right, then, come on, Mike. Say "Bye-bye Daddy."'

'Bye-bye Daddy,' the little boy said, and she led him out of the apartment and slammed the door.

Bill settled back on the couch and picked up the magazine again, but the rankling memory of her words made it impossible to read. 'Rest, or whatever it is you're doing.' And just what did she *expect* him to be doing, two weeks out of the hospital? He was on doctor's *orders* to rest, wasn't he? Angrily he shut the magazine and flipped it toward the coffee table. It missed and splayed out on the rug, calling his attention to a number of cigarette ashes – his – that had fallen there too. Well, maybe she *was* overworked, but what did she

111

expect? She was pretty lucky not to be a widow, wasn't she, after an operation like that? Using the magazine as a dustpan he scraped up most of the ashes and dropped them in an ashtray, and then rubbed the remnants into the carpet with his slipper. It wasn't until he went to the kitchen for a glass of milk (he was on doctor's orders to drink a lot of milk too) that he remembered about the teacups. She had lined them up on the side of the sink for washing – four plain little cups and saucers that she'd brought home the night before. 'I couldn't resist them, Bill,' she'd said, 'and we do *need* new cups. You don't think it was terribly extravagant, do you?' He smiled as he lathered up the sink brush. This was her idea of a big extravagance now – four cups – when last year she'd have put them on the charge account without even thinking about it. A long illness certainly did change your attitude about money. But in another month he'd be on his feet again, bringing home a man-sized check every payday, and *then* she could begin to relax. They could do the kind of things they'd almost forgotten about – buy clothes they didn't need and go to the theater and throw parties and stay up late when they felt like it. Then maybe she'd get over this dreary business of watching every nickel. Then maybe she'd – Suddenly there was a sharp noise and a little mess of broken china in the sink. It was all over so fast that it took him a full minute, standing there with trembling hands, to figure out what had happened. The porcelain soap dish had given way under his brush, dropped from the wall and smashed, breaking the cup and saucer he'd just washed. He picked up the broken soap dish and scrutinized the place on the wall from which it had fallen, and his first consecutive thought was, Well it certainly wasn't *my* fault. The stupid thing had been hanging there by two little rusty hooks – almost any pressure would have broken it, and the remarkable thing was that it hadn't broken long ago. It certainly wasn't *my* fault, he told himself again. He gathered all the pieces and put them in the garbage. Then very carefully he washed the other cups and saucers, dried them and put them away. But his hands were still trembling as he hung up the dish towel, and his knees were weak when he went back into the living room.

He sat down and lit a cigarette, turning the defiant little phrase over and over in his mind – wasn't *my* fault, wasn't *my* fault – with less and less conviction. Things like this had been happening nearly every day since he came home from the hospital. First there had been the discovery that he'd left his silver fountain pen behind, in the locker beside his hospital bed, and Jean had to make a special trip back to get it from the nurses. Then on the second or third day, when he'd insisted on helping with the housework, he had shaken the dust mop out the window so hard that the head of the thing fell off, five stories down into the courtyard, and left him absurdly shaking the naked stick over the windowsill. And there was the time he'd let the bathroom sink overflow, and the time he'd split the side of Mike's wagon wide open trying to nail the wheel back in place, and the terrible morning when he'd not only cut his thumb on the unwinding strip of a coffee can but spilled the coffee all over the floor. At first Jean had laughed about it ('Poor darling, you're just out of *touch* with things, aren't you?') but lately her reactions had alternated between elaborate kindliness and tight-lipped silence, and he didn't know which was worse. How, exactly, could he tell her about this? A pleasant little apology was out of the question; he absolutely could not say 'Sorry, darling, I broke one of the cups,' and expect to retain a shred of dignity. But what else was there to say?

Sweat prickled his scalp, and his fingers drummed convulsively on the table. He stamped out his cigarette decisively, smoothed his hair and forced himself to sit back and relax. You could drive yourself crazy taking little things so hard; he would have to pull himself together. The soap dish hadn't been fastened securely, it could have happened to anybody, and there was nothing to apologize for. And there was certainly no point in trying to tell her about it all at once, the minute she came in. Obviously, the only way was to let her discover it herself, and then give her the explanation sensibly and calmly, when she asked for it. He pictured the scene.

She would come in with her load of groceries, and Mike would probably be whimpering. He'd get up from the couch to take the bundles from her, of course, but she'd say, 'No, that's all right. Bill. You sit still. Mike, stop that, now.' He would try to take the bundles anyway, and she'd say, 'No, Bill, don't be silly. Do you want to get sick again?' So he would sit down and watch her go into the kitchen with Mike tagging along. She might discover it right away, but more likely she'd be too busy at first. It wouldn't happen until after she'd gotten the food put away and Mike attended to, perhaps not until she'd started to make lunch. Then there would be an abrupt silence from the kitchen, and he would hear her polite, questioning voice: 'Bill?'

'Yes, honey?'

'What happened to the soap dish?'

'It wasn't put up properly.'

'It wasn't *what?*'

'Well, I can't shout,' he would say, with dignity. 'You'll have to come in if you want to hear me.' And when she came to the kitchen door, with her expression of sorely tried patience, he would say, judiciously, 'The soap dish wasn't put up properly, Jean. Didn't you ever notice that before? I don't see how you could've *helped* noticing it. There were only these two little rusty hooks, and—'

'You mean you broke it?'

'*No,* I didn't break it. I mean it wasn't my *fault.* Now look, do you want to hear what happened or don't you?'

She would sigh, perhaps even roll her eyes and then sit down with a great display of attention. 'Well,' he would begin, 'I was washing the cups, you see, and when I lathered up the brush – just using the soap dish the way it's intended to be used – these two little rusty hooks gave way and the whole thing fell into the sink. And there was this cup and saucer that I'd just finished washing, you see, and—'

'Oh, no,' she would say, closing her eyes. 'Bill, did you break one of the new cups too?'

'*I* didn't break it! It was an accident, don't you understand? I didn't break it any more than you did!'

'Don't shout!'

'I'm *not* shouting!' And by that time Mike would probably be in tears again.

Bill sprang from the couch and stalked the floor, wrenching the sash of his bathrobe into angry knots. That would be exactly the *wrong* way to go about it. Why did he always play the fool? Why should he always set himself up for little humiliations like this? Oh, and she'd love every minute of it, wouldn't she, with that endless act she put on about bearing her burden with a smile. He'd had just about as much of that as he could take – that and all her little wisecracks about 'resting.' It was time she found out once and for all who *did* wear the pants in this family, bathrobe or no bathrobe.

Suddenly he stopped, breathless, poised on the brink of a new idea. With a grin he tore off the robe and strode into the bathroom to shave. At first, the idea was only a reckless blur in his mind, but in the slow process of shaving he developed it into an orderly, perfect plan of action. When he had finished shaving he would get fully dressed, in real clothes, and leave the apartment. She couldn't be back for another hour, and that gave him plenty of time. He'd take a taxi to the store where she'd bought the cups (luckily he knew which store it was) and buy a cup and saucer to replace the broken ones. Then he'd buy a soap dish with a decent, sturdy wall attachment, and on the way home he'd pick up a dozen long-stemmed roses – and a bottle of wine. He smiled as the extra idea of the wine leaped into his mind. That would be perfect – a bottle of really good wine, maybe even champagne, to celebrate. Then he would hurry home in time to get everything set, and this was how it would happen.

She would come in tired, loaded down with groceries, with Mike bawling and pulling at her skirt. 'Mike, *stop* that!' she'd say, and as she bent to detach him from her legs a couple of grapefruit would probably topple from an overstuffed paper bag. 'Oh—' she'd say, but before she could say anything else the load of bundles would be swept out of her arms, the rolling grapefruit snatched from the floor. 'Bill!' she'd say, aghast, 'what're you *doing?*'

'That should be obvious,' he would say smiling, perhaps even bowing, controlling all the bundles in one arm while he pulled Mike off her with the other. 'Won't you come in?' Then he would turn to Mike. 'Go to your room, son, and cut out that sniveling. I won't have it.' The boy's eyes would widen with respect as he sidled off toward his room. 'Hurry up!' Bill would command, and Mike would disappear. 'Now,' he would say to his wife, 'will you excuse me a moment, darling? Just make yourself comfortable.'

'But Bill, you're *dressed*.'

He would stop on his way to the kitchen, turn, and make another little bow. 'Obviously.' He'd stay in the kitchen only a second, just long enough to put the bundles down, and then he'd return, wheeling the tea cart on which he would have previously arranged the box of roses, the bottle of champagne in its ice bucket, two stemmed glasses and perhaps a little dish of salted nuts.

'Bill,' she would say, 'have you gone out of your *mind*?'

'On the contrary, darling.' He would laugh softly. 'One might almost say I've regained my sanity. Oh, here – these are for you.' And when he had her sitting on the couch with the roses in her lap and a glass in her hand, he would dry the bottle with a flourish, pop the cork and serve it up. 'Now,' he would say. 'May I propose a toast? To the noble memory of your courage and sacrifice throughout my illness; to the celebration of my complete recovery, which occurred today; and to the continuation of my excellent health' – here he would smile winningly – 'and yours.'

But before she drank she would certainly say, with fear in her voice: 'Bill, how much did all this *cost*?'

'Cost?' he'd say. 'Cost? Don't be absurd, darling. All that's over now. Drink!'

Exultant, he gave the razor a final sweep across his cheek and cut himself badly, just above the lip. His thoughts were interrupted by the business of washing the soap away and fixing a piece of tissue on the wound, and by the time he returned to the plan it had lost much of its luster. He persisted doggedly anyway, like a man trying to return to sleep for the completion of a dream.

'I'll explain it all from the beginning,' he would tell her, 'but not until you drink some of this.'

Stunned, suspicious, she would take a tiny sip.

'Now. When you left here this morning, darling, I became very fed up with this stupid convalescence of mine – this "resting," as you chose so appropriately to call it. So fed up, in fact, that I got clumsy, and the very first thing I did was break one of your new cups. Yes! Smashed it to pieces, and I wouldn't blame you a bit if you're angry. But listen. Breaking that cup had a remarkable, therapeutic effect on me. Made me realize all at once that if I went on much longer that way I'd *really* be sick. Yes, and you'd be plenty sick too, of living with a man like that. So I decided to declare the whole thing over and done with, as of today. Go back to work and everything. And right away I began to feel like a million dollars. Never been so well in my life. Drink!'

'Now wait a minute,' she would say. 'Just try to calm down and let me—'

'I *am* calmed down.'

'All right. Just let me get this straight. You broke a cup and so you steamed out of here and bought all these crazy things – spent more money than I've spent on food in the past two weeks. Right?'

'Darling,' he would say, 'I'll have earned it all back by tomorrow at this time. One half-day at the office will cover everything, and I have every intention of spending all my days – full days – at the office from now on.'

'Oh, don't be a fool. You know perfectly well you're not allowed to work for another month.'

'I know nothing of the sort. All I know is—'

'All *I* know,' she would say, 'is that I come home and find my budget ruined for weeks to come, you carrying on like a madman, *and* one of the new cups broken.'

'The cup,' he would say icily, 'needn't bother you any more. It's been replaced. *And* so has the soap dish.'

'Oh, no,' she would say, closing her eyes. 'You mean you broke the soap dish *too*?'

'Listen,' he'd say, or probably shout. 'I'm going to the office tomorrow, is that clear?'

'You're going to bed,' she would say, getting to her feet. 'Is that clear? And I'm going to make lunch, and then I'm going to see if the florist will take these roses back. That'll recover some of the loss, anyway. And I think I'll call the doctor too, and have him look at you. You've probably done yourself a great deal of damage this morning. You're hysterical, Bill.'

By the time the scene had played itself out in his mind he was staring fiercely into the mirror, breathing hard. That was how she'd win, all right, as easily as that. She always won. And even if he did go to work in the morning the whole thing would be ruined, the whole point lost. He was blocked every way he turned. He slouched out of the bathroom and began absently putting on the robe as he walked around the carpet. But wait a minute, he thought, stopping in his tracks again. What if he wasn't *here* when she came home? What if he went to the office now, before she had a chance to stop him? It was only a little after eleven – he could leave now, get in a full half-day's work and *then* come home with the new cup and the soap dish, the flowers and champagne. What could she say to that? How could there be any argument when he confronted her with the accomplished fact? The beautiful logic of the thing was suddenly clear, and he nearly laughed as he tore the robe off for the second time and headed for his dresser. He yanked the pins out of a clean shirt and began dressing with brisk efficiency – dressing to go to work like any normal man, just as he'd once done every morning of his life. It was as if there had never been any illness, any hospital, any operation or any convalescence. Everything seemed in order for the first time in many months. He still felt a little weak in the knees, but that would go away as soon as he'd had a decent lunch. When he straightened up from tying his shoes, he almost blacked out in a rush of dizziness. He blinked and sat down on the bed, shaking his head. He was probably a little overexcited; he'd have to get a grip on himself, so that when he walked into the office he would look fit and rested. Already he could picture their faces when he got off the elevator. 'Bill!' his boss would say, looking as if he'd seen a ghost, and Bill would grin at him and shake hands – 'Hi, George' – and sit casually on the edge of his desk.

'But your wife said you wouldn't be back for another month at *least.*'

'Oh,' he would say, 'you know women, George. She exaggerates everything. Anyway, here I am. Cigarette?'

'Well, it's certainly great to see you, boy, but how do you feel?'

'Like a million dollars, George. Never better in my life. How's everything here in the shop?' It would be as simple as that. Then as soon as he'd straightened up his desk and shaken hands with everybody and answered all their questions he'd be back in commission again; doing a job and on the payroll.

But he'd have to hurry now, if he wanted to get out of here before she came home. Knotting his tie in the mirror, he planned the note he would leave for her: something short and to the point. 'Decided to stop fooling around. Gone to the office. Feeling great. See you later. What kind of champagne do you like?' Or maybe it would be better to let the champagne be a complete surprise, when he made his triumphal return. He hurried over to the desk and wrote it out, omitting the part about the champagne, making the whole thing look very casual. Inspired, he finished it off with 'P.S. – Cup, soap dish broken. Sorry. Will replace both on way home tonight.' Then he propped it on the coffee table where she couldn't miss it, and chuckled.

She would come in loaded down with clumsy bundles, exhausted, with Mike howling and dirty and hanging on her skirt. 'Mike, *stop* that! Stop it this instant! Bill?' she would call plaintively, 'would you mind getting up for just a minute and giving me a hand? Bill, do you hear me?' And she'd stagger into the living room, enraged, dragging Mike and spilling half her groceries. 'Look, Bill, I *hate* to tear you away from your—' But then she would stop, amazed, finding him gone and the apartment empty, and the little note propped on the table.

She probably wouldn't be able to do anything for an hour or so, until after she'd made Mike's lunch and gotten him settled for his nap, but after that the first thing she'd do would be to call him frantically on the telephone. He would take the call at his desk, leaning back in the swivel chair and answering the phone in a crisp, businesslike way.

'Bill?' she'd say. 'Is that *you*?'

He would feign surprise. 'Oh, hi, baby. What's on your mind?'

'Bill, have you gone *mad* ? Are you all right?'

'Never better, honey. Say, I'm sorry about that cup, and the other thing, the soap dish. That what you called about?'

'Listen to me, Bill. I don't know what this is all about, but you're going to get right on the bus and come home. Do you hear me? No, better take a taxi. This instant. Do you hear me?'

'But *baby*,' he'd say, 'you know I can't quit work in the middle of the day. Want me to get fired?'

He laughed aloud – the line about getting fired was a hot one. He was all ready to go now, except for the piece of tissue on his lip. He pulled it off carefully, but the cut was still fresh and started to bleed again. Cursing, he dabbed at it with his handkerchief and stood by the door, waiting for it to heal. What would she say next, after the line about getting fired? Probably something like 'Look. Just what is all this supposed to prove? Would you mind telling me?'

'Sure,' he'd say. 'Proves I'm well, that's all. Well man's got no business moping around the house all day making work for his wife. Ought to be out earning a living, providing a little security for her. Anything wrong in that?'

'Oh, nothing at all,' she would say. 'That's just lovely. You stay right there and make yourself ill, and come home tonight and collapse, and go to work tomorrow and come home in an *ambulance*. That's just *fine*, isn't it. That'll give me lots and *lots* of security, won't it?'

'Aw, now, honey, you're all excited about nothing. You've just got this stubborn idea in your head that I'm—' But probably about this point George would walk into his office, the way he always used to do when Jean was on the phone. 'Say, Bill, here's a couple of reports you might want to look— oh, sorry.' And he'd sit down, well within earshot, to wait until Bill was free.

'All right, Bill,' Jean's voice would say coldly in the receiver. 'I'll put it this way; either you come home right now—'

'Okay,' he'd say, cheerily, trying to convey by the false tone that he was no longer alone, 'okay, then, honey, I'll see you at six o'clock.'

'Either you come home right now—'

'Right, honey. Six o'clock.'

'—Or don't expect to find me here when you *do* come home. I'll be on the train for Mother's, and so will Mike. I've had just about enough of your kind of security.' And there would be a little dry click as she hung up the phone.

Bill rubbed his head, sweating, looking at the note. He had never felt more thoroughly beaten in his life. He walked over to the table, crumpled the note and threw it into the wastebasket. That was that. And suddenly he stopped caring about the whole thing. Let her say or do whatever she wanted. Let anything happen. He was through. He surrendered. All he wanted was to go out and sit down in a bar and have a drink. Or two drinks or three. He grabbed his hat out of the hall closet, wrenched open the front door and stopped short. There she was, just coming in, about to put her key in the door he had flung open, looking up startled into his face. She was carrying only a few light packages, and Mike was neither crying nor pulling her skirt – he was grinning, in fact, and eating an apple.

'Well!' she said. 'Where are *you* going?'

He jammed on his hat and brushed past them. 'Out for a drink.'

'Like that? With your suspenders hanging down?'

One sickening glance confirmed the fact: the suspenders hung in loops against his trouser legs. He spun around and glared at her, then started back toward her at a slow and menacing gait. 'Listen. It's a good thing you came back before I left, because I've got a few things to tell you.'

'Is it necessary to tell the neighbors too?' she inquired.

Grimly, controlling himself with a supreme effort of will, he followed her back into the apartment, took off his hat and followed her around while she disposed of the groceries and shooed Mike off to his room. Then she confronted him with a prim smile. 'Now.'

He planted his fists on his hips, rocked on his heels a few times and grinned evilly at her. 'You know that soap dish? Well, it's broken.'

'Oh.' Annoyance flickered briefly on her face; then she resumed her thin little smile. 'So *that's* what it is.'

'Whaddya *mean* that's what it is? Another thing. You know those new cups? One of *them's* broken too! And the *saucer* too!'

She closed her eyes for an instant and sighed. 'Well,' she said. 'I guess we don't need to discuss it. I'm sure you feel bad enough about it already.'

'Feel *bad*? Feel *bad*? Why the hell should I feel *bad*? It wasn't my *fault!*'

'Oh,' she said.

'Whatsa matter, don'tcha believe me? Don'tcha believe me? Huh? No, of *course* you don't. You're like a Communist *court*, aren'tcha? Everybody's guilty until proved innocent, aren't they? Huh? Oh no, not everybody, I forgot. Just me, right? Just poor stupid old Bill who drops ashes on the rug all day, right? Who's always "resting," right? Pretending to be sick while you bear your burdens with a smile, right? Oh, you *like* that, don'tcha? Love every minute of it, don'tcha? Huh? Don'tcha?'

'I will *not* take this, Bill,' she said, her eyes blazing. 'I will *not* take—'

'*Is that so? Is that so?* Because there's a couple things *I'm* not gonna take any more, and you better get 'em straight right now. I'm not gonna take any more of your wisecracks about "resting," understand? That's one thing. And I'm not gonna take any more of your—' His voice failed; he was out of breath. 'Ah, never mind,' he said at last. 'You wouldn't understand.' He took off his jacket, flung it on the couch and started to fix his suspenders; then with a gesture of disgust he let them fall again and plunged his hands in his pockets, staring out the window. He didn't even want a drink, now. He just wanted to stand here and look out the window and wait for the storm to pass.

'I certainly *wouldn't* understand,' she said. 'I'm afraid I *don't* understand why I should have to come home and find everything broken, and then get all this raging abuse from you *too*. Really, Bill, you *do* expect a lot.'

The only thing to do was stand there and let her get it out of her system. He was spent now, unable to strike back or even to defend himself, a fighter hanging groggy on the ropes.

'What *does* go on in that mind of yours, anyway?' she demanded. 'You're just like a child! A big, spoiled, stubborn child . . .'

It went on and on, but her voice lacked the shrill, nagging quality he had expected – instead it sounded hurt and almost tearful, which was worse. In the small part of his mind that remained clear he decided grimly that this quarrel would probably be a long one, the kind that lasted two or three days. The shouting and recriminations would stop soon, but there would be a long interval of cold silence, of polite little questions and answers over meals, of going to sleep without even saying goodnight, before he could decently go to her and say the big, simple thing that might have averted it all in the first place: 'I'm sorry, darling.'

Her tirade came to an end, and he heard her flounce off into the kitchen. Then there was a series of curt, businesslike kitchen noises – the refrigerator opened and shut, pots rattled, carrots scraped – and in a little while she came back again and started briskly straightening a slipcover right behind the place where he stood. What would she do, he wondered tensely, if I turned around and said it right now?

But at that moment a remarkable thing happened behind his back. Her fingers took hold of the dangling suspenders, pulled them up and deftly slipped them over his shoulders, and her voice – a new voice with laughter in it – said, 'Fix your suspenders, mister?' Then her arms went around him and squeezed, tight, and her face pressed warm between his shoulder blades. 'Oh Bill, I *have* been awful since you came home, haven't I? I'm so busy being tired and heroic I haven't given you a *chance* to get well – I haven't even let you know how terribly glad I am to have you *back*. Oh Bill, you ought to break *all* the dishes, right over my dumb head.'

He didn't trust himself to speak, but he turned around and took her in his arms, and there was nothing sick and nothing tired about the way they kissed. This was the one thing he hadn't figured on, in all his plans – the one slim chance he had overlooked completely.

An Anxious Man
by
James Lasdun

James Lasdun was born in London and now lives in upstate New York. He has published two collections of short stories, three books of poetry and two novels, *The Horned Man* and *Seven Lies*. His story 'The Siege' was adapted by Bernardo Bertolucci for his film *Beseiged*. He co-wrote the screenplay for the film *Sunday* (based on another of his stories) which won Best Feature and Best Screenplay awards at Sundance, 1997. He is the recipient of a Guggenheim Fellowship in poetry, and currently teaches poetry and fiction workshops at Princeton. In 2006 he won the inaugural National Short Story competition with 'An Anxious Man'.

An Anxious Man

JOSEPH NAGEL SLUMPED forward, head in hands.
  'My God,' he groaned.
Elise snapped off the car radio.
'Calm down, Joseph.'
'That's four straight days since we got here.'
'Joseph, please.'
'What do you think we're down now? Sixty? Eighty thousand?'
'It'll come back.'
'We should have sold everything after the first twenty. That would have been an acceptable loss. Given that we were too stupid to sell when we were actually ahead—'
Joseph felt the petulant note in his voice, told himself to shut up, and plunged on:
  'I did say we should get out, didn't I? Frankly, it was irresponsible committing all that money—' shut *up, shut up* '—not to mention the unseemliness of buying in when you did—'
  Oh God . . .
His wife spoke icily: 'I didn't hear you complain when we were ahead.'
'All right, but that's not the point. The point is—'
'What?'
Her face had tightened angrily on itself, all line and bone.
'The point is . . .' But he had lost his train of thought and sat blinking, walled in a thick grief that seemed for a moment

127

unaccounted for by money or anything else he could put his finger on.

Elise got out of the car.

'Let's go for a swim, shall we, Darcy?'

She opened the rear door for their daughter and led her away.

Glumly, Joseph watched them walk hand in hand down through the scrub oaks and pines to the sandy edge of the kettle pond.

He gathered the two bags from the shopping expedition into his lap, but remained in the car, heavily immobile.

Money . . . For the first time in their lives they had some capital. It had come from the sale of an apartment Elise had inherited, and it had aroused volatile forces in their household. Though not a vast amount – under a quarter of a million dollars after estate taxes – it was large enough, if considered as a stake rather than a nest egg, to form the basis of a dream of real riches, and Joseph had found himself unexpectedly susceptible to this dream. The money he had made as a dealer in antique prints and furniture was enough, combined with Elise's income from occasional web-design jobs, to keep them in modest comfort – two cars, an old brick house in Aurelia with lilac bushes and a grape arbour, the yearly trip up here to the Cape – but there wasn't much left over for Darcy's college fund, let alone their retirement. In the past such matters hadn't troubled him greatly, but with the advent of Elise's inheritance he had felt suddenly awoken into new and urgent responsibilities. At their age they shouldn't be worrying about how to pay for medical coverage every year, should they? Or debating whether they could afford the dental and eye-care package too? And wasn't it about time they built a studio so that Elise could concentrate on her painting?

The more he considered these things, the more necessary, as opposed to merely desirable, they had seemed, until he began to think that to go on much longer without them would be to accept failure – a marginal existence that would doubtless grow more pinched as time went by, and end in squalor.

After probate had cleared and Elise had sold the apartment, they had gone to a man on Wall Street, a money manager who didn't as a rule handle accounts of less than a million dollars, but who, as a special favour to the mutual acquaintance who had recommended him, had agreed to consider allowing the Nagels to invest their capital in one of his funds.

Morton Dowell, the man's name was. Gazing out at the pond glittering through the pines, Joseph recalled him vividly: a tanned, smiling, sapphire-eyed man in a striped shirt with white collar and cuffs, and a pair of elasticized silver sleevelinks circling his arms.

A young assistant, balding and grave, had shown them into Dowell's cherry-panelled bower overlooking Governor's Island. There, sunk in dimpled leather armchairs, Joseph and Elise had listened to Dowell muse in an English-accented drawl on his 'extraordinary run of good luck' these past twenty years, inclining his head in modest disavowal when the assistant murmured that he could think of a better word for it than luck, while casually evoking image after image of the transformations he had wrought upon his clients' lives, and hinting casually at the special intimacies within the higher circles of finance that had enabled him to accomplish these transformations.

'I think it's just so much *fun* to help people attain the things they want from life,' he had said, 'be it a yacht or a house on St Bart's or a Steinway for their musical child . . .'

Joseph had listened, mesmerised, hardly daring to hope that this mighty personage would consent to sprinkle his magic upon their modest capital. He was almost overcome with gratitude when at the end of the meeting Dowell appeared to have decided they would make acceptable clients, sending his assistant to fetch his Sovereign Mutual Fund prospectus for them to take home.

'What a creep,' Elise had murmured as they waited for the elevator outside. 'I wouldn't leave him in a room with Darcy's piggy bank.'

Stunned, Joseph had opened his mouth to defend the man, but at once found himself hesitating. Perhaps she was right . . . He knew himself to be a poor judge of people. He, who could detect the most skilfully faked Mission desk or Federal-era sleigh bed merely by standing in its presence for a moment, was less sure of himself when it came to human beings. He tended to like them on principle, but his sense of what they were essentially was vague, unstable – qualities he suspected might be linked to some corresponding instability in himself. Whereas Elise, who had little interest in material things (and who had been altogether less unsettled by her inheritance than he had), took a keen if somewhat detached interest in other people, and was shrewd at assessing them.

Even as their elevator began descending from Dowell's office, Joseph had found his sense of the man beginning to falter. And by the time they got home it had reversed itself entirely. *Of course,* he had thought, picturing the man's tanned smile and sparking armbands again; *what an obvious phony! A reptile!* He shuddered to think how easily he had been taken in.

'You know what? You should invest the money yourself,' he had told Elise.

'That had crossed my mind.'

'You should do it, Elise! It can't be that hard.' He was brimming with sudden enthusiasm for the idea.

'Perhaps I will give it a try.'

'You should! You have good instincts. That's all that matters. These money managers are just guessing like anyone else. You'd be as good as any of them.'

And this in fact had appeared to be the case. After biding her time for several weeks, Elise had made her move with an audacity that stunned him. It was right after the September 11 attacks, when the shell-shocked markets reopened. Over ten days, as the Dow reeled and staggered, she bought and bought and bought, icily resolute while Joseph flailed around her, wrenched between his fearful certainty that the entire capitalist system was about to collapse, his guilty terror of being punished by the gods for attempting to profit from disaster, and his rising excitement, as the tide turned and he could see, on the Schwab web page over his wife's shoulder, the figure in the Total Gain column swelling day after day in exuberant vindication of her instincts. An immense contentment had filled him. Thank God she had kept the money out of that fiend Dowell's clutches!

But then the tide had turned again. The number that had been growing so rapidly in the Total Gain column, putting out a third, fourth, then a fifth figure, like a ship unfurling sails in the great wind of prosperity that had seemed set to blow once again across America, had slowed to a halt, lowered its sails one by one, and then, terrifyingly, begun to sink. And suddenly Elise's shrewdness, the innate financial acumen he had attributed to her, had begun to look like nothing more than beginner's luck, while in place of his contentment, a mass of anxieties began teeming inside him.

How exhausting it all was. How he hated it! It was as though, in investing the money, Elise had unwittingly attached him by invisible filaments to some vast, seething collective psyche that never rested. Having paid no attention to financial matters before, he now appeared to be enslaved by them. When the Dow or NASDAQ went down, he was dragged with them, unable to enjoy a beautiful day, a good meal, or even his nightly game of chequers with his daughter. Almost worse, on the rare occasions when the indices went up, a weird stupor of happiness would seize him, no matter what awful things might be going on around him. And more than just his mood, the management of his entire sense of reality seemed to have been handed over to the markets. Glimpsing in the *Times* Business Section (pages that would formerly have gone straight into the recycling bin) an article on mutual funds bucking the downward trend, he had seen Morton Dowell's Sovereign Fund among the lucky few, and felt suddenly a fool for having allowed what at once seemed an act of astoundingly poor judgment to steer him away from that sterling, agile man . . .

God! All that and the nightmarish discovery that you could never get out once you were in anyway – couldn't sell when you were ahead because you might miss out on getting even further ahead, couldn't sell when you were down because the market might come surging back the next week, leaving you high and dry with your losses, though of course when it merely continued tanking you wanted to tear your hair out for not having had the humility to acknowledge your mistake, and salvage, sadder but wiser, what you could.

Whatever you did, it seemed you were bound to regret doing it, or not having done it sooner. It was as though some malicious higher power, having inspected the workings of the human mind, had calibrated a torment for it based on precisely the instincts of desire and caution that were supposed to enable it to survive. One could no more help oneself than the chickadee that nested in the lilacs outside their living room could stop attacking its own reflection in the window all day long every spring, however baffling and terrible every headlong slam against the glass must have felt.

Wearily, Joseph climbed out of the car. In the kitchen, as he unpacked the grocery bags, he made a conscious effort to flight off his gloom. Four days into the vacation and he had yet to relax. It was absurd. The weather was perfect, the rented house peaceful, the freshwater pond it stood by clear as glass, the ocean beaches beyond it magnificent. And at three hundred dollars a day for the house alone he couldn't afford *not* to be enjoying himself.

His hand made contact with a soft, cold package inside one of the bags. Ah yes. Here was something one could contemplate with unequivocal relish: a pound and a half of fresh queen scallops for the grill tonight.

He had bought them at Taylor's, while Elise and Darcy shopped at the produce store next door.

Taylor's was one of the glories of the Cape, and as always, it had been packed that afternoon, vacationers crushed up against the zinc slope, anxiously eyeing the diminishing piles of snowy white bass fillets or glistening pink tuna steaks, guarding their place in line with one foot while peering ahead to see what sandy gold treasures lay in the day's salver of smoked seafood.

There had been an incident: two women had each laid claim to the last pair of lobsters in the tank. The woman who was first in line had been distracted, searching for something in her purse, when the teenage server came over. The other woman, tall and bronzed, in an outfit of some tissuey material slung weblike between thin chains of beaded gold, had silently held up two fingers and pointed to the lobsters, which the boy was already weighing for her when the first woman realized what was happening. She protested that she had been first in line, but the other woman simply ignored her, handing the boy several bills with an intense smile and telling him to keep the change, while the boy himself stood in a kind of paralysis that seemed as much to do with her immaculately constructed glamour training itself upon him at full beam as with the awkwardness of the situation. 'We'll be getting more in later,' he had muttered lamely to the first woman. 'Well, gosh . . .' she had said breathily as the other woman, still smiling, strode serenely out, the two live lobsters swinging from her hand in their bag of crushed ice.

Joseph, who had observed it all, had felt vaguely that he ought to stand up for the woman in front. But nobody else had stirred and it didn't after all seem a matter of great importance, so that in the end he had done nothing, a fact of which he had felt fractionally ashamed as he left the store.

At any rate he had his scallops – huge, succulent ones, with their delicate-tasting pink corals still attached. Lucky he'd bought them before hearing the day's numbers, he thought, smiling a little. Otherwise he might have balked at the astronomical price Taylor's charged per pound. He stowed them away with a feeling of minor triumph, as if he had snatched them from the very jaws of the NASDAQ.

There was no sign of his wife and daughter when he made his way down to the pond. He stood on the small private jetty that came with the house, wondering if he were being punished for his comment about the timing of Elise's investments. Elise did have a punitive streak, and his comment had undoubtedly been offensive. Still, it was unlike her to vanish altogether without telling him.

A slight anxiety stirred in him. He fought it: he had noticed a growing tendency to worry recently, and he was aware that he needed to get a grip on it. They must have gone off to pick blackberries, he told himself, or maybe they had decided to walk over the dunes to the ocean. At any rate he would have his swim – across the pond and back – before he allowed himself to become concerned.

He stepped into the clear water, walked out up to his knees, then plunged in, drawing himself forward with leisurely strokes. The top few inches of water were sun-warmed; below that it was abruptly cold. There were no other people around. Thumbnail-sized water skimmers teemed on the surface ahead of him, thousands of them, jetting twitchily in every direction.

The 'pond' (he would have called it a lake) was a quarter mile wide. It took him twenty minutes to cross it, and by a determined effort of will he managed not to look back once to see whether Elise and Darcy had returned. At the far shore he climbed out to touch land, then turned around, half-believing that he would be rewarded for his self-control by the sight of figures on the jetty below their house.

There were none.

Easy now, he instructed himself as he waded in again. There was still the journey back before he was officially allowed to worry. But knowing that in twenty minutes you were going to legitimately succumb to anxiety was not very different from succumbing to it right now. He could feel in advance how, as he passed the halfway point on the pond, he would be seized by a mounting anger at Elise for not informing him of her plans, and how, as he swam on, the anger would change gradually to fear, which was worse because it indicated, did it not, that one's mind had reached some limit of reasonable hope and switched its bet from her and Darcy being perfectly, if irresponsibly, safe somewhere to their being caught up in some disaster.

How wearying, how humiliating it was to have so little faith in anything, to be so abjectly at the mercy of every tremor of fear in one's mind . . . Unballasted by any definite convictions of his own (convictions, he liked to joke, were for convicts), he appeared to have gone adrift in a realm of pure superstition. If I avoid listening to *Marketplace* for three days, the Dow will miraculously recover. It did not. If I close my eyes and hold my breath for seventeen strokes Elise and Darcy will be there on the jetty . . .

They were not.

He swam on, thrusting out violently from his shoulders, ropes of cooler water slipping around his ankles as he kicked back and down, as hard as he could, in an effort to annihilate the drone of his own thoughts.

The sun was low in the sky, banding every ripple he made with a creamy glaze. The light here! That was something else to relish. In the early morning it seemed to glow from inside the trees, spilling out from one leaf after another as the sun rose, a rich, gold-tinted green. In the afternoon it turned to this creamy silver. Then, it was the light itself one became aware of, rather than the things it lit. Right now, in fact, as Joseph looked across the pond, the glare of direct and water-reflected light was so bright he could no longer see the far shore. This seemed propitious, and he deliberately refrained from trying to squint through the dazzle, surrendering to it. He had caught this moment once or twice before on the pond, and it did have some mysterious, elevating splendour about it that took you out of yourself. Everything seemed purely an occurrence of light: the water streaming glassily as he raised each arm for its stroke, bubbles sliding over the curving ripples, the water-skimmers registering no longer as frantic insect hordes but careening saucers of light, the whole glittering mass of phenomena so absorbing it emptied your sense of anything but itself, and for a moment you had the impression you could not only see the light but taste it, smell it, feel it on your skin, and hear it ringing all around you like shaken bells.

Darcy was standing at the end of the jetty when he came through the glare. She was leaning over the water with a fishing net in her hand. Another girl was beside her, shorter and plumper, holding a yellow bucket. Behind them, a little further off along the beach, sat Elise, drawing in her sketchpad.

For a moment Joseph tried to resist the joyful relief that the sight offered (relief being just the obverse of the irrational anxiety of which he was trying to cure himself, and therefore equally undesirable), but it flooded into him. They were there! No harm had come to them! He swam on happily. How lithe and supple his daughter looked in her swimsuit, her legs growing long now, beautifully smooth, her brown hair already streaked gold from the sun.

· A surge of love came into him, and with it a feeling of shame. How crazily out of perspective he had let things get, to have allowed money to loom larger in his mind than his own daughter! A few evenings ago she had been telling him in detail the plot of a film she had seen. He had pretended to be paying attention, but so preoccupied had he been with the day's losses that even his pretence had been a failure. With a pang he remembered the look of dismay on Darcy's face as she realised he wasn't listening to a word she was saying. How could he have done that? It was unforgivable!

The girls darted off as he approached the jetty, running down a path that led around the pond. Elise remained on her deck chair. She greeted him with a friendly look.

'Did you make it all the way across?' she asked.

'All the way. I see Darcy found a friend.'

'Yes. She's staying in the next house down. We're invited over for cocktails later on.'

'Cocktails. My!'

'I said we'd go. Darcy's so excited to have a playmate.'

'Is she bored here?'

'No, but you know how it is . . .'

'I thought we might rent bikes tomorrow, and go whalewatching.'

'Interesting concept.'

'What? Oh!'

She was smiling at him. He laughed. Another of life's unequivocal pleasures: being reinstated in his wife's good graces. He rubbed himself dry. He felt refreshed, light on his feet.

An hour later and he and Elise walked over to join their daughter at her new friend's house. A tall woman carrying a pitcher of purplish liquid greeted them on the deck.

'They call this a Cape Codder,' she said, holding her free hand out to Joseph. 'Hi, I'm Veronica.'

She was the woman he had seen earlier on in Taylor's.

She had changed out of the tissuey top into a sleeveless robe of flowing, peach-coloured linen, but Joseph had recognised her at once as the victor in the incident with the lobsters.

She poured the drinks and called into the house:

'Sugar . . .'

An older man came out onto the deck, sunburned, with a strong, haggard face and vigorous silvery tufts sprouting at his open shirt. 'Hal Kaplan,' he said, gripping Joseph's hand and baring a row of shiny white teeth in a broad smile.

Veronica poured drinks and the four adults sat at a steel table on the deck, while the girls played down by the pond. She spoke rapidly, her large eyes moving with an intent sociability between Elise and Joseph. Within minutes, she had sped the conversation past the conventional pleasantries to more intimate questions and disclosures, in which she took an unashamedly flagrant delight. She and Hal were each other's third spouse, she volunteered; they had met on a helicopter ride into the Grand Canyon. The girl, Karen, was Hal's daughter by his second wife, who had died in a speedboat crash. He and Veronica had been trying for a year to have a child of their own. There wasn't anything physically wrong with either of them, but because she was approaching forty and they didn't want to risk missing out, they had decided to sign up at an expensive clinic for in vitro fertilisation, a process she described in droll detail, down to her husband's twenty-minute sojourns in the 'masturbatorium'. *Don't mind me,* her tone seemed to signal as she probed and confided, *I'm not someone you have to seriously* . . . 'How about you guys . . . ?' she asked. 'How did you meet?' As he answered, Joseph found himself thinking that if he hadn't seen her in Taylor's earlier on, he would have taken her for precisely the charmingly frivolous and sweet-natured person she seemed intent on appearing. And in fact he so disliked holding a negative view of people that he rapidly allowed his present impression of her to eclipse the earlier one.

Hal, her husband, had been an eye surgeon in Miami for twenty-five years. Now he was living, as he put it, on his 'wits'. Judging from the house they'd rented – bigger, sleeker and glassier than Elise and Joseph's – he was doing all right on them.

'Karen is in love with your daughter,' Veronica said to Elise, 'she is in *love* with her.'

Elise murmured that Darcy was thrilled too.

Swallows were diving over the pond, picking off skimmers. As the sun went down behind the trees the water turned a greenish black, with a scattering of fiery ripples. The girls came up, wrapped in towels, shivering a little. Elise looked at her watch.

'Why don't you stay and eat dinner with us?' Veronica asked.

Elise smiled: 'Oh no, we couldn't possibly . . .'

'It'd be no trouble, really.'

'Say yes, Mommy!' Darcy cried.

'We're just throwing some things on the grill. It seems a shame to break these two up . . .'

'Daddy could bring over our scallops . . .'

Elise turned to Joseph. Assuming her hesitancy to be nothing more than politeness, he made what he thought was the expected gesture of tentative acceptance.

'Well . . .'

And a few minutes later he was bringing the scallops over from their kitchen, along with a bottle of wine.

Hal had lit the grill. Joseph poured himself another Cape Codder and joined him.

'Lousy day on the markets,' he said, with a rueful chuckle.

The older man's long, rectangular face, full of leathery corrugations, hoisted itself into a grin.

'You play them?'

'We have a few little investments here and there.'

'Time to buy more, is what I say.'

'Oh? You think it'll go back up?'

'Like a rocket.'

'Really? Even the NASDAQ?'

'No question. The smart money's all over it. I'm buying like crazy right now.'

'You are?' Joseph's heart had given a little leap.

'You bet! Intel at twenty? Lucent under four dollars? These are bargain-basement prices by any estimation. Nortel at two fifty? Not buy Nortel at two dollars and fifty cents a share?' He gave another grin, the centres of his lips staying together while the edges flew apart, showing his teeth.

'That's extremely interesting,' Joseph said, enjoying the unexpected feeling of well-being that had come into him. 'So you think a recovery's imminent?'

'Right around the corner, my friend. Right around the corner.'

It was like drinking a draught of some fiery, potent liquor!

Hal jostled at the coals in the barbecue with a two-pronged fork. He called over to Veronica:

'Bring 'em on, sweetheart!'

Veronica went into the kitchen and came out with the bag from Taylor's. Setting it on the table, she reached into the crushed ice and pulled out the two lobsters, one in each hand, and brought them over to the grill.

'Joseph, do me a favour and take the bands off, would you?'

She was holding the creatures out towards him.

Gingerly, he removed the yellow elastic bands from the flailing blue claws.

'Careful', the woman said.

She caught his eye, giving him a sly, unexpected smile. Then she placed the living lobsters on the grill. Joseph had never seen this done before. The sight of them convulsing and hissing over the red-hot coals sent a reflexive shudder of horror through him, though a few minutes later he was happily eating his share.

At three that morning he woke up with a dry mouth and a full bladder. He got out of bed and walked unsteadily toward the bathroom. Through the open door to the living room he glimpsed the sofa bed where Darcy slept, and was momentarily stalled by the realisation that it was empty. Then he remembered that she was sleeping over at her new friend's house.

A murky sensation, compounded of guilt and dim apprehension, stirred in him at the recollection of how this had come about.

He stumbled on into the bathroom, relieved himself, then stood in darkness, looking out at the pond. The moon had risen and the surface of the water, dimpled here and there by rising fish, shone brightly in its ring of black trees.

He had drunk too much, that was for sure, and overeaten. He recalled the weirdly euphoric mood that had mounted in him over the course of the evening: an unaccustomed exuberance. Partly it was Hal's amazing confident predictions for the market. Several times Joseph had found himself steering the conversation back to the subject, raising various objections to the optimistic view, but purely for the joy of hearing this weather-beaten old oracle shrug them off. And partly, too, it was Veronica. With a few glances and touches she had deftly set a little subterranean current flowing between the two of them over dinner. He was a faithful husband, not even seriously tempted by actual bodily infidelity, but it gave him a tremendous lift to be flirted with by an attractive woman. Actually she wasn't, inherently, as attractive as he had first thought. Her chin was long and her nose looked as though it had been broken. But her evident conviction that she was desirable appeared to be more than enough to make her so. By the end of the evening he had been in an exhilarated state – drunk, aroused, glutted, his vanity flattered, his head spinning with the thought of the markets shooting back up 'like a rocket'.

As they stood up to leave, Elise had called Darcy, only to be informed by the girls that Karen had invited her for a sleepover, and that she had accepted.

'Not tonight,' Elise had said, with more firmness than Joseph had thought altogether polite to their hosts.

The girls began appealing at once to the other adults. Veronica took up their case, assuring Elise that Darcy would be more than welcome.

'We *love* having kids stay over. Anyway, we're only a hundred yards away . . .'

Elise had looked to Joseph for support. Simultaneously Veronica had turned to him: 'It'll be so much fun for them, don't you think . . . ?' She had laid her hand on his arm, and in the flush of his dilated spirits, he had announced imperiously that since they were on vacation, he saw no reason why Darcy should not sleep over.

Elise said nothing; it wasn't her style to argue in public. But as soon as they were out of earshot, leaving their daughter behind with her new friend, she had turned on Joseph with a cold fury:

'First you force us to have dinner with those people, then you walk right over me with this sleepover. You are *un*believable.'

More than the fierceness of her tone, more than the aggrieved wish to remind her that it was she, not himself, who had accepted the original invitation to go over for cocktails, more than the bewilderment at her objecting so strongly to Darcy sleeping over with her new friend, it was her phrase 'those people' that had startled him. All this time, he realised, while he had been blithely enjoying himself, she had been assessing this couple, sitting in judgment on them, and quietly forming a verdict against them. On what grounds? he had wanted to know. But as he opened his mouth to demand an explanation he had felt once again the familiar sense of uncertainty about his own instincts.

And now, as he listened to the insomniac bullfrogs croaking down at the pond, the image of Veronica walking calmly out of Taylor's with the lobsters came back to him, and, with a guilty wonder at his wife's powers of intuition, he went uneasily back to bed.

The day was overcast when he awoke later. He was alone. As he opened the curtains he saw Elise striding up the steps from the pond. She burst in through the kitchen door.

'I am beyond angry.'

'What happened?'

'They've gone.'

'What do you mean?'

'They've gone. The car's not there.'

'With Darcy?'

'Yes, with Darcy.'

'No.'

'Yes.'

He felt a loosening sensation inside him.

'You checked inside the house?'

'The doors are locked. I yelled. There's no one there.'

Joseph threw on his bathrobe and ran outside, racing down the steps to the path. Rain had begun pattering onto the bushes. Reaching the other house, he blundered about the deck, beating on doors and windows and calling Darcy's name. The place was empty. The windows had screens on the inside, making it hard to see into the unlit interior, but what he couldn't see with his eyes his imagination supplied vividly: empty rooms, everything packed swiftly and surreptitiously in the dead of night, Darcy bundled into the car with the rest of them, then off out into the vastness of the country.

A feeling of terror swelled up inside him. He staggered back along the path and up the steps, legs shaking, heart pounding in his chest. Elise was on the phone.

'Are you calling the police?'

She frowned, shaking her head.

If she wasn't calling the police that must mean she didn't think things were as serious as he did. This calmed Joseph, though the calm had an artificial sheen to it that was familiar to him from the rare positive days on the Dow, as though some essential fact had been temporarily left out of the reckoning. Then he remembered again that Elise hadn't witnessed the scene in Taylor's, and it seemed to him suddenly that his wife had no idea of what kind of people they were dealing with.

She hung up the phone and dialled another number. He realized she was calling nearby restaurants to see if their daughter's abductors had perhaps just gone out for breakfast. The idea seemed unbearably naïve to him. He stood there, helpless, immobilised, looking out through the thickening rain.

She hung up again:

'So much for that.'

'What are we going to do?'

'What do you propose, Joseph?'

'I think we should call the police. What kind of car did they have?'

'For god's sake! I don't even know their surname.'

'Call the police.'

'And say what? You call them.'

He picked up the receiver, but found himself reluctant to dial, as though to do so would be to confer more reality on the situation than he was ready to bear.

'Maybe just one of them went out and the other's still around here somewhere with the girls.'

'Doing what?'

'I don't know. Picking blackberries – or maybe they went to the ocean . . .'

'In this?'

'It wasn't raining earlier. Why don't I go check? You wait here . . .'

He ran out of the house again. The sandy path wound around the pond to a series of dunes – the trees giving way to wild roses, then sea grass with sharp edges that cut against his ankles. The sand crumbled under his feet as he climbed, half a step down for every step up. He was panting heavily as he reached the high point, his heart pounding in his ears. Wind whipped rain and salt spray into his face. He looked down at the shore. On sunny mornings the narrow margin between the dunes and the waves would already be covered with towels and fluttering beach umbrellas and little human figures in bright swimsuits – a touching image, it always seemed to Joseph: life blossoming fraily between two inhospitable elements. It was empty now, not a figure visible on the mile-long stretch of wet sand. Black waves came racing in with the wind, exploding onto the shore. Gulls flew screeching over the surf.

Was this it? Was this the catastrophe he had felt preparing itself inside him? His obscure, abiding sense of himself as a flawed and fallen human being seemed suddenly clarified: he was guilty and he was being punished. A feeling of dread gripped him. Childlike thoughts arose in his mind: propitiation, sacrifice . . . There was a clock, a valuable Crystal Regulator clock that he had bought for a bargain in Asheville earlier that year. If their daughter was at the house by the time he got back, he would sacrifice the clock. He would destroy it: smash it into pieces in the back room of his store. Or no, better, he would return it to the dealer who had sold it to him, ask his forgiveness for taking advantage of him . . . And meanwhile, to show he wasn't only prepared to make a sacrifice in return for a guaranteed reward (the primitive religious state he had fallen into appeared to come complete with its own finer points of dogma), he vowed, right there and then, to change his entire life. Yes: he would devote himself to the poor and needy, give up drinking, overeating, flirting, obsessing about the markets, in fact he would tell Elise to sell off the shares and they would swallow the losses . . . The thought of this filled him with a sharp, almost painful elation: he seemed to glimpse in it the possibility of a new existence, one of immense and joyous calm. And even though he was aware in another part of himself that there was no prospect of his keeping a single one of these vows (that clock was earmarked to pay for this vacation), he turned back along the path full of faith and hope.

Veronica was at the house with the two girls when he arrived back. She was talking to Elise on the deck outside the kitchen. Seeing Joseph, she waved, laughing.

'We were playing in a tree house in the woods,' she called out. 'Hal drove into town to buy pastries.'

'Ah!'

'We always lock the door. Hal likes to keep a lot of cash around.'

'I see. I see.'

'We headed back as soon as we heard you guys yelling . . .'

She grinned at Joseph as he stepped onto the deck. She was wearing a white T-shirt and gold sneakers, her bare legs golden against the grey rain. A mischievous look appeared on her face:

'What were you thinking?'

He had had a moment of relief on seeing his daughter, but now he felt embarrassed.

'Nothing . . . We were just, you know, wondering where you were.'

She touched his arm, her eyes sparkling with hilarity.

'We freaked you out, huh?'

'No, no . . .'

He turned away, as though from an uncomfortably bright glare. Mumbling an excuse, he went on into the kitchen. Already his panic on the beach seemed absurd, shameful almost. What a state to get into! He turned on the radio. The *Marketplace* morning report was about to come on. Lifting a watermelon from the fridge, he set it on the counter and cut himself a thick slice. He ate it nervously while he listened.

The Moons of Jupiter
by
Alice Munro

Alice Munro was born in 1931 in Ontario. She began writing as a teenager and published her first story, 'The Dimensions of a Shadow', while a student at the University of Western Ontario in 1950. Her first collection of stories, *Dance of the Happy Shades* (1968), was highly acclaimed and won that year's Governor General's Award, Canada's highest literary prize. She has received many awards and prizes, including two Giller Prizes, the Rea Award for the Short Story, the Lannan Literary Award, the W.H. Smith Book Award in the UK, the National Book Critics Circle Award in the US, and was shortlisted for the Booker Prize for *The Beggar Maid*. In 2009 she won the Man Booker International Prize for her body of work. Her stories have appeared in *The New Yorker*, *Atlantic Monthly*, *The Paris Review*, and other publications, and her collections have been translated into thirteen languages. She lives with her husband in Clinton, Ontario, near Lake Huron in Canada.

The Moons of Jupiter

I FOUND MY FATHER in the heart wing, on the eighth floor of Toronto General Hospital. He was in a semi-private room. The other bed was empty. He said that his hospital insurance covered only a bed in the ward, and he was worried that he might be charged extra.

'I never asked for a semi-private,' he said.

I said the wards were probably full.

'No. I saw some empty beds when they were wheeling me by.'

'Then it was because you had to be hooked up to that thing,' I said. 'Don't worry. If they're going to charge you extra, they tell you about it.'

'That's likely it,' he said. 'They wouldn't want those doohickeys set up in the wards. I guess I'm covered for that kind of thing.'

I said I was sure he was.

He had wires taped to his chest. A small screen hung over his head. On the screen a bright jagged line was continually being written. The writing was accompanied by a nervous electronic beeping. The behavior of his heart was on display. I tried to ignore it. It seemed to me that paying such close attention – in fact, dramatizing what ought to be a most secret activity – was asking for trouble. Anything exposed that way was apt to flare up and go crazy.

My father did not seem to mind. He said they had him on tranquillizers. You know, he said, the happy pills. He did seem calm and optimistic.

149

It had been a different story the night before. When I brought him into the hospital, to the emergency room, he had been pale and closemouthed. He had opened the car door and stood up and said quietly, 'Maybe you better get me one of those wheelchairs.' He used the voice he always used in a crisis. Once, our chimney caught on fire; it was on a Sunday afternoon and I was in the dining room pinning together a dress I was making. He came in and said in that same matter-of-fact, warning voice, 'Janet. Do you know where there's some baking powder?' He wanted it to throw on the fire. Afterwards he said, 'I guess it was your fault – sewing on Sunday.'

I had to wait for over an hour in the emergency waiting room. They summoned a heart specialist who was in the hospital, a young man. He called me out into the hall and explained to me that one of the valves of my father's heart had deteriorated so badly that there ought to be an immediate operation.

I asked him what would happen otherwise.

'He'd have to stay in bed,' the doctor said.

'How long?'

'Maybe three months.'

'I meant, how long would he live?'

'That's what I meant too,' the doctor said.

I went to see my father. He was sitting up in bed in a curtained-off corner. 'It's bad, isn't it?' he said. 'Did he tell you about the valve?'

'It's not as bad as it could be,' I said. Then I repeated, even exaggerated, anything hopeful the doctor had said. 'You're not in any immediate danger. Your physical condition is good, otherwise.'

'Otherwise,' said my father gloomily.

I was tired from the drive – all the way up to Dalgleish, to get him, and back to Toronto since noon – and worried about getting the rented car back on time, and irritated by an article I had been reading in a magazine in the waiting room. It was about another writer, a woman younger, better-looking, probably more talented than I am. I had been in England for two months and so I had not seen this article before, but it crossed my mind while I was reading that my father would have. I could hear him saying, Well, I didn't see anything about you in *Maclean's*. And if he had read something about me he would say, Well, I didn't think too much of that write-up. His tone would be humorous and indulgent but would produce in me a familiar dreariness of spirit. The message I got from him was simple: Fame must be striven for, then apologized for. Getting or not getting it, you will be to blame.

I was not surprised by the doctor's news. I was prepared to hear something of the sort and was pleased with myself for taking it calmly, just as I would be pleased with myself for dressing a wound or looking down from the frail balcony of a high building. I thought, Yes, it's time; there has to be something, here it is. I did not feel any of the protest I would have felt twenty, even ten, years before. When I saw from my father's face that he felt it – that refusal leapt up in him as readily as if he had been thirty or forty years younger – my heart hardened, and I spoke with a kind of badgering cheerfulness. 'Otherwise is plenty,' I said.

The next day he was himself again.

That was how I would have put it. He said it appeared to him now that the young fellow, the doctor, might have been a bit too eager to operate. 'A bit knife-happy,' he said. He was both mocking and showing off the hospital slang. He said that another doctor had examined him, an older man, and had given it as his opinion that rest and medication might do the trick.

I didn't ask what trick.

'He says I've got a defective valve, all right. There's certainly some damage. They wanted to know if I had rheumatic fever when I was a kid. I said I didn't think so. But half the time then you weren't diagnosed what you had. My father was not one for getting the doctor.'

The thought of my father's childhood, which I always pictured as bleak and dangerous – the poor farm, the scared sisters, the harsh father – made me less resigned to his dying. I thought of him running away to work on the lake boats, running along the railway tracks, toward Goderich, in the evening light. He used to tell about that trip. Somewhere along the track he found a quince tree. Quince trees are rare in our part of the country; in fact, I have never seen one. Not even the one my father found, though he once took us on an expedition to look for it. He thought he knew the crossroad it was near, but we could not find it. He had not been able to eat the fruit, of course, but he had been impressed by its existence. It made him think he had got into a new part of the world.

The escaped child, the survivor, an old man trapped here by his leaky heart. I didn't pursue these thoughts. I didn't care to think of his younger selves. Even his bare torso, thick and white – he had the body of a workingman of his generation, seldom exposed to the sun – was a danger to me; it looked so strong and young. The wrinkled neck, the age-freckled hands and arms, the narrow, courteous head, with its thin gray hair and mustache, were more what I was used to.

'Now, why would I want to get myself operated on?' said my father reasonably. 'Think of the risk at my age, and what for? A few years at the outside. I think the best thing for me to do is go home and take it easy. Give in gracefully. That's all you can do, at my age. Your attitude changes, you know. You go through some mental changes. It seems more natural.'

'What does?' I said.

'Well, death does. You can't get more natural than that. No, what I mean, specifically, is not having the operation.'

'That seems more natural?'

'Yes.'

'It's up to you,' I said, but I did approve. This was what I would have expected of him. Whenever I told people about my father I stressed his independence, his self-sufficiency, his forbearance. He worked in a factory, he worked in his garden, he read history books. He could tell you about the Roman emperors or the Balkan wars. He never made a fuss.

Judith, my younger daughter, had come to meet me at Toronto Airport two days before. She had brought the boy she was living with, whose name was Don. They were driving to Mexico in the morning, and while I was in Toronto I was to stay in their apartment. For the time being, I live in Vancouver. I sometimes say I have my headquarters in Vancouver.

'Where's Nichola?' I said, thinking at once of an accident or an overdose. Nichola is my older daughter. She used to be a student at the Conservatory, then she became a cocktail waitress, then she was out of work. If she had been at the airport, I would probably have said something wrong. I would have asked her what her plans were, and she would have gracefully brushed back her hair and said, 'Plans?' – as if that was a word I had invented.

'I knew the first thing you'd say would be about Nichola,' Judith said.

'It wasn't. I said hello and I—'

'We'll get your bag,' Don said neutrally.

'Is she all right?'

'I'm sure she is,' said Judith, with a fabricated air of amusement. 'You wouldn't look like that if I was the one who wasn't here.'

'Of course I would.'

'You wouldn't. Nichola is the baby of the family. You know, she's four years older than I am.'

'I ought to know.'

Judith said she did not know where Nichola was exactly. She said Nichola had moved out of her apartment (that dump!) and had actually telephoned (which is quite a deal, you might say, Nichola phoning) to say she wanted to be incommunicado for a while but she was fine.

'I told her you would worry,' said Judith more kindly on the way to their van. Don walked ahead carrying my suitcase. 'But don't. She's all right, believe me.'

Don's presence made me uncomfortable. I did not like him to hear these things. I thought of the conversations they must have had, Don and Judith. Or Don and Judith and Nichola, for Nichola and Judith were sometimes on good terms. Or Don and Judith and Nichola and others whose names I did not even know. They would have talked about me. Judith and Nichola comparing notes, relating anecdotes; analyzing, regretting, blaming, forgiving. I wished I'd had a boy and a girl. Or two boys. They wouldn't have done that. Boys couldn't possibly know so much about you.

I did the same thing at that age. When I was the age Judith is now I talked with my friends in the college cafeteria or, late at night, over coffee in our cheap rooms. When I was the age Nichola is now I had Nichola herself in a carry-cot or squirming in my lap, and I was drinking coffee again all the rainy Vancouver afternoons with my one neighborhood friend, Ruth Boudreau, who read a lot and was bewildered by her situation, as I was. We talked about our parents, our childhoods, though for some time we kept clear of our marriages. How thoroughly we dealt with our fathers and mothers, deplored their marriages, their mistaken ambitions or fear of ambition, how competently we filed them away, defined them beyond any possibility of change. What presumption.

I looked at Don walking ahead. A tall ascetic-looking boy, with a St Francis cap of black hair, a precise fringe of beard. What right did he have to hear about me, to know things I myself had probably forgotten? I decided that his beard and hairstyle were affected.

Once, when my children were little, my father said to me, 'You know those years you were growing up – well, that's all just a kind of a blur to me. I can't sort out one year from another.' I was offended. I remembered each separate year with pain and clarity. I could have told how old I was when I went to look at the evening dresses in the window of Benbow's Ladies' Wear. Every week through the winter a new dress, spotlit – the sequins and tulle, the rose and lilac, sapphire, daffodil – and me a cold worshipper on the slushy sidewalk. I could have told how old I was when I forged my mother's signature on a bad report card, when I had measles, when we papered the front room. But the years when Judith and Nichola were little, when I lived with their father – yes, *blur* is the word for it. I remember hanging out diapers, bringing in and folding diapers; I can recall the kitchen counters of two houses and where the clothesbasket sat. I remember the television programs – *Popeye the Sailor, The Three Stooges, Funorama.* When *Funorama* came on it was time to turn on the lights and cook supper. But I couldn't tell the years apart. We lived outside Vancouver in a dormitory suburb: Dormir, Dormer, Dormouse – something like that. I was sleepy all the time then; pregnancy made me sleepy, and the night feedings, and the west coast rain falling. Dark dripping cedars, shiny dripping laurel; wives yawning, napping, visiting, drinking coffee, and folding diapers; husbands coming home at night from the city across the water. Every night I kissed my homecoming husband in his wet Burberry and hoped he might wake me up; I served up meat and potatoes and one of the four vegetables he permitted. He ate with a violent appetite, then fell asleep on the living-room sofa. We had become a cartoon couple, more middle-aged in our twenties than we would be in middle age.

Those bumbling years are the years our children will remember all their lives. Corners of the yards I never visited will stay in their heads.

'Did Nichola not want to see me?' I said to Judith.

'She doesn't want to see anybody, half the time,' she said. Judith moved ahead and touched Don's arm. I knew that touch – an apology, an anxious reassurance. You touch a man that way to remind him that you are grateful, that you realize he is doing for your sake something that bores him or slightly endangers his dignity. It made me feel older than grandchildren would to see my daughter touch a man – a boy – this way. I felt her sad jitters, could predict her supple attentions. My blunt and stocky, blonde and candid child. Why should I think she wouldn't be susceptible, that she would always be straightforward, heavy-footed, self-reliant? Just as I go around saying that Nichola is sly and solitary, cold, seductive. Many people must know things that would contradict what I say.

In the morning Don and Judith left for Mexico. I decided I wanted to see somebody who wasn't related to me, and who didn't expect anything in particular from me. I called an old lover of mine, but his phone was answered by a machine: 'This is Tom Shepherd speaking. I will be out of town for the month of September. Please record your message, name, and phone number.'

Tom's voice sounded so pleasant and familiar that I opened my mouth to ask him the meaning of this foolishness. Then I hung up. I felt as if he had deliberately let me down, as if we had planned to meet in a public place and then he hadn't shown up. Once, he had done that, I remembered.

I got myself a glass of vermouth, though it was not yet noon, and I phoned my father.

'Well, of all things,' he said. 'Fifteen more minutes and you would have missed me.'

'Were you going downtown?'

'Downtown Toronto.'

He explained that he was going to the hospital. His doctor in Dalgleish wanted the doctors in Toronto to take a look at him, and had given him a letter to show them in the emergency room.

'Emergency room?' I said.

'It's not an emergency. He just seems to think this is the best way to handle it. He knows the name of a fellow there. If he was to make me an appointment, it might take weeks.'

'Does your doctor know you're driving to Toronto?' I said.

'Well, he didn't say I couldn't.'

The upshot of this was that I rented a car, drove to Dalgleish, brought my father back to Toronto, and had him in the emergency room by seven o'clock that evening.

Before Judith left I said to her, 'You're sure Nichola knows I'm staying here?'

'Well, I told her,' she said.

Sometimes the phone rang, but it was always a friend of Judith's.

'Well, it looks like I'm going to have it,' my father said. This was on the fourth day. He had done a complete turnaround overnight. 'It looks like I might as well.'

I didn't know what he wanted me to say. I thought perhaps he looked to me for a protest, an attempt to dissuade him.

'When will they do it?' I said.

'Day after tomorrow.'

I said I was going to the washroom. I went to the nurses' station and found a woman there who I thought was the head nurse. At any rate, she was gray-haired, kind, and serious-looking.

'My father's having an operation the day after tomorrow?' I said.

'Oh, yes.'

'I just wanted to talk to somebody about it. I thought there'd been a sort of decision reached that he'd be better not to. I thought because of his age.'

'Well, it's his decision and the doctor's.' She smiled at me without condescension. 'It's hard to make these decisions.'

'How were his tests?'

'Well, I haven't seen them all.'

I was sure she had. After a moment she said, 'We have to be realistic. But the doctors here are very good.'

When I went back into the room my father said, in a surprised voice, '*Shore*-less seas.'

'What?' I said. I wondered if he had found out how much, or how little, time he could hope for. I wondered if the pills had brought on an untrustworthy euphoria. Or if he had wanted to gamble. Once, when he was talking to me about his life, he said, 'The trouble was I was always afraid to take chances.'

I used to tell people that he never spoke regretfully about his life, but that was not true. It was just that I didn't listen to it. He said that he should have gone into the Army as a tradesman – he would have been better off. He said he should have gone on his own, as a carpenter, after the war. He should have got out of Dalgleish. Once, he said, 'A wasted life, eh?' But he was making fun of himself, saying that, because it was such a dramatic thing to say. When he quoted poetry too, he always had a scoffing note in his voice, to excuse the showing-off and the pleasure.

'Shoreless seas,' he said again. '"Behind him lay the gray Azores, / Behind the Gates of Hercules; / Before him not the ghost of shores, / Before him only shoreless seas." That's what was going through my head last night. But do you think I could remember what kind of seas? I could not. Lonely seas? Empty seas? I was on the right track but I couldn't get it. But there now when you came into the room and I wasn't thinking about it at all, the word popped into my head. That's always the way, isn't it? It's not all that surprising. I ask my mind a question. The answer's there, but I can't see all the connections my mind's making to get it. Like a computer. Nothing out of the way. You know, in my situation the thing is, if there's anything you can't explain right away, there's a great temptation to – well, to make a mystery out of it. There's a great temptation to believe in – You know.'

'The soul?' I said, speaking lightly, feeling an appalling rush of love and recognition.

'Oh, I guess you could call it that. You know, when I first came into this room there was a pile of papers here by the bed. Somebody had left them here – one of those tabloid sort of things I never looked at. I started reading them. I'll read anything handy. There was a series running in them on personal experiences of people who had died, medically speaking – heart arrest, mostly – and had been brought back to life. It was what they remembered of the time when they were dead. Their experiences.'

'Pleasant or un-?' I said.

'Oh, pleasant. Oh, yes. They'd float up to the ceiling and look down on themselves and see the doctors working on them, on their bodies. Then float on further and recognize some people they knew who had died before them. Not see them exactly but sort of sense them. Sometimes there would be a humming and sometimes a sort of – what's that light that there is or color around a person?'

'Aura?'

'Yes. But without the person. That's about all they'd get time for; then they found themselves back in the body and feeling all the mortal pain and so on – brought back to life.'

'Did it seem – convincing?'

'Oh, I don't know. It's all in whether you want to believe that kind of thing or not. And if you are going to believe it, take it seriously, I figure you've got to take everything else seriously that they print in those papers.'

'What else do they?'

'Rubbish – cancer cures, baldness cures, bellyaching about the younger generation and the welfare bums. Tripe about movie stars.'

'Oh, yes. I know.'

'In my situation you have to keep a watch,' he said, 'or you'll start playing tricks on yourself.' Then he said, 'There's a few practical details we ought to get straight on,' and he told me about his will, the house, the cemetery plot. Everything was simple.

'Do you want me to phone Peggy?' I said. Peggy is my sister. She is married to an astronomer and lives in Victoria.

He thought about it. 'I guess we ought to tell them,' he said finally. 'But tell them not to get alarmed.'

'All right.'

'No, wait a minute. Sam is supposed to be going to a conference the end of this week, and Peggy was planning to go along with him. I don't want them wondering about changing their plans.'

'Where is the conference?'

'Amsterdam,' he said proudly. He did take pride in Sam, and kept track of his books and articles. He would pick one up and say, 'Look at that, will you? And I can't understand a word of it!' in a marvelling voice that managed nevertheless to have a trace of ridicule.

'Professor Sam,' he would say. 'And the three little Sams.' This is what he called his grandsons, who did resemble their father in braininess and in an almost endearing pushiness – an innocent energetic showing-off. They went to a private school that favored old-fashioned discipline and started calculus in Grade 5. 'And the dogs,' he might enumerate further, 'who have been to obedience school. And Peggy . . .'

But if I said, 'Do you suppose she has been to obedience school too?' he would play the game no further. I imagine that when he was with Sam and Peggy he spoke of me in the same way – hinted at my flightiness just as he hinted at their stodginess, made mild jokes at my expense, did not quite conceal his amazement (or pretended not to conceal his amazement) that people paid money for things I had written. He had to do this so that he might never seem to brag, but he would put up the gates when the joking got too rough. And of course I found later, in the house, things of mine he had kept – a few magazines, clippings, things I had never bothered about.

Now his thoughts travelled from Peggy's family to mine. 'Have you heard from Judith?' he said.

'Not yet.'

'Well, it's pretty soon. Were they going to sleep in the van?'

'Yes.'

'I guess it's safe enough, if they stop in the right places.'

I knew he would have to say something more and I knew it would come as a joke.

'I guess they put a board down the middle, like the pioneers?'

I smiled but did not answer.

'I take it you have no objections?'

'No,' I said.

'Well, I always believed that too. Keep out of your children's business. I tried not to say anything. I never said anything when you left Richard.'

'What do you mean, "said anything"? Criticize?'

'It wasn't any of my business.'

'No.'

'But that doesn't mean I was pleased.'

I was surprised – not just at what he said but at his feeling that he had any right, even now, to say it. I had to look out the window and down at the traffic to control myself.

'I just wanted you to know,' he added.

A long time ago, he said to me in his mild way, 'It's funny. Richard when I first saw him reminded me of what my father used to say. He'd say if that fellow was half as smart as he thinks he is, he'd be twice as smart as he really is.'

I turned to remind him of this, but found myself looking at the line his heart was writing. Not that there seemed to be anything wrong, any difference in the beeps and points. But it was there.

He saw where I was looking. 'Unfair advantage,' he said.

'It is,' I said. 'I'm going to have to get hooked up too.'

We laughed, we kissed formally; I left. At least he hadn't asked me about Nichola, I thought.

The next afternoon I didn't go to the hospital, because my father was having some more tests done, to prepare for the operation. I was to see him in the evening instead. I found myself wandering through the Bloor Street dress shops, trying on clothes. A preoccupation with fashion and my own appearance had descended on me like a raging headache. I looked at the women in the street, at the clothes in the shops, trying to discover how a transformation might be made, what I would have to buy. I recognized this obsession for what it was but had trouble shaking it. I've had people tell me that waiting for life-or-death news they've stood in front of an open refrigerator eating anything in sight – cold boiled potatoes, chili sauce, bowls of whipped cream. Or have been unable to stop doing crossword puzzles. Attention narrows in on something – some distraction – grabs on, becomes fanatically serious. I shuffled clothes on the racks, pulled them on in hot little changing rooms in front of cruel mirrors. I was sweating; once or twice I thought I might faint. Out on the street again, I thought I must remove myself from Bloor Street, and decided to go to the museum.

I remembered another time, in Vancouver. It was when Nichola was going to kindergarten and Judith was a baby. Nichola had been to the doctor about a cold, or maybe for a routine examination, and the blood test revealed something about her white blood cells – either that there were too many of them or that they were enlarged. The doctor ordered further tests, and I took Nichola to the hospital for them. Nobody mentioned leukemia but I knew, of course, what they were looking for. When I took Nichola home I asked the baby-sitter who had been with Judith to stay for the afternoon and I went shopping. I bought the most daring dress I ever owned, a black silk sheath with some laced-up arrangement in front. I remembered that bright spring afternoon, the spike-heeled shoes in the department store, the underwear printed with leopard spots.

I also remembered going home from St. Paul's Hospital over the Lions Gate Bridge on the crowded bus and holding Nichola on my knee. She suddenly recalled her baby name for *bridge* and whispered to me, 'Whee – over the whee.' I did not avoid touching my child – Nichola was slender and graceful even then, with a pretty back and fine dark hair – but realized I was touching her with a difference, though I did not think it could ever be detected. There was a care – not a withdrawal exactly but a care – not to feel anything much. I saw how the forms of love might be maintained with a condemned person but with the love in fact measured and disciplined, because you have to survive. It could be done so discreetly that the object of such care would not suspect, any more than she would suspect the sentence of death itself. Nichola did not know, would not know. Toys and kisses and jokes would come tumbling over her; she would never know, though I worried that she would feel the wind between the cracks of the manufactured holidays, the manufactured normal days. But all was well. Nichola did not have leukemia. She grew up – was still alive, and possibly happy. Incommunicado.

I could not think of anything in the museum I really wanted to see, so I walked past it to the planetarium. I had never been to a planetarium. The show was due to start in ten minutes. I went inside, bought a ticket, got in line. There was a whole class of schoolchildren, maybe a couple of classes, with teachers and volunteer mothers riding herd on them. I looked around to see if there were any other unattached adults. Only one – a man with a red face and puffy eyes, who looked as if he might be here to keep himself from going to a bar.

Inside, we sat on wonderfully comfortable seats that were tilted back so that you lay in a sort of hammock, attention directed to the bowl of the ceiling, which soon turned dark blue, with a faint rim of light all around the edge. There was some splendid, commanding music. The adults all around were shushing the children, trying to make them stop crackling their potato-chip bags. Then a man's voice, an eloquent professional voice, began to speak slowly, out of the walls. The voice reminded me a little of the way radio announcers used to introduce a piece of classical music or describe the progress of the Royal Family to Westminster Abbey on one of their royal occasions. There was a faint echo-chamber effect.

The dark ceiling was filling with stars. They came out not all at once but one after another, the way the stars really do come out at night, though more quickly. The Milky Way appeared, was moving closer; stars swam into brilliance and kept on going, disappearing beyond the edges of the sky-screen or behind my head. While the flow of light continued, the voice presented the stunning facts. A few light-years away, it announced, the sun appears as a bright star, and the planets are not visible. A few dozen light-years away, the sun is not visible, either, to the naked eye. And that distance – a few dozen light-years – is only about a thousandth part of the distance from the sun to the center of our galaxy, one galaxy, which itself contains abut two hundred billion suns. And is, in turn, one of millions, perhaps billions, of galaxies. Innumerable repetitions, innumerable variations. All this rolled past my head too, like balls of lightning.

Now realism was abandoned, for familiar artifice. A model of the solar system was spinning away in its elegant style. A bright bug took off from the earth, heading for Jupiter. I set my dodging and shrinking mind sternly to recording facts. The mass of Jupiter two and a half times that of all the other planets put together. The Great Red Spot. The thirteen moons. Past Jupiter, a glance at the eccentric orbit of Pluto, the icy rings of Saturn. Back to Earth and moving in to hot and dazzling Venus. Atmospheric pressure ninety times ours. Moonless Mercury rotating three times while circling the sun twice; an odd arrangement, not as satisfying as what they used to tell us – that it rotated once as it circled the sun. No perpetual darkness after all. Why did they give out such confident information, only to announce later that it was quite wrong? Finally, the picture already familiar from magazines: the red soil of Mars, the blooming pink sky.

When the show was over I sat in my seat while the children clambered across me, making no comments on anything they had just seen or heard. They were pestering their keepers for eatables and further entertainments. An effort had been made to get their attention, to take it away from canned pop and potato chips and fix it on various knowns and unknowns and horrible immensities, and it seemed to have failed. A good thing too, I thought. Children have a natural immunity, most of them, and it shouldn't be tampered with. As for the adults who would deplore it, the ones who promoted this show, weren't they immune themselves to the extent that they could put in the echo-chamber effects, the music, the churchlike solemnity, simulating the awe that they supposed they ought to feel? Awe – what was that supposed to be? A fit of the shivers when you looked out the window? Once you knew what it was, you wouldn't be courting it.

Two men came with brooms to sweep up the debris the audience had left behind. They told me that the next show would start in forty minutes. In the meantime, I had to get out.

'I went to the show at the planetarium,' I said to my father. 'It was very exciting – about the solar system.' I thought what a silly word I had used: *exciting*. 'It's like a slightly phony temple,' I added.

He was already talking. 'I remember when they found Pluto. Right where they thought it had to be. Mercury, Venus, Earth, Mars,' he recited. 'Jupiter, Saturn, Nept – no, Uranus, Neptune, Pluto. Is that right?'

'Yes,' I said. I was just as glad he hadn't heard what I said about the phony temple. I had meant that to be truthful, but it sounded slick and superior. 'Tell me the moons of Jupiter.'

'Well, I don't know the new ones. There's a bunch of new ones, isn't there?'

'Two. But they're not new.'

'New to us,' said my father. 'You've turned pretty cheeky now I'm going under the knife.'

'"Under the knife." What an expression.'

He was not in bed tonight, his last night. He had been detached from his apparatus, and was sitting in a chair by the window. He was bare-legged, wearing a hospital dressing gown, but he did not look self-conscious or out of place. He looked thoughtful but good-humored, an affable host.

'You haven't even named the old ones,' I said.

'Give me time. Galileo named them. Io.'

'That's a start.'

'The moons of Jupiter were the first heavenly bodies discovered with the telescope.' He said this gravely, as if he could see the sentence in an old book. 'It wasn't Galileo named them, either; it was some German. Io, Europa, Ganymede, Callisto. There you are.'

'Yes.'

'Io and Europa, they were girlfriends of Jupiter's, weren't they? Ganymede was a boy. A shepherd? I don't know who Callisto was.'

'I think she was a girlfriend too,' I said. 'Jupiter's wife – Jove's wife – changed her into a bear and stuck her up in the sky. Great Bear and Little Bear. Little Bear was her baby.'

The loudspeaker said that it was time for visitors to go.

'I'll see you when you come out of the anesthetic,' I said.

'Yes.' When I was at the door, he called to me, 'Ganymede wasn't any shepherd. He was Jove's cupbearer.'

When I left the planetarium that afternoon, I had walked through the museum to the Chinese garden. I saw the stone camels again, the warriors, the tomb. I sat on a bench looking toward Bloor Street. Through the evergreen bushes and the high grilled iron fence I watched people going by in the late-afternoon sunlight. The planetarium show had done what I wanted it to after all – calmed me down, drained me. I saw a girl who reminded me of Nichola. She wore a trenchcoat and carried a bag of groceries. She was shorter than Nichola – not really much like her at all – but I thought that I might see Nichola. She would be walking along some street maybe not far from here – burdened, preoccupied, alone. She was one of the grown-up people in the world now, one of the shoppers going home.

If I did see her, I might just sit and watch, I decided. I felt like one of those people who have floated up to the ceiling, enjoying a brief death. A relief, while it lasts. My father had chosen and Nichola had chosen. Someday, probably soon, I would hear from her, but it came to the same thing.

I meant to get up and go over to the tomb, to look at the relief carvings, the stone pictures, that go all the way around it. I always mean to look at them and I never do. Not this time, either. It was getting cold out, so I went inside to have coffee and something to eat before I went back to the hospital.

*Stories
to intrigue
and excite*

The Coincidence of the Arts
by
Martin Amis

Martin Amis was born on 29 August, 1949 in Oxford and is
the son of Booker prize-winning novelist, Kingsley Amis. His
stepmother, the novelist Elizabeth Jane Howard, introduced
him to Jane Austen, whom he often names as his earliest
influence. He graduated from Exeter College, Oxford and at
age 27 became literary editor of *The New Statesman*. His first
novel *The Rachel Papers* (1973) won the Somerset Maugham
Award. His subsequent novels include *London Fields* (1989),
Time's Arrow (1991), *Night Train* (1997) and *House of Meetings*
(2006). In February 2007, Amis was appointed as a Professor
of Creative Writing at The Manchester Centre for New Writing
in the University of Manchester.

The Coincidence of the Arts

'THIS IS A farce, man. Have you read my novel yet?'
  'No.'
'Well why's that now?'
'I've been terribly —'
Across the road a fire truck levered itself backwards into its bay
with a great stifled sneeze. Round about, a thousand conversations
missed a beat, gulped, and then hungrily resumed.
'The thing is I've been terribly busy.'
'Aren't those the exact same words you used last time I asked you?'
'Yes.'
'Then how many more times do I got to hear them?'
The two men stood facing each other on the corner: that mess
of streets, of tracks and rinks, where Seventh Avenue collapses into
the Village . . . He who posed the questions was thirty-five years
old, six foot seven, and built like a linebacker in full armour. His
name was Pharsin Courier, and he was deeply black. He who
tendered the answers was about the same age; but he was five foot
eight, and very meagre. Standing there, confronted by his interrogator,
he seemed to be lacking a whole dimension. His name was Sir
Rodney Peel, and he was deeply white.
  They were shouting at each other, but not yet in exasperation or
anger. The city was getting louder every day: even the sirens had to
throw a tantrum, just to make themselves heard.
  'Find time for my novel,' said Pharsin. He continued to urge such

a course on Rodney for a further twenty minutes, saying, in conclusion, 'I gave you that typescript in good faith, and I need your critique. You and I, we're both artists. And don't you think that counts for something?'

In this city?

The sign said: Omni's Art Material – For the Artist in Everyone. But everyone was *already* an artist. The coffeeshop waiters and waitresses were, of course, actors and actresses; and the people they served were all librettists and scenarists, harpists, pointillists, ceramicists, caricaturists, contrapuntalists. The little boys were bladers and jugglers, the little girls all ballerinas (bent over the tables in freckly discussions with their mothers or mentors). Even the babies starred in ads and had agents. And it didn't stop there. Outside, sculptors wheelbarrowed chunks of rock over painted pavements past busking flautists, and a troupe of clowns performed mime, watched by kibitzers doing ad lib and impro. And on and on and up and up. Jesters teetered by on ten-foot stilts. Divas practised their scales from tenement windows. The AC installers were all installationists. The construction workers were all constructivists.

And, for once, Sir Rodney Peel happened to be telling the truth: he *was* terribly busy. After many soggy years of artistic and sexual failure, in London, SW3, Rodney was now savouring their opposites, in New York. You could still see this failure in the darkened skin around his eyes (stained, scarred, blinded); you could still nose it in his pyjamas, unlaundered for fifteen years (when he got out of bed in the morning he left them leaning against the wall). But America had reinvented him. He had a title, a ponytail, a flowery accent, and a pliant paintbrush. He was an unattached heterosexual in Manhattan: something had to give. And Rodney now knew the panic of answered prayers. Like a bit-part player in a dream, he looked on as his prices kept doubling: all you needed was an aristocratic wag of the head, and a straight face. Under the floorboards of his studio, in brown envelopes, lurked ninety-five thousand dollars: cash. And every afternoon he was climbing into an aromatic bed, speechless, with his ears whistling like seashells.

Rodney still felt that he had a chance of becoming a serious painter. Not a good chance – but a chance. Even he could tell that his artistic universe, after ten months in New York, had undergone drastic contraction. The journey into his own nervous system, the groping after spatial realtionships, the trawl for his own talent – all this, for the time being, he had set aside. And now he specialised. He did wives. Wives of wealthy professionals and executives: wives of the lions of Madison Avenue, wives of the heroes of Wall Street. His brush flattered and rejuvenated them, naturally; but this wasn't especially arduous or even dishonest, because the wives were never first wives: they were second wives, third wives, subsequent wives. They gazed up at him righteously, at slender Sir Rodney in his smudged smock. 'Perfect,' he would murmur. 'No. Yes. That's quite lovely . . .' One thing sometimes led to another thing; but never to the real thing. Meekly, his lovelife imitated his art. This wife, that wife. Rodney flattered, flirted, fumbled, failed. Then change came. Now, when he worked, his paint coagulated along traditional lines, and conventional curves. In between the sheets, though, Rodney felt the terrible agitation of the innovator.

'There's been a breakthrough,' he told Rock Robville, his agent or middleman, 'on the uh, "carnal knowledge" front.'

'Oh? Do tell.'

'Quite extraordinary actually. Never known anything quite . . .'

'The fragrant Mrs Peterson, mayhap?'

'Good God no.'

'The bodacious Mrs Havilland then, I'll wager.'

Twenty-eight, sleek, rosy, and darkly balding, Rock, too, was English, and of Rodney's class. The Robvilles were not as old and grand as the Peels; but they were much richer. Rock was now accumulating another fortune as an entrepreneur of things British: holiday castles in Scotland, Cumbrian fishing rights, crests, titles, nannies, suits of armour. Oh, and butlers. Rock did much trafficking in butlers.

'No. She's not a wife,' said Rodney. 'I don't want to say too much about it in case it breaks the spell. Early days and all that.'

'Have you two actually slimed?'

Rodney looked at him, frowning, as if in effortful recall. Then his face cleared and he answered in the negative. Rock seemed to enjoy scattering these phrases of the moment – these progeriac novelties – in Rodney's path. There was another one he used: 'playing Hide the Salami'. Hide the Salami sounded more fun than the game Rodney usually played with women. That game was called *Find* the Salami. 'We uh, "retire" together. But we haven't yet done the deed.'

'The act of darkness,' said Rock, causing Rodney to contemplate him strangely. 'How sweet. And how retro. You're getting to know each other first.'

'Well that's just it. She doesn't . . . We don't . . .'

Rock and Rod were leaning backwards on a mahogany bar, drinking Pink Ladies, in some conservatorial gin-palace off Lower Park Avenue. Inspecting his friend's anxious leer, Rock felt a protective pang and said suddenly,

'Have you done anything about your money yet? Talk to Mr Jaguar about it. Soon. Americans are very fierce about tax. You could get locked up.'

They fell silent. Both of them were thinking about the four or five seconds Rodney would last in an American jail. Now Rodney stirred and said,

'I'm in a mood to celebrate. It's all very exciting. Let me get you another one of those.'

'Ah. You're a white man,' said Rock absentmindedly. 'And do let me know,' he added, 'when you've slimed.'

Rodney was one of those Englishmen who had to get out of England. He had to get out of England and grow his hair. Helpless against his mother, his grandmother, helpless against each dawdling, prating, beaming milady they somehow conscripted him to squire. When he tried to break out they always easily reclaimed him, drawing him back to what was theirs. They owned him . . . Rodney had a fat upper lip which, during those soggy years, often wore a deep lateral crease of resignation – of vapid resignation. In the Chinese restaurants of Chelsea you might have glimpsed him, being lunched and lectured by a heavy-smoking aunt, his arms folded in the tightness of his jacket, his upper lip philosophically seamed.

'You get to my novel yet?'
'What?'
'Have you read my novel yet?'
'Ah. Pharsin.' Rodney collected himself. 'The thing is, I've been trying to make time for it in the afternoons. But the thing is . . .' He gazed unhappily down Greenwich Avenue. Sunday morning, and everyone was staggering around with their personal burden of prolixity, of fantastic garrulity, of uncontainable communicativeness: the *Sunday Times*. 'The thing is . . .'

The thing was that Rodney worked every morning and drunkenly socialised every evening, and in the afternoons – the only time of day he might conceivably pick up a book, or at any rate a magazine or a catalogue – he went to bed. With humming ears. And perpendicular in his zeal.

'Come on, man. This is getting insane.'

Rodney remembered a good tip about lying: stay as close to the truth as you dare. 'I've been trying to make time for it in the afternoons. But in the afternoons . . . My lady friend, do you see. I uh, "entertain" her in the afternoons.'

Pharsin assumed a judicious air.

'For instance,' Rodney enthused, 'on Friday afternoon I was just settling down to it. And in she came. I had your novel on my lap.'

This was of course untrue. Pharsin's ruffled, slewing typescript had never made it on to Rodney's lap. It was still under the piano, or in whatever corner or closet he had booted it into, months ago.

'She come every day?'
'Except weekends.'
'So what's your solution, Rod?'
'I'm going to clear some evenings. Settle down to it.'
'You say Friday afternoon you had my novel on your lap?'
'Just settling down to it.'
'Okay. What's the title?'

Pharsin stood there, skyscrapering over him. Each of his teeth was about the size of Rodney's head. When he leant over to spit in the gutter, you'd think someone had voided a bucket from the third floor.

'Give it up! What's the fucking title!'

'Um,' said Rodney.

Pharsin he had first encountered in the southwest corner of Washington Square Park, that inverted parliament of chess, where the junkies were all Experts, the winos were all Grand Masters, and the pizza-bespattered babblers and bums were all ex-World Champions. Rodney, who for a year had played second board for the University of Suffolk, approached the marble table over which Pharsin showily presided. In half an hour he lost a hundred dollars.

Never in his dealings with the thirty-two pieces and the sixty-four squares had Rodney been so hilariously outclassed. He was a mere centurion, stupidly waiting, in his metal miniskirt, his short-sword at his side; whereas Pharsin was the career gladiator, hideously experienced with the weighted net and the bronze trident. After half a dozen moves Rodney could already feel the grip of the cords, the bite of the tines. In the third game Pharsin successfully dispensed with the services of his queen: things looked good until Black drove the first of his rooks into the groin of White's defence.

They got talking as they loped together, serenaded by saxophones and sirens, past the bobbing dopedealers of the northwest corner and out on to Eighth Street.

'Do you uh, "make a living" at it?'

'Used to,' said Pharsin through the backbeat of nineteen different boomboxes and radios turned out on to the road. 'Chess hustling is down with the economy. Forcing me to diversify.'

Rodney asked him what kind of thing.

'It's like this: chess is an art. You can do one art, you can do them all.'

Rodney said how interesting, and toddled on after him. It seemed to Rodney that he could walk through Pharsin's legs and out the other side. No, not enough room: muscles stood like heavies leaning against the tunnel walls. Pharsin's head, perched up there on that body, could only look to be the shape and size of a car neckrest. Rodney experienced respect for Pharsin's head. Whatever chess was (an art, a game, a fight), chess was certainly a mountain. Rodney strolled its foothills. Whereas the forward-leaning cliff face that closed out the sky had Pharsin halfway up it.

'You see this?'

Halting, Pharsin from inside his hoodie produced a fistful of scrolled paper: an essay, a polemic, entitled 'The Co-Incidence of the Arts, Part I: The Indivisibility of Poetry, Photography, and Dance'. Rodney ran his eye down the opening sentence. It was the kind of sentence that spent a lot of time in reverse gear before crunching itself into first.

'Are you sure you mean "coincidence"? Not uh, "correspondence"?'

'No. Co-incidence. The arts happen in the same part of the brain. That's how come I hyphenate. Co-incidence.'

Rodney had a lot of time for coincidence. Everything he now had he owed to coincidence. It happened on a country lane half a mile from his grandmother's house: a head-on collision between two Range Rovers, both of them crammed with patrilinear Peels. All else followed from this: title, nerve, Rock, America, sex, and the five thousand twenty-dollar bills underneath his studio floor. And talent too, he thought: maybe.

'You English?'

'Oh, very much so.'

'My wife is English also. The oppressiveness of the class system caused her to leave your shores.'

'I sympathise. It can be very wearing. Is she in the arts too, your wife?'

'Yeah. She does –'

But Pharsin's monosyllable was quite cancelled by city stridor – someone detonating a low-yield nuclear weapon or dropping a dumpster from a helicopter. 'And yourself?' said Rodney.

'Sculptor. Mathematician. Choreographer. Percussionist. Essayist. Plus the art you and I engaged in some while ago.'

'Oh, I remember,' said Rodney humbly. 'I'm a painter. With other interests.' And he said what he usually said to Americans, because it was virtually true, geographically (and what would *they* know?): 'I studied literature at Cambridge.'

Pharsin gave a jolt and said, 'This intrigues me. Because I've recently come to think of myself as primarily a novelist. Now, my friend. There's something I'm going to ask you to do for me.'

He listened, and said yes. Why not? Rodney reckoned that Pharsin, after all, would be incredibly easy to avoid.

Pharsin said, 'I'll be in an excellent position to monitor your progress with it.'

Rodney waited.

'You don't recognise me. I work the door of your building. Weekends.'

'Oh of course you do.' In fact, Rodney had yet to begin the task of differentiating the three or four black faces that scowled and glinted through the gloom of his lobby. 'The coincidence,' he mused, 'of the arts. Tell me, are you all a little family down there?'

'Why would we be? I don't associate with those animals. Now. I'll bring you my novel early tomorrow. Casting all false modesty aside, I don't believe you'll have a problem falling under its spell.'

'Um,' said Rodney.

'Three months you been sitting on it, and you don't even know the fucking *title*?'

'Um,' he repeated. Like the novel itself, the title, Rodney recalled, was very *long*. Pharsin's typescript ran to more than eleven hundred pages: single-spaced. Pharsin said it comprised exactly one million words – a claim (Rodney felt) that few would ever call him on. 'It's very *long*.' He looked up into Pharsin's blood-spoked eyes and said, '"The . . ."'

'*The* what?'

'"The Words of . . ." Wait. "The Noise of the . . ."'

'Sound.'

'"The Noise of the Sound . . ."'

'Bullshit! *The Sound of the Words, the Sound of the Words*, man. *The Sound of the Words, the Sound of the Words.*'

'Exactly. *The Sound of the Words, the Sound of the Words.*'

'Commit the fucking energy, man. I say this because I'm convinced that your effort will be rewarded. The structure you'll particularly relish. And also the theme.'

After another forty column-inches of reproach, dissimulated threat, moral suasion and literary criticism, Pharsin wrapped things up, adding, as an audible afterthought,

'Thirteen weeks. And he doesn't even know its *name*?'

'Forgive me. I'm stupefied by, uh, "amorous excess".'

'That I can believe. You look totally fucked out. Man, take care: you're going to blow away on the wind. My marriage has survived thus far, but woman action and woman trouble I know all about. What's her name?'

Rodney murmured some feminine phoneme: Jan or Jen or June. But the truth was he didn't know *her* name either.

'We've slimed.'

'Good man. Tell all.'

This time Rod and Rock were to be found in some kind of *Irish* restaurant high up on Lexington Avenue. They occupied two places near the head of a table laid for eighteen. Their practice on such occasions was to meet an hour early, to chat and drink cocktails, before some Americans showed up and paid for it all. This night, in Rock's comfortable company, Rodney belied his eight-and-a-half stone. Pared down to the absolute minimum (carrying just two or three extra grams in that buxom upper lip), he nevertheless seemed to share in his friend's bland rotundity; they both wore the cummerbund of inner fatness conferred by their class. Black Velvet, quaffed from pewter tankards, was their tipple of the hour.

'What's there to say?' said Rodney. 'Frankly, I'm speechless. Words cannot . . .'

'Dear oh dear. Well describe her body at least.'

'Actually I'd rather not. I mean there's nothing to say, is there, when things go so gloriously?'

'. . . It's Mrs Peterson, isn't it?' Rock paused unkindly. 'No. Far too swarthy for you. You like the dairy-product type. Raised on curds and whey. They have to look like English roses. Or you get culture shock.'

'How very wrong you are,' said Rodney in a strained voice. 'It may interest you to know that my inamorata happens to be . . . "bleck".'

'Bleck?'

'Bleck,' said Rodney with emphasis. It sounded more like *blick* than *black*. A year or two ago they might have said *bluhck*. But having largely shed their class signatures, the two men were now recultivating them.

'Bleck?' repeated Rock. 'You mean a proper . . . ? What are they calling themselves these days. A proper American-African?'

'African-American.' As he continued, Rodney's voice grew drowsy, and it was with a haggard sensuality – slow inhalations, feeding some inner fire – that he relished his nightly cigarette. 'Well, African. I sense Africa in her. I taste Africa in her. One of the French bits, probably. Senegal, perhaps. Sierra Leone. Guinea-Bissau.'

Rock was looking at him.

'She moves like an empress. A Dahomey Amazon. Cleopatra was very dark, you know.'

'So she's posh, too, is she? As well as bleck. Where does *she* say she's from?'

Simultaneously ignoring this and rousing himself, Rodney said, 'It's what's so wonderful about America. There *aren't* any good bleck girls in London. All they've got there are those squeaky Cockneys. Magnificent creatures, some of them, but – quite impossible. Simply not on the cards, over there. But over here, in the great uh, "melting pot" . . .'

'The salad bowl.'

'I beg your pardon?' said Rodney, looking around for the salad bowl.

'They call it the salad bowl now. Not the melting pot.'

'Do they indeed.'

'In a way, you could say that English blecks are posher than their American cousins.'

'How so?'

'How *so*?'

Here were two men living in a silent movie: when they were alone together, the millennium seemed about a century away. Rock was now about to speak of the historical past; but his urbanity faltered, and he suddenly sounded sober.

'Oh come on. We know a *little* bit about this, don't we? The English contingent, they were shipped in after the war. To run the tubes and so on. And the buses. Contract labour. But not – but not like American blecks.'

'Same stock, though. One imagines.'

Rod and Rock: their family trees stood tall. Their family trees stood tall and proud. But what kind of trees were they – weeping willow, sallow, mahogany, ash? And something ailed or cankered them, shaping their branches all arthritic and aghast ... The Peels had been among the beneficiaries when, on a single day in 1661, Charles II created thirteen baronetcies on the plantation island of Barbados. Rock's lot, the Robvilles, rather disappointingly (rather puzzlingly, from Rodney's point of view), didn't go back quite so far. But the Peels and the Robvilles alike had flourished at a time when every English adult with cash or credit owned a piece of it: a piece of slavery. The place where Rock's dad lived had been assembled by massive shipwright profits out of Liverpool, *circa* 1750. Intelligence of these provenanaces could never be openly acknowledged by either of the two men. Lifelong inhibition protected them: in their childhood it was like something terrible hiding under the bed. Still, Rock was a businessman. And he had never expected business to be pretty. He said,

'There's not much in it, I suppose. But the English contingent were freed longer ago.'

'Yes, well,' pondered Rodney, 'I suppose you can't get much less posh than being a slave. But that's to forget what they might have been originally.'

'Posh in Africa.'

'In a way. You know, Africa was quite advanced for a while. I mean, look at African art. Exquisite. Ancient, but immediate. Immediate. They had great civilisations there when England was just a sheepdip. Ages ago.'

'What have you been reading? The *Amsterdam News*?'

'No. *Ebony*. But it's true! We're just upstarts and counterjumpers compared to them. Scum, Rock. Anyway I have a hunch my one came direct from Africa. The Sudan, quite possibly. Timbuktu was apparently an incredible city. Crammed with princes and poets and amazing *houris*. Jezebel was of –'

'Did you say amazing hoorays? Sorry? Oh never *mind*. What sort of accent does she have? Your one.'

'I don't know.'

'What's her name?'

'I don't know.'

Rock paused and said, 'Pray describe this relationship. How did you meet? Or don't you know that either?'

'We met in a bar. But it wasn't like that.'

They met in a bar but it wasn't like that.

It was like this.

Rodney had just asked for a Bullshot. Consisting of vodka and consommé, a Bullshot is arguably a bullshit drink; but Rodney, his eyes lurking and cowering behind his dark glasses, badly needed his Bullshot. What he really felt like was a Bloodshot. He wore a pinched seersucker suit and a grimy cravat. He had spent the morning in a sepulchral brownstone on East Sixty-Fifth Street, doing what he could with the long upper lip and ridiculously interproximate eyebrows of a Mrs Sheehan – wife to the chat-show king.

'Worcestershire sauce, if you please, and the juice of at least one lemon.'

'You know something? I could listen to your voice all day.'

It was not the first time Rodney had been paid this compliment. Sequestered in a deceptively mild cocaine hangover, he said, 'How sweet of you to say so.'

'No. Really.'

'So kind.'

This waitress at some point or other might have wanted to be an actress. She might have had the odd prompting towards the stage. But not recently. And anyway Rodney was looking past her, Rodney was flinching past her . . .

So. She was up on a stool at the counter – and up on the turret of her swivelling haunches, rising in her seat whenever they crossed or uncrossed, uncrossed or crossed. Rodney stared. There she sat, drinking milky tea from a braced glass, being bawled at by some ballgame on the perched TV, and exchanging vigorous but inaudible smalltalk with a hidden figure behind the bar. Unquestionably she was a person of colour, and that colour – or so it seemed to Rodney – was *american*. As in black, brown, american; then beige, white, pink . . . Beyond this room lay another room, where some kind of talent contest was being noisily disputed. Poetry readings. Monologues. Stand-up.

Rodney was staring at her with a pang of recognition, although he knew she was a stranger. He thought he had seen her before, in the neighbourhood. But never fully seen her. Because she was the woman on the street whom you never see fully, sent here to elude you, always turning away or veering off, or exactly maintaining parallax with mailbox or tree bole, or vanishing for ever behind the burning glass of a phonebooth or under the black shadow of a truck. Indignant poems have been written about these women – about these *desaparacidas*. Even the douce Bloom grew petulant about them. Men mind, because for once they are demanding so little, no contact, just a free gaze at the moving form. And this was Rodney's initial disposition. He didn't want to date her. He wanted to paint her.

'There you go, sir.'

'Thank you most awfully.'

'That voice!'

Even now, at the bar, she always seemed to be occluded or eclipsed. In particular a pink lady, a Germanic middle-aged blonde with a whole reef of freckles and moles on her bared throat (how Rodney struggled, each day, with such imperfections in his sitters) kept masking her, kept hiding her and then revealing her. Suddenly the view cleared, and he absorbed the lavish power of her thighs – then her face, her glance, her unspecific smile. What she said to him was Talent. Not just *her* talent. His talent, too.

'Waitress! Waitress! Ah. Thank you. I wonder if you would very kindly lend me your pen there. For just a couple of minutes.'

'Certainly!'

'Thank you *so* much.'

He knew what to do. At his agent's prompting, Rodney had had some cards printed up, headed: Sir Rodney Peel (Baronet): Portraitist. The flipside gave an example of the portraitist's art: looking like non-identical twins, the wife and daughter of a burglar-alarm tycoon were pooling their repose on a pair of French armchairs. Rodney started writing. He still wasn't entirely reconciled to that bracketed 'Baronet'. At first he had argued for the more discreet and conventional abbreviation, '(Bt)'. But he had eventually submitted to the arguments of his agent: according to Rock, Americans might think that Bt was short for Bought.

In the great wreaths and plumes of his embarrassing calligraphy Rodney said that he was an English painter, come to America; said how rare it was, even in this city, with its famed diversity, to encounter a face so *paintable* as her own; said he would, of course, remunerate her for her indulgence; said his rates were high. Rodney then used up a second card and most of a third with a fantastic array of apologies and protestations, of microscopic diffidences – and then added a fourth, for her reply.

'Waitress? Excuse me! Excuse me!' Rodney's voice was having to contend with the espresso machine and the robust applause coming from the back room, as well as with the gasps and hiccups of human communion, all around: like a schoolyard. But Rodney's voice was bigger than he was. Trained by centuries of hollering across very large rooms.

'Ah. There you are.'

The waitress stood by as Rodney outlined her mission. And it seemed that her avowed preparedness to listen to Rodney's voice all day came under immediate strain. Her face toughened, and she knocked a fist into her hip as her shoulders gave a single shrug or shudder. But Rodney just tapped his calling-cards into alignment and contentedly added,

'Now, not the orange-haired one, do you see, with all the freckles. Behind her. The dark one.' Rodney had a witty notion. His interlocutor was a cocktail waitress: why not speak her language? 'The Pink Lady: no. By no means. Rather, the Black Velvet. The Black Velvet.'

He tried to watch as the waitress delivered his note. Its recipient, again, seemed to glance and smile his way; but then a wall of new bards or jokesmiths, heading for the back room, interposed itself, and when the room cleared she was gone.

The shadow of the waitress dropped past him. He looked down at the tray she had placed on his table: the check, plus the fourth postcard, which said tersely and in neat small caps: 'You talk too much.'

Triple-lipped, Rodney paid and added fifteen per cent and took his leave.

It was as he crossed Tenth Street that he realised she was following him. Realised, too, in the light of day, that she was as black as night. And twice his size. His first impulse (one not quickly overcome) was to make a run for it. On Eleventh Street the darkened window of Ray's Pizza told Rodney that she was still behind him. He halted and turned, weakly squinting, and she halted, intelligently smiling, and he took a step towards her, and she took a step back, and he moved on, and she followed. Across Twelfth Street. Now with every step his legs were getting heavier and tenderer; it felt like the marrow-ache of adolescent growth. Despairingly he turned left on Thirteenth Street. She stopped following him. She overtook him.

And as her pace slowed and slackened, and as he attended to the amazing machine of her thighs and buttocks, the parts accommodating themselves so equably in the close quarters of her skirt, all his fears (and all thoughts of his easel) gave way to a reptile vacuity. For the first time in his life Rodney was ready for anything. No questions asked.

When she reached his building she turned and waited. He summoned breath to speak – but she smoothly raised a vertical forefinger to her lips. And he understood, and felt like a child. He talked too much. He talked too much . . . Mounting the steps, he pushed the inner glass door and held it open behind him; when he felt the transfer of its weight he withstood a rush of intimacy, as intimate as the press of boiling breasts on his spine. Dismissing the elevator as an impossibility, he began the long ascent, afraid to turn but minutely alert to her tread. His door. His keys all jammed and tangled in their ring, which he weepily picked at. Each lock turned a different way, the English way, the American way. He pushed, and felt the air rearrange itself as her shape moved past his back.

Many times, during that first half hour, speech gulped up in Rodney's throat – and just as often her forefinger sought her lips (and there would be a frown of real warning). The finger side-on, always. But then they were standing near the piano, when she had completed her tour of his space; Rodney swallowed his most recent glottal stop, and her finger was once again raised; only now she turned it, rotating her whole hand through ninety degrees, showing him the bruised pink of the nail. After a beat or two Rodney took this as an invitation. He hovered nearer still and strained upwards. He kissed.

'Well what the fuck's the story, Rod? You read my novel yet or what?'

Jesus: the guy was like a neighbour's dog that just kept on hating you. You never gave him an instant's thought until there he was, balanced upright on the tautness of his leash, and barking in your face.

'Not yet,' Rodney conceded, as he stepped out of the elevator.

'Now this is basically some *rude shit* we're looking at here. Why the contempt, Rod? What's your answer?'

Rodney wrongly regarded himself as an expert at excuses. After all, he and excuses had been through a lot together. Gazing upwards, with tubed lips, he softly said,

'You're going to hate me for this.'

'I hate you already.'

Feeling a furry hum in either armpit, Rodney decided to change tack. The occasion called for something more than a negligent simper. 'But there was nothing I could do,' he found himself saying. 'My aunt died, do you see. Suddenly. And I had to compose the uh, "eulogy" for her funeral.'

'Your aunt where? In England?'

'No. She lives in . . .' This was not the verb Rodney wanted. 'She was in uh, Connecticut. It was all very awkward. I took the train to, to Connecticut, do you see. Now normally I'd have put up with Auntie Jean, but her, her son was there, with his family, and I . . .'

When he wasn't talking, which wasn't often, Pharsin had a stunned look. As if he couldn't believe he was listening to a voice other than his own. Rodney's agonising tale had brought them out on to Thirteenth Street. In the middle distance the Empire State seemed to sway for a moment, and was then restiffened by its stress equations.

'. . . and *that* train was cancelled too. So with one thing and another I've had my hands full all week.'

Pharsin's expression had softened to something more quizzical, even indulgent. He said, 'I see it. I see what you're doing here, Rod. You're digging yourself into a situation. You *want* to read my novel. But it's like you left it so long you can only see it coming back the other way.' Pharsin tapped his temple. 'I understand the mind. I know the mind. Last year I took a lot of –'

He paused as if to listen. Rodney was expecting the next word to be *Prozac*. But Pharsin went on quickly,

'– psychology courses and I know how we do this, how we set these traps for ourselves and walk right into them. I understand. Rod?'

'Yes, Pharsin?'

'You're going to read my book next week. Isn't that right?'

'Pharsin, I will.'

'One more thing. You got to imagine that novel is written in my blood. In my blood, Rod. It's all there. Everything I am is in that –'

Rodney tuned out for a while and listened to Manhattan. Listened to Manhattan, playing its concerto for horn.

'– the trauma and the wounds. Written in my *blood*, Rod. Written in my blood.'

That night (it was Sunday, and Rock was out of town) Rodney faced a void of inactivity. He was so at a loss that for the first time ever he contemplated digging out his typescript of *The Sound of the Words, the Sound of the Words*. But there turned out to be a reasonably diverting documentary about synchronised swimmers on TV. And he managed to kill the rest of the evening by washing his hair and rolling around in twenty-dollar bills.

'I see her in an Abyssinian setting. Or Ancient Ethiopia. She's a Nefertiti. Or one of the Candaces. Here'll do. Actually I think it's a gay place but they don't seem to mind me coming here.'

No irony was intended or understood by this last remark, and Rock followed Rodney unsmilingly down the steps.

Rock's older brother Inigo had known Rodney at Eton; and in his schooldays Rodney had apparently been famed for his lending library of glamour magazines and his prolific onanism. So Rock sensed no sexual ambiguity in his friend. But others did. For instance, it had never occurred to any of his sitters' husbands that Rodney was straight. And Rodney himself had entertained inevitable doubts on this score, in the past, in London, lying on his side and apologetically stroking the back of yet another unslain giantess of the gentry.

They ordered their Highballs. The clientele was all-male but also middle-aged (woollen, paunchy), and Rodney received no more than his usual deal of stares.

He said, 'This'll amuse you. The first time we uh, "hid the salami"

. . . No. The first time I *revealed* the salami – I felt a real pleb. A real cur. Like an Untouchable.'

'How so?'

'I'm a Cavalier.'

'Me too.'

'Of course. We're English. But over here they're all Roundheads. It's posh to be a Roundhead here. Only the hicks and Okies are Cavaliers.' Rodney well remembered Mrs Vredevoort, wife to the construction grandee: how, when at last she had found the salami (the salami having been located and identified), she gave a little mew of surprised distaste, and immediately came up for air. 'Ours look like joints. As opposed to cigarettes. Which is what they're used to. I bet they're all Roundheads in Africa.'

'But there's not much difference, is there, when you've got the horn.'

'Exactly! That's *exactly* it. Exactly. Mine didn't seem to mind. She didn't say anything.'

'She *never* says anything.'

'True,' said Rodney. 'You know, there's just one thing she won't let me do. No, nothing like that. She won't let me *paint* her. Or even photograph her.'

'Superstitious.'

'And I feel if I could just paint her . . .'

'All slime,' said Rock, 'and no paint. A reversal of your usual setup.'

'Balls. I did pretty well with the wives. All slime and no speech. That's what's really weird.'

'Come out to the house this weekend. It's finished now.'

'Ooh. That does sound like a good idea.'

Love without words. A caveman could do it. And it sounded like something that Picasso or Beckett might have pulled off. But Sir Rodney Peel? He had never shown any sign of pretending to such masterful purity. More scavenger than predator, in matters of the heart, Rodney was the first on the scene after the big cats had eaten their fill. He liked his women freshly jilted. His lips knew the sweet tang of liquefying mascara; his eyes knew the webby rivulets it formed on the blotting-paper of a powdered cheek. He was an old hand at the consoling caress. Rhythmically he would smooth the sideswell of the breast, murmuring *there there* . . . It suited him. Sexual expectation, in such circumstances, was generally low. In such circumstances, impotence could almost be taken as a gallantry.

Love without voices. Usually she came around half past two. Flushed and blotchy from his shower, wearing his long blue robe, Rodney would be lying on the chaise longue, trying to skim a magazine or else just dumbly waiting. Sometimes he went and stuck his head out of the window and tried to glimpse her as she glided under the ginko trees; once he saw her out there in the middle of the street, sharply questioning the driver of the cab from which she had slid. When he heard her keys in the locks, he felt, beneath his robe, the ceremony of painless circumcision.

A smile was all she wanted by way of greeting. Humbly he looked on as she walked the room, her head dipped over her folded arms. She had arrived at his place; but it took time for her to get around to him in her thoughts. Then she would move towards the two lacquered screens that bowered the bed. She undressed matter-of-factly, laying her clothes on the chair (as if ready for school). Around now a switch would be thrown in Rodney's head, immersing him in greater gravity. His ears were trained inwards only, and he listened to the muscles creaking in the root of his tongue.

There *was* something primitive about it – about what followed. Not least in the startling elevations engineered by his blood. But she was one thing and he was the other. Rodney Peel had come to Africa. Her body seemed preternatural in its alternations of the soft and the hard; and her skin, unlike his own, did not reflect the light but absorbed it, confidently annexing its powers. As for her scent, it seemed to Rodney to be of a higher proof, or just more concentrated. And his thoughts went further – to her volcanic breasts, her zebra-ripping teeth! Sun-helmeted and canvas-shoed (and settling down to his task of tribute), Sir Rodney parts the lianas and the sweating fronds and sees . . . Actually it reminded him of a barbecue at Rock's place in Quogue, when he pierced the charred surface of the beef and saw that the flesh was still very rare.

Afterwards she rested. She never slept. Quite often, and increasingly cravenly, he would point to his easel or his brushes; but she always swiped a finger through the air and turned away. And once, early on, when he sat on the bed with his cocked sketch pad, she wrenched it from his grasp with an awful severity in her snuff-coloured eyes. With real strength, too a strength he knew all about. Still, she had created or revealed something in him, and he thought it might be talent. Rodney's loft contained no internal walls, so he was allowed to watch her as she used the bathroom or made the milky tea she liked. She had the overdeveloped upward-surging calf muscles of a dancer. All her movements showed the mechanical security and high definition of intense technique. Rodney thought about it: of course she was an artist. A non-businesswoman under thirty-five living in Manhattan? Of course she was an artist. A dancer. Maybe a *singer*. The performing arts, without question. But which one?

She never slept. She drank her tea, and rested, sighing sometimes and powerfully yawning, but she never slept. Her thoughtfulness seemed centralised and assiduous, as if she were following an argument taking place on the near side of her eyes. Rodney worried about interrupting this argument when he later returned to the bed, but her body always fully admitted him to its heat. He often imagined, as he squirmed and bounced above her, that the first word he would ever hear her say would be the forename of another man . . . All the same, what they did and made together had nothing to do with art. No play: sheer earnest. It felt like honest work.

'Hey. Hey! Ain't no damn use you sneaking out like that. Have you read my novel yet?'

'*Yes*,' said Rodney.

Rodney said Yes, not because it was true or anything like that, but to make a change from saying No. It was an impulse thing. And Rodney was surprised it worked so well.

Pharsin stepped back. For several seconds he wore a plugged expression. Then with his brow softly working he bent and lowered his head. Rodney almost reached up a hand to stroke the black filings of Pharsin's hair.

'So, man. What did you think?'

It was gently said. What a welcome change this makes, thought Rodney (putting all that unpleasantness behind him): these chaps are exceptionally sweet and reasonable. He laughed, saying,

'Ho no, my friend. With a novel like that . . . with a *writer* like that, I'm not going to stand here in a doorway as if I'm talking about the weather. Oh no.'

'But you saying it measures up?'

'*Oh* no. Pharsin, don't try and do this! You my friend are going to come up to my studio. One day very soon. We're going to take the phone uh, "off the hook", put a log on the fire, and open a bottle of good red wine. A claret, I rather think – a nice sharp Morgon. *Then* we'll talk.'

'When?' said Pharsin, with familiar vigilance.

'Actually there's a good reason why we can't do it this weekend.'

'What's that?'

'I'm *re*reading it.'

'. . . I applaud your rigour. Such works seldom render up their secrets on a first absorption.'

'Exactly so.'

'As I've said, Rod, a great deal hinges on your critique. It's been suggested to me that I'm not cut out for fiction, and I'm impatient for a second response. I'm at a stage in my life where . . . You got a minute to hear this?'

Half an hour later Rodney said, 'Of course. On second thoughts, perhaps we'd be better off with something thicker – like a Margaux. We'll have some Stilton. And black olives . . .'

On parting, the two men performed an old ritual (now long disused): a series of street-guy handshakes. Rodney, as ever, looked like someone slowly and painfully learning how to play Paper, Scissors, Stone.

*

It was a gallery opening near Tompkins Square Park – an occasion sponsored by a new brand of vodka, and marked by a nostalgic deluge of Martinis. Rod and Rock had established themselves near the caterers' table. Sexually at peace, and additionally numbed by cocaine, Rodney was temporarily under the impression that everybody loved him. Now he bantered with the barman, affecting interest in the lot of barmen everywhere. Though invariably polite to servants, Rodney never differentiated them. Failing to see, for example, that this waiter was definitely an actor who had waited way too long.

'I have reached a bold conclusion,' he said, swinging round on Rock. 'All my troubles with women come from . . . from words. From speech.'

And there was something in this. Surprisingly, for such a fragile and ingratiating presence, Rodney, over the years, had had his face slapped practically out of alignment, so often had his patter gone awry. He was a flatterer – by profession. He believed in flattery and was always trying to deploy it. But something went wrong with the words: they came out, as his mother would say, just a bit *off*. If conversation was an art, then Rodney was no artist. He created ratty atmospheres around himself. 'Put a sock in it, Rodney,' they would say. 'Oh shut up, Rodney, do.' And the fat beak of his upper lip, after framing its latest unwelcome bauble, would stoically self-transect. Prose wasn't any better. His scented notes routinely caused year-long *froideurs*: 'non-speaks', as in 'She and I are now on non-speaks.' Non-speaks: that's how they should have *started* . . .

'Silence,' he went on, 'was the only reason I got anywhere with the wives. You can't speak while you paint.'

'I thought women liked the kind of rot you talk.'

'Me too. But they don't. I always seem to say the wrong thing.'

A while ago, as an experiment, Rodney had reopened his flirtations with two of the wives: Mrs Globerman, wife to the telecommunications tycoon, and Mrs Overbye, wife to the airline boss. The idea was to see if his new puissance was transferable and could be tried out elsewhere. Both efforts were failures – impossibilities. The things he said and the things they said. The things they all said. It seemed far stranger than silence. With these women Rodney had felt the utter superfluity of human speech. So the rain held off. So tell me about your week. So how have you been? Oh, you know: so-so. So-and-so said this and so-and-so said that. So tired. So soon? And so on and so on.

'You and your bleck girl seem to be made for each other.'

'We do. We are. Capital cocktails, these. Blimey, though. Bit strong, aren't they? Feeling rather tight. It's loosening my tongue. Rock, can I ask you something? Why do I *know* it's going to end in tears? Why do I feel all this anxiety? And all this guilt?'

'Because you're getting something for nothing. Yet again.'

Rodney's eyes widened. He thought about the first time: the fraudulent feeling, when he watched her undress. As if he had reached his objective not by normal means (flattery, false promises, lies) but by something worse: black magic, or betrayal. For a moment he had the strange suspicion that she was his cousin, and they were playing doctors.

'Because you've bucked the work ethic. Yet again. Oh. I'm seeing Jaguar tomorrow. Have you done something with that money yet?'

'Yes,' said Rodney. He *had* done something with that money, if you counted counting it and rolling around in it and spending a lot of it on cocaine.

'I'll check with Jagula. I mean Jaguar. Whew, that last one just hit me.' Rock went on in a smudged voice, '*I* sometimes feel like a trader in slaves. A white-slaver. Onna butlers. Anna nannies. Maybe that's what's worrying you. It's just because she's bleck.'

Rodney said suddenly, 'Blick? No.'

Could that be it? No. No, because he had always felt that she was a woman who carried freedom around with her. On her person. Somewhere in the jaws it seemed to lurk.

Soon afterwards he started to find the bruises.

Nothing florid or fulminant. Just a different kind of dark beneath the dark. The hip, the shoulder, the upper arm. On noticing a new one, Rodney would arrest his movements and attempt to meet her eye – but he never achieved this, and, having faltered, went back to what he was doing before; and afterwards he didn't smile at her in praise and gratitude, as he usually did, turning instead to the stain on the wall, oval and the colour of nicotine, where his head had rested these many months.

He thought he knew something about women and silence. There they would sit before him, the wives, engaged in self-conscious smalltalk as he made his preliminary sketches – as he situated the human posture against the just and rake of the chair, the wall cabinet, the low table. Artists of course crave silence. They wish their sitters dead, stilled: a bowl of apples, a wineglass, a cold fish. But the sitter is alive, and must talk, perhaps sensing that speech is needed to bring colour and indignation to the throat, the cheeks, the eyes. And the painter chats back with his skeleton staff of words until the moment comes when he is incapable of vocalisation: when, in short, he is getting the head. Even Rodney knew this moment of deafened concentration (it felt like talent). And the sensitive sitter would come to note such moments, maintaining a pious hush until her next thricehourly intermission. Her breather, when it was okay for her to be alive again.

He thought he knew something about women and silence. But this? Rodney slipped from the bed and, in his blue robe, set about the preparation of English Breakfast Tea. He watched her through the gap between the two screens: the pillow clutched to her breast like a baby. And always she was following the argument inside her own head. The bruise on her shoulder, tinged with betel or cinnabar, looked artificially applied – caste mark, war paint. Rodney assessed it with a professional eye. It was no accident that he worked in oil. Oil was absolutely right. His brush, he realised, was not an artist's wand so much as a cosmeticist's tweezer. Oil, in his hands, was the elixir of youth. It would be different with her, he felt. Because everything else was different with her. But he would never dare broach it now.

For an instant she loomed over him and then moved past, to the shower. Rodney had never supposed that he was her single – or even her principal – erotic interest. How could he own *her*? He thought of a scene in a huge American novel he had read, years back, where a young man comes of age, pleasantly, in a Chicago bordello. And it went something like, He had used what others used. So what? That's what cities are.

On the other hand he suddenly knew what he wanted to say to her. Three words: a verb flanked by two personal pronouns.

'Hey. *Hey.*'

No black shape – no roller or mugger, no prison-yard rapist, no Hutu warrior, no incensed Maroon on the blazing cane fields of Saint Domingue – could be as fearful to Rodney, now, as the man who occasionally guarded his building: namely Pharsin. Rodney's weekends were entirely devoted to avoiding him: four of the last five had been spent in Quogue. He had even made a couple of phone calls about the possibility of moving. There was apparently a place in midtown, quite near Rock's offices . . .

'Ah, Pharsin. There you are.'

Rodney turned, physically wincing, but only from the rain. He was afraid of Pharsin, and generally well attuned to threat. But his anguish here was almost wholly social.

'What's the latest, Rod?'

'Yes it's high time we uh, "broke bread". I find myself leaning towards a Chambertin-Clos de Beze. And a swampy Camembert.'

'I keep hearing about these goddamn wines you got. But I'm thinking these are the exact same hoops we were going through before. What do I got to do, Rod? It's not just me who's hurting – it's everyone around me. I never thought a man could do this to me. I never thought a man could reduce me to this.'

It was raining. Raining on the terrible city, with people suffering through it and giving voice to their pain, groaning, swearing, babbling. In New York, if you had no one to talk to or shout at, then there was always yourself: always yourself. As Rodney debarked his umbrella he noticed the way the raindrops fell from the lobes of Pharsin's childishly small ears.

'Friday at five.'

'That's in stone?'

'On my mother's life. Hock and smoked salmon might be more the thing. Or some Gewurtztraumeiner. Or what about some Trockenbeerenauslcse, with Turkish Delight?'

'Friday at five.'

'Busy week?' said Rock on Thursday evening.

They were drinking in a bar they usually went to only very late at night: Jimmy's. Although he had been there perhaps a dozen times, it turned out that Rodney had no idea where it was. 'Where *is* Jimmy's?' he asked, as Rock guided him there. The place looked different, in the happy hour.

'Not really,' Rodney answered. 'But you know how it is in New York. You've got nothing on and you think, I know: I'll stay home and read a book. Then the next thing you know . . . there's an opening or something. And then you're bawling your head off across some restaurant.'

'Got anything on tonight? There's a freebie at some punk club in Brooklyn. I've got all-you-can-drink coupons. It doesn't start for hours and it'll be a bugger to get to.'

'Oh all right,' said Rodney.

The next day he left for Quogue rather earlier than usual. He rose at noon and, held upright only by the strata of dried come in his pyjamas, made tea. He took a fifty-minute shower. He performed surprisingly creditably during his tryst (she seemed relieved that afternoon, but expeditious) and he practically joined her in the elevator. To the weekday janitoriat he entrusted a long note for Pharsin about his aunt's exhumation and reburial in another plot; by way of a PS he switched their date to the same time on Monday. Only when the Jitney was idling outside that cincma on its stop near the airport did Rodney question the packing choices in his garment bag: the three new magazines, along with his standard weekend kit.

*

Just gone one on Monday afternoon.

He was sitting at the kitchen table and reading – in preparation
for his task – the back of a cereal packet. Lifting his head and
blinking, he thought of the corpulent Victorian novels he had gaped
his way through at university, the *Middlemarches* and *Bleak Houses*:
they had taken him at least a month each. Still, he had never
contemplated spending more than about half an hour with *The
Sound of the Words, the Sound of the Words*. He was just beginning
to reread the back of the cereal packet when he heard the keys in
the door.

Her appearance almost shocked him into speech. What had
happened was this. The argument which for months had been taking
place inside her head, illegibly, was now written on the outside. For
all to see. Her eyes steadily invited him to register this change: the
nether lip all smudged and split, and the right cheekbone loudly
marked, as if swiped with a hot daub of rouge. The thing that was
wrong had now been stated, not by her but by the thing that was
wrong.

Aghast, he tottered towards her. And found himself leniently
received. He kissed her neck, her jaw, and, with circumspection,
her mouth – but then all circumspection was lost. Fearfully and
ardently, and for the last time, Sir Rodney Peel stoked the tarry
blood of Eve.

Afterwards she did something she'd never done before. She didn't
speak. No. She slept.

Rodney got to work, and quite noisily.

He dragged his easel across the floor, shifted the screens, and
rattled around with his brushes. There was no sense of tiptoe in
his body or his mind: her sleep seemed elementally sure, like
hibernation. He pulled off the cover. She was lying on her side, the
upper knee raised, one hand beneath the pillow and the other placed
flat between her thighs. First get the head, he thought. Then get
the neck. Then get the body.

'Artists are waiters!' he said. Waiting for the right thing in the right place at the right time. And with that he said goodbye to his discursive mind – until the painting was about done and somebody seemed to be banging on his door.

And Rodney spoke. In a childishly lucid voice he said, 'Oh dear. That will be Pharsin.'

She was looking up at him over her shoulder. And she spoke too. What she said was obliterating; but it wasn't the content. It was the style. Heard by him before only on English high streets, in supermarket checkout bays, in cauldrons of drycleaning. Maybe, too, in the squawk of the minicab switchboard, endured from the back seat, late at night. She said, 'Eez me yusband.'

'OPEN THIS FUCKING DOOR RIGHT NOW.'

Rodney would later describe the events that followed as 'something of a blur'. But in fact these events were clear. It was good that he was feeling so talented. And enormous chemicals were igniting his brain.

'YOU GOT ONE MINUTE. THEN I RIP THIS DOOR OFF THE FUCKING WALL. SIXTY. FIFTY-NINE. FIFTY-EIGHT.'

In an ideal world Rodney would have liked rather more than a minute to read *The Sound of the Words, the Sound of the Words*. But before he could read it he first had to *find* it.

Mrs Pharsin Courier having been shushed, and sealed off behind the twin screens, Rodney went and thrashed around in the double-doored closet (FIFTY-ONE), then bent himself under the piano (FORTY-FIVE), then wriggled about among the low shelves and shadows of the kitchen (THIRTY-FOUR). On the half-minute mark he paused to take stock – and to hoist a lumpy brown rug over the gap between the screens, noticing, as he did so, a suspicious wedge in the heap of death-grey newspapers silting up the corner beyond the bed. Rodney pounced (THIRTEEN): A Novel by Pharsin J Courier (NINE, EIGHT). Skilfully he flipped it on to the table (SIX, FIVE), read half a phrase from page one ('Around noon Cissy thought she'd') and, as he rose to answer the door

(THREE, TWO), half a phrase from page 1,123 ('seemed that way to Cissy'). And that was all he had time for.

'Ah, Pharsin. You respond to our cries of 'Author! Author!' Step forward, sir, and be recognised. Now. If you'll just sit yourself there, I'll just . . .

'Now I'm not a writer,' said Rodney sternly, laying before Pharsin a glass of flat Pepsi. And a saucer with most of a Graham Cracker on it. Heartier and more various fare could have been plucked from the surface of Rodney's burred blue robe. 'I'm a painter, a visual artist. But as you have written elsewhere there is a certain . . . affinity between the arts. Now. The *first* time I read your book I was quite overwhelmed by this cascade of visual images. These things you describe – I felt I could reach out and touch them, smell them, taste them. Only on a second reading and, may I say, a third uh, 'perusal' did I see that these images were, in fact, connected. In very intricate ways.'

Admiringly hefting the typescript in his hands, Rodney gave Pharsin a candid stare. So far so good. Pharsin's wrath, while still manifest, had reached some trancelike register. Rodney knew enough about novels to know that they all *tried* to do something like that – to connect image with theme. Cautiously he continued with his own variations, feeling the spasms of unused muscles: his lits, his crits. Yes, he could still swim in that pool. He could still ride that old bike.

'. . . shaping the whole composition. I could step back from the fretwork, the mouldings, the beadings, the uh, flutings and so on. I could step back from the gargoyles and see the whole cathedral.'

It looked for a moment as if Pharsin was going to ask a question about this cathedral: what it looked like or where it stood. So with a woozy roll of his head Rodney proceeded,

'And where did you find those *characters*? Quite incredible. I mean – take Cissy, for instance. How did you dream *her* up?'

'You like Cissy?'

'Cissy? Oh, Cissy! Cissy . . . By the time I was finished I felt I'd never known *anyone* as intimately as I knew her.' As he talked he started riffling fondly through the pages. 'Her thoughts. Her hopes and dreams. Her doubts. Her fears. I *know* Cissy. Like you'd know a sister. Or a lover.'

Rodney looked up. Pharsin's face was a screen of tears. Thoroughly emboldened, Rodney hunched himself forward and leafed through the text.

'That bit . . . that bit where she . . . when Cissy –'

'When she comes to the States?'

'Yes. When she comes to America.'

'The thing with Immigration?'

'Yes. Now *that scene* . . . Incredible. But so true! And then, after that – I'm trying to find it – the bit when she . . .'

'When she meets the guy?'

'Yes. The guy: now there's another character. And there's that great scene when they . . . Here it is. No. When they . . .'

'At the rent tribunal?'

'Oh now that scene. Can you believe that?'

'The judge?'

'Please,' said Rodney. 'Don't get me started on the judge.'

And so, for forty-five minutes, always a beat late, he somehow sang along with a song he didn't know. It seemed like scurvy work, of course; and it was strangely shaming to see Pharsin's face awaken out of hunger into vivid varieties of animation and delight (as at the chess board, Rodney felt dwarfed by a superior force of life). It was scurvy work, but it was *easy*. He wondered why he hadn't done it months ago. Then Pharsin said,

'Enough. Forget the laughter, the characters, the images. What's *The Sound of the Words, the Sound of the Words* actually *saying*, Rod?'

'*The Sound of the Words, the Sound of the Words?*'

'What's it *saying*?'

'What's it saying? Well, it's a love story. It's about love in the modern world. How love gets hard to do.'

'But what's it *saying*?'

Ten seconds passed. And Rodney thought *fuck it* and said, 'It's about race. It's about the agony of the African-American male. It's about the need, the compulsion, to express that agony.'

Pharsin slowly reached out a hand towards him. Once more tears shone in the bloodbaths of his eyes.

'Thanks, Rod.'

'It's been a pleasure, Pharsin. Hello, is that the time? Shouldn't you be uh . . . ?'

Until that moment Pharsin had seemed insensible of his surroundings. But now he jerked himself upright and began to move around the room with purposeful curiosity, one arm folded, the other crooked, a forefinger tapping on his chin, pausing to inspect a nicknack here, a doodad there. Rodney wasn't thinking about his other guest (who, he assumed, would still be wedged behind the bed). He was thinking of her simulacrum: her portrait, arrayed on its stand, in blazing crime. Redigesting a mouthful of vomit, Rodney watched as Pharsin loped up to the easel and paused.

The black shape on the white sheet. The beauty and power of the rump and haunches. The sleeping face, half-averted. Rodney, out of sheer habit, had salved and healed her bruises. That was probably a good idea, he thought.

'This a real person pose for this?' Pharsin turned, artist to artist, and added, 'Or you take it from a book.'

'A book?'

'Yeah, like a magazine?'

'Yes. From a magazine.'

'Know who this kind of reminds me of? Cassie. My wife Cassie.' Pharsin smiled ticklishly as he followed the resemblance for another second or two. Then he rejected it. 'Maybe ten years ago. And she never had an ass like that in *all* her born days. Well, Rod. I want you to know what this last hour has meant to me. There was a man crying out in the dark here. You my friend have answered that cry. You've given me what I wanted: a hearing. I sent that novel to every registered publisher and agent in the city. All I got was a bunch of printed slips. Know what I think? They didn't read it. They didn't even *read* it, Rod.'

'That's a terrible thing, Pharsin. A terrible thing. Oh, by the way. You once told me that your wife was an artist. What kind is she?'

Then for a second their eyes met: horribly. And in Pharsin's face you could see the ageless and awful eureka of every stooge and sap and cinch. He said,

'You read my book and you're asking me what Cassie *does*?'

But it came to Rodney and he said, 'I know what *Cissie* does. In the book. I was just wondering how close you were sticking to life. I know what Cissie does.'

Pharsin's voice had Rodney by the lapels. It said, 'What?'

And he told him: 'Mime.'

With Pharsin caged and dropping in the elevator, and all loaded up with his typescript like a bearer, Rodney's head remained limp and bent, hangdog with relief. Even the strengthening conviction – not yet entire, needing more thought – that he, Rodney, had no talent: this brought relief. He let his head hang there a little longer, before he faced the music of human speech.

She said, 'You fucking done it now.'

He said, 'Oh dear. Have I said the wrong thing?'

'All a slight nightmare, really. She couldn't leave, do you see, because Pharsin was on the door. So she rather let me have it.' Rodney was no stranger to the experience of being denounced from dawn to dusk; but he wasn't used to accents such as hers. 'A terrible way for things to end. Our first night together and it was all talk and no sex. And such talk. She was *livid*.'

'What about? I wish those people would go away.'

Cocktails *al fresco* in Rockefeller Plaza: Amber Dreams under a cold blue sky. The square was punctuated by people dressed as mannequins and posing as statues. Just standing there with painted smiles.

'Oh God, don't ask,' said Rodney – for her grievances had been legion. 'She knew someone or something had been driving him nuts. She didn't know it was me. He'd never been violent before. It was me. *I* put those marks on her.'

'Oh come on. It's in their culture.'

Rodney coughed and said, 'Oh yeah. And she said, "He'll write another one now." She'd been moonlighting for two years. As a waitress. To support him. And she could tell I hadn't read it. By my voice.'

Rock looked on, frowning, as Rodney talentlessly imitated her imitating him. It sounded something like: Ooh, ah say, wort simplay dezzling imagereh. Rodney said,

'She thought I was sneering at him. Him being bleck, do you see.'

'Yes, well, they can be quite chippy about that over here. Do you think his novel might have been *good*?'

'No one will ever know. But I do know this. She won't have to support him while he writes the second one.'

'Why not?'

'Because she stole my money.'

'Oh you *tit*. How many times did I tell you? Jesus Christ, what a silly old tart you are.'

'I know. I know. Waitress? If you please? Two Amber Dreams. No. *Four* Amber Dreams.'

'Are you telling me you just left it lying around?'

'In the middle of the night I . . . Wait. When I first met her, in the bar, do you see, I offered her five hundred dollars. No, as a sitter's fee. So I reckoned I owed her that. Went and got it out for her. Thought she was sleeping.'

'Oh you *tit*.'

'She did leave me the five hundred. Ah. Thank you most awfully.'

And on her way to the door she paused in front of the easel and whispered a single word (stressed as a menacing and devastating spondee): 'Wan*ker*.' And that was the end of that, he thought. That was the end of that.

Rock said, 'Were they in it together, do you think?'

'No no. No. It was all pure . . . coincidence.'

'Why aren't you angrier?'

'I don't know.'

*

Pharsin he never saw again. But he did see Pharsin's wife, once, nearly two years later, in London Town.

Rodney was consuming a tragic tea of crustless sandwiches in a dark café near Victoria Station. He had just left the Pimlico offices of the design magazine he worked part-time for, and was girding himself to catch a train for Sussex, where he would be met at the station by a childless divorcee in a Range Rover. He no longer wore a ponytail. And he no longer used his title. That sort of thing didn't seem to play very well in England any more. Besides, for a while Rodney had become very interested in his family tree; and this was his puny protest. The scars had deepened around his eyes. But not much else had changed.

Weatherless Victoria, and a café in the old style. Coffee served in leaky steel pots, and children eating Banana Splits and Knickerbocker Glories and other confections the colour of traffic lights. In this place the waitresses were waitresses by caste, contemplating no artistic destiny. Outside, the city dedicated itself to the notion of mobility, fleets of buses and taxis, herds of cars, and then the trains.

She was several tables away, facing him, with her slender eyebrows raised and locked in enquiry. Rodney glanced, blinked, smiled. Then it was dumbshow all over again. May I? Well if you. No I'll just . . .

'Well well. It *is* a small world, isn't it.'

'. . . So you're not going to murder me? You're not going to slag me off?'

'What? Oh no. No no. No.'

'. . . So you're back here now.'

'Yes. And you, you're . . .'

'Me mum died.'

'Oh, I'm so sorry. So you're just here for the . . .'

'For the funeral and that, yeah . . .'

She said that her mother had been very old and had had a good life. Rodney's mother was also very old and had had a good life, at least on paper. But she wasn't dead. On the contrary she was, as the saying had it, 'very much alive'. He was back with his mother.

There was nothing he could do about that. He had to talk to her a lot but everything he said enraged her. Better to seal up your lips, he thought. Mum's the word. Seal up your lips, and give no words but – mum. She said,

'I can't believe you're being so sweet about the money. Have you got loads more?'

'No. What? Sweet? No no. I was upset at first, of course. But I . . . What did you do with it in the end?'

'I told him I *found* it. In a cab. It's New York, right?' She shrugged and said, 'Went upstate and got a place in the Poconos. We were there twenty-two months. It was handsome. Look. A boy. Julius. Not quite one.'

As he considered the photograph Rodney was visited by a conventional sentiment: the gift of life! And stronger, according to his experience, in the black than in all the other planetary colours. 'Can he talk yet? When do they talk?' And he pressed on, 'Our code of silence. What was that – sort of a game?'

'You were a Sir. And me with my accent.'

The implication being that he wouldn't have wanted her if she'd talked like she talked. And it was true. He looked at Cassie. Her shape and texture sent the same message to his eyes and his mind. But the message stopped there. It no longer travelled down his spine. Sad and baffling, but perfectly true. 'Well I'm not a Sir any more,' he said, and he almost added 'either'. 'Did uh –?'

'It was nice though, wasn't it. Restful. Uncomplicated.'

'Yes, it was very nice.' Rodney felt close to tears. He said, 'Did uh, Pharsin continue with his . . . ?'

'He got it out of his system. Let's put it like that. He's himself again now.'

She spoke with relief, even with pride. It had not escaped Rodney's plodding scrutiny that her face and her long bare arms were quite free of contusion. Violence: it's in their culture, Rock had said. And Rodney now asked himself: Who put it there?

'He's back doing the chess,' she said. 'Doing okay. It's up with the economy.'

Rodney wanted to say, 'Chess is a high calling' – which he believed. But he was afraid it might be taken amiss. All he could think to offer was the following: 'Well. A fool and his money are soon parted.'

'That's what they say.'

'Take it as . . .' He searched for the right word. Would 'reparations' answer? He said, 'Still doing the mime?'

'Doing well. We tour now. How about you? Still doing the painting?'

'Got fed up with it. Don't know why really.'

Although Rodney was not looking forward to his rendezvous in Sussex, he was looking forward to the drinks he would have on the train to prepare himself for it. He turned to the window. His upper lip did its thing: slowly folding into two. He said,

'So the rain held off.'

'Yeah. It's been nice.'

'Thought it looked like rain earlier.'

'Me too. Thought it was going to piss down.'

'But it held off.'

'Yeah,' she said. 'It held off.'

On Seeing the 100% Perfect Girl
One Beautiful April Morning
by
Haruki Murakami

Haruki Murakami was born in Kyoto in 1949. Following the publication of his first novel in Japanese in 1979, he sold the jazz bar he ran with his wife and became a full-time writer. It was with the publication of *Norwegian Wood* – which has, to date, sold more than 4 million copies in Japan alone – that the author was truly catapulted into the limelight. Known for his surrealistic world of mysterious (and often disappearing) women, cats, earlobes, wells, Western culture, music and quirky first-person narratives, he is now Japan's best-known novelist abroad. Nine novels, three short story collections and one work of non-fiction are currently available in English translation.

ONE BEAUTIFUL APRIL morning, on a narrow side street in Tokyo's fashionable Harajuku neighborhood, I walk past the 100% perfect girl.

Tell you the truth, she's not that good-looking. She doesn't stand out in any way. Her clothes are nothing special. The back of her hair is still bent out of shape from sleep. She isn't young, either – must be near thirty, not even close to a 'girl,' properly speaking. But still, I know from fifty yards away: She's the 100% perfect girl for me. The moment I see her, there's a rumbling in my chest, and my mouth is as dry as a desert.

Maybe you have your own particular favorite type of girl – one with slim ankles, say, or big eyes, or graceful fingers, or you're drawn for no good reason to girls who take their time with every meal. I have my own preferences, of course. Sometimes in a restaurant I'll catch myself staring at the girl at the table next to mine because I like the shape of her nose.

But no one can insist that his 100% perfect girl correspond to some preconceived type. Much as I like noses, I can't recall the shape of hers – or even if she had one. All I can remember for sure is that she was no great beauty. It's weird.

'Yesterday on the street I passed the 100% perfect girl,' I tell someone.

'Yeah?' he says. 'Good-looking?'

'Not really.'

211

'Your favorite type, then?'

'I don't know. I can't seem to remember anything about her – the shape of her eyes or the size of her breasts.'

'Strange.'

'Yeah. Strange.'

'So anyhow,' he says, already bored, 'what did you do? Talk to her? Follow her?'

'Nah. Just passed her on the street.'

She's walking east to west, and I west to east. It's a really nice April morning.

Wish I could talk to her. Half an hour would be plenty: just ask her about herself, tell her about myself, and – what I'd really like to do – explain to her the complexities of fate that have led to our passing each other on a side street in Harajuku on a beautiful April morning in 1981. This was something sure to be crammed full of warm secrets, like an antique clock built when peace filled the world.

After talking, we'd have lunch somewhere, maybe see a Woody Allen movie, stop by a hotel bar for cocktails. With any kind of luck, we might end up in bed.

Potentiality knocks on the door of my heart.

Now the distance between us has narrowed to fifteen yards.

How can I approach her? What should I say?

'Good morning, miss. Do you think you could spare half an hour for a little conversation?'

Ridiculous. I'd sound like an insurance salesman.

'Pardon me, but would you happen to know if there is an all-night cleaners in the neighborhood?'

No, this is just as ridiculous. I'm not carrying any laundry, for one thing. Who's going to buy a line like that?

Maybe the simple truth would do. 'Good morning. You are the 100% perfect girl for me.'

No, she wouldn't believe it. Or even if she did, she might not want to talk to me. Sorry, she could say, I might be the 100% perfect girl for you, but you're not the 100% perfect boy for me. It could happen. And if I found myself in that situation, I'd probably go to pieces. I'd never recover from the shock. I'm thirty-two, and that's what growing older is all about.

We pass in front of a flower shop. A small, warm air mass touches my skin. The asphalt is damp, and I catch the scent of roses. I can't bring myself to speak to her. She wears a white sweater, and in her right hand she holds a crisp white envelope lacking only a stamp. So: She's written somebody a letter, maybe spent the whole night writing, to judge from the sleepy look in her eyes. The envelope could contain every secret she's ever had.

I take a few more strides and turn: She's lost in the crowd.

Now, of course. I know exactly what I should have said to her. It would have been a long speech, though, far too long for me to have delivered it properly. The ideas I come up with are never very practical.

Oh, well. It would have started 'Once upon a time' and ended 'A sad story, don't you think?'

Once upon a time, there lived a boy and a girl. The boy was eighteen and the girl sixteen. He was not unusually handsome, and she was not especially beautiful. They were just an ordinary lonely boy and an ordinary lonely girl, like all the others. But they believed with their whole hearts that somewhere in the world there lived the 100% perfect boy and the 100% perfect girl for them. Yes, they believed in a miracle. And that miracle actually happened.

One day the two came upon each other on the corner of a street. 'This is amazing,' he said. 'I've been looking for you all my life. You may not believe this, but you're the 100% perfect girl for me.'

'And you,' she said to him, 'are the 100% perfect boy for me, exactly as I'd pictured you in every detail. It's like a dream.'

They sat on a park bench, held hands, and told each other their stories hour after hour. They were not lonely anymore. They had found and been found by their 100% perfect other. What a wonderful thing it is to find and be found by your 100% perfect other. It's a miracle, a cosmic miracle.

As they sat and talked, however, a tiny, tiny sliver of doubt took root in their hearts: Was it really all right for one's dreams to come true so easily?

And so, when there came a momentary lull in their conversation, the boy said to the girl, 'Let's test ourselves – just once. If we really are each other's 100% perfect lovers, then sometime, somewhere, we will meet again without fail. And when that happens, and we know that we are the 100% perfect ones, we'll marry then and there. What do you think?'

'Yes,' she said, 'that is exactly what we should do.'

And so they parted, she to the east, and he to the west.

The test they had agreed upon, however, was utterly unnecessary. They should never have undertaken it, because they really and truly were each other's 100% perfect lovers, and it was a miracle that they had ever met. But it was impossible for them to know this, young as they were. The cold, indifferent waves of fate proceeded to toss them unmercifully.

One winter, both the boy and the girl came down with the season's terrible influenza, and after drifting for weeks between life and death they lost all memory of their earlier years. When they awoke, their heads were as empty as the young D. H. Lawrence's piggy bank.

They were two bright, determined young people, however, and through their unremitting efforts they were able to acquire once again the knowledge and feeling that qualified them to return as full-fledged members of society. Heaven be praised, they became truly upstanding citizens who knew how to transfer from one subway line to another, who were fully capable of sending a special-delivery letter at the post office. Indeed, they even experienced love again, sometimes as much as 75% or even 85% love.

Time passed with shocking swiftness, and soon the boy was thirty-two, the girl thirty.

One beautiful April morning, in search of a cup of coffee to start the day, the boy was walking from west to east, while the girl, intending to send a special-delivery letter, was walking from east to west, both along the same narrow street in the Harajuku neighborhood of Tokyo. They passed each other in the very center of the street. The faintest gleam of their lost memories glimmered for the briefest moment in their hearts. Each felt a rumbling in the chest. And they knew:

She is the 100% perfect girl for me.

He is the 100% perfect boy for me.

But the glow of their memories was far too weak, and their thoughts no longer had the clarity of fourteen years earlier. Without a word, they passed each other, disappearing into the crowd. Forever.

A sad story, don't you think?

Yes. that's it, that is what I should have said to her.

—translated by Jay Rubin

The Tiger's Bride
by
Angela Carter

Angela Carter was born in 1940 in Eastbourne. Her first novel, *Shadow Dance*, was published in 1965. Her next book, *The Magic Toyshop*, won the John Llewellyn Rhys Prize and the next, *Several Perceptions*, the Somerset Maugham Award. Carter used the proceeds of the Somerset Maugham Award to travel to Japan, where she lived for two years. She then travelled throughout Asia, Europe and the United States and spent much of the late 1970s and 1980s as a writer in residence at universities. As well as her novels she also wrote short stories, articles for the *Guardian*, *Independent* and *New Statesman*, two original radio dramas, a libretto for an opera of Virginia Woolf's *Orlando* and was actively involved in the film adaptations of two of her works: *The Company of Wolves* and *The Magic Toyshop*. She died in February 1992.

The Tiger's Bride

M Y FATHER LOST me to The Beast at cards.
There's a special madness strikes travellers from the North
when they reach the lovely land where the lemon trees grow. We
come from countries of cold weather; at home, we are at war with
nature but here, ah! you think you've come to the blessed plot
where the lion lies down with the lamb. Everything flowers; no
harsh wind stirs the voluptuous air. The sun spills fruit for you.
And the deathly, sensual lethargy of the sweet South infects the
starved brain; it gasps: 'Luxury! more luxury!' But then the snow
comes, you cannot escape it, it followed us from Russia as if it
ran behind our carriage, and in this dark, bitter city has caught
up with us at last, flocking against the windowpanes to mock my
father's expectations of perpetual pleasure as the veins in his
forehead stand out and throb, his hands shake as he deals the
Devil's picture books.

The candles dropped hot, acrid gouts of wax on my bare shoulders.
I watched with the furious cynicism peculiar to women whom
circumstances force mutely to witness folly, while my father, fired
in his desperation by more and yet more draughts of the firewater
they call 'grappa', rids himself of the last scraps of my inheritance.
When we left Russia, we owned black earth, blue forest with bear
and wild boar, serfs, cornfields, farmyards, my beloved horses, white
nights of cool summer, the fireworks of the northern lights. What
a burden all those possessions must have been to him, because he

laughs as if with glee as he beggars himself; he is in such a passion to donate all to The Beast.

Everyone who comes to this city must play a hand with the *grande seigneur*; few come. They did not warn us at Milan, or, if they did, we did not understand them – my limping Italian, the bewildering dialect of the region. Indeed, I myself spoke up in favour of this remote, provincial place, out of fashion two hundred years, because, oh irony, it boasted no casino. I did not know that the price of a stay in its Decembral solitude was a game with Milord.

The hour was late. The chill damp of this place creeps into the stones, into your bones, into the spongy pith of the lungs; it insinuated itself with a shiver into our parlour, where Milord came to play in the privacy essential to him. Who could refuse the invitation his valet brought to our lodging? Not my profligate father, certainly; the mirror above the table gave me back his frenzy, my impassivity, the withering candles, the emptying bottles, the coloured tide of the cards as they rose and fell, the still mask that concealed all the features of The Beast but for the yellow eyes that strayed, now and then, from his unfurled hand towards myself.

'*La Bestia!*' said our landlady, gingerly fingering an envelope with his huge crest of a tiger rampant on it, something of fear, something of wonder in her face. And I could not ask her why they called the master of the place, *La Bestia* – was it to do with the heraldic signature – because her tongue was so thickened by the phlegmy, bronchitic speech of the region I scarcely managed to make out a thing she said except, when she saw me: '*Che bella!*'

Since I could toddle, always the pretty one, with my glossy, nutbrown curls, my rosy cheeks. And born on Christmas Day – her 'Christmas rose', my English nurse called me. The peasants said: 'The living image of her mother', crossing themselves out of respect for the dead. My mother did not blossom long; bartered for her dowry to such a feckless sprig of the Russian nobility that she soon died of his gaming, his whoring, his agonising repentances. And The Beast gave me the rose from his own impeccable if outmoded buttonhole when he arrived, the valet brushing the snow off his black cloak. This white rose, unnatural, out of season, that now my nervous fingers ripped, petal by petal, apart as my father magnificently concluded the career he had made of catastrophe.

This is a melancholy, introspective region; a sunless, featureless landscape, the sullen river sweating fog, the shorn, hunkering willows. And a cruel city; the sombre piazza, a place uniquely suited to public executions, under the beetling shadow of that malign barn of a church. They used to hang condemned men in cages from the city walls; unkindness comes naturally to them, their eyes are set so close together, they have thin lips. Poor food, pasta soaked in oil, boiled beef with sauce of bitter herbs. A funereal hush about the place, the inhabitants huddled up against the cold so you can hardly see their faces. And they lie to you and cheat you, innkeepers, coachmen, everybody. God, how they fleeced us.

The treacherous South, where you think there is no winter but forget you take it with you.

My senses were increasingly troubled by the fuddling perfume of Milord, far too potent a reek of purplish civet at such close quarters in so small, a room. He must bathe himself in scent, soak his shirts and underlinen in it; what can he smell of, that needs so much camouflage?

I never saw a man so big look so two-dimensional, in spite of the quaint elegance of The Beast, in the old-fashioned tailcoat that might, from its looks, have been bought in those distant years before he imposed seclusion on himself; he does not feel he need keep up with the times. There is a crude clumsiness about his outlines, that are on the ungainly, giant side; and he has an odd air of self-imposed restraint, as if fighting a battle with himself to remain upright when he would far rather drop down on all fours. He throws our human aspirations to the godlike sadly awry, poor fellow; only from a distance would you think The Beast not much different from any other man, although he wears a mask with a man's face painted most beautifully on it. Oh, yes, a beautiful face; but one with too much formal symmetry of feature to be entirely human: one profile of his mask is the mirror image of the other, too perfect, uncanny. He wears a wig, too, false hair tied at the nape with a bow, a wig of the kind you see in old-fashioned portraits. A chaste silk stock stuck with a pearl hides his throat. And gloves of blond kid that are yet so huge and clumsy they do not seem to cover hands.

He is a carnival figure made of papier-mâché and crêpe hair; and yet he has the Devil's knack at cards.

His masked voice echoes as from a great distance as he stoops over his hand and he has such a growling impediment in his speech that only his valet, who understands him, can interpret for him, as if his master were the clumsy doll and he the ventriloquist.

The wick slumped in the eroded wax, the candles guttered. By the time my rose had lost all its petals, my father, too, was left with nothing.

'Except the girl.'

Gambling is a sickness. My father said he loved me yet he staked his daughter on a hand of cards. He fanned them out; in the mirror, I saw wild hope light up his eyes. His collar was unfastened, his rumpled hair stood up on end, he had the anguish of a man in the last stages of debauchery. The draughts came out of the old walls and bit me, I was colder than I'd ever been in Russia, when nights are coldest there.

A queen, a king, an ace. I saw them in the mirror. Oh, I know he thought he could not lose me; besides, back with me would come all he had lost, the unravelled fortunes of our family at one blow restored. And would he not win, as well, The Beast's hereditary palazzo outside the city; his immense revenues; his lands around the river; his rents, his treasure chest, his Mantegnas, his Giulio Romanos, his Cellini saltcellars, his titles . . . the very city itself.

You must not think my father valued me at less than a king's ransom; but at *no more* than a king's ransom.

It was cold as hell in the parlour. And it seemed to me, child of the severe North, that it was not my flesh but, truly, my father's soul that was in peril.

My father, of course, believed in miracles; what gambler does not? In pursuit of just such a miracle as this, had we not travelled from the land of bears and shooting stars?

So we teetered on the brink.

The Beast bayed; laid down all three remaining aces.

The indifferent servants now glided smoothly forward as on wheels to douse the candles one by one. To look at them you would think that nothing of any moment had occurred. They yawned a little resentfully; it was almost morning. We had kept them out of bed. The Beast's man brought his cloak. My father sat amongst these preparations for departure, staring on at the betrayal of his cards upon the table.

The Beast's man informed me crisply that he, the valet, would call for me and my bags tomorrow, at ten, and conduct me forthwith to The Beast's palazzo. *Capisco?* So shocked was I that I scarcely did *capisco*; he repeated my orders patiently, he was a strange, thin, quick little man who walked with an irregular jolting rhythm upon splayed feet in curious, wedge-shaped shoes.

Where my father had been red as fire, now he was white as the snow that caked the windowpane. His eyes swam; soon he would cry.

"'Like the base Indian,'" he said; he loved rhetoric. "'One whose hand,/Like the base Indian, threw a pearl away/Richer than all his tribe . . .' I have lost my pearl, my pearl beyond price.'

At that, The Beast made a sudden, dreadful noise, halfway between a growl and a roar; the candles flared. The quick valet, the prim hypocrite, interpreted unblinkingly: 'My master says: If you are so careless of your treasures, you should expect them to be taken from you.'

He gave us the bow and smile his master could not offer us and they departed.

I watched the snow until, just before dawn, it stopped falling; a hard frost settled, next morning there was a light like iron.

The Beast's carriage, of an elegant if antique design, was black as a hearse and it was drawn by a dashing black gelding who blew smoke from his nostrils and stamped upon the packed snow with enough sprightly appearance of life to give me some hope that not all the world was locked in ice, as I was. I had always held a little towards Gulliver's opinion, that horses are better than we are, and, that day, I would have been glad to depart with him to the kingdom of horses, if I'd been given the chance.

The valet sat up on the box in a natty black and gold livery, clasping, of all things, a bunch of his master's damned white roses as if a gift of flowers would reconcile a woman to any humiliation. He sprang down with preternatural agility to place them ceremoniously in my reluctant hand. My tear-beslobbered father wants a rose to show that I forgive him. When I break off a stem, I prick my finger and so he gets his rose all smeared with blood.

The valet crouched at my feet to tuck the rugs about me with a strange kind of unflattering obsequiousness yet he forgot his station sufficiently to scratch busily beneath his white periwig with an over-supple index finger as he offered me what my old nurse would have called an 'old-fashioned look', ironic, sly, a smidgen of disdain in it. And pity? No pity. His eyes were moist and brown, his face seamed with the innocent cunning of an ancient baby. He had an irritating habit of chattering to himself under his breath all the time as he packed up his master's winnings. I drew the curtains to conceal the sight of my father's farewell; my spite was sharp as broken glass.

Lost to The Beast! And what, I wondered, might be the exact nature of his 'beastliness'? My English nurse once told me about a tiger-man she saw in London, when she was a little girl, to scare me into good behaviour, for I was a wild wee thing and she could not tame me into submission with a frown or the bribe of a spoonful of jam. If you don't stop plaguing the nursemaids, my beauty, the tiger-man will come and take you away. They'd brought him from Sumatra, in the Indies, she said; his hinder parts were all hairy and only from the head downwards did he resemble a man.

And yet The Beast goes always masked; it cannot be his face that looks like mine.

But the tiger-man, in spite of his hairiness, could take a glass of ale in his hand like a good Christian and drink it down. Had she not seen him do so, at the sign of The George, by the steps of Upper Moor Fields when she was just as high as me and lisped and toddled, too. Then she would sigh for London, across the North Sea of the lapse of years. But, if this young lady was not a good little girl and did not eat her boiled beetroot, then the tiger-man would put on his big black travelling cloak lined with fur, just like your daddy's, and hire the Erl-King's galloper of wind and ride through the night straight to the nursery and –

Yes, my beauty! GOBBLE YOU UP!

How I'd squeal in delighted terror, half believing her, half knowing that she teased me. And there were things I knew that I must not tell her. In our lost farmyard, where the giggling nursemaids initiated me into the mysteries of what the bull did to the cows, I heard about the waggoner's daughter. Hush, hush, don't let on to your nursie we said so; the waggoner's lass, hare-lipped, squint-eyed, ugly as sin, who would have taken her? Yet, to her shame, her belly swelled amid the cruel mockery of the ostlers and her son was born of a bear, they whispered. Born with a full pelt and teeth; that proved it. But, when he grew up, he was a good shepherd, although he never married, lived in a hut outside the village and could make the wind blow any way he wanted to besides being able to tell which eggs would become cocks, which hens.

The wondering peasants once brought my father a skull with horns four inches long on either side of it and would not go back to the field where their poor plough disturbed it until the priest went with them; for this skull had the jaw-bone of a *man*, had it not?

Old wives' tales, nursery fears! I knew well enough the reason for the trepidation I cosily titillated with superstitious marvels of my childhood on the day my childhood ended. For now my own skin was my sole capital in the world and today I'd make my first investment.

We had left the city far behind us and were now traversing a wide, flat dish of snow where the mutilated stumps of the willows flourished their ciliate heads athwart frozen ditches; mist diminished the horizon, brought down the sky until it seemed no more than a few inches above us. As far as eye could see, not one thing living. How starveling, how bereft the dead season of this spurious Eden in which all the fruit was blighted by cold! And my frail roses, already faded. I opened the carriage door and tossed the defunct bouquet into the rucked, frost-stiff mud of the road. Suddenly a sharp, freezing wind arose and pelted my face with a dry rice of powdered snow. The mist lifted sufficiently to reveal before me an acreage of half-derelict façades of sheer red brick, the vast man-trap, the megalomaniac citadel of his palazzo.

It was a world in itself but a dead one, a burned-out planet. I saw The Beast bought solitude, not luxury, with his money.

The little black horse trotted smartly through the figured bronze doors that stood open to the weather like those of a barn and the valet handed me out of the carriage on to the scarred tiles of the great hall itself, into the odorous warmth of a stable, sweet with hay, acrid with horse dung. An equine chorus of neighings and soft drummings of hooves broke out beneath the tall roof, where the beams were scabbed with last summer's swallows' nests; a dozen gracile muzzles lifted from their mangers and turned towards us, ears erect. The Beast had given his horses the use of the dining room. The walls were painted, aptly enough, with a fresco of horses, dogs and men in a wood where fruit and blossom grew on the bough together.

The valet tweaked politely at my sleeve. Milord is waiting.

Gaping doors and broken windows let the wind in everywhere. We mounted one staircase after another, our feet clopping on the marble. Through archways and open doors, I glimpsed suites of vaulted chambers opening one out of another like systems of Chinese boxes into the infinite complexity of the innards of the place. He and I and the wind were the only things stirring; and all the furniture was under dust sheets, the chandeliers bundled up in cloth, pictures taken from their hooks and propped with their faces to the walls as if their master could not bear to look at them. The palace was dismantled, as if its owner were about to move house or had never properly moved in; The Beast had chosen to live in an uninhabited place.

The valet darted me a reassuring glance from his brown, eloquent eyes, yet a glance with so much queer superciliousness in it that it did not comfort me, and went bounding ahead of me on his bandy legs, softly chattering to himself. I held my head high and followed him; but for all my pride, my heart was heavy.

Milord has his eyrie high above the house, a small, stifling, darkened room; he keeps his shutters locked at noon. I was out of breath by the time we reached it and returned to him the silence with which he greeted me. I will not smile. He cannot smile.

In his rarely disturbed privacy, The Beast wears a garment of Ottoman design, a loose, dull purple gown with gold embroidery round the neck that falls from his shoulders to conceal his feet. The feet of the chair he sits in are handsomely clawed. He hides his hands in his ample sleeves. The artificial masterpiece of his face appals me. A small fire in a small grate. A rushing wind rattles the shutters.

The valet coughed. To him fell the delicate task of transmitting to me his master's wishes.

'My master –'

A stick fell in the grate. It made a mighty clatter in that dreadful silence, the valet started, lost his place in his speech, began again.

'My master has but one desire.'

The thick, rich, wild scent with which Milord had soaked himself the previous evening hangs all about us, ascends in cursive blue from the smoke hole of a precious Chinese pot.

'He wishes only –'

Now, in the face of my impassivity, the valet twittered, his ironic composure gone, for the desire of a master, however trivial, may yet sound unbearably insolent in the mouth of a servant and his role of go between clearly caused him a good deal of embarrassment. He gulped; he swallowed, at last contrived to unleash an unpunctuated flood.

'My master's sole desire is to see the pretty young lady unclothed nude without her dress and that only for the one time after which she will be returned to her father undamaged with bankers' orders for the sum which he lost to my master at cards and also a number of fine presents such as furs, jewels and horses –'

I remained standing. During this interview, my eyes were level with those inside the mask that now evaded mine as if, to his credit, he was ashamed of his own request even as his mouthpiece made it for him. *Agitato, molto agitato*, the valet wrung his white-gloved hands.

'Desnuda —'

I could scarcely believe my ears. I let out a raucous guffaw; no young lady laughs like that! my old nurse used to remonstrate. But I did. And do. At the clamour of my heartless mirth, the valet danced backwards with perturbation, palpitating his fingers as if attempting to wrench them off, expostulating, wordlessly pleading. I felt that I owed it to him to make my reply in as exquisite a Tuscan as I could master.

'You may put me in a windowless room, sir, and I promise you I will pull my skirt up to my waist, ready for you. But there must be a sheet over my face, to hide it; though the sheet must be laid over me so lightly that it will not choke me. So I shall be covered completely from the waist upwards, and no lights. There you can visit me once, sir, and only the once. After that I must be driven directly to the city and deposited in the public square, in front of the church. If you wish to give me money, then I should be pleased to receive it. But I must stress that you should give me only the same amount of money that you would give to any other woman in such circumstances. However, if you choose not to give me a present, then that is your right.'

How pleased I was to see I struck The Beast to the heart! For, after a baker's dozen heart-beats, one single tear swelled, glittering, at the corner of the masked eye. A tear! A tear, I hoped, of shame. The tear trembled for a moment on an edge of painted bone, then tumbled down the painted cheek to fall, with an abrupt tinkle, on the tiled floor.

The valet, ticking and clucking to himself, hastily ushered me out of the room. A mauve cloud of his master's perfume billowed out into the chill corridor with us and dissipated itself on the spinning winds.

A cell had been prepared for me, a veritable cell, windowless, airless, lightless, in the viscera of the palace. The valet lit a lamp for me; a narrow bed, a dark cupboard with fruit and flowers carved on it bulked out of the gloom.

'I shall twist a noose out of my bed linen and hang myself with it,' I said.

'Oh, no,' said the valet, fixing upon me wide and suddenly melancholy eyes. 'Oh, no, you will not. You are a woman of honour.'

And what was *he* doing in my bedroom, this jigging caricature of a man? Was he to be my warder until I submitted to The Beast's whim or he to mine? Am I in such reduced circumstances that I may not have a lady's maid? As if in reply to my unspoken demand, the valet clapped his hands.

'To assuage your loneliness, madame . . .'

A knocking and clattering behind the door of the cupboard; the door swings open and out glides a soubrette from an operetta, with glossy, nut-brown curls, rosy cheeks, blue, rolling eyes; it takes me a moment to recognise her, in her little cap, her white stockings, her frilled petticoats. She carries a looking glass in one hand and a powder puff in the other and there is a musical box where her heart should be; she tinkles as she rolls towards me on her tiny wheels.

'Nothing human lives here,' said the valet.

My maid halted, bowed; from a split seam at the side of her bodice protrudes the handle of a key. She is a marvellous machine, the most delicately balanced system of cords and pulleys in the world.

'We have dispensed with servants,' the valet said. 'We surround ourselves instead, for utility and pleasure, with simulacra and find it no less convenient than do most gentlemen.'

This clockwork twin of mine halted before me, her bowels churning out a settecento minuet, and offered me the bold carnation of her smile. Click, click – she raises her arm and busily dusts my cheeks with pink, powdered chalk that makes me cough, then thrusts towards me her little mirror.

I saw within it not my own face but that of my father, as if I had put on his face when I arrived at The Beast's palace as the discharge of his debt. What, you self-deluding fool, are you crying still? And drunk, too. He tossed back his grappa and hurled the tumbler away.

Seeing my astonished fright, the valet took the mirror away from me, breathed on it, polished it with the ham of his gloved fist, handed it back to me. Now all I saw was myself, haggard from a sleepless night, pale enough to need my maid's supply of rouge.

I heard the key turn in the heavy door and the valet's footsteps patter down the stone passage. Meanwhile, my double continued to powder the air, emitting her jangling tune but, as it turned out, she was not inexhaustible; soon she was powdering more and yet more languorously, her metal heart slowed in imitation of fatigue, her musical box ran down until the notes separated themselves out of the tune and plopped like single raindrops and, as if sleep had overtaken her, at last she moved no longer. As she succumbed to sleep, I had no option but to do so too. I dropped on the narrow bed as if felled.

Time passed but I do not know how much; then the valet woke me with rolls and honey. I gestured the tray away but he set it down firmly beside the lamp and took from it a little shagreen box, which he offered to me.

I turned away my head.

'Oh, my lady!' Such hurt cracked his high-pitched voice! He dextrously unfastened the gold clasp; on a bed of crimson velvet lay a single diamond earring, perfect as a tear.

I snapped the box shut and tossed it into a corner. This sudden, sharp movement must have disturbed the mechanism of the doll; she jerked her arm almost as if to reprimand me, letting out a rippling fart of gavotte. Then she was still again.

'Very well,' said the valet, put out. And indicated it was time for me to visit my host again. He did not let me wash or comb my hair. There was so little natural light in the interior of the palace that I could not tell whether it was day or night.

You would not think the Beast had budged an inch since I last saw him; he sat in his huge chair, with his hands in his sleeves, and the heavy air never moved. I might have slept an hour, a night, or a month, but his sculptured calm, the stifling air remained just as it had been. The incense rose from the pot, still traced the same signature on the air. The same fire burned.

Take off my clothes for you, like a ballet girl? Is that all you want of me?

'The sight of a young lady's skin that no man has seen before –' stammered the valet.

I wished I'd rolled in the hay with every lad on my father's farm, to disqualify myself from this humiliating bargain. That he should want so little was the reason why I could not give it; I did not need to speak for The Beast to understand me.

A tear came from his other eye. And then he moved; he buried his cardboard carnival head with its ribboned weight of false hair in, I would say, his arms; he withdrew his, I might say, hands from his sleeves and I saw his furred pads, his excoriating claws.

The dropped tear caught upon his fur and shone. And in my room for hours I heard those paws pad back and forth outside my door.

When the valet arrived again with his silver salver, I had a pair of diamond earrings of the finest water in the world; I threw the other into the corner where the first one lay. The valet twittered with aggrieved regret but did not offer to lead me to The Beast again. Instead, he smiled ingratiatingly and confided: 'My master, he say: invite the young lady to go riding.'

'What's this?'

He briskly mimicked the action of a gallop and, to my amazement, tunelessly croaked: 'Tantivy! tantivy! a-hunting we will go!'

'I'll run away, I'll ride to the city.'

'Oh, no,' he said. 'Are you not a woman of honour?'

He clapped his hands and my maidservant clicked and jangled into the imitation of life. She rolled towards the cupboard where she had come from and reached inside it to fetch out over her synthetic arm my riding habit. Of all things. My very own riding habit, that I'd left behind me in a trunk in a loft in the country house outside Petersburg that we'd lost long ago, before, even, we set out on this wild pilgrimage to the cruel South. Either the very riding habit my old nurse had sewn for me or else a copy of it perfect to the lost button on the right sleeve, the ripped hem held up with a pin. I turned the worn cloth about in my hands, looking for a clue. The wind that sprinted through the palace made the door tremble in its frame; had the north wind blown my garments across Europe to me? At home, the bear's son directed the winds at his pleasure; what democracy of magic held this palace and the fir forest in common? Or, should I be prepared to accept it as proof of the axiom my father had drummed into me: that, if you have enough money, anything is possible?

'Tantivy,' suggested the now twinkling valet, evidently charmed at the pleasure mixed with my bewilderment. The clockwork maid held my jacket out to me and I allowed myself to shrug into it as if reluctantly, although I was half mad to get out into the open air, away from this deathly palace, even in such company.

The doors of the hall let the bright day in; I saw that it was morning. Our horses, saddled and bridled, beasts in bondage, were waiting for us, striking sparks from the tiles with their impatient hooves while their stablemates lolled at ease among the straw, conversing with one another in the mute speech of horses. A pigeon or two, feathers puffed to keep out the cold, strutted about, pecking at ears of corn. The little black gelding who had brought me here greeted me with a ringing neigh that resonated inside the mist roof as in a sounding box and I knew he was meant for me to ride.

I always adored horses, noblest of creatures, such wounded sensitivity in their wise eyes, such rational restraint of energy at their high-strung hindquarters. I lirruped and hurrumphed to my shining black companion and he acknowledged my greeting with a kiss on the forehead from his soft lips. There was a little shaggy pony nuzzling away at the *trompe l'oeil* foliage beneath the hooves of the painted horses on the wall, into whose saddle the valet sprang with a flourish as of the circus. Then The Beast wrapped in a black fur-lined cloak, came to heave himself aloft a grave grey mare. No natural horseman he; he clung to her mane like a shipwrecked sailor to a spar.

Cold, that morning, yet dazzling with the sharp winter sunlight that wounds the retina. There was a scurrying wind about that seemed to go with us, as if the masked, immense one who did not speak carried it inside his cloak and let it out at his pleasure, for it stirred the horses' manes but did not lift the lowland mists.

A bereft landscape in the sad browns and sepias of winter lay all about us, the marshland drearily protracting itself towards the wide river. Those decapitated willows. Now and then, the swoop of a bird, its irreconcilable cry.

A profound sense of strangeness slowly began to possess me. I knew my two companions were not, in any way, as other men, the simian retainer and the master for whom he spoke, the one with clawed forepaws who was in a plot with the witches who let the winds out of their knotted handkerchiefs up towards the Finnish border. I knew they lived according to a different logic than I had done until my father abandoned me to the wild beasts by his human carelessness. This knowledge gave me a certain fearfulness still; but, I would say, not much . . . I was a young girl, a virgin, and therefore men denied me rationality just as they denied it to all those who were not exactly like themselves, in all their unreason. If I could see not one single soul in that wilderness of desolation all around me, then the six of us – mounts and riders, both – could boast amongst us not one soul, either, since all the best religions in the world state categorically that not beasts nor women were equipped with the flimsy, insubstantial things when the good Lord opened the gates of Eden and let Eve and her familiars tumble out. Understand, then, that though I would not say I privately engaged in metaphysical speculation as we rode through the reedy approaches to the river, I certainly meditated on the nature of my own state, how I had been bought and sold, passed from hand to hand. That clockwork girl who powdered my cheeks for me; had I not been allotted only the same kind of imitative life amongst men that the doll-maker had given her?

Yet, as to the true nature of the being of this clawed magus who rode his pale horse in a style that made me recall how Kublai Khan's leopards went out hunting on horseback, of that I had no notion.

We came to the bank of the river that was so wide we could not see across it, so still with winter that it scarcely seemed to flow. The horses lowered their heads to drink. The valet cleared his throat, about to speak; we were in a place of perfect privacy, beyond a brake of winter-bare rushes, a hedge of reeds.

'If you will not let him see you without your clothes –'

I involuntarily shook my head –

'– you must, then, prepare yourself for the sight of my master, naked.'

The river broke on the pebbles with a diminishing sigh. My composure deserted me; all at once I was on the brink of panic. I did not think that I could bear the sight of him, whatever he was. The mare raised her dripping muzzle and looked at me keenly, as if urging me. The river broke again at my feet. I was far from home.

'You,' said the valet, 'must.'

When I saw how scared he was I might refuse, I nodded.

The reed bowed down in a sudden snarl of wind that brought with it a gust of the heavy odour of his disguise. The valet held out his master's cloak to screen him from me as he removed the mask. The horses stirred.

The tiger will never lie down with the lamb; he acknowledges no pact that is not reciprocal. The lamb must learn to run with the tigers.

A great, feline, tawny shape whose pelt was barred with a savage geometry of bars the colour of burned wood. His domed, heavy head, so terrible he must hide it. How subtle the muscles, how profound the tread. The annihilating vehemence of his eyes, like twin suns.

I felt my breast ripped apart as if I suffered a marvellous wound.

The valet moved forward as if to cover up his master now the girl had acknowledged him, but I said: 'No.' The tiger sat still as a heraldic beast, in the pact he had made with his own ferocity to do me no harm. He was far larger than I could have imagined. From the poor, shabby things I'd seen once, in the Czar's menagerie at Petersburg, the golden fruit of their eyes dimming, withering in the far North of captivity. Nothing about him reminded me of humanity.

I therefore, shivering, now unfastened my jacket, to show him I would do him no harm. Yet I was clumsy and blushed a little, for no man had seen me naked and I was a proud girl. Pride it was, not shame, that thwarted my fingers so; and a certain trepidation lest this frail little article of human upholstery before him might not be, in itself, grand enough to satisfy his expectations of us, since those, for all I knew, might have grown infinite during the endless time he had been waiting. The wind clattered in the rushes, purled and eddied in the river.

I showed his grave silence my white skin, my red nipples, and the horses turned their heads to watch me, also, as if they, too, were courteously curious as to the fleshly nature of women. Then the Beast lowered his massive head; Enough! said the valet with a gesture. The wind died down. All was still again.

Then they went off together, the valet on his pony, the tiger running before him like a hound, and I walked along the river bank for a while. I felt I was at liberty for the first time in my life. Then the winter sun began to tarnish, a few flakes of snow drifted from the darkening sky and, when I returned to the horses, I found The Beast mounted again on his grey mare, cloaked and masked and once more, to all appearances, a man, while the valet had a fine catch of waterfowl dangling from his hand and the corpse of a young roebuck slung behind his saddle. I climbed up on the black gelding in silence and so we returned to the palace as the snow fell more and more heavily, obscuring the tracks that we had left behind us.

The valet did not return me to my cell but, instead, to an elegant, if old-fashioned boudoir with sofas of faded pink brocade, a jinn's treasury of Oriental carpets, tintinnabulation of cut-glass chandeliers. Candles in antlered holders struck rainbows from the prismatic hearts of my diamond earrings, that lay on my new dressing table at which my attentive maid stood ready with her powder puff and mirror. Intending to fix the ornaments in my ears, I took the looking glass from her hand, but it was in the midst of one of its magic fits again and I did not see my own face in it but that of my father; at first I thought he smiled at me. Then I saw he was smiling with pure gratification.

He sat, I saw, in the parlour of our lodgings, at the very table where he had lost me, but now he was busily engaged in counting out a tremendous pile of banknotes. My father's circumstances had changed already; well-shaven, neatly barbered, smart new clothes. A frosted glass of sparkling wine sat convenient to his hand beside an ice bucket. The Beast had clearly paid cash on the nail for his glimpse of my bosom and paid up promptly, as if it had not been a sight I might have died of showing. Then I saw my father's trunks were packed, ready for departure. Could he so easily leave me here?

There was a note on the table with the money, in a fine hand. I could read it quite clearly. 'The young lady will arrive immediately.' Some harlot with whom he'd briskly negotiated a liaison on the strength of his spoils? Not at all. For, at that moment, the valet knocked at my door to announce that I might leave the palace at any time hereafter, and he bore over his arm a handsome sable cloak, my very own little gratuity, The Beast's morning gift, in which he proposed to pack me up and send me off.

When I looked at the mirror again, my father had disappeared and all I saw was a pale, hollow-eyed girl whom I scarcely recognised. The valet asked politely when he should prepare the carriage, as if he did not doubt that I would leave with my booty at the first opportunity while my maid, whose face was no longer the spit of my own, continued bonnily to beam. I will dress her in my own clothes, wind her up, send her back to perform the part of my father's daughter.

'Leave me alone,' I said to the valet.

He did not need to lock the door, now. I fixed the earrings in my ears. They were very heavy. Then I took off my riding habit, left it where it lay on the floor. But, when I got down to my shift, my arms dropped to my sides. I was unaccustomed to nakedness. I was so unused to my own skin that to take off all my clothes involved a kind of flaying. I thought The Beast had wanted a little thing compared with what I was prepared to give him; but it is not natural for humankind to go naked, not since first we hid our loins with fig leaves. He had demanded the abominable. I felt as much atrocious pain as if I was stripping off my own underpelt and the smiling girl stood poised in the oblivion of her balked simulation of life, watching me peel down to the cold, white meat of contract and, if she did not see me, then so much more like the market place, where the eyes that watch you take no account of your existence.

And it seemed my entire life, since I had left the North, had passed under the indifferent gaze of eyes like hers.

Then I was flinching stark, except for his irreproachable tears.

I huddled in the furs I must return to him, to keep me from the lacerating winds that raced along the corridors. I knew the way to his den without the valet to guide me.

No response to my tentative rap on his door.

Then the wind blew the valet whirling along the passage. He must have decided that, if one should go naked, then all should go naked; without his livery, he revealed himself, as I had suspected, a delicate creature, covered with silken moth-grey fur, brown fingers supple as leather, chocolate muzzle, the gentlest creature in the world. He gibbered a little to see my fine furs and jewels as if I were dressed up for the opera and, with a great deal of tender ceremony, removed the sables from my shoulders. The sables thereupon resolved themselves into a pack of black squeaking rats that rattled immediately down the stairs on their hard little feet and were lost to sight.

The valet bowed me inside The Beast's room.

The purple dressing gown, the mask, the wig, were laid out on his chair; a glove was planted on each arm. The empty house of his appearance was ready for him but he had abandoned it. There was a reek of fur and piss; the incense pot lay broken in pieces on the floor. Half-burned sticks were scattered from the extinguished fire. A candle stuck by its own grease to the mantelpiece lit two narrow flames in the pupils of the tiger's eyes.

He was pacing backwards and forwards, backwards and forwards, the tip of his heavy tail twitching as he paced out the length and breadth of his imprisonment between the gnawed and bloody bones.

He will gobble you up.

Nursery fears made flesh and sinew; earliest and most archaic of fears, fear of devourment. The beast and his carnivorous bed of bone and I, white, shaking, raw, approaching him as if offering, in myself, the key to a peaceable kingdom in which his appetite need not be my extinction.

He went still as stone. He was far more frightened of me than I was of him.

I squatted on the wet straw and stretched out my hand. I was now within the field of force of his golden eyes. He growled at the back of his throat, lowered his head, sank on to his forepaws, snarled, showed me his red gullet, his yellow teeth. I never moved. He snuffled the air, as if to smell my fear; he could not.

Slowly, slowly he began to drag his heavy, gleaming weight across the floor towards me.

A tremendous throbbing, as of the engine that makes the earth turn, filled the little room; he had begun to purr.

The sweet thunder of this purr shook the old walls, made the shutters batter the windows until they burst apart and let in the white light of the snowy moon. Tiles came crashing down from the roof; I heard them fall into the courtyard far below. The reverberations of his purring rocked the foundations of the house, the walls began to dance. I thought: 'It will all fall, everything will disintegrate.'

He dragged himself closer and closer to me, until I felt the harsh velvet of his head against my hand, then a tongue, abrasive as sandpaper. 'He will lick the skin off me!'

And each stroke of his tongue ripped off skin after successive skin, all the skins of a life in the world, and left behind a nascent patina of shining hairs. My earrings turned back to water and trickled down my shoulders; I shrugged the drops off my beautiful fur.

*Stories
to remind you that
love conquers all*

The Story of an Hour
by
Kate Chopin

Kate Chopin was born in 1850 in Missouri. She married Oscar
Chopin in 1870 and gave birth to six children before she was
28. Her husband died of complications arising from swamp-
fever in 1883 and her mother died a year later. Chopin's
physician suggested she turn to writing as a way of dealing
with her grief and anger, as well as providing a source of
income for the young family. By the early 1890s, she was
writing short stories, articles, and translations but in 1899,
her second novel, *The Awakening*, was published to widespread
criticism from male reviewers. Chopin, deeply discouraged by
the criticism, returned to short story writing. In 1900 she
wrote *The Gentleman from New Orleans*, and that same year
she was listed in the first edition of *Who's Who*. She died in
1904.

The Story of an Hour

KNOWING THAT Mrs Mallard was afflicted with a heart trouble, great care was taken to break to her as gently as possible the news of her husband's death.

It was her sister Josephine who told her, in broken sentences; veiled hints that revealed in half concealing. Her husband's friend Richards was there, too, near her. It was he who had been in the newspaper office when intelligence of the railroad disaster was received, with Brently Mallard's name leading the list of 'killed.' He had only taken the time to assure himself of its truth by a second telegram, and had hastened to forestall any less careful, less tender friend in bearing the sad message.

She did not hear the story as many women have heard the same, with a paralyzed inability to accept its significance. She wept at once, with sudden, wild abandonment, in her sister's arms. When the storm of grief had spent itself she went away to her room alone. She would have no one follow her.

There stood, facing the open window, a comfortable, roomy armchair. Into this she sank, pressed down by a physical exhaustion that haunted her body and seemed to reach into her soul.

She could see in the open square before her house the tops of trees that were all aquiver with the new spring life. The delicious breath of rain was in the air. In the street below a peddler was crying his wares. The notes of a distant song which some one was singing reached her faintly, and countless sparrows were twittering in the eaves. There were patches of blue sky showing here and there through the clouds that had met and piled one above the other in the west facing her window.

She sat with her head thrown back upon the cushion of the chair, quite motionless, except when a sob came up into her throat and shook her, as a child who has cried itself to sleep continues to sob in its dreams.

She was young, with a fair, calm face, whose lines bespoke repression and even a certain strength. But now there was a dull stare in her eyes, whose gaze was fixed away off yonder on one of those patches of blue sky. It was not a glance of reflection, but rather indicated a suspension of intelligent thought.

There was something coming to her and she was waiting for it, fearfully. What was it? She did not know; it was too subtle and elusive to name. But she felt it, creeping out of the sky, reaching toward her through the sounds, the scents, the color that filled the air.

Now her bosom rose and fell tumultuously. She was beginning to recognize this thing that was approaching to possess her, and she was striving to beat it back with her will – as powerless as her two white slender hands would have been. When she abandoned herself a little whispered word escaped her slightly parted lips. She said it over and over under her breath: 'free, free, free!' The vacant stare and the look of terror that had followed it went from her eyes. They stayed keen and bright. Her pulses beat fast, and the coursing blood warmed and relaxed every inch of her body. She did not stop to ask if it were or were not a monstrous joy that held her. A clear and exalted perception enabled her to dismiss the suggestion as trivial.

She knew that she would weep again when she saw the kind, tender hands folded in death; the face that had never looked save with love upon her, fixed and gray and dead. But she saw beyond that bitter moment a long procession of years to come that would belong to her absolutely. And she opened and spread her arms out to them in welcome. There would be no one to live for during those coming years; she would live for herself. There would be no powerful will bending hers in that blind persistence with which men and women believe they have a right to impose a private will upon a fellow-creature. A kind intention or a cruel intention made the act seem no less a crime as she looked upon it in that brief moment of illumination.

And yet she had loved him – sometimes. Often she had not. What did it matter! What could love, the unsolved mystery, count for in face of this possession of self-assertion which she suddenly recognized as the strongest impulse of her being!

'Free! Body and soul free!' she kept whispering.

Josephine was kneeling before the closed door with her lips to the keyhole, imploring for admission. 'Louise, open the door! I beg, open the door – you will make yourself ill. What are you doing, Louise? For heaven's sake open the door.'

'Go away. I am not making myself ill.' No; she was drinking in a very elixir of life through that open window. Her fancy was running riot along those days ahead of her. Spring days, and summer days, and all sorts of days that would be her own. She breathed a quick prayer that life might be long. It was only yesterday she had thought with a shudder that life might be long.

She arose at length and opened the door to her sister's importunities. There was a feverish triumph in her eyes, and she carried herself unwittingly like a goddess of Victory. She clasped her sister's waist, and together they descended the stairs. Richards stood waiting for them at the bottom.

Someone was opening the front door with a latchkey. It was Brently Mallard who entered, a little travel-stained, composedly carrying his grip-sack and umbrella. He had been far from the scene of the accident, and did not even know there had been one. He stood amazed at Josephine's piercing cry; at Richards' quick motion to screen him from the view of his wife.

But Richards was too late.

When the doctors came they said she had died of heart disease – of the joy that kills.

The Half-Brothers
by
Elizabeth Gaskell

Elizabeth Stevenson was born in London on 29 September 1810, the daughter of a Unitarian minister, and, after her mother's early death, was raised by an aunt who lived in Knutsford in Cheshire. She married William Gaskell, a Unitarian minister, in 1832 and the death of their only son inspired her to write her first novel, *Mary Barton*, which was published anonymously in 1848. It was an immediate success, winning the praise of Charles Dickens and Thomas Carlyle. Dickens invited her to contribute to his magazine, *Household Words*, where her next major work, *Cranford*, appeared in 1853. *North and South* was published the following year and *Wives and Daughters*, her last novel, was published after her death in 1865.

The Half-Brothers

MY MOTHER WAS twice married. She never spoke of her first husband, and it is only from other people that I have learnt what little I know about him. I believe she was scarcely seventeen when she was married to him: and he was barely one-and-twenty. He rented a small farm up in Cumberland, somewhere towards the sea-coast; but he was perhaps too young and inexperienced to have the charge of land and cattle: anyhow, his affairs did not prosper, and he fell into ill health, and died of consumption before they had been three years man and wife, leaving my mother a young widow of twenty, with a little child only just able to walk, and the farm on her hands for four years more by the lease, with half the stock on it dead, or sold off one by one to pay the more pressing debts, and with no money to purchase more, or even to buy the provisions needed for the small consumption of every day. There was another child coming, too; and sad and sorry, I believe, she was to think of it. A dreary winter she must have had in her lonesome dwelling, with never another near it for miles around; her sister came to bear her company, and they two planned and plotted how to make every penny they could raise go as far as possible. I can't tell you how it happened that my little sister, whom I never saw, came to sicken and die; but, as if my poor mother's cup was not full enough, only a fortnight before Gregory was born the little girl took ill of scarlet fever, and in a week she lay dead. My mother was, I believe, just stunned with this last blow. My aunt has told me that she did not cry; aunt Fanny would have been thankful if she had; but she sat holding the poor wee lassie's hand and looking in her pretty, pale, dead face, without so much as shedding a tear. And it was all the same, when they had to take her away to be buried. She just kissed the child, and sat her down in the window-seat to watch the little black train of people (neighbours – my aunt, and one far-off cousin, who were all the friends they could muster) go winding away amongst the snow, which had fallen thinly over the country the night before. When my aunt came back from the funeral, she found my mother in the same place, and as dry-eyed as ever. So she continued until after Gregory was born; and, somehow, his coming seemed to loosen the tears, and she cried day and night, till my aunt and the other watcher looked at each other in dismay, and would fain have stopped her if they had but known how. But she bade them let her alone, and not be over-anxious, for every drop she shed eased her brain, which had been in a terrible state before for want of the power to cry. She seemed after that to think of nothing but her new little baby; she had hardly appeared to remember either her husband or her little daughter that lay dead in Brigham churchyard – at least so aunt Fanny said, but she was a great talker, and my mother was very silent by nature, and I think aunt Fanny may have been mistaken in believing that my mother never thought of her husband and child just because she never spoke about them. Aunt Fanny was older than my mother, and had a way of treating her like a child; but, for all that, she was a kind, warm-hearted creature, who thought more of her sister's welfare than she did of her own and it was on her bit of money that they principally lived, and on what the two could earn by working for the great Glasgow sewing-merchants. But by-and-by my mother's eye-sight began to fail. It was not that she was exactly blind, for she could see well enough to guide herself about the house, and to do a good deal of domestic work; but she could no longer do fine sewing and earn money. It must have been with the heavy crying she had had in her day, for she was but a young creature at this time, and as pretty a young woman, I have heard people say, as any on the country side. She took it sadly to heart that she could no longer gain anything towards the keep of herself and her child. My aunt Fanny would fain have persuaded her that she had enough to do in managing their cottage and minding Gregory; but my mother knew that they were pinched, and that aunt Fanny herself had not as much to eat, even of the commonest kind of food, as she could have done with; and as for Gregory, he was not a strong lad, and needed, not more food – for he always had enough, whoever went short – but better nourishment, and more flesh-meat. One day – it was aunt Fanny who told me all this about my poor mother, long after her death – as the sisters were sitting together, aunt Fanny working, and my mother hushing Gregory to sleep, William Preston, who was afterwards my father, came in. He was reckoned an old bachelor; I suppose he was long past forty, and he was one of the wealthiest farmers thereabouts, and had known my grandfather well, and my mother and my aunt in their more prosperous days. He sat down, and began to twirl his hat by way of being agreeable; my aunt Fanny talked, and he listened and looked at my mother. But he said very little, either on that visit, or on many another that he paid before he spoke out what had been the real purpose of his calling so often all along, and from the very first time he came to their house. One Sunday, however, my aunt Fanny stayed away from church, and took care of the child, and my mother went alone. When she came back, she ran straight upstairs, without going into the kitchen to look at Gregory or speak any word to her sister, and aunt Fanny heard her cry as if her heart was breaking; so she went up and scolded her right well through the bolted door, till at last she got her to open it. And then she threw herself on my aunt's neck, and told her that William Preston had asked her to marry him, and had promised to take good charge of her boy, and to let him want for nothing, neither in the way of keep nor of education, and that she had consented. Aunt Fanny was a good deal shocked at this; for, as I have said, she had often thought that my mother had forgotten her first husband very quickly, and now here was proof positive of it, if she could so soon think of marrying again. Besides as aunt Fanny used to say, she herself would have been a far more suitable match for a man of William Preston's age than Helen, who, though she was a widow, had not seen her four-and-twentieth summer. However, as aunt Fanny said, they had not asked her advice; and there was much to be said on the other side of the question. Helen's eyesight would never be good for much again, and as William Preston's wife she would never need to do anything, if she chose to sit with her hands before her; and a boy was a great charge to a widowed mother; and now there would be a decent steady man to see after him. So, by-and-by, aunt Fanny seemed to take a brighter view of the marriage than did my mother herself, who hardly ever looked up, and never smiled after the day when she promised William Preston to be his wife. But much as she had loved Gregory before, she seemed to love him more now. She was continually talking to him when they were alone, though he was far too young to understand her moaning words, or give her any comfort, except by his caresses.

At last William Preston and she were wed; and she went to be mistress of a well-stocked house, not above half-an-hour's walk from where aunt Fanny lived. I believe she did all that she could to please my father; and a more dutiful wife, I have heard him himself say, could never have been. But she did not love him, and he soon found it out. She loved Gregory, and she did not love him. Perhaps, love would have come in time, if he had been patient enough to wait; but it just turned him sour to see how her eye brightened and her colour came at the sight of that little child, while for him who had given her so much, she had only gentle words as cold as ice. He got to taunt her with the difference in her manner, as if that would bring love: and he took a positive dislike to Gregory, – he was so jealous of the ready love that always gushed out like a spring of fresh water when he came near. He wanted her to love him more, and perhaps that was all well and good; but he wanted her to love her child less, and that was an evil wish. One day, he gave way to his temper, and cursed and swore at Gregory, who had got into some mischief, as children will; my mother made some excuse for him; my father said it was hard enough to have to keep another man's child, without having it perpetually held up in its naughtiness by his wife, who ought to be always in the same mind that he was; and so from little they got to more; and the end of it was, that my mother took to her bed before her time, and I was born that very day. My father was glad, and proud, and sorry, all in a breath; glad and proud that a son was born to him; and sorry for his poor wife's state, and to think how his angry words had brought it on. But he was a man who liked better to be angry than sorry, so he soon found out that it was all Gregory's fault, and owed him an additional grudge for having hastened my birth. He had another grudge against him before long. My mother began to sink the day after I was born. My father sent to Carlisle for doctors, and would have coined his heart's blood into gold to save her, if that could have been; but it could not. My aunt Fanny used to say sometimes, that she thought that Helen did not wish to live, and so just let herself die away without trying to take hold on life; but when I questioned her, she owned that my mother did all the doctors bade her do, with the same sort of uncomplaining patience with which she had acted through life. One of her last requests was to have Gregory laid in her bed by my side, and then she made him take hold of my little hand. Her husband came in while she was looking at us so, and when he bent tenderly over her to ask her how she felt now, and seemed to gaze on us two little half-brothers, with a grave sort of kindness, she looked up in his face and smiled, almost her first smile at him; and such a sweet smile! as more besides aunt Fanny have said. In an hour she was dead. Aunt Fanny came to live with us. It was the best thing that could be done. My father would have been glad to return to his old mode of bachelor life, but what could he do with two little children? He needed a woman to take care of him, and who so fitting as his wife's elder sister? So she had the charge of me from my birth; and for a time I was weakly, as was but natural, and she was always beside me, night and day watching over me, and my father nearly as anxious as she. For his land had come down from father to son for more than three hundred years, and he would have cared for me merely as his flesh and blood that was to inherit the land after him. But he needed something to love, for all that, to most people, he was a stern, hard man, and he took to me as, I fancy, he had taken to no human being before – as he might have taken to my mother, if she had had no former life for him to be jealous of. I loved him back again right heartily. I loved all around me, I believe, for everybody was kind to me. After a time, I overcame my original weakness of constitution, and was just a bonny, strong-looking lad whom every passer-by noticed, when my father took me with him to the nearest town.

At home I was the darling of my aunt, the tenderly-beloved of my father, the pet and plaything of the old domestics, the 'young master' of the farm-labourers, before whom I played many a lordly antic, assuming a sort of authority which sat oddly enough, I doubt not, on such a baby as I was.

Gregory was three years older than I. Aunt Fanny was always kind to him in deed and in action, but she did not often think about him, she had fallen so completely into the habit of being engrossed by me, from the fact of my having come into her charge as a delicate baby. My father never got over his grudging dislike to his stepson, who had so innocently wrestled with him for the possession of my mother's heart. I mistrust me, too, that my father always considered him as the cause of my mother's death and my early delicacy; and utterly unreasonable as this may seem, I believe my father rather cherished his feeling of alienation to my brother as a duty, than strove to repress it. Yet not for the world would my father have grudged him anything that money could purchase. That was, as it were, in the bond when he had wedded my mother. Gregory was lumpish and loutish, awkward and ungainly, marring whatever he meddled in, and many a hard word and sharp scolding did he get from the people about the farm, who hardly waited till my father's back was turned before they rated the stepson. I am ashamed – my heart is sore to think how I fell into the fashion of the family, and slighted my poor orphan step-brother. I don't think I ever scouted him, or was wilfully ill-natured to him; but the habit of being considered in all things, and being treated as something uncommon

and superior, made me insolent in my prosperity, and I exacted more
than Gregory was always willing to grant, and then, irritated, I
sometimes repeated the disparaging words I had heard others use
with regard to him, without fully understanding their meaning.
Whether he did or not I cannot tell. I am afraid he did. He used
to turn silent and quiet – sullen and sulky, my father thought it:
stupid, aunt Fanny used to call it. But every one said he was stupid
and dull, and this stupidity and dullness grew upon him. He would
sit without speaking a word, sometimes, for hours; then my father
would bid him rise and do some piece of work, maybe, about the
farm. And he would take three or four tellings before he would go.
When we were sent to school, it was all the same. He could never
be made to remember his lessons; the schoolmaster grew weary of
scolding and flogging, and at last advised my father just to take him
away, and set him to some farm-work that might not be above his
comprehension. I think he was more gloomy and stupid than ever
after this, yet he was not a cross lad; he was patient and good-natured,
and would try to do a kind turn for any one, even if they had been
scolding or cuffing him not a minute before. But very often his
attempts at kindness ended in some mischief to the very people he
was trying to serve, owing to his awkward, ungainly ways. I suppose
I was a clever lad; at any rate, I always got plenty of praise; and
was, as we called it, the cock of the school. The schoolmaster said
I could learn anything I chose, but my father, who had no great
learning himself, saw little use in much for me, and took me away
betimes, and kept me with him about the farm. Gregory was made
into a kind of shepherd, receiving his training under old Adam, who
was nearly past his work. I think old Adam was almost the first
person who had a good opinion of Gregory. He stood to it that my
brother had good parts, though he did not rightly know how to bring
them out; and, for knowing the bearings of the Fells, he said he
had never seen a lad like him. My father would try to bring Adam
round to speak of Gregory's faults and shortcomings; but, instead
of that, he would praise him twice as much, as soon as he found
out what was my father's object.

One winter-time, when I was about sixteen, and Gregory nineteen, I was sent by my father on an errand to a place about seven miles distant by the road, but only about four by the Fells. He bade me return by the road, whichever way I took in going, for the evenings closed in early, and were often thick and misty; besides which, old Adam, now paralytic and bedridden, foretold a downfall of snow before long. I soon got to my journey's end, and soon had done my business; earlier by an hour, I thought, than my father had expected, so I took the decision of the way by which I would return into my own hands, and set off back again over the Fells, just as the first shades of evening began to fall. It looked dark and gloomy enough; but everything was so still that I thought I should have plenty of time to get home before the snow came down. Off I set at a pretty quick pace. But night came on quicker. The right path was clear enough in the day-time, although at several points two or three exactly similar diverged from the same place; but when there was a good light, the traveller was guided by the sight of distant objects, – a piece of rock, – a fall in the ground – which were quite invisible to me now. I plucked up a brave heart, however, and took what seemed to me the right road. It was wrong, nevertheless, and led me whither I knew not, but to some wild boggy moor where the solitude seemed painful, intense, as if never footfall of man had come thither to break the silence. I tried to shout – with the dimmest possible hope of being heard – rather to reassure myself by the sound of my own voice; but my voice came husky and short, and yet it dismayed me; it seemed so weird and strange, in that noiseless expanse of black darkness. Suddenly the air was filled thick with dusky flakes, my face and hands were wet with snow. It cut me off from the slightest knowledge of where I was, for I lost every idea of the direction from which I had come, so that I could not even retrace my steps; it hemmed me in, thicker, thicker, with a darkness that might be felt. The boggy soil on which I stood quaked under me if I remained long in one place, and yet I dared not move far. All my youthful hardiness seemed to leave me at once. I was on the point of crying, and only very shame seemed to keep it down. To save myself from shedding tears, I shouted – terrible, wild shouts for bare life they were. I turned sick as I paused to listen; no answering sound came but the unfeeling echoes. Only the noiseless, pitiless snow kept falling thicker, thicker – faster, faster! I was growing numb and sleepy. I tried to move about, but I dared not go far, for fear of the precipices which, I knew, abounded in certain places on the Fells. Now and then, I stood still and shouted again; but my voice was getting choked with tears, as I thought of the desolate helpless death I was to die, and how little they at home, sitting round the warm, red, bright fire, wotted what was become of me, – and how my poor father would grieve for me – it would surely kill him – it would break his heart, poor old man! Aunt Fanny too – was this to be the end of all her cares for me? I began to review my life in a strange kind of vivid dream, in which the various scenes of my few boyish years passed before me like visions. In a pang of agony, caused by such remembrance of my short life, I gathered up my strength and called out once more, a long, despairing, wailing cry, to which I had no hope of obtaining any answer, save from the echoes around, dulled as the sound might be by the thickened air. To my surprise I heard a cry – almost as long, as wild as mine – so wild that it seemed unearthly, and I almost thought it must be the voice of some of the mocking spirits of the Fells, about whom I had heard so many tales. My heart suddenly began to beat fast and loud. I could not reply for a minute or two. I nearly fancied I had lost the power of utterance. Just at this moment a dog barked. Was it Lassie's bark – my brother's collie? – an ugly enough brute, with a white, ill-looking face, that my father always kicked whenever he saw it, partly for its own demerits, partly because it belonged to my brother. On such occasions, Gregory would whistle Lassie away, and go off and sit with her in some outhouse. My father had once or twice been ashamed of himself, when the poor collie had yowled out with the suddenness of the pain, and had relieved himself of his self-reproach by blaming my brother, who, he said, had no notion of training a dog, and was enough to ruin any collie in Christendom with his stupid way of allowing them to lie by the kitchen fire. To all which Gregory would answer nothing, nor even seem to hear, but go on looking absent and moody.

Yes! there again! It was Lassie's bark! Now or never! I lifted up my voice and shouted 'Lassie! Lassie! for God's sake, Lassie!' Another moment, and the great white-faced Lassie was curving and gambolling with delight round my feet and legs, looking, however, up in my face with her intelligent, apprehensive eyes, as if fearing lest I might greet her with a blow, as I had done oftentimes before. But I cried with gladness, as I stooped down and patted her. My mind was sharing in my body's weakness, and I could not reason, but I knew that help was at hand. A grey figure came more and more distinctly out of the thick, close-pressing darkness. It was Gregory wrapped in his maud.

'Oh, Gregory!' said I, and I fell upon his neck, unable to speak another word. He never spoke much, and made me no answer for some little time. Then he told me we must move, we must walk for the dear life – we must find our road home, if possible; but we must move, or we should be frozen to death.

'Don't you know the way home?' asked I.

'I thought I did when I set out, but I am doubtful now. The snow blinds me, and I am feared that in moving about just now, I have lost the right gait homewards.'

He had his shepherd's staff with him, and by dint of plunging it before us at every step we took – clinging close to each other, we went on safely enough, as far as not falling down any of the steep rocks, but it was slow, dreary work. My brother, I saw, was more guided by Lassie and the way she took than anything else, trusting to her instinct. It was too dark to see far before us; but he called her back continually, and noted from what quarter she returned, and shaped our slow steps accordingly. But the tedious motion scarcely kept my very blood from freezing. Every bone, every fibre in my body seemed first to ache, and then to swell, and then to turn numb with the intense cold. My brother bore it better than I, from having been more out upon the hills. He did not speak, except to call Lassie. I strove to be brave, and not complain; but now I felt the deadly fatal sleep stealing over me.

'I can go no farther,' I said, in a drowsy tone. I remember I suddenly became dogged and resolved. Sleep I would, were it only for five minutes. If death were to be the consequence, sleep I would. Gregory stood still. I suppose, he recognised the peculiar phase of suffering to which I had been brought by the cold.

'It is of no use,' said he, as if to himself. 'We are no nearer home than we were when we started, as far as I can tell. Our only chance is in Lassie. Here! roll thee in my maud, lad, and lay thee down on this sheltered side of this bit of rock. Creep close under it, lad, and I'll lie by thee, and strive to keep the warmth in us. Stay! hast gotten aught about thee they'll know at home?'

I felt him unkind thus to keep me from slumber, but on his repeating the question, I pulled out my pocket-handkerchief, of some showy pattern, which Aunt Fanny had hemmed for me – Gregory took it, and tied it round Lassie's neck.

'Hie thee, Lassie, hie thee home!' And the white-faced ill-favoured brute was off like a shot in the darkness. Now I might lie down – now I might sleep. In my drowsy stupor I felt that I was being tenderly covered up by my brother; but what with I neither knew nor cared – I was too dull, too selfish, too numb to think and reason, or I might have known that in that bleak bare place there was nought to wrap me in, save what was taken off another. I was glad enough when he ceased his cares and lay down by me. I took his hand.

'Thou canst not remember, lad, how we lay together thus by our dying mother. She put thy small, wee hand in mine – I reckon she sees us now; and belike we shall soon be with her. Anyhow, God's will be done.'

'Dear Gregory,' I muttered, and crept nearer to him for warmth. He was talking still, and again about our mother, when I fell asleep. In an instant – or so it seemed – there were many voices about me – many faces hovering round me – the sweet luxury of warmth was stealing into every part of me. I was in my own little bed at home. I am thankful to say, my first word was 'Gregory?'

A look passed from one to another – my father's stern old face strove in vain to keep its sternness; his mouth quivered, his eyes filled slowly with unwonted tears.

'I would have given him half my land – I would have blessed him as my son, – oh God! I would have knelt at his feet, and asked him to forgive my hardness of heart.'

I heard no more. A whirl came through my brain, catching me back to death.

I came slowly to my consciousness, weeks afterwards. My father's hair was white when I recovered, and his hands shook as he looked into my face.

We spoke no more of Gregory. We could not speak of him; but he was strangely in our thoughts. Lassie came and went with never a word of blame; nay, my father would try to stroke her, but she shrank away; and he, as if reproved by the poor dumb beast, would sigh, and be silent and abstracted for a time.

Aunt Fanny – always a talker – told me all. How, on that fatal night, my father, – irritated by my prolonged absence, and probably more anxious than he cared to show, had been fierce and imperious, even beyond his wont, to Gregory; had upbraided him with his father's poverty, his own stupidity which made his services good for nothing – for so, in spite of the old shepherd, my father always chose to consider them. At last, Gregory had risen up, and whistled Lassie out with him – poor Lassie, crouching underneath his chair for fear of a kick or a blow. Some time before, there had been some talk between my father and my aunt respecting my return; and when aunt Fanny told me all this, she said she fancied that Gregory might have noticed the coming storm, and gone out silently to meet me. Three hours afterwards, when all were running about in wild alarm, not knowing whither to go in search of me – not even missing Gregory, or heeding his absence, poor fellow – poor, poor fellow! – Lassie came home, with my handkerchief tied round her neck. They knew and understood, and the whole strength of the farm was turned out to follow her, with wraps, and blankets, and brandy, and every thing that could be thought of. I lay in chilly sleep, but still alive, beneath the rock that Lassie guided them to. I was covered over with my brother's plaid, and his thick shepherd's coat was carefully wrapped round my feet. He was in his shirt-sleeves – his arm thrown over me – a quiet smile (he had hardly ever smiled in life) upon his still, cold face.

My father's last words were, 'God forgive me my hardness of heart towards the fatherless child!'

And what marked the depth of his feeling of repentance, perhaps more than all, considering the passionate love he bore my mother, was this: we found a paper of directions after his death, in which he desired that he might lie at the foot of the grave, in which, by his desire, poor Gregory had been laid with OUR MOTHER.

Mabel
by
W. Somerset Maugham

William Somerset Maugham was born in 1874 at the British Embassy in Paris, and lived in France until he was ten. He was educated at King's School, Canterbury, and at Heidelberg University. He spent some time at St. Thomas's Hospital studying medicine while writing in the evenings, and his first novel, *Liza of Lambeth*, was published in 1897. The first print run sold out in a matter of weeks and Maugham, by this stage qualified as a doctor, left medicine to become a full-time writer. He wrote short stories, novels and plays – in 1908 he had four plays running simultaneously in London – including *Of Human Bondage* (1915), *The Moon and Sixpence* (1919) and *The Razor's Edge* (1944). *Ashenden* (1918) is partly based on his experiences as a spy during the First World War. He died in 1965.

Mabel

I WAS AT PAGAN, in Burma, and from there I took the steamer
to Mandalay, but a couple of days before I got there, when the
boat tied up for the night at a riverside village, I made up my mind
to go ashore. The skipper told me that there was there a pleasant
little club in which I had only to make myself at home; they were
quite used to having strangers drop off like that from the steamer,
and the secretary was a very decent chap; I might even get a game
of bridge. I had nothing in the world to do, so I got into one of the
bullock-carts that were waiting at the landing-stage and was driven
to the club. There was a man sitting on the verandah and as I
walked up he nodded to me and asked whether I would have a
whisky and soda or a gin and bitters. The possibility that I would
have nothing at all did not even occur to him. I chose the longer
drink and sat down. He was a tall, thin, bronzed man, with a big
moustache, and he wore khaki shorts and a khaki shirt. I never
knew his name, but when we had been chatting a little while another
man came in who told me he was the secretary, and he addressed
my friend as George.

'Have you heard from your wife yet?' he asked him.

The other's eyes brightened.

'Yes, I had letters by this mail. She's having no end of a time.'

'Did she tell you not to fret?'

George gave a little chuckle, but was I mistaken in thinking that
there was in it the shadow of a sob?

'In point of fact she did. But that's easier said than done. Of course I know she wants a holiday, and I'm glad she should have it, but it's devilish hard on a chap.' He turned to me. 'You see, this is the first time I've ever been separated from my missus, and I'm like a lost dog without her.'

'How long have you been married?'

'Five minutes.'

The secretary of the club laughed.

'Don't be a fool, George. You've been married eight years.'

After we had talked for a little George, looking at his watch, said he must go and change his clothes for dinner and left us. The secretary watched him disappear into the night with a smile of not unkindly irony.

'We all ask him as much as we can now that he's alone,' he told me. 'He mopes so terribly since his wife went home.'

'It must be very pleasant for her to know that her husband is as devoted to her as all that.'

'Mabel is a remarkable woman.'

He called the boy and ordered more drinks. In this hospitable place they did not ask you if you would have anything; they took it for granted. Then he settled himself in his long chair and lit a cheroot. He told me the story of George and Mabel.

They became engaged when he was home on leave, and when he returned to Burma it was arranged that she should join him in six months. But one difficulty cropped up after another; Mabel's father died, the war came, George was sent to a district unsuitable for a white woman; so that in the end it was seven years before she was able to start. He made all arrangements for the marriage, which was to take place on the day of her arrival, and went down to Rangoon to meet her. On the morning on which the ship was due he borrowed a motor-car and drove along to the dock. He paced the quay.

Then, suddenly, without warning, his nerve failed him. He had not seen Mabel for seven years. He had forgotten what she was like. She was a total stranger. He felt a terrible sinking in the pit of his stomach and his knees began to wobble. He couldn't go through with it. He must tell Mabel that he was very sorry, but he couldn't, he really couldn't marry her. But how could a man tell a girl a thing like that when she had been engaged to him for seven years and had come six thousand miles to marry him? He hadn't the nerve for that either. George was seized with the courage of despair. There was a boat at the quay on the very point of starting for Singapore; he wrote a hurried letter to Mabel, and without a stick of luggage, just in the clothes he stood up in, leaped on board.

The letter Mabel received ran somewhat as follows:

Dearest Mabel, I have been suddenly called away on business and do not know when I shall be back. I think it would be much wiser if you returned to England. My plans are very uncertain. Your loving George.

But when he arrived at Singapore he found a cable waiting for him.

Quite understand. Don't worry. Love. Mabel.

Terror made him quick-witted.

'By Jove, I believe she's following me,' he said.

He telegraphed to the shipping-office at Rangoon and sure enough her name was on the passenger list of the ship that was now on its way to Singapore. There was not a moment to lose. He jumped on the train to Bangkok. But he was uneasy; she would have no difficulty in finding out that he had gone to Bangkok and it was just as simple for her to take the train as it had been for him. Fortunately there was a French tramp sailing next day for Saigon. He took it. At Saigon he would be safe; it would never occur to her that he had gone there; and if it did, surely by now she would have taken the hint. It is five days journey from Bangkok to Saigon and the boat is dirty, cramped and uncomfortable. He was glad to arrive and took a rickshaw to the hotel. He signed his name in the visitors' book and a telegram was immediately handed to him. It contained but two words: *Love. Mabel.* They were enough to make him break into a cold sweat.

'When is the next boat for Hong-Kong?' he asked.

Now his flight grew serious. He sailed to Hong-Kong, but dared not stay there; he went to Manila; Manila was ominous; he went on to Shanghai: Shanghai was nerve-racking; every time he went out of the hotel he expected to run straight into Mabel's arms; no, Shanghai would never do. The only thing was to go to Yokohama. At the Grand Hotel at Yokohama a cable awaited him.

'*So sorry to have missed you at Manila. Love. Mabel.'*

He scanned the shipping intelligence with a fevered brow. Where was she now? He doubled back to Shanghai. This time he went straight to the club and asked for a telegram. It was handed to him.

'*Arriving shortly. Love. Mabel.'*

No, no, he was not so easy to catch as all that. He had already made his plans. The Yangtze is a long river and the Yangtze was falling. He could just about catch the last steamer that could get up to Chungking and then no one could travel till the following spring except by junk. Such a journey was out of the question for a woman alone. He went to Hankow and from Hankow to Ichang, he changed boats here and from Ichang through the rapids went to Chungking. But he was desperate now, he was not going to take any risks: there was a place called Cheng-tu, the capital of Szechuan, and it was four hundred miles away. It could only be reached by road, and the road was infested with brigands. A man would be safe there.

George collected chair-bearers and coolies and set out. It was with a sigh of relief that he saw at last the crenellated walls of the lonely Chinese city. From those walls at sunset you could see the snowy mountains of Tibet.

He could rest at last: Mabel would never find him there. The consul happened to be a friend of his and he stayed with him. He enjoyed the comfort of a luxurious house, he enjoyed his idleness after that strenuous escape across Asia, and above all he enjoyed his divine security. The weeks passed lazily one after the other.

One morning George and the consul were in the courtyard looking at some curios that a Chinese had brought for their inspection when there was a loud knocking at the great door of the Consulate. The doorman flung it open. A chair borne by four coolies entered, advanced, and was set down. Mabel stepped out. She was neat and cool and fresh. There was nothing in her appearance to suggest that she had just come in after a fortnight on the road. George was petrified. He was as pale as death. She went up to him.

'Hulloa, George, I was so afraid I'd missed you again.'

'Hulloa, Mabel,' he faltered.

He did not know what to say. He looked this way and that: she stood between him and the doorway. She looked at him with a smile in her blue eyes.

'You haven't altered at all,' she said. 'Men can go off so dreadfully in seven years and I was afraid you'd got fat and bald. I've been so nervous. It would have been terrible if after all these years I simply hadn't been able to bring myself to marry you after all.'

She turned to George's host.

'Are you the consul?' she asked.

'I am.'

'That's all right. I'm ready to marry him as soon as I've had a bath.'

And she did.

King Thrushbeard
by
The Brothers Grimm

Jacob Grimm (1785–1863) and Wilhelm Grimm (1786–1859) were born in Hanau, Germany. They published the first of their many collections of fairy tales in 1812. The story that they wandered about Germany collecting their tales from the lips of peasants is a fairy tale itself. In fact, they invited educated middle class women into their home to tell them the stories they had heard from their governesses and servants. The point of their collection of folklore was to study the German language and they also did important work on the German dictionary. The stories were revised to be more appropriate for children in 1819 and were published under the title *Children's and Household Tales*. By the beginning of the twentieth century *Children's and Household Tales* was second only to the Bible in the German bestseller lists.

King Thrushbeard

A KING HAD A daughter whose beauty was beyond comparison, but she was so proud and haughty that no suitor was good enough for her. Indeed, she rejected one after the other and ridiculed them as well. Once her father held a great feast and invited all the marriageable young men from far and wide to attend. They were all lined up according to their rank and class: first came the kings, then the dukes, princes, counts, and barons, and finally the gentry. The king's daughter was conducted down the line, and she found fault with each one of the suitors there. One was too fat for her. 'That wine barrel!' she said. Another was too tall. 'Tall and thin, he looks like a pin!' The third was too short. 'Short and fat, he's built like a vat!' The fourth was too pale. 'He resembles death!' The fifth was too red. 'What a rooster!' The sixth did not stand straight enough. 'Green wood, dried behind the stove!'

There was not a single man whom she did not criticise, but she made the most fun of a good king who stood at the head of the line and had a chin that was a bit crooked.

'My goodness!' she exclaimed, and laughed. 'He's got a chin like a thrush's beak!' From then on, everyone called him Thrushbeard.

When her father saw that she did nothing but ridicule people, and that she scorned all the suitors who were gathered there, he was furious and swore that she would have to marry the very first beggar who came to his door. A few days later a minstrel came and began singing beneath the windows to earn some money. When the

273

king heard him, he said, 'Have him come up here.'

The minstrel, who was dressed in dirty, tattered clothes, entered the hall and sang in front of the king and his daughter. When he was finished, he asked for a modest reward.

'Your singing has pleased me so much,' the king said, 'that I shall give you my daughter for your wife.'

The king's daughter was horrified, but the king said, 'I swore I'd give you to the very first beggar who came along, and I intend to keep my word.'

All her objections were to no avail. The minister was fetched, and she was compelled to wed the minstrel. When that was done, the king said, 'It's not fitting for you to stay in my palace any longer since you're now a beggar woman. I want you to depart with your husband.'

The beggar took her by the hand, and she had to go with him on foot. When they came to a huge forest, she asked:

'Tell me, who might the owner of this forest be?'
'King Thrushbeard owns the forest and all you can see.
If you had taken him, it would belong to you.'
'Alas, poor me! What can I do?
I should have wed King Thrushbeard. If only I knew!'

Soon they crossed a meadow, and she asked again:

'Tell me, who might the owner of this meadow be?'
'King Thrushbeard owns the meadow and all you can see.
If you had taken him, it would belong to you.'
'Alas, poor me! What can I do?
I should have wed King Thrushbeard. If only I knew!'

Then they came to a large city, and she asked once more:

'Tell me, who might the owner of this city be?'
'King Thrushbeard owns the city and all you can see.
If you had taken him, it would belong to you.'

'Alas, poor me! What can I do?
I should have wed King Thrushbeard. If only I knew!'

'I'm not at all pleased by this,' said the minstrel. 'Why are you always wishing for another husband? Do you think I'm not good enough for you?'

Finally, they came to a tiny cottage, and she said:

'Oh, Lord! What a wretched tiny house!
It's not even fit for a mouse.'

The minstrel answered, 'This house is mine and yours, and we shall live here together.'

She had to stoop to get through the low doorway.

'Where are the servants?' the king's daughter asked.

'What servants?' answered the beggar. 'You must do everything yourself if you want something done. Now, make a fire at once and put the water on so you can cook me my meal. I'm very tired.'

However, the king's daughter knew nothing about making a fire or cooking, and the beggar had to lend a hand himself if he wanted anything done in a tolerable fashion. After they had eaten their meagre meal, they went to bed. But the next morning he got her up very early because she had to take care of the house. For a few days they lived like this and managed as best they could. When they had consumed all their provisions, the man said, 'Wife, we can't go on this way any longer. We've used everything up, and we're not earning a thing. You've got to weave baskets.'

He went out to cut some willows and brought them home, but the rough willows bruised her tender hands.

'I see that won't work,' said the man. 'Let's try spinning. Perhaps you'll be better at that.'

She sat down at the spinning wheel and tried to spin, but the hard thread soon cut her soft fingers, and blood began to flow.

'See now,' said the man. 'You're not fit for any kind of work. I made a bad bargain when I got you. But let's see how things go if

I start a business with pots and earthenware. You're to sit in the marketplace and sell the wares.'

Oh, she thought, if some people from my father's kingdom come to the marketplace and see me selling wares, they'll surely make fun of me!

But there was no way to avoid it. She had to obey her husband if she did not want to die of hunger. The first time everything went well. People gladly bought her wares because she was beautiful, and they paid what she asked. Indeed, many gave her money and did not even bother to take the pots with them. So the couple lived off their earnings as long as they lasted. Then her husband bought a lot of new earthenware. His wife sat down with it at a corner in the marketplace, set her wares around her, and offered them for sale. Suddenly, a drunken hussar came galloping along and rode right over the pots so that they were all smashed to pieces. She began to weep and was paralysed with fear.

'Oh, what's going to happen to me!' she exclaimed. 'What will my husband say?'

She ran home and told him about the accident, and he responded by saying, 'In heaven's name, who would ever sit down at a corner in the marketplace with earthenware? Now stop your weeping. I see full well that you're not fit for proper work. I've already been to the king's castle and have asked whether they could use a kitchen maid, and they've promised me to take you on. In return you'll get free meals.'

Now the king's daughter became a kitchen maid and had to assist the cook and do the lowest kind of work. She sewed two little jars inside her pockets and carried home the leftovers so they could have some food to live on. One day it happened that the king's oldest son was celebrating his wedding, and the poor woman went upstairs, stood outside the door of the large hall, and wanted to look inside. When the candles were lit, each guest entered, one more exquisitely dressed than the next, and everything was full of splendour. With a sad heart she thought about her fate and cursed her pride and arrogance for bringing about her humiliation and great poverty. Sometimes the servants threw her pieces of the delicious dishes they were carrying in and out of the hall, and she could also smell the aroma of the food. She put the pieces into her pockets and intended to carry them home.

Suddenly the king's son entered. He was dressed in velvet and silk and had a golden chain around his neck. And, when he saw the beautiful woman standing in the doorway, he grabbed her by the hand and wanted to dance with her, but she refused. Indeed, she was horrified because she saw it was King Thrushbeard, who had courted her and whom she had rejected with scorn. Although she struggled, it was to no avail, for he pulled her into the hall. Then the string that held her pockets together broke, and the jars fell out, causing the soup to spill and the scraps of food to scatter on the floor. When the people saw that, they laughed a good deal and poked fun at her. She was so ashamed that she wished she were a thousand fathoms under the earth. She ran out the door and tried to escape, but a man caught up with her on the stairs and brought her back. When she looked at him, she saw it was King Thrushbeard again, and he said to her in a friendly way, 'Don't be afraid. I and the minstrel who lived with you in the wretched cottage are one and the same person. I disguised myself out of love for you, and I was also the hussar who rode over your pots and smashed them to pieces. I did all that to humble your proud spirit and to punish you for the insolent way you behaved toward me.'

Then she shed bitter tears and said, 'I've done a great wrong and don't deserve to be your wife.'

However, he said, 'Console yourself. The bad days are over. Now we shall celebrate our wedding.'

The chambermaids came and dressed her in splendid clothes, and her father came along with his entire court, and they wished her happiness in her marriage with King Thrushbeard. Then the real rejoicing began, and I wish that you and I had been there too.

*And stories
to celebrate
the joys of
growing old*

Hermitage
by
Julian Barnes

Julian Barnes was born in Leicester in 1946. He studied at Magdalen College, Oxford and was a lexicographer for the *Oxford English Dictionary*, before working as a literary editor and critic. His first novel, *Metroland* was published in 1980 and his third novel, *Flaubert's Parrot* (1984) was shortlisted for the Booker Prize, as were *England, England* (1998) and *Arthur & George* (2005). His short story collections include *Cross Channel* and *The Lemon Table*. In France, he is the only writer to have won both the Prix Médicis and the Prix Fémina, and in 2004 he became a Commandeur de l'Ordre des Arts et des Lettres. He lives in London.

Hermitage

THEY SAW IT from the Pauillac steamer, its pocked façade still quarter-lit by the early afternoon sun. They had embarked at Bordeaux, near the Place des Quinconces, at eleven, taking their place in cane seats beneath a striped awning. On the foredeck immediately below them clustered the third-class passengers, equipped with livestock, energy and noise. Florence felt debilitated by the evidence of normal vivacity undiscouraged by the heat; yet Emily seemed to feed from it.

'Look at that man, Florence. He does not just talk. He . . . he *dances* his conversation.'

'I expect he is saying something very mundane.'

'If so,' Emily came back, undaunted, 'if so, then his manner permits him to transcend the mundane.' She took out her sketch-book and began to draw the capering, sharp-nosed fellow, with his bare head, blue blouse, stubby pipe and liquid hands.

'I wish I discovered as much transcending as you, my dear Emily. It seems all around you. Now you transcend the man some more by turning him into art.'

'You shan't put me out of humour. And besides, we all believe in transcendence. You merely disguise it by calling it practical improvement.'

They sat quietly, two Englishwomen in their thirties, sailor-hats and brown shoes apiece, while the steamer headed past a winter woodland of ships' masts. Steam whistles were the loudest birdsong here. A tugboat named *Ercule* churned froth on the *café au lait* river; lesser ferries scudded across their bows like water-spiders. They had been away three weeks, and were at the most southerly point of their journey. Soon, as every year, they would be heading back to their separate Essex villages, to winds from the Urals and the chill conversation of turnip-farmers. Of course, these dinner clods cultivated other crops, but this was how, in their private conversations, Florence and Emily invariably designated them.

'I shall never marry,' said Florence suddenly. She made it sound a matter of fact but not regret.

'In any case,' her friend replied, continuing, or perhaps duplicating, the thought, 'it is well known that a turnip-farmer is beyond any possible transcendence.'

The little steamer tacked from bank to bank, picking up and depositing merchants and peasants, livestock and priests. The Garonne embraced the Dordogne and became the Gironde. Emily's skirt bulged with the wind until she pressed down on it a map marked with the châteaux of the Médoc. She settled a small pair of field-glasses over her spectacles and adopted a scholarly hunch familiar to her fellow-traveller. Alongside Beychevelle, Emily explained that the château had once belonged to an admiral, that every ship passing along the river had been at one time obliged to lower its sail, or *baisser la voile*, in homage, and that this phrase had been corrupted into the present name.

'Quite fanciful,' commented Florence cheerfully.

Emily indicated Margaux and Ducru-Beaucaillou, Léoville-las-Cases and Latour, appending Baedeker embellishments to each name. Beyond Latour, the boat ran close to the bank as it headed up towards Pauillac. Ribbed vineyards ran away from them like green corduroy. A broken-down pier came into sight, followed by a patch of corduroy stained half-black. Then, a little higher up, a flat façade made biscuity by the sun, with a brief terrace half-obscuring the ground-floor windows. After a nudge of focusing, Emily detected that several balusters were missing from the balcony of the terrace, and others badly askew. Florence took the glasses. The façade had large holes gouged into it, there were some broken upper window-panes, while the roof appeared to have been given over to experimental agriculture.

'Not exactly our hermitage,' she commented.

'So we shall visit tomorrow?'

This teasing pastime had evolved during the last two years of their French excursions. Idling glances proposed a different life: in a timbered Normandy farmhouse, a trim Burgundy *manoir*, a backwater château of the Berry. Lately, a new gravity of intention had arisen, which neither woman could quite admit. So Florence would announce that their hermitage had again not been found, and soon afterwards they would visit.

Château Dauprat-Bages had not been listed in the great Classification of 1855. It was a modest *cru bourgeois*, 16 hectares planted with cabernet sauvignon, merlot and petit verdot. During the last decade phylloxera had blackened its green corduroy, and some hesitant replanting had begun under its enfeebled and impoverished owner. Three years previously he had died, leaving all to a young nephew in Paris, who snobbishly preferred Burgundy and sought to divest himself of Château Dauprat-Bages as quickly as possible. But no neighbouring estate could be persuaded to take on the blighted vineyards; the *régisseur* and the *homme d'affaires* had therefore struggled on with casual labour, producing a wine which even they admitted had sunk to the level of a *cru artisan*.

When Florence and Emily returned for their second visit, Monsieur Lambert, the *homme d'affaires*, a short, black-suited man with a felt cap and a spiky moustache, his manner both fussy and domineering, turned suddenly to Emily, whom he judged the younger, and therefore the more dangerous of the two, and demanded, 'Êtes-vous Américaniste?'

Misunderstanding him, she replied, 'Anglaise.'

'Américaniste?' he reiterated.

'Non,' she replied, and he grunted approval. She felt she had passed some test without having been told what the test might be.

Next morning, over a breakfast of oysters and hot sausages at the Hôtel d'Angleterre in Pauillac, Florence said musingly, 'You cannot say that they have landscape here. It is more that they have contours.'

'Then it will not seem entirely a change from Essex.'

Both observed the seduction of *might* and *could* into *is* and *will*. They had travelled in France together for five summers now. In hotels they shared the same bed; at meals they permitted themselves wine; after dinner Florence would smoke a single cigarette. Each year had been a heady escape, both a justification of their life among the turnip-farmers and a rebuke to it. Their excursions among the French had so far been light-hearted, flirtatious. Emily now felt as if something – not destiny, but the lesser organisation that directed their lives – was calling her bluff.

'However, it is your money,' she said, acknowledging that things had become very serious indeed.

'It was my father's money and I shall have no children.'

Florence, the larger and slightly older of the two, had an oblique way of announcing decisions. She was dark and sturdy, with a deceptive style of down-to-earth discouragement. In truth, she was both more capable and more benign than she appeared, despite a docile preference for only the broader aspects of any project. Emily could always be relied upon to take care of the particularities; Emily, slim, blonde, neatly fussy, peering through gold-wired spectacles at notebook, sketch-pad, timetable, newspaper, menu, Baedeker, map, ticket and legal fine print; Emily, fretful yet optimistic, who now said wonderingly, 'But we know nothing of making wine.'

'We are not applying for posts as vendangeuses,' Florence replied, with a lazy hauteur that was not wholly self-mocking. 'Father did not understand how the saw-mill operated, but he knew that gentlemen required desks. Besides, I am sure that you will study the matter. It cannot be more complicated than . . . cathedrals.' She threw this out as a recent example, since in her view they had spent excessive time beneath the statue of Bertrand de Goth, Archbishop of Bordeaux and later Pope Clement V, while Emily expounded on 12th-century Romanesque arches in the nave and a choir with double stalls from some other – no doubt earlier, or later – century.

The Burgundian nephew accepted Florence's offer, and she sold her house in Essex; Emily informed brother Lionel, the solicitor, that he would have to find himself another housekeeper (news she had longed to impart for some years). In the spring of 1890 the two women transplanted themselves irrevocably to France, taking with them no specific reminders of England except the grandfather-clock which had marked every hour of Florence's childhood. As their train pulled away from the quai d'Austerlitz at the Gare d'Orléans, Emily yielded up a final anxiety.

'You shall not be bored? I mean, with my company. This is not just an excursion.'

'I have decided the château will bear your name,' Florence replied. 'I have always thought Dauprat-Bages quite lacking in romance.' She re-pinned her hat, as if to ward off any protest. 'In the matter of the turnip-farmers, I do not think their memory will fade so quickly. Such dancers! The clods scarcely noticed when they trod upon one!'

Mme Florence and Mme Emily re-engaged M. Lambert as *homme d'affaires* and M. Collet as *régisseur* on improved terms. M. Lambert then found them a housekeeper, three estate workers, a maid and a gardener. The shrubbery was dug out of the roof, the balusters mended, the pock-marked façade filled in, the pier rebuilt. Florence occupied herself with the house and presided over the newly-planted *potager*; Emily directed relations with the vineyard. The commune of Dauprat welcomed the women: they brought employment, and wished to restore a damaged vineyard to prosperity. No one objected when Château Dauprat-Bages became Château Haut Railly. *Les Anglaises* may have lacked religion, but they entertained the curé to tea each November, and solemnly attended his annual benediction of the vines in April. Such eccentricities as were observed could be lightly ascribed to the impoverished existence they must have previously endured on that distant island in whose cold, wet climate not even an Alsatian vine could flourish. It was noted, for instance, that they were great enthusiasts for domestic economy. A roast fowl might last them a week; soap and string were used until their final centimetre; linen was spared by the women's sharing a bed.

In late September a band of genial ruffians descended for the *vendange*; they were awarded huge dinners, and allowed to drink as much of the previous year's *petit vin* as they wished. Florence and Emily were impressed that drunkenness did not ensue. They were also surprised to see men and women working harmoniously alongside one another in the vineyard. M. Lambert explained that the women were paid less on the grounds that they talked more. With a few sly shakes of the head, he then described a particular local tradition. It was strictly forbidden for any of the *vendangeurs* to eat the grapes they were picking, and at the end of each morning the women were obliged to put out their tongues for inspection. If the proof was purple, then the overseer would be entitled to claim a kiss in punishment. Florence and Emily kept to themselves the reflection that this sounded a little primitive, while the *homme d'affaires* concluded, with a wink bordering on impertinence, 'Of course, sometimes they eat deliberately.'

When the first vintage was safely gathered in, the *bal des vendangeurs* ensued. Trestle tables were laid out in the courtyard, and on this occasion the effects of alcohol were more readily apparent. Two fiddles and a squeezebox goaded the heavy-kneed vintagers into some dancing which, even so, displayed a grace and energy way beyond those of the most teetotal turnip-farmer. There being insufficient women present, Florence enquired of M. Lambert as to the propriety of his partnering the château's new owner. The *homme d'affaires* pronounced the suggestion an honour, but felt, if he was being invited to offer guidance to Madame, that others in the same situation would choose to watch from the head of the table. Florence therefore tapped her foot in irritated resignation as slight and wiry Frenchmen slung around women who for the most part were taller, plumper and older. After an hour or so, M. Lambert clapped his hands, and the youngest *vendangeuse* shyly brought Florence and Emily each a bunch of heliotropes. Emily delivered a short speech of thanks and congratulations, whereupon the two women retired to bed, listening through their open window to the whirl and stamp from the courtyard, to the scratch of the fiddles and the indefatigable jauntiness of the squeezebox.

Emily became, to Florence's indulgent dismay, even more learned in viticulture than in church architecture. The matter was the more confusing since Emily rarely knew the correct English word for the terms she was employing. Sitting in a cane chair on the terrace with the sun glistening the loose hair at the nape of her neck, she would lecture Florence on the parasitical enemies and cryptogamic maladies of the vine. *Altise*, Florence heard, and *rhynchite; cochinelle, grisette, érinose*; there were monstrous beasts called *l'ephippigère de Béziers* and *le vespère de Xatart*; then there was *le mildiou* and *le black-rot* (those at least she understood), *l'anthracnose* and *le rot blanc*. Emily saw these disasters in coloured illustration as she spoke: shredded leaves, noxious spottings and wounded branches filled her spectacles. Florence tried to show the proper concern.

'What is a cryptogamic malady?' she asked dutifully.

'Cryptogamia, according to Linnaeus, comprise those plants which have no stamens or pistils, and therefore no flowers, such as mosses, algae, funghi. Mosses and lichens too. From the Greek, meaning concealed wedlock.'

'Cryptogamia,' Florence repeated like a pupil.

'It is Linnaeus's last class of plants,' Emily added. She was now at the extremity of her knowledge, but pleased that Florence seemed for once to be following her there.

'Last, but I am sure not least.'

'I do not know if the categories imply moral judgment.'

'Oh, I am sure not,' Florence asserted firmly, though she was no botanist. 'But how sad that some of our enemies are cryptogamic,' she added.

Emily's discussion of these selfsame maladies with M. Lambert was more complete but less satisfactory. It seemed evident to her that the researches of L'École Nationale d'Agriculture at Montpellier were convincing, and that the ravages of phylloxera should be repaired with vines grafted upon American rootstocks. Professor Millardet of Bordeaux agreed, even if there had been lively differences of opinion in the viticultural press.

To M. Lambert the matter was not at all so evident; indeed, quite the contrary. He reminded Mme Emily, who was a recent arrival in the Médoc, that the European vine, for all its many variations, consisted of but a single species, *vinis vitifera*, whereas the American vine comprised nearly two dozen different species. The European vine had existed in a state of almost perfect health for more than two millennia, and the maladies now afflicting it were entirely due, as had been proved beyond the least doubt, to the introduction of the American vines into France. Thus, he continued – and at this juncture Emily began to suspect that they had read the same volume – thus, there had been the appearance of oïdium in 1845, of phylloxera in 1867, of mildew in 1879, and of black-rot in 1884. Whatever professors in universities might believe, his colleagues in the vineyards had the opinion that you did not, when confronted by a disease, cure it by importing its cause. To put matters as plainly as possible, if you had a child with pneumonia, you did not seek to cure it by putting into its bed another child already suffering from influenza.

When Emily pressed the argument for grafting, M. Lambert's face tightened, and he banged his felt cap against his thigh. 'Vous avez dit que vous n'étiez pas Américaniste,' he said plainly, as if forcing an end to the discussion.

Only now, with her studies behind her, did Emily appreciate the question she had been asked on their second tour of inspection. The world here divided into *sulfureurs* and *Américanistes*: those for whom salvation from phylloxera lay in rescuing and restoring pure French vines by chemical treatment, and those who wished to turn the vineyards into some new California. Her earlier reply to M. Lambert had unwittingly confirmed to him that she was a *sulfureur*, or rather, as he now put it, with what might have been either linguistic correctness or light sarcasm, a *sulfureuse*. If she was now telling him that she had changed her mind and was an *Américaniste* after all, then he and M. Collet, grateful though they were to Mme Florence and Mme Emily, would feel, to say the least, deceived.

'Who are we to say?' was Florence's response when Emily explained the dilemma.

'Well, we – you – are the owner. And I have been reading the very latest viticultural press.'

'My father never knew how the saw-mill worked.'

'Even so, the legs of his desks did not, I trust, fall off.'

'Dear Emily,' said Florence, 'you do worry so.' She smiled, then gave an indulgent chuckle. 'And I shall think of you from now on as my *sulfureuse*. Yellow has always suited you.' She chuckled again. The matter, Emily realised, had been both avoided and concluded by Florence: such was often her way.

What Florence called 'worrying' was to Emily a proper concern for husbandry. She proposed extending the estate by planting the lower meadows close to the river; but was told they were too saturated. She replied that they should import bog-draining fen-men from East Anglia – indeed, she knew just which trenchers to appoint; but was told that even were the slopes to be drained, the subsoil was inhospitable to vines. Next she proposed the use of English horses to work the vineyard in place of oxen. M. Lambert took her into the estate and they waited at the end of a row of petit verdot as a pair of harnessed oxen, their heads cowled like nuns against the flies, progressed towards them. 'Look,' he said, his eyes shining, 'look how they pick up and put down their feet. Is it not as graceful as any minuet that has been danced in the ballrooms of Europe?' Emily responded with praise of the strength, docility and intelligence of English horses; and in this matter she had the bump of perseverance. A few months later a pair of sturdy, feather-footed shires arrived at Haut Railly. They were stabled, rested and praised. What went wrong thereafter she never quite discovered: were the horses too clumsy-footed, or the workers too little skilled at directing them? Whichever the case, the shires were soon living out a peaceful early retirement on the unplanted lower meadows of the estate, the frequent aim of pointed fingers from the Pauillac steamer.

This ferry, when not over-burdened, could sometimes be persuaded to put in at the château's bright new stone pier. Such piers, Emily discovered, were locally called *ports*. They were so named, she naturally deduced, because their intended function was

not as a tying-up place for pleasure-craft, but as an embarkation
point for goods: specifically and obviously, the estate's wine must
in the past have been sent to Bordeaux for bottling by the direct
water-route rather than being hauled overland. She therefore
instructed M. Lambert to move the next vintage by this method,
and he seemingly accepted the order. But a week later Florence
informed her that the housekeeper had offered her resignation amid
spectacular tears, because if Madame did not wish to employ her
brother the haulier then she herself was unable to work for Madame,
since her brother was a widower with many children, and reliant
for their bread upon the haulage contract from the château. Florence
had of course replied that they had known none of this, and Mme
Merle was not to fret.

'Can the lazy fellow not turn to river haulage as well?' Emily
asked rather snappishly.

'My dear, we did not come here to disturb their lives. We came
for the tranquillity of our own.'

Florence had adapted to the Médoc with a swift content that
was close to indolence. For her the year now ran not from January
to December, but from one harvest to the next. In November they
cleared the vineyard and manured; in December they lightly ploughed
as protection against winter frosts; on January 22nd, St Vincent's
Day, they started to prune; in February and March they ploughed
to open up the vines; and in April they planted. June saw the
flowering; July the spraying and trimming; August contained the
véraison, that annually miraculous passage of the grapes from green
to purple; September and October brought the *vendange.* As Florence
watched these events from the terrace, she was aware of constant
disquiet over rain and hail, frost and drought; but country folk were
universally possessed by weather, and she decided as proprietor to
exempt herself from such anxieties. She preferred to concentrate
on what she loved: the vines draping their octopus arms over the
supporting wires; the slow creak and tinkle as the sandy oxen made
their stately way through the vineyard; the winter smell of a fire
constructed from prunings. On late-autumn mornings when the sun

rose low, she would sit in her cane chair with a bowl of chocolate, and from her flattened angle of vision all the rusting colours intensified: flame, ochre, and pale burgundy. This is our hermitage, she thought.

Each year for her therefore ended on the moveable feast of the *bal des vendangeurs*. Mindful of M. Lambert's earlier strictures, Florence had in the summer of 1891 made several mysterious trips into Bordeaux. Their purpose became plain when she celebrated the second vintage of Château Haut Railly in resplendent evening dress: black barathea jacket and trousers, with white silk waistcoat underneath, all cut with an elegant eccentricity by a bemused French tailor. Emily wore the same yellow dress as the first year, and when the trestle-table feast was over, and the fiddles and squeezebox started up, *les dames anglaises* rose and danced to unfamiliar tunes of furious friskiness. Mme Florence threw Mme Emily around in passable imitation of the wiry, mustachioed *vendangeurs*, who for their part asserted the democracy of the dance-floor by defending their territory with shoulder and hip. At the end of an hour the two women found, in mid-dance, that everyone else had faded to the edge of their awareness, and they were the proprietors of empty space. When the music stopped, the other dancers applauded, M. Lambert drily clapped his hands, the youngest *vendangeuse* brought two bunches of heliotropes, Emily made her speech, which was not substantially different, except for an improved accent, from the previous year, and *les dames anglaises* retired to bed. Florence hung up her evening suit, which would not be taken down until the following year. In the dark, she yawned heavily and summoned up a final picture of Emily, half-blinded without her spectacles, being tossed and whirled about the courtyard in her yellow dress. 'Goodnight, *ma petite sulfureuse*,' she said with a sleepy chuckle.

The great crisis in the management of Château Haut Railly came in the summer of 1895. One morning Emily noticed the housekeeper's brother unloading barrels at the door of the *chai*. She watched the haulier without at first realising there was something inapposite about the way he heaved them from his cart and thudded them down on to the courtyard. Of course, it was obvious – it should have been immediately obvious – that the barrels were full.

When the haulier had departed she went to see the *régisseur*. 'Monsieur Collet, I have always understood that we make wine here.' The *régisseur*, a lanky, taciturn man, had fond respect for his employers, but knew that they preferred to approach any subject by an ironical or indirect route. He therefore smiled and waited for Mme Emily to arrive at the matter in hand.

'Come with me.' She led the way out into the courtyard and stood before the evidence. A dozen small barrels, neatly stacked, bearing no obvious stamp of identification. 'Where are they from?'

'The Rhone Valley. They should be, anyway.' When Mme Emily failed to respond, he went on helpfully, 'Of course, in the old days it was more difficult. My father had to bring Cahors down the Dordogne. Then they opened the railway from Sète to Bordeaux. That was a great advance.'

'Monsieur Collet. Forgive me, my question is this: if we make wine here, why are we importing it?'

'Ah, I see. *Pour le vinage.*'

Emily had not come across the term before. '*Vinage?*'

'To be added to our wine. To make it better.'

'Is this . . . is it . . . legal?'

M. Collet shrugged. 'In Paris people make laws. In the Médoc people make wine.'

'Monsieur Collet, let me get this clear. You, who are in charge of making our wine, you adulterate Château Haut Railly with filth from the Rhône Valley? You do this without permission? You do this every year?'

The *régisseur* could see that more than factual explanation was being called for. It was always the younger Madame who caused the problems. She had, in his opinion, a capacity for hysteria. Whereas Mme Florence was much more calm. 'Tradition is permission,' he replied. From Mme Emily's face he could see that the hallowed words of his father were not working their trick. 'No, Madame, not every year. Last year was a very poor vintage, as you know, so it is necessary. Otherwise no one will buy the wine. If it was a little better, we might be able to improve it with some of our own wine, a few barrels of the '93. That we call *le coupage*,' he added apprehensively, unsure whether he was compounding or diminishing his supposed sin. 'But last year was truly mediocre, so we need these helpful barrels . . . *pour le vinage.*'

He was unprepared for Mme Emily's next action. She ran to the store-house, returning with a mallet and chisel. A few moments later, a dozen holes had been made, and the lower part of Emily's dress was stained with a pungent, spicy red liquor of considerably greater vivacity than the 1894 Château Haut Railly stored a few dozen metres away.

M. Lambert, attracted by the mallet blows, ran from his office and attempted to calm Mme Emily by introducing an historical perspective to the situation. He told her about *les vins d'aide*, as they were called, and the preparation of wine for *le goût anglais*, as it was known in the Médoc, and how the wine that the English gentleman served at his dinner table was very rarely the same liquid that had left a particular estate a few months or years previously. He spoke of a Spanish brew called Benicarlo.

Emily's disbelief was like heat. 'Monsieur Lambert, I do not understand you. In the past you have lectured me severely about the purity of the Médoc vineyards, about how French vines must not be adulterated with American rootstocks. Yet you blithely throw barrels of . . . of *this* into what those self-same vines produce.'

'Madame Emily, let me put it like this.' His manner became avuncular, almost clerical. 'What is the best wine of the Médoc?'

'Château Latour.'

'Of course. And do you know the verb *hermitager*?'

'No.' Her vocabulary was certainly being broadened today.

'It means to put the wine of Hermitage, a wine of the Rhône as you perhaps know, into a red Bordeaux. To give it weight. To accentuate its virtues.'

'They do this at Latour?'

'Perhaps it does not happen at the château itself. On the

Chartrons, in London . . . The négociant, the shipper, the bottler
. . .' M. Lambert's hands sketched a conspiracy of necessary virtue.
'In poor years it has to be done. It has always been done. Everyone
knows.'

'Do they do it there, next door, at Latour?' Emily pointed south,
into the sun. 'Do the owners do it? Do they have barrels delivered
like this, in broad daylight?'

The *homme d'affaires* shrugged. 'Perhaps not.'

'Then we shall not do this here either. I forbid it. We forbid it.'

On the terrace that evening, while her dress was still in the soak,
Emily remained adamant. Florence at first tried to tease her into a
good humour, expressing surprise that an enthusiast for transcendence should not wish her wines to enjoy this quality as well.
But Emily was not to be humoured or flattered.

'Florence, you cannot say that you approve of this process. If the
label of our wine proclaims it to be of a certain vintage, and it is
in fact a mixture of two vintages, you cannot say that you approve?'

'No.'

'And you must therefore approve even less when our bottles
contain wine from hundreds of kilometres away, grown God knows
where and by God knows whom?'

'Yes. But . . .'

'*But?*'

'Even I, my dear Emily, have grasped that it is permitted to add
sugar to our wine, and what is the name of that acid . . . ?'

'Citric acid, yes, and tartaric acid, and tannins. I am not
sentimental enough to imagine that the process is not in some ways
one of manufacturing. It is an industrial as well as an agricultural
process nowadays. What I cannot abide, Florence, is fraud. Fraud
on those who buy our wine, who drink it.'

'Surely people buy a wine because they know what taste it has.
Or should have.' Emily did not reply, and Florence pursued her
thought. 'An Englishman buys Château Latour with a certain
expectation, does he not? So those who provide the taste he requires
are merely giving him what he wants.'

'Florence, I did not expect to hear you taking the devil's position. I am perfectly serious about this matter. It seems to me of the utmost, the final importance.'

'So I can see.'

'Florence, we do not talk about such things, and I am happy that it should remain that way, but when we moved here, when we gave up the turnip-farmers, we did so, as I understand it, because we could not live pretendingly, shut up in all that cold formality, waiting for those four weeks of the year in which we might escape. We could not bear the fraud in our lives.' Emily by now had a lively blush and a stern stillness to her posture. Florence had seen her like this before, when she had the bump of perseverance about a matter.

'Yes, my dear.'

'You like to say that this is our hermitage. Well, so it is, but only if it is we who make the rules.'

'Yes.'

'Then we must not live pretendingly, or with fraud, or believe, as Monsieur Collet expressed it to me this morning, that "tradition is permission". We must not live like that. We must believe in truth. We must not live pretendingly.'

'You are perfectly right, my dear, and I love you for it.'

For once, M. Lambert and M. Collet were quite unable to prevail upon either of the Mesdames. Normally they knew to intervene with Mme Florence once Mme Emily was safely out of the way. They would address her with pathos or pride, invoke local or national considerations, and appeal to what they regarded as her essential complacency. But this time Mme Florence proved as obdurate as Mme Emily. Arguments from necessity and from tradition, references to the implied authority of the great vineyards, were placed before her in vain. There was to be no *vinage* and no *coupage*. There were to be no secretive deliveries of anonymous barrels, and, for that matter, no consequent obfuscations in M. Lambert's account books. Florence feared another threat of resignation, though far less than she feared the possibility of Emily's censure. But the two men, after several days of sulking and some growled conversations which seemed to contain more *patois* than usual, agreed that what had been ordered would be done.

The decade continued. The 1890s were kindlier years in the Médoc than the 1880s, and the last years of the century brought no sense of ending. Florence would reflect that their glass as yet contained no lees. They had settled comfortably into middle age, perhaps she more comfortably than Emily; and they had no regrets for England. Their stewardship of Château Haut Railly grew lighter. The replanting of the vineyard with ungrafted stock was complete; the oxen danced their minuets, the *vendangeurs* went through their ruffianly rituals. The old curé retired, but his successor respected the ancestral duties: tea in November, benediction of the vines in April. Forence took to tapestry work, Emily to pickling; they frequented the Bordeaux steamer more rarely. *Les dames anglaises* had ceased to be a novelty, or even an eccentricity; they had become a fixture.

Emily would sometimes reflect on how little impact they had truly made upon the estate; how little transcendence had occurred. They had brought money, to be sure, but this had merely allowed the vineyard to reassert itself, the better to take its chance against parasitical enemies and cryptogamic maladies. And at times like this, when she felt that personal will was less significant than philosophers claimed, she liked to think of human life as following its own viticultural cycle. Childhood was full of frosts and pruning, of wrist-cracking labour at the plough: it was hard to imagine that the weather would ever change. But it did, and June brought the flowering. Flowers led to fruit, and with August came the *véraison* that miraculous colour-turn, the sign and promise of maturity. She and Florence had now reached the August of their lives. She shuddered to admit how much their maturity had depended upon the fortunes of the weather! She had known many who never recovered from the savagery of early frosts; others fell to mildew, rot, disease; others again to hail, rain, drought. They – she and Florence – had been lucky with their weather. That was all there was to say. And there the analogy ended, she thought. They may be now in their maturity, but there was no wine to be pressed from their lives. Emily believed in transcendence, but not in the soul. This was their patch of land, their patch of life. Then, at some point, the oxen came, dancing an unfamiliar dance, with the blade behind them cutting more deeply into the soil.

On the last evening of the century, as midnight approached, Florence and Emily sat alone on the terrace at Château Haut Railly. Even the familiar silhouette of the two elderly shires down in the lower meadows was missing. The horses had grown fat and nervous lately, and had been stabled close this night in case the fireworks alarmed them. *Les dames anglaises* had naturally been invited to attend the festivities in Pauillac, but had declined. There were times when the world shifted and you needed public comfort. But there were also great instants better savoured in private. Not for them tonight the official speeches, the municipal ball, the first purple-tongued riot of the new century.

Wrapped in rugs, they gazed down towards the Gironde, which was occasionally illumined by a premature rocket. A shuddery, but more reliable light came from the storm lantern set on the table between them. Emily could see that the balusters they had renewed a decade earlier had now quite blended in with the old ones: she could not now recognise, or remember, which was which.

Florence refilled their glasses with the 1898 vintage. It had been a small crop, reduced by lack of rain after a dry summer. The 1899, currently brooding in the *chai*, was known already to be magnificent, a grand finale to the century. But the 1898 had its virtues: a pretty robe, ample fruit, a proper length. Whether all these virtues were entirely its own was another matter. Florence, though essentially complacent, could not help being intrigued by the idea that their wine appeared to acquire a certain additional solidity between its journey in cask to Bordeaux and its return thence in bottle. Once, with a cheerful recklessness, she had ventured this notion to Emily, who had sharply replied that all good wine put on weight in the bottle. Florence had acquiesced in this declaration, and sworn to herself that she would never go near the subject again.

'You can be proud of this vintage,' she said.

'We can both be proud.'

'Then I give you a toast. To Château Haut Railly.'

'To Château Haut Railly.'

They drank, and walked to the front of the terrace, adjusting their rugs. They placed their glasses on the balustrade. The English grandfather-clock struck twelve, and the first fireworks of the new century climbed into the sky. Florence and Emily played at trying to guess their firing-points. Château Latour, obviously, that ruby explosion close at hand. Château Haut Brion, the browny-gold susurrus in the distance. Château Lafite, the elegant pattern to the north. Between the scatterings of light and the unfearsome crackles, they proposed a series of toasts. They turned towards England and drank; towards Paris; towards Bordeaux. Then they faced one another on the silent terrace with the storm lantern tickling their skirts and toasted the new century. A last, misguided rocket flew low across the water and exploded above their little *port*. Arm in arm, they walked towards the house, leaving their undrained glasses on the balustrade, and the lantern to burn itself out at some untenanted hour. Florence hummed a waltz, and they skittishly danced the last few yards to the French windows.

In the hallway, under the burner at the foot of the stairs, Florence said, 'Let me see your tongue.' Emily rather delicately extruded a centimetre and a half. 'Just as I thought,' said Florence. 'Stealing the grapes. Every year the same disobedience, *ma petite sulfureuse*.' Emily dropped her head in mock contrition. Florence tut-tutted, and turned down the light.

Clementina
by
John Cheever

John Cheever was born in Massachusetts in 1912. In 1935 he sold his first story to *The New Yorker* for $45 and in 1938 he began work for the Federal Writers' Project in Washington, D. C. His first collection of stories, *The Way Some People Live*, was published in 1943 and his first novel, *The Wapshot Chronicle*, won the 1958 National Book Award. In 1965 he received the Howells Medal for Fiction and in 1978 he won the National Book Critics Circle Award and the Pulitzer Prize for *The Stories of John Cheever*. Shortly before his death in 1982 he was awarded the National Medal for Literature.

Clementina

SHE WAS BORN and brought up in Nascosta, in the time of the wonders – the miracle of the jewels and the winter of the wolves. She was ten years old when thieves broke into the shrine of the Holy Virgin after the last Mass on San Giovanni and stole the jewels that had been given to the Madonna by a princess who was cured there of a malady of the liver. On the next day, when Uncle Serafino was walking up from the fields, he saw, in the mouth of the cave where the Etruscans had buried their dead, a youth of great radiance, who beckoned to him, but he was afraid and ran away. Then Serafino was stricken with a fever, and he called for the priest and told him what he had seen, and the priest went to the cave and found the jewels of the Madonna there in the dead leaves where the angel had been standing. That same year, on the road below the farm, her cousin Maria saw the devil, with horns, a pointed tail, and a tight red suit, just as in the pictures. She was fourteen at the time of the big snow, and she went that night after dark to the fountain and, turning back toward the tower where they then lived, she saw the wolves. It was a pack of six or seven, trotting up the stairs of the Via Cavour in the snow. She dropped her pitcher and ran into the tower, and her tongue was swollen with terror, but she looked out the cracks in the door and saw them, more churlish than dogs, more ragged, their ribs showing in their mangy coats and the blood of the sheep they had murdered falling from their mouths. She was terrified and she was rapt, as if the sight of the wolves

303

moving over the snow was the spirits of the dead or some other part of the mystery that she knew to lie close to the heart of life, and when they had passed she would not have believed she had seen them if they had not left their tracks in the snow. She was seventeen when she went to work as a *donna di servizio* for the baron of little importance who had a villa on the hill, and it was the same summer that Antonio, in the dark field, called her his dewy rose and made her head swim. She confessed to the priest and did her penance and was absolved, but when this had happened six times the priest said they should become engaged, and so Antonio became her *fidanzato*. The mother of Antonio was not sympathetic, and after three years Clementina was still his rose and he was still her *fidanzato* and whenever the marriage was mentioned the mother of Antonio would hold her head and scream. In the autumn, the baron asked her to come to Rome as a *donna* and how could she say no when she had dreamed all the nights of her life of seeing the Pope with her own eyes and walking on streets that were lighted after dark with electricity?

In Rome she slept on straw and washed in a bucket, but the streets were a spectacle, although she had to work such hours that she was not often able to walk in the city. The baron promised to pay her twelve thousand lire a month, but he paid her nothing at the end of the first month and nothing at the end of the second, and the cook said that he often brought girls in from the country and paid them nothing. Opening the door for him one evening, she asked with great courtesy for her wages, and he said he had given her a room, a change of air, and a visit to Rome and that she was badly educated to ask for more. She had no coat to wear in the street, and there were holes in her shoes, and all she was given to eat was the leftovers from the baron's table. She saw that she would have to find another post, because she didn't have the money to go back to Nascosta. That next week, the cousin of the cook found her a place where she was both seamstress and *donna*, and here she worked even harder, but when the month was over there were no wages. Then she refused to finish a dress the signora had asked her to make for a reception. She said she would not finish the dress until she had her wages. The signora angered herself and tore her hair, but she paid the wages. Then that night the cousin of the cook said that some Americans needed a *donna*. She put all the dirty dishes in the oven to give a false appearance of cleanliness, said her prayers in San Marcello's, and flew across Rome to where the Americans lived, feeling that every girl on the street that night was looking for the same post. The Americans were a family with two boys – well-educated people, although she could see that they were sad and foolish. They offered her twenty thousand lire in wages and showed her a very commodious room where she would live and said they hoped she would not be uncomfortable, and in the morning she moved her things to the Americans'.

She had heard much about Americans, about how they were generous and ignorant, and some of this was true, for they were very generous and treated her like a guest in the house, always asking her if she had time to do this and that and urging her to take a passage in the streets on Thursdays and Sundays. The signore was meager and tall and worked in the Embassy. His hair was cropped close like a German or a prisoner or someone recovering from an operation of the brain. His hair was black and strong, and if he had let it go and waved it with *frissone* the girls in the street would have admired him, but he went each week to the barber and had himself disfigured. He was very modest in other things and wore at the beach a concealing bathing costume, but he walked through the streets of Rome with the shape of his head naked for everyone to see. The signora was fine, with a skin like marble and many clothes, and it was a commodious and a diverting life, and Clementina prayed at San Marcello's that it would never end. They left all the lights burning as if electricity cost nothing, and they burned wood in the fireplace only to take off the evening chill, and they drank iced gin and vermouth before dinner. They smelled different. It was a pale smell, she thought – a weak smell – and it might have had something to do with the blood of northerners, or it might be because they took so many hot baths. They took so many hot baths that she could not understand why they were not neurasthenics. They ate Italian food and drank wine, and she hoped that if they ate enough pasta and oil they would have a strong and wholesome smell. Sometimes when she waited on table, she smelled them, but it was always a very weak smell and sometimes nothing. They spoiled their children, and sometimes the children spoke sharply or in an ill temper to their *genitori*, for which they should have been whipped, but they never whipped their children, these strangers, or even raised their voices in anger, or did anything else that would explain to the children the importance of their *genitori*, and once when the smallest boy was very badly disposed and should have been whipped, his mother took him instead to a toy store and bought him a sailboat. And sometimes when they were dressing to go out in the evening the signore would fasten his wife's clothes or her pearls, like a *cafone*, instead of ringing for Clementina. And once when there was no water in the flat and she had gone down the stairs to the fountain to get some, he came after her to help, and when she said that it was not possible for him to carry water, he said that it was not possible for him to sit by his fire while a young woman carried a heavy demijohn up and down the stairs. Then he took the demijohn out of her hands and went down to the fountain, where he could be seen getting water by the porter and all the other servants in the place, and she watched this from the kitchen window and was so angry and ashamed that she had to take some wine for her stomach, for everyone would say that she was lazy and that she worked for a vulgar and badly educated family. And they did not believe in the dead. Once, walking down the *sala* in the dusk, she saw the spirit of a dead man before her so clearly that at first she thought it was the signore, until she saw him standing in the door. Then she screamed and dropped the tray with the glasses and bottles on it, and when the signore asked her why she had screamed and she said it was because she had seen a ghost he was not sympathetic. And once, in the back hall, she saw another ghost, the ghost of a bishop with a miter, and when she screamed and told the signore what she had seen he was not sympathetic.

But the children were sympathetic, and in the evening, when they were in bed, she told them the stories of Nascosta. The story they liked best was of the young farmer in Nascosta who was married to a beautiful woman named Assunta. When they had been married a year, they had a fine son with dark curls and a golden skin, but from the first he was sickly, and he cried, and they thought there was a spell on him, and they took him to the doctor in Conciliano, riding all the way there on an *asino*, and the doctor said the baby was dying of starvation. But how could this be, they asked, for the breasts of Assunta were so full of milk they stained her blouse. But the doctor said to watch at night, and they went home by *asino* and ate their supper, and Assunta fell asleep, but the husband stayed awake to watch, and then at midnight he saw in the moonlight a great viper come over the threshold of the farmhouse and come into the bed and suck the milk from the breasts of the woman, but the husband could not move, for if he moved, the viper would have put his fangs into her breast and killed her, and when the serpent had sucked her breasts dry he went back across the floor and over the threshold in the moonlight, and then the farmer gave the alarm, and all the farmers from around came, and they found against the wall of the farm a nest of eight great serpents, fat with milk, who were so poisonous that even their breath was mortal, and they beat them to death with clubs, and this was a true story, because she had passed the farm where it happened a hundred times. And the story they preferred after this was of the lady in Conciliano who became the lover of a handsome stranger from America. But one night she noticed on his back a small mark like a leaf and remembered that the son who had been taken away from her many years ago was so marked, and knew then that this lover was her son. She ran then to the church to ask forgiveness in the confessional, but the priest – he was a fat and a haughty man – said there was no forgiveness for her sin and, *subito*, there was in the confessional a loud clatter of bones. Then the people came and opened the confessional and saw that where there had been a proud and a haughty priest there was nothing but bones. And she also told the children about the miracle of the jewels of the Madonna, and the *tempo infame* when she had seen the wolves coming up the Via Cavour, and the time her cousin Maria had seen the devil in his red suit.

She went with this American family to the mountains in July, and in August to Venice, and, coming back to Rome in the fall, she understood them to say that they were leaving Italy, and they had the trunks brought up from the cellar, and she helped the signora with the packing. Now she had five pairs of shoes and eight dresses and money in the bank, but the thought of looking for another post with a Roman signora who might spit in her eye whenever she felt like it was discouraging, and one day when she was repairing a dress for the signora she became so discouraged that she cried. Then she explained to the signora how hard the life of a *donna* was working for Romans, and the signora said they would take her to the new world if she liked. They would take her for six months on an impermanent visa; it would be diverting for her and a help to them. Then all the arrangements were made, and she went to Nascosta, and the mamma cried and asked her not to go, and everyone in the village said she should not go, but this was jealousy, because they had never had a chance to go anywhere – not even Conciliano. And for once the world where she had lived and been so happy seemed to her truly to be an old world where the customs and the walls were older than the people, and she felt that she would be happier in a world where the walls were all new, even if the people were savage.

When the time came to go, they drove to Naples, stopping whenever the signore felt like it to have a little coffee and cognac, traveling very commodiously like millionaires and staying in a *di lusso* hotel in Naples, where she had a room to herself. But on the morning when they sailed she felt a great sadness, for who can live out a good life but in his own country? Then she told herself that it was only a voyage – she would come home in six months – and what had the good God made the world so strange and various for if it was not to be seen? She had her passport stamped and went aboard the ship feeling very emotional. It was an American ship, as cold as winter, and at lunch there was ice water on the table, and what was not cold was flavorless and badly cooked, and she came back to her deep feeling that, while these people were kind and generous, they were ignorant and the men fastened their wives' pearls and, with all their money, they did not know any better than to eat platcfuls of raw steak washed down with coffee that tasted like medicine. They were not beautiful or elegant and they had pale eyes, but what disgusted her most on the ship were the old women, who in her country would be wearing black in memory of their numerous dead and, as suited their time of life, would move slowly and inspire dignity. But here the old ladies spoke in shrill voices and wore bright clothes and as much jewelry, all of it false, as you find on the Madonna of Nascosta, and painted their faces and tinted their hair. But who was deceived, for you could see how haggard under the paint were their cheeks, and that their necks were rucked and seamed like the necks of turtles, and although they smelled like the *campagna* in spring they were as withered and dry as the flowers on a tomb. They were like straw, and this must be a savage country where the old had no wisdom or taste and did not deserve or receive the respect of their children and their grandchildren and had forgotten their dead.

But it would be beautiful, she thought, because she had seen in magazines and newspapers photographs of the towers of the city of New York, towers of gold and silver, against the blue sky, in a city that had never once been touched by the damage of war. But it was raining when they came up the Narrows, and when she looked for the towers they were not to be seen, and when she asked for the towers she was told they were lost in the rain. She was disappointed, for what she could see of this new world seemed ugly, and all the people who dreamed of it were deceived. It was like Naples in the time of the war, and she wished she had not come. The customs man who went through her bags was badly educated. They took a taxi and a train to Washington, the capital of the new world, and then another taxi, and she could see out of the window that all the buildings were copies of the buildings of Imperial Rome, and they looked ghostly to her in the night lights, as if the Forum had risen again from the dust. They drove into the country, where the houses were all of wood and all new and where the washbasins and bathtubs were very commodious, and in the morning her signora showed her the machines and how to work them.

At first she was suspicious of the washing machine, for it used a fortune in soap and hot water and did not clean the clothes, and it reminded her of how happy she had been at the fountain in Nascosta, talking with her friends and making everything as clean as new. But little by little the machine seemed to her more *carina*, for it was after all only a machine, and it filled itself and emptied itself and turned around and around, and it seemed marvelous to her that a machine could remember so much and was always there, ready and waiting to do its work. And then there was the machine for washing the dishes, and you could wash the dishes in a costume for the evening without getting a drop of water on your gloves. When the signora was away and the boys were at school, first she would put some dirty clothes in the washing machine and start that, and then she would put some dirty dishes in the other machine and start that, and then she would put a nice *saltimbocca alla romana* in the electric frying pan and start that, and then she would sit in the *salone* in front of the TV and listen to all the machines around her doing the work, and it delighted her and made her feel powerful. Then there was the *frigidario* in the kitchen, making ice and keeping the butter as hard as stone, and there was the deep freeze full of lamb and beef as fresh as the day when they had been killed, and there was an electric egg beater, and a machine for squeezing the oranges, and a machine for breathing in the dust, and she would have them all going at once, and a machine for making the toast – all bright silver – where you put in the plain bread and turned your back and *allora*, there were two pieces of toast just the color you had asked for, and all done by the machine.

During the day, her signore was away at the office, but her signora, who in Rome had lived like a princess, seemed in the new world to be a secretary, and she thought perhaps that they were poor and the signora must work. She was always talking on the telephone and making computations and writing letters like a secretary. She was always hurried during the day and tired at night, like a secretary. Because they were both tired at night, the house was not as peaceful as it had been in Rome. Finally she asked the signora to explain what she was a secretary for, and the signora said that she was not a secretary but that she was kept busy raising money for the poor and the sick and the mad. This seemed to Clementina very strange. The climate also seemed to her strange and humid, bad for the lungs and the liver, but the trees at that season were very colorful – she had never seen this before; they were gold and red and yellow, and their leaves fell through the air as in some great hall in Rome or Venice where the paint is flaking from the pictures on the ceiling.

There was a *paisano*, an old man they called Joe, from bas-Italia, who delivered the milk. He had sixty years or more and was bent with carrying milk bottles, but she went with him to the movies, where he could explain the story to her in Italian and where he pinched her and asked her to marry him. This was a joke, as far as Clementina was concerned. There were strange *feste* in the new world – one with a turkey and no saints – and then there was the *festa* of the *Natale*, and she herself had never seen anything so discourteous to the Holy Virgin and the sainted baby. First they bought a green tree and then they put it up in the *salone* and hung it with shining necklaces, as if it were a holy saint with the power of curing evil and hearing prayers. *Mamma mia!* A tree! She was confessed by a priest who gave her the tail of the devil for not coming to church every Sunday of her life and who was very rigid. When she went to Mass, they took the collection three times. She thought that when she returned to Rome she would write an article for the paper about the church in this new world where there was not even the wristbone of a saint to kiss and where they made offerings to a green tree and forgot the travail of the Holy Virgin and took the collection three times. And then there was the snow, but it was more *carina* than the snow in Nascosta – there were no wolves, and the signori skied in the mountains, and the children played in the snow and the house was always warm.

She still went with Joe every Sunday to the movies, where he told her the story, asked her to marry him, and pinched her. Once, before the movies, he stopped at a fine house all made of wood and neatly painted, and he unlocked the door and took her upstairs to a nice apartment with paper on the walls, the floor shining with varnish, and five rooms in all, with a modern bathroom, and he said that if she would marry him it would all be hers. He would buy her a machine for washing the dishes and a machine for beating the eggs and a frying pan like the signora had that knew when to turn off the *saltimbocca alla romana*. When she asked him where he would find all the money to do this, he said that he had saved seventeen thousand dollars, and he took a book out of his pocket, a bankbook, and there was stamped in it seventeen thousand two hundred and thirty dollars and seventeen cents. It would all be hers if she would come and be his wife. She said no, but after the movies, when she was in bed, it made her sad to think of all the machinery and she wished that she had never come to the new world. Nothing would ever be the same again. When she went back to Nascosta and told them that a man – not a beautiful man, but one who was honest and gentle – had offered her seventeen thousand dollars and a place with five rooms, they would never believe her. They would think she was crazy, and how could she lie again on straw in a cold room and be contented? Her impermanent visa expired in April and she would have to go home then, but the signore said that he could apply for an extension if she liked, and she begged him to do this. In the kitchen one night, she heard them speaking in low voices and she guessed they were speaking about her affairs, but he did not speak to her until much later when the others had gone up and she came into the room to say good night.

'I'm very sorry, Clementina,' he said, 'but they won't give me an extension.'

'It doesn't matter,' she said. 'If I am not wanted in this country, I will go home.'

'It isn't that, Clementina, it's the law. I'm very sorry. Your visa expires on the twelfth. I'll get your passage on a boat before then.'
'Thank you, signore,' she said. 'Good night.'

She would go back, she thought. She would take the boat, she would debark at Naples, she would catch a train at the Mergellina and in Rome a *pullman,* and go out the Tiburtina with the curtains of the bus swaying and the purple clouds of exhaust rolling out behind them when they climbed the hill at Tivoli. Her eyes filled with tears when she thought of kissing Mamma and giving her the silver-framed photograph of Dana Andrews that she had bought at Woolworth's for her present. Then she would sit on the piazza with such a ring of people around her as would form for an accident, speaking in her own tongue and drinking the wine they had made and talking about the new world where there were frying pans with brains and where even the powder for cleaning the *gabinetti* smelled of roses. She saw the scene distinctly, the fountain spray blowing on the wind, but then she saw gathering in the imagined faces of her townsmen a look of disbelief. Who would believe her tales? Who would listen? They would have admired her if she had seen the devil, like Cousin Maria, but she had seen a sort of paradise and no one cared. In leaving one world and coming to another she had lost both.

Then she opened and reread a package of letters written from Nascosta by her Uncle Sebastiano. That night, his letters all seemed dolorous. The autumn had come on quickly, he wrote; and it was cold, even in September, and many of the olives and the grapes were lost, and *la bomba atomica* had ruined the seasons of Italy. Now the shadow of the town fell over the valley earlier, and she remembered herself the beginnings of winter – the sudden hoarfrost lying on the grapes and wild flowers, and the *contadini* coming in at dark on their *asini,* loaded down with roots and other scraps of wood, for wood was hard to find in that country and one would ride ten *kilometri* for a bundle of green olive cuttings, and she could remember the cold in her bones and see the *asini* against the yellow light of evening and hear the lonely noise of stones falling down the steep path, falling away from their hooves. And in December Sebastiano wrote that it was again the time of the wolves. The *tempo infame* had come to Nascosta, and wolves had killed six of the padrone's sheep, and there was no *abbacchio*, and no eggs, either, for pasta, and the piazza was buried in snow up to the edge of the fountain, and they knew hunger and cold, and she could remember both.

The room where she read these letters was warm. The lights were pink. She had a silver ashtray like a signora, and, if she had wanted, in her private bathroom she could have drawn a hot bath up to her neck. Did the Holy Virgin mean for her to live in a wilderness and die of starvation? Was it wrong to take the comforts that were held out to her? The faces of her people appeared to her again, and how dark were their skin, their hair, and their eyes, she thought, as if through living with fair people she had taken on the dispositions and the prejudices of the fair. The faces seemed to regard her with reproach, with earthen patience, with a sweet, dignified, and despairing regard, but why should she be compelled to return and drink sour wine in the darkness of the hills? In this new world they had found the secret of youth, and would the saints in heaven have refused a life of youthfulness if it had been God's will? She remembered how in Nascosta even the most beautiful fell quickly under the darkness of time, like flowers without care; how even the most beautiful became bent and toothless, their dark clothes smelling, as the mamma's did, of smoke and manure. But in this country she could have forever white teeth and color in her hair. Until the day she died she would have shoes with heels and rings on her fingers, and the attention of men, for in this new world one lived ten lifetimes and never felt the pinch of age; no, never. She would marry Joe. She would stay here and live ten lives, with a skin like marble and always the teeth with which to bite the meat.

On the next night, her signore told her when the boats were leaving, and when he had finished she said, 'I am not going back.'

'I don't understand.'

'I will marry Joe.'

'But Joe's a great deal older than you, Clementina.'

'Joe is sixty-three.'

'And you?'

'I am twenty-four.'

'Do you love Joe?'

'Oh no, signore. How could I love him, with his big paunch like a sackful of apples and so many wrinkles at the back of his neck you could tell your fortune there? It is not possible.'

'Clementina, I admire Joe,' the signore said. 'He's an honest man. If you marry him, you must care for him.'

'Oh, I'll care for him, signore. I'll make his bed and cook his supper, but I will never let him touch me.'

He deliberated, looked down at the floor, and finally said, 'I will not let you marry Joe, Clementina.'

'But why?'

'I won't let you marry him unless you'll be his wife. You must love him.'

'But, signore, in Nascosta there would be no sense in marrying a man whose land did not adjoin yours, and does that mean then that your heart will fly out to him?'

'This is not Nascosta.'

'But all marriages are like this, signore. If people married for love, the world would not be a place in which to live, it would be a hospital for the mad. Did not the signora marry you because of the money and the conveniences you bring her?' He did not answer, but she saw his face flush dark with blood. 'Oh, signore, my signore,' she said, 'you talk like a boy with stars in your eyes, a thin boy at the fountain, his head full of the *poesia*. I am only trying to unfold to you that I am only marrying Joe so that I can stay in this country, and you are talking like a boy.'

'I am not talking like a boy,' he said. Then he rose from the chair. 'I am not talking like a boy. Who do you think you are? When you came to us in Rome you didn't have shoes or a coat.'

'Signore, you do not understand me. Perhaps I will love him, but I am only trying to unfold to you that I am not marrying for love.'

315

'And that's what I'm trying to explain to you. I won't stand for it.'

'I will leave your house, signore.'

'I'm responsible for you.'

'No, signore. Joe is responsible for me now.'

'Then get out of my house.'

She went upstairs to her room and cried and cried, in anger and pity for this grown fool, but she packed her things. In the morning she cooked the breakfast, but she stayed in the kitchen until the signore had gone to work, and then the signora came down and cried, and the children cried, and at noon Joe came to get her in his car and took her to the Pelluchis', who were *paisani* and with whom she would stay until she and Joe were married. Maria Pelluchi explained to her that in the new world one was married like a princess, and this was so. For three weeks she was in and out of the stores with Maria – first to buy the wedding dress for herself, all white and the latest mode, with a tail of satin to drag along the ground, but economical, too, because the tail could be adjusted, making the dress like a costume for the grand evening. Then there were the costumes for Maria and her sister, who would be the attendants, and these were yellow and lavender and could be used later as costumes for the evening. Then there were the shoes and the flowers and the clothes for traveling and the suitcase, and nothing was rented. And when the day of the wedding arrived she was so tired that she had milk in the knees and walked through it all like a dream, of which she could remember very little. There were many *paisani* at the reception and much wine, food, and music, and then she took with Joe a train to New York, where the buildings were so tall they made her feel homesick and of little importance. In New York, they spent the night in a hotel, and the next day they took a *di lusso* train, only for signori who were going to Atlantic City, with a special chair for each passenger and a waiter to bring things to eat and drink. She hung behind her chair the mink stole that Joe had given her for a present, and everyone saw it and admired it and judged her to be a rich signora. Joe called the waiter over and told him to bring some whiskey and seltz, but the waiter pretended not to understand what Joe was saying and to be so busy waiting on other people that they would have to be the last, and she felt again that shame, and anger at discovering that because they could not speak elegantly the language of this new country they would be treated with great discourtesy, as if they were pigs. And that is the way they were treated on the passage, for the waiter did not come near them again, as if their money was not as good as the money of the others. They went first through a great, dark *galleria* and then out into a country that was ugly and potent with fire exploding from many chimneys, and there were trees and rivers and places for boating. She looked out of the window at the country that streamed by as swiftly and gently as water, to see if it was as fair as Italy, but what she saw was that it was not her country, her earth. Near the cities they passed those places where the poor lived and where washing was hung on lines, and she thought that this was the same – that washing on lines must be the same all over the world. And the houses of the poor were the same, too, the way they leaned against one another and had gardens that were not commodious but that were cultivated, you could see, with gentleness and love. It was in the middle of the day or later when they left, and, as they sped through the country and the afternoon, she saw that the schools were closing and that on the streets there were many children carrying books and riding bicycles and playing games, and many of them waved to the train as it rolled along and she waved back to them. She waved to some children who were walking through the high grass in a field, and she waved to two boys on a bridge, and she waved to an old man, and they all waved back to her, and she waved to three girls, and she waved to a lady who was pushing a baby carriage, and she waved to a little boy who was wearing a yellow coat and carrying a valise, and he waved back. They all waved back. Then she could see that they were coming close to the ocean, for there was a bareness in the air and not so many trees and many pictures of hotels painted on wood saying how many hundreds of rooms they had and how many different kinds of places for drinking cocktails, and she was happy to see the name of their hotel on one of these signs and to be sure that it was *di lusso*. Then the train stopped and it was the end of the passage and she felt shy and timid, but Joe said *andiamo*, and the waiter who had been so discourteous to them took their bags away and reached for her mink stole, but she said, 'No, thank you,' and got it away from him, the pig. And then there was the largest black car she had ever seen in her life, with a sign on it saying the name of their hotel, and they got into this with some other people, but they did not speak to one another on the passage, because she did not want the others to know that she could not speak the language of this country.

The hotel was very *di lusso*, and they ascended in an elevator, and walked down a hall that was covered with thick carpet, into a fine room, also with thick carpet everywhere, and a toilet – only with no bidet – and when the waiter had gone Joe got a bottle of whiskey out of his valise and had a drink and asked her to come and sit in his lap, and she said a little later, later, for it was unlucky in the daylight, and it would be better to wait for the moon to rise, and she would like to go down and see the dining rooms and lounges. She wondered if the salt air would be bad for the mink, and Joe had another drink, and out of the window she could see the ocean and the lines of white waves coming in, and because the windows were closed and she could not hear the sound the waves made when they broke it seemed like something she was dreaming. They went down again, not speaking, because she had distinctly come to feel that it was better not to speak the *bella lingua* in such a luxurious place, and they looked in the bars and dining rooms, which were grand, and they went out onto a broad walk beside the sea and there was salt in the air, like Venice, and it smelled like Venice, and there was also a smell of frying food in the air, which reminded her of the feast of San Giuseppe in Rome. On one side of them was the green, cold sea, which she had crossed to come to this new world, and on the other side of them there were many diverting things. They walked along until they came to the gypsies, where there was in the window a drawing of the human hand and where one's fortune could be told, and when she asked if they could speak Italian they said, '*Si, si, si, non c'e' dubbio!*' and Joe gave her a dollar, and she went behind a curtain with the gypsy, who looked at her hand and began to tell her fortune, but it was not Italian she was speaking, it was a bastard language of a little Spanish and a little something that Clementina had never heard before, and she could only understand a word here and there, like 'the sea' and 'the voyage,' but she could not tell if this was a voyage she would make or a voyage she had made, and she became impatient with the gypsy, who had made a lie in saying that she spoke in Italian, and she asked for her money back, but the gypsy said that if the money was given back there would be a curse on it. And, knowing what strong curses the gypsies make, she did not create a further disturbance, and went out where Joe was waiting for her on the wooden walk, and walked along again between the green sea and the diversion of frying food, where people called to them to come in and spend their money, smiling and beckoning wickedly like the angels of hell. And then there was the *tramonto*, and the lights went on gloriously like pearls, and, looking back, she could see the pink windows of the hotel where they were known, where they had a room of their own they could return to when they pleased, and the noise of the sea sounded like distant blasting in the mountains.

She was a good wife to him, and in the morning he was so grateful that he bought her a silver dish for the butter and a cover for the ironing board and a pair of red pants, laced with gold. The mother would give her the tail of the devil, she knew, for wearing pants, and in Rome she herself would spit in the eye of a woman who was so badly educated as to wear pants, but this was a new world and it was no sin, and in the afternoon she wore the mink stole and the red pants and went with Joe up and down the wooden walk above the sea. On Saturday they went home, and on Monday they bought the furniture, and on Tuesday it was delivered, and on Friday she put on the red pants and went to the supermarket with Maria Pelluchi, who explained the labels on the boxes to her, and she looked so much like an American that people were surprised when she could not speak the language.

But if she could not speak the language she could do everything else, and she even learned to drink whiskey without coughing and spitting. In the morning, she would turn on all the machines and watch the TV, learning the words of the songs, and in the afternoons Maria Pelluchi came to her house and they watched the TV together, and in the evening she watched it with Joe. She tried to write the mother about the things she had bought – much finer things than the Pope possessed – but she realized that the letter would only bewilder the mother, and in the end she sent her nothing but postcards. No one could describe how diverting and commodious her life had become. In the summer, in the evenings, Joe took her to the races in Baltimore, and she had never seen anything so *carina* – the little horses and the lights and the flowers and the red coat of the marshal with his bugle. That summer, they went to the races every Friday and sometimes oftener, and it was one night there, when she was wearing her red pants and drinking whiskey, that she saw her signore for the first time since they had quarreled.

She asked him how he was, and how was his family, and he said, 'We are not together. We are divorced.' Looking into his face then, she saw not the end of his marriage but the end of his happiness. The advantage was hers, because hadn't she explained to him that he was like a boy with stars in his eyes, but some part of his loss seemed to be hers as well. Then he went away, and, although the race was beginning, she saw instead the white snow and the wolves of Nascosta, the pack coming up the Via Cavour and crossing the piazza as if they were bent on some errand of that darkness that she knew to lie at the heart of life, and, remembering the cold on her skin and the whiteness of the snow and the stealth of the wolves, she wondered why the good God had opened up so many choices and made life so strange and diverse.